SERVANTS of the CROWN

THE TURKISH PRETENDER

This is an IndieMosh book

brought to you by MoshPit Publishing
an imprint of Mosher's Business Support Pty Ltd

PO Box 4363
Penrith NSW 2750

indiemosh.com.au

A catalogue record for this work is available from the National Library of Australia

https://www.nla.gov.au/collections

Title: Servants of the Crown

Subtitle: The Turkish Pretender

Author: Jones, Garrick (1948–)

ISBNs: 978-1-922703-91-0 (paperback)
978-1-922703-92-7 (ebook – epub)
978-1-922703-93-4 (ebook – mobi)

Subjects: FICTION: LGBT / Gay. Action & Adventure; Thrillers / Historical; LGBTQ+ / General

Cover design by Garrick Jones.

Cover images Library of Congress, public domain.

Editing by Nick Taylor, Just Write Right at https://justwriteright.co.uk

Servants of the Crown

THE TURKISH PRETENDER

Garrick Jones

Contents

ACKNOWLEDGEMENTS AND AUTHOR'S NOTES

The author wishes to thank the following people and organisations for their input, advice, and very kind and generous support, especially the archivists at the museums and the Royal institutions:

Aleksandr Voinov, JLT, Pontus Aleryd, The British Museum, The Imperial War Museum, The Royal Collection, the National Maritime Museum, and The Queen's Archives.

The author wishes to stress that this book is historical fiction, not an actual diary of events in Victorian London in 1855. Events, names, places, dates, and the activities of real people may have occasionally been tweaked to advance the narrative.

... and as we, a crowd of perhaps twenty men, let forth a huge cry of dismay, the longboat foundered, discharging its crew of six rowers, the naval lieutenant who'd been standing in its bow, the three government officials, and our two civilian passengers into the sea.

The shell had hit not five yards or more from its stern and the huge spout brought about by its landing had caused the boat to capsize. Even from where I stood, my knuckles white as I clutched the deck rail, one foot on the paddle-wheel housing to retain my balance in the rough sea swell, I could see small figures, black dots, thrashing around in the water, heading for the Firefly, *not more than fifty yards from where the longboat had gone down.*

By that point, we'd been under fire for not more than ten minutes, shells landing closer both to us and to the Firefly *as the Russians gauged the range of their cannons. I was torn between returning to my cabin to retrieve my short, telescopic spy glass, and staying where I was, watching with fear and trepidation for all those who'd been aboard the longboat, when the* Firefly *seemed to keel violently to starboard, away from us. A large puff of white smoke arose from somewhere amidships, a few yards above the waterline.*

"She's been hit!" someone yelled from behind me. I held my breath, hoping it was either an old-fashioned iron ball or perhaps a charged shell that had not ignited.

But then, with an almighty roar, the ship rose high in the water, disintegrating into a mass of smoke, flying timbers, and other debris. My immediate instinct was to fling myself to the deck, but at the very moment that I loosened my grip on the handrail, the Sisley *rocked violently beneath my feet, a massive explosion issuing from behind in the aft section of the vessel.*

I fell to my knees, debris from the Firefly *raining down over us and, as I looked up, sheltering my face with my forearm, the last thing I saw was the mainmast, its rigging tangled around our tall smokestack, both of them falling directly toward where I lay on my back.*

Someone grabbed my leg and pulled me, I remember no more.

Excerpt from the Admiralty report by Travis Holland, ship's surgeon aboard H.M.S. *Sisley*, the sole survivor of the sinking of the *Sisley* and H.M.S. *Firefly* during the Battle of Varna on Tuesday, the sixth of February, 1855. Given this day at Gibraltar Naval Hospital, Monday, the twenty-sixth of February, 1855.

1. AN UNTIMELY DEATH

He stood in the drawing room window of Birch House, his forearm resting against one of the internal shutters of the large, twelve-paned window, his forehead pressed against the back of his hand.

Behind him, the room was a shroud of covered furniture, the house long closed-up and unaired. Shapes of cabinets, comfortable armchairs, a large sofa, and a sideboard were swathed in coarse, cream-coloured linen. The air smelled softly of staleness; the same scent of things neglected, once loved, and yet forgotten over the course of time. It reminded him of the smell of the sea chest his father had left behind, intending Lennard to bring with him two months after he and Lennard's mother, younger brother, and baby sister had departed for the great southern continent. Occasionally, Lennard would open it and gently press each garment, wooden box, and leather pouch back into its place. His eyes always misted with tears. Had he not been diagnosed with scarlatina and denied passage on the *Castle Howard* two days before she sailed, he too might have drowned alongside his parents and siblings. These were the memories the smell of the room evoked … and they caught in his throat.

He checked his timepiece. It was fifteen minutes before ten.

Casting his glance out into the garden evoked more pleasant memories. Although a little unkempt, it was still as beautiful as ever. The twin rose gardens on either side of the broad central pathway that led up to the house were neglected but needed no more than a week's hard work. Come summer, they'd look as delightful and abundant as he'd always remembered them being.

He walked to the grate and stoked the coals, surprised the chimney hadn't smoked when Elam had lit it not more than two hours ago. They'd exchanged a quick smile. How long had it been since his grandfather had last sat in front of this fire, warming his shins at the same time of year? Five years could it be? Early March was always cold, oft-times colder than the dead of winter, due to the icy winds that frequently blew down from the north.

The house had been named after the wonderful stand of silver birch trees, planted in a close thicket on the western side of the building. As a small child, when visiting with his parents, his grandfather had often hoisted him into his arms in that very room, pointing out their beautiful white bark, striated with horizontal turf-coloured lines and patches. By the age of six, his grandfather had taught him the name of every species of bird that sat in the trees' drooping branches, or that foraged in the close-clipped grass below.

He didn't know quite how long he'd spent gazing out of the side window, lost in memories—again, more agreeable ones—of times when his family was still alive, when he was young, before the world had taught him the lesson that not every man alive was kind and generous as his grandfather Trefford had been.

"Lennard?" a voice asked from his side.

"Yes, Elam, what is it?" Lennard turned to face him. Elam had been deaf since the age of twelve but was the most excellent "hearer" of the spoken word, merely by watching mouth movements and lip shapes. They'd also been intimates, not just master and servant, since the summer of 1837, nearly twenty years ago.

"They're here. Robert's been banging on the door. Didn't you hear it? He came down to the kitchen when you didn't respond to his knock at the front door and scared the living daylights out of me."

"I'm sorry, I heard nothing. I was completely lost in thought. Where's your brother? He's supposed to be keeping watch."

"There was nothing in the house, so I sent Miles to the bakery in Oxford Street. No tea, milk, or sugar ... the pantry is completely bare. And since neither of us has eaten since last evening, I've asked him to bring back some meat and vegetable turnovers, and something sweet for everyone else. I remembered they have those biscuits we all were once so fond of."

"That's very thoughtful of you, Elam. I'm sorry, I didn't think of tea. Did you have money?"

"I had a few shillings in my pocket but Miles told me not to worry. He told me Sir Hugh had kept an account with them."

"An account in Oxford Street, so far from Clarence Gardens? What's wrong with his cook?"

"He let Mr Huilot go, not long after your grandfather passed away."

"Dear God, don't tell me your brother has been cooking for him?"

"I think that hardly likely, Lennard. I doubt even Sir Hugh would have eaten what Miles might have prepared. He either sent out for food or ate in public houses. Said it was cheaper than keeping a chef."

"A false economy if you ask me, Elam. Now, you said the others had arrived and that Robert is downstairs?"

"He's attending to the range. As you might remember, it's a cranky old thing but Robert was always able to wrestle it into submission."

"He was always able to use the same device on us, if you remember."

Elam smiled. "I do indeed. Now, I know your mind is still reeling but your guests are waiting outside in the carriage."

Lennard strode back to the front window, craning his head to see past the twin gate posts, which had been added just before his grandfather had died. They were tall and made from sandstone, each topped with a gas lantern, but the combination blocked any view of Soho Square, except through the bars of the wrought iron gate.

He turned back to Elam and beckoned him to his side. "I see your brother has returned and is talking to them."

"Shall I fetch them in?" Elam asked.

"No, Robert can do that. Where is he anyway? The kitchen stove must be behaving particularly badly."

"I'm right here behind you, Lennard. The kitchen range has been duly tamed and the kettle is on the boil. Now, what the blasted hell is going on? Fetched here with no explanation—"

"Would you mind bringing the others inside, Robbie? There is news, and I think it should be told when we're all gathered."

"Very well, but there'll be hell to pay when I get back to the office. There's a—"

"Business can wait, Robert. The office will continue without your presence for a few hours. You have an assistant, don't you? He can handle whatever's going on. I wouldn't have asked all four of you to come were it not important. Just be patient a little longer. I promise you, I'm not ill, if that's what has you worried."

"Very well, Lenn, I know better than to press you when you wish to make some great *dénouement*, so I shall wait, as you ask."

Robert quickly insinuated his hand into Lennard's and squeezed it. "It's been far too long, Lenn. All of us scattered every which where."

"Indeed. I can't remember the last time we four have all been in the same place at the same time. The Brothers all together, will wonders never cease?"

"And it's for that very reason I'm anxious. What can be so important that we were all variously pulled from our beds and told to be here at ten? What couldn't wait until this evening?"

Lennard smiled then led Robert to the drawing room door. "Well, my dear cousin, in five minutes, you, Angus, and Gerald will find out."

"If this is some sort of terrible adventure that's going to have us wandering through the sewers looking for French spies like the last time you brought us together, I think I might send someone in my place."

Lennard chuckled, kissing his cousin's cheek quickly.

"No spies, no sewers, I promise. Now, please, bring the others into the warm."

Robert hesitated in the doorway, casting his eyes around the room. "Birch House, Lennard. What fun we all had here ..."

"Maybe we shall again in the future, Robbie. Now, please, I'm anxious to get this over and done with."

Maybe we shall again in the future? Robert Fahey couldn't get the words out of his mind as he made his way down to the street to tell the other two men that Lennard was ready for them.

*****

Lennard knew his friends as well as any man did another—any man who enjoyed an intimate and close relationship with another, that is.

They'd been called "The Brothers" since adolescence, and although Robert was his only true blood relative—their French mothers were sisters—they had known Angus and Gerald ever since the two young men had arrived to spend the summer of 1838 at his grandfather's estate, Gresting, just before going up to Cambridge.

These days, their erstwhile boyhood friends were men of note: Angus Spratt, the Viscount Fallerton, personal private secretary to the Home Secretary; and the Right Honourable Gerald Langbourne, recently returned from the Crimea, a captain in Her Majesty's armed forces. Lennard loved them both, equally. It had been inevitable that they'd formed friendships during that summer, seventeen years ago. Thereafter, over time, they'd grown to be the truest companions. The epithet of Brothers suited all four, as it allowed the very closeness of their relationships with each other to be considered familial affection, and not the awkward intimacy of men in society who were not kin.

Lennard smiled. He'd noticed Angus's fingers were drumming on his knee, a sign of his friend's impatience. "I suppose you're anxious to know why you were dragged from the warmth of your covers, gentlemen?"

"Oh, blast you, Lennard! Being summoned at eight in the morning is hardly being dragged out of bed," Angus said, feigning annoyance, betrayed by his broad smile. "I was already at my desk. Get on with it, please."

"Very well, Angus, since you're so insistent ... he's dead," Lennard announced.

"Who's dead, Lennard?"

"Sir Hugh."

"Your uncle is dead?" Angus asked, his teacup suspended an inch from his lips such was his amazement. "Are you sure?"

"If you don't believe me, you can go upstairs and see for yourself, Angus. Although, I warn you, it's not a pretty sight."

"Dear God! Was he murdered?"

Lennard almost laughed, and might have other than for the serious nature of the situation. "No, he wasn't murdered. It seems he suffered an infarction last night mid-coitus, staggered off the woman, then called out to Miles, before tumbling head first down the stairs, coming to rest on the first-floor landing."

"You left the body *in situ*?" Angus asked.

"What else should I do with it at one o'clock in the morning, Angus? Bury him in the compost heap next to the icehouse?"

Lennard waited until the silence became almost unbearable.

"Hugh had a mistress?" Gerald asked, his voice hovering on mirth and incredulity. Not one of The Brothers had held a modicum of affection for Sir Hugh.

Lennard glanced at Miles, whom he'd asked to remain in the room, indicating he should speak. "Mistress is not a word I might use to describe his companion," Miles said, awkwardly.

"Where is this creature, Miles?" Angus asked.

"She fled, my lord. She nearly knocked me down the stairs in her urgency to leave the house as I was coming upstairs to see what the noise was. She's one of a dozen or so he sees ... sorry, used to see, here regularly. A different one every fourteen days or so."

"Do you know where we can find her? Perhaps she poisoned him for his money or some such thing."

"I paid her when she arrived. That's the way he did business. He never kept money about his person."

"*You* paid her?"

"He gave me two crowns before I left Clarence Gardens. I always got here an hour before the time of his assignation to light a fire in the largest of the servant's bedrooms. She'd arrive at the back door, I'd give her the coins, then take her up with a candle. Always punctual they were, those women, invariably arriving at half past eleven. He'd stride in the door at a quarter to midnight and they'd be done by quarter past the hour. None of them ever stayed."

"Hugh Malloray was swiving a ten-shilling whore once a fortnight in your grandfather Trefford's empty house?" Gerald said, laughter clearly threatening in his voice. "Which of them was the man, do you suppose?"

"Gerald, please," Angus said, glancing over Lennard's shoulder at Elam, who Lennard suspected had not tried to contain his amusement.

Gradually, one by one, they began to understand why Lennard had summoned them. They all detested Hugh, everyone did. He was a pompous, choleric man who had apparently—according to both Lennard's father and his uncle, Arthur—struggled with an inability to curb offensive behaviour and bad manners from childhood. No one ever seemed to have had a good word to say about him.

"That means …"

"Yes, Robert, it means that unwillingly, although rather sooner than I'd anticipated, I am now the apparent eighth Baron Betteridge of Hazlemere, and presumed inheritor of my grandfather's estate and business holdings."

"You've seen Hugh's will?"

"He left none. I pulled Simeon Drudge, the family solicitor, out of bed at five this morning after Miles came to rouse me shortly after one. I came straight here, sent Miles for a doctor, then after death had been confirmed, sat with Elam for a few hours before I went to see Drudge. It was Elam who suggested I should summon you all. For, despite my apparent good fortune, if given time, I'm sure each of you will see there are complications."

"Why would someone in Hugh's position make no legal provisions?"

"If I may answer that, Mr Fahey?" Miles said. He'd been Sir Hugh's valet since Lennard's grandfather had died, five years beforehand. "He thought writing a will was tempting fate. I went with him to Mr Drudge twice, but both times he became anxious and couldn't go ahead. I believe he left a letter with his intentions, but no official will."

"A letter of intent? Did you know that, Lenn? Did our solicitor say anything about that?"

"Yes, I read it," Lennard said.

"Then where is it?"

Lennard stared at the fireplace, and his three friends followed his gaze.

"He intended to sell everything by auction—and I mean everything—then distribute the proceeds among his hangers-on, and use the rest to establish a colony named after himself somewhere in the wilds of Canada. He could do nothing about the title passing to me, one which he never used in the five years after my grandfather's death, preferring to be called 'Sir Hugh'. To his warped sense of what was right and what was not, it seemed more deferential than the way a baron is addressed, by the name of the title."

"Were you to get nothing, Lennard? Not a penny?"

"A sum of four hundred pounds. 'To find myself a suitable country cottage of four rooms with a vegetable garden, and no annuity'—those were more or less his words. I'm not fabricating what he wrote."

"There was no signature on the letter, or witness, Lenn?" Gerald asked. He'd studied law at Cambridge, leaving in his final year to take up a commission in the army.

"No. It was in Drudge's hand, so it must have been dictated."

"Will Drudge hold his tongue?"

"Would you, Gerald, if you might lose the business of the new Lord Betteridge, a wealthy shipping magnate and landholder? I think not. Anyway, you can ask him yourself. He'll be here at eleven."

"May I ask why?"

"What do you think Elam and I were doing for hours in the dark?"

"*Ce que vous faites, tous les deux, très probablement tous les soirs sous les couvertures, mon cher cousin,*" Robert said with a smile and a wink, knowing that Miles spoke not one word of French and Elam could not read-hear in any language other than his own.

Angus and Gerald, however, roared with laughter. It was no secret among The Brothers that Elam not only looked after Lennard's needs as his manservant but also kept his bed warm.

At Elam's puzzled look, Lennard turned at an angle and mouthed in English what Robert had said in French. "Robert just remarked," he said, voicelessly, "in answer to what I thought we might be doing for four hours in the dark, that if was most likely what we did every night in the dark under the bedsheets."

Elam, although amused, contained it completely, yet he did colour rather spectacularly. "I'll get more tea, shall I, sir?" he said, a little more loudly than he might normally have done. Then, with a slight gesture, beckoned his brother to follow him to the kitchen.

"I must say, I haven't seen Elam since before I went to the Crimea, Lennard," Gerald said after the brothers had closed the drawing room door behind them. "He's remarkably handsome now he's a few years older. Filled out mightily in the chest ... and those very neat mutton chops accentuate the beauty of his cheekbones and the brightness of his smile."

"You're welcome to join us, whenever you wish, Gerald. Just like old times, eh?"

"It does my heart good to hear you're still ...?"

"There's no great love affair going on between us. As you all know, I had my heart broken once and, as much as I care for him, we have an intimacy born from friendship, needs of the flesh, and mutual convenience. Besides, he's as dear to me as any of you. Who couldn't care for him?"

"And you, Robert? I'm sorry I haven't called, but I've been quite busy since I returned. Do you have anyone special in your life?"

"I do keep up with one or two gentlemen of discretion from time to time, Gerald," Robert replied. "But I have a lady friend these days, and I work very long hours. However, sometimes, when the moon is in the right cycle ... well, I've been known to spend time with one of my two admirers."

"What about you, Gerald?" Lennard asked. "Find a strapping guardsman with thick thighs and abundant energy while you were abroad?"

"Alas no, Lenn. Not that there weren't handsome men aplenty, but I had no appetite for it, to be honest. War and carnage tend to make one's mind turn to other things."

*****

At eleven o'clock, Miles announced that Simeon Drudge had arrived and was clearing a space on the desk in the study. Angus asked Lennard if they might have a quick turn in the garden. He needed a breath of fresh air, explaining glibly that the particulates in the room had caused his sinuses to ache.

Lennard knew it to be a pretext to have a word in private, so excused himself from his friends and showed Angus into the back garden.

"Of all the men in the world, it's you I know the best," Angus said, taking Lennard's hand in his own. "How are you faring, my friend?"

"I'm rather petrified, to be honest."

"There's no need to put on a mask in front of us friends."

"If you say you know me best, Angus, then you realise it's my way. I do what I'm best at. I take control in difficult situations, no matter what's happening, and deal with the crisis. I don't want this, you must understand. You've been a titled member of the gentry since you were born. My association has been oblique. The eldest son of the third son, I never expected this so soon and I—"

"You still haven't told me how you feel. That's typical of you."

"My feelings are best kept to myself, Angus. I demonstrate what I feel in deeds rather than using words, for those are simply said.

"However, sometimes those few words, sincerely meant, carry a far greater weight than all the deeds in the world."

"I shall take your word for it, my friend. Perhaps one day …?"

Angus sighed, knowing the conversation on this subject would proceed no further and offered Lennard a cheroot, quickly forgetting his excuse to flee had been due to the dusty air inside.

"I love this time of year, you know," he said, "the feeling that, at any moment, one might spy the first purple crocus poking through the snow."

"There's no snow this year, nor has there been for three weeks, Angus."

"It was a metaphor, Lennard."

"I see … due to my change in circumstance, you spy an opportunity?"

"Indeed, I do. The thought is embryonic at this stage but, by Wednesday, when you are summoned to the Home Secretary's office—

it's not arranged as yet, but I shall make it so—it will be fully formed and ready to exit the womb of my fertile imagination."

Lennard laughed. Angus was prone to unnecessarily florid turns of phrase, and when he was trying to make Lennard laugh they usually took on a somewhat grotesque form.

"I'll send something around for you later today. Where shall you be?"

"I'll be at my lodgings," Lennard replied. "Most likely trying to catch up on lost sleep."

"Jermyn Street, isn't it? I've never been invited."

"You know damned well where it is, Angus. And, if truth be told, you've turned up more than once ... although, I will admit, it was without invitation."

Angus winked then lit Lennard's cheroot with a sulphur match.

"Those damned things make my eyes sting something dreadful," Lennard complained, wiping the tears with his pocket kerchief.

"What I'll send around later this evening will include something that will make your eyes sting even more, Lenn. We heard late yesterday that there was a survivor of the *Sisley* disaster."

"What?"

"For some reason, the man, when plucked from the ocean, was believed to be one of the civilian passengers who'd abandoned ship when the *Minotaur* was badly hit, about four miles away from where the *Sisley* and the *Firefly* went down. He was found clinging to a wooden hatch cover and had drifted quite close to Varna. A local fisherman found him."

"Surely he must have told someone what vessel he was from."

"Well, it seems he took a large section of a splintered spar through the fleshy part of his thigh and had suffered severe blood loss as a result. That, together with an enormous contusion and swelling of the side of his head, kept him insensible for over a week. Varna came under attack so the wounded were shipped off to other ports. Our survivor was thought to be a civilian by his dress so was sent to Gibraltar. It was only when he became lucid as they were crossing the Mediterranean that he revealed he'd been the surgeon about the *Sisley*."

"What a story! It's like something Daniel Defoe might have written."

"Well, the long and short of it is that he wrote a report for the Admiralty on the twenty-sixth of last month, a partial copy of which reached us yesterday. The full report and the good doctor himself are due to arrive Monday next, a week from today."

"Who will interview him?"

"You, most likely. But let's talk of that later, shall we? I don't want to spend too long out here. Even though we work together at the Home Office it would appear more than strange to be discussing affairs of state at a time like this. I'll send the letter this evening."

"You might have to get the porter to pound on the door."

"That won't be necessary, Lennard."

"And why not, Angus?"

"Because I'll send it with someone you know, who may, or may not have a key."

"Why must you always speak in riddles, Angus?"

"Because I know it infuriates you! Besides, now that Sir Hugh is dead, it's about time you learned something. There was some speculation about the company your late uncle kept, Lennard, so the Home Secretary thought it wise to have an eye kept on him."

"You had an intelligencer working in his household? One I know nothing of?"

"I think you mean *we* had an intelligencer working in his household, Lennard. No matter what you think, you're still my best and favourite spy."

"You know how much I hate that word. It's intelligence gathering, Angus. Spy sounds so vulgar. This person in my uncle's household …?"

"Someone I used to be quite fond of before my marriage."

"No!" Lennard said, at once amazed and amused. "Not—?"

"Yes, the most handsome coachman in all of the country. Your grandfather's and my favourite handler of horses, carriages, and their equipage."

Christopher Hoskins. Lennard couldn't quite believe what he'd heard. Christopher's forbears had worked for generations of the Betteridge barons. A few years younger than Lennard and his friends, he had no small reputation for being a stallion himself, some young woman always pining for his attention, but his heart securely and firmly attached to his wife and three young children.

"Take my word for it, Lennard. If you want to know anything about a man's movements when you haven't got someone following him, or you lose him in the crowds, the best information is always best heard from his stablemaster or his coachman."

"How long has he been working for … us?"

"He was recruited at the age of sixteen, when the Marquess of Normanby was Home Secretary in 1839. A little over sixteen years."

"So he spied on my grandfather Trefford and later on Sir Hugh? Shall I be next?"

"My dear boy, do you keep secrets from me? Of course not. He'll be spying *for* you, not *on* you. If I wanted to know anything you got up to and didn't want anyone to know, I'd just ask Elam."

"Please don't call me your boy, Angus. I'm nigh on three years older than you, remember?"

"Well, as you no longer allow me the privilege of calling you sweetheart, one can only try epithets until they fit, *n'est-ce pas*?"

"Back to Christopher, you flirt. Spying *for* me, you said?"

"Men in Christopher's position have access to information that might cause us no end of trouble to discover. Christopher has a collection of fellow coachmen who, for sums of money or other favours, can deliver information almost irretrievable for the likes of you and me."

"Other favours?"

"Not every man is swayed by carnal propositions, as easy as they are to arrange from our office, be it man, woman, or whatever. There are other enticements that loosen men's tongues, as well you know."

"Angus, you have been sitting behind your desk for far too long. As someone who works among the general population plying our trade as an intelligencer, I can tell you the quickest way to loosen a man's tongue is usually by means of what's in his trousers."

"And your knowledge of that, Lennard? Is it firsthand?"

"I'm paid to be a servant of the Crown, Angus. How I come by my intelligence is my own business."

2. THE INHERITANCE

After returning to the house, and to avoid further dust storms caused by the removal of sheets that covered the various items of furniture in the study, Gerald suggested they move the writing desk into the drawing room, which was also considerably warmer.

"I asked Mr Drudge to come here this morning to take notes, in order to prepare some documents based on what I've decided since learning of Sir Hugh's death and my inheritance," Lennard said once his friends had settled. "How long will probate take, Simeon?"

"As there are no encumbrances, up to two months, my lord. However, as you have highly placed friends, it could be expedited to say three or four weeks? Sir Hugh was sparing with his money and had no debts. It should be a matter quickly dealt with."

"Very well," Lennard said. "The complication of no testament will play to my advantage. My grandfather's estate, business holdings, properties, and investments will remain intact, as they were at the time of his death and when my uncle inherited them. As I am the next in line to the title, I suspect that everything else will pass on to me too. Is that not so, Mr Drudge?"

"Indeed, sir. There are no other contenders. I am mindful that your uncle Arthur, God rest his soul, dead not twelve months since, was next in line after Sir Hugh, and your father, had he survived, after Arthur Malloray. However, I'm mindful that your very good fortune must also be accompanied by no small amount of associated sadness. I both congratulate you, my lord, and at the same time, condole with you on such poignant, personal losses, which, under the circumstances, must be foremost in your mind."

"It's terrible that such great prosperity should come your way by means of other past, tragic misfortunes," Gerald said. "Although none of us knew your parents, we were all immensely fond of your grandfather and Arthur. I'm sure I speak for all of us when I say we're here for you, Lennard, for whatever you need. Any inheritance must involve a degree of mourning. In your case, there has been too much in your life."

"Thank you, Gerald," Lennard said. "As usual, you are very thoughtful and I appreciate your kind words greatly. However, I have to admit that, this morning, after having dragged poor Mr Drudge from his bed, I returned here and spent some time weeping. My tears were neither grief for my uncle Hugh, whom I loved as little as he did me, nor for the memory of my grandfather, my uncle Arthur, or my parents and siblings."

"You wept for your unexpected good fortune, Lennard?" Robert asked. "The shock would do that to any man."

"No, I'm still feeling far too overwhelmed to have any genuine acceptance of the change of my situation just yet. I was weeping because of Hugh's duplicity, avarice, and mean spirit. Perhaps you could explain to the others what you revealed to me this morning, Drudge?"

"Of course, my lord. Twelve months ago, Sir Hugh showed me a letter from his younger brother, Arthur, dictated as he lay dying in Calicut. In the letter, Arthur Malloray expressed his wishes that his nephew, Lennard Alexandre Malloray, be the sole beneficiary of his personal estate. In it, he begged his brother, Hugh, to seek him out, to have death duties dealt with, then see to it that not only his goods and chattel were passed onto his nephew, but also the substance of his fortune, once death duties had been discharged. Sir Hugh—"

"Not only did I *not* receive any of my uncle's personal possessions, but also neither did I see a penny of his estate of forty thousand pounds, as directly expressed in Uncle Arthur's letter to Sir Hugh," Lennard shouted, his face red with rage.

"Dear Heavens, Lennard," Gerald said, "forty thousand? That's an absolute fortune! Where is it now?"

"Still sitting untouched in the Bank of England, in the special account I first drew up for it while we waited for probate to be granted, Captain Langbourne," Drudge explained. "I wrote to Sir Hugh as soon as I'd learned duty had been paid, advising him the funds were free of any encumbrance and now ready for disbursement. However, no matter how many times I enquired whether there was anything I needed to do to expedite the disbursal, I was forced to come to the conclusion he'd either forgotten about it or hadn't got around to it yet."

"Hadn't got around to it yet?" Angus was outraged. "It wasn't his to do nothing with. The money was Lennard's. What was wrong with the man?"

"Sir Hugh never bothered to attend to any business," Drudge replied. "He lived more than frugally, drawing one hundred pounds a month from a personal bequest left to him by his grandfather. He seemed unwilling to touch the vast fortune he'd inherited from his own father."

"Why did you not mention this to Lennard earlier, Mr Drudge?" Gerald said. "As Angus has just pointed out, it was Lennard's money, not Sir Hugh's."

"I've already mentioned that I enquired frequently, Captain Langbourne," the solicitor replied. "However, my queries were always brushed aside. As I am retained by the barony, and not by any individual, it was not my business to mention affairs that were dealt with in confidence, as this matter was at the time Sir Hugh first showed me the letter."

The solicitor shifted uncomfortably before continuing. "For some time, I've been torn between my legal obligations of confidentiality and my earnest wish to tell his lordship what I knew. Anyway, as soon as he'd revealed the nature of his unannounced visit to my home this morning, I confessed that I'd reluctantly been keeping a confidence and now that he was the barony personified, I was able to discharge news of the inheritance. I expressed my sorrow, not only at hearing of Sir Hugh's passing but also my remorse over being forced to keep secrets that were not mine to divulge earlier. I hasten to add that I was truly mortified and begged his forgiveness."

"And it is for that reason, I've decided to keep Mr Drudge as my lawyer," Lennard announced. "Any legal man who can hold his tongue is a rare bird indeed."

"I thank you, my lord," Drudge replied. "And to your credit, sir, you did not show me the back of your hand, something I might have done had I been in your shoes."

"Please don't tell me you've been doing it hard, Lennard," Angus said. "It's none of my business, but I'd have hoped you'd always realised my purse is your own. I should be devastated to learn that you've been going without."

"I've hardly been penniless, Angus," Lennard replied. "However, twelve months ago I could sorely have done with even a small percentage of what my uncle Arthur had left me. Although, as you said, it's no one's business but my own. For the past five years, I've managed a spartan existence, living on the annual payment I received from Her Majesty's government as a third secretary in the Home Office. When my grandfather was alive, I sought for nothing. However, since his death, I've had to survive on my government stipend and what little was left in my father's account. There was little of that, to tell the truth, for he had converted nearly all of his savings into gold bullion to take with him to the colonies. It is still lying in a coffer at the bottom of the ocean somewhere, and Hugh, out of neglect, spite, or whatever, neither enquired about my situation, nor offered to help. Twelve months ago, when my dear uncle Arthur died, I was in a precarious situation, no longer able to keep up the rent on the small cottage in which Elam and I were living. My uncle's bequest would have made all the difference. Uncle Arthur's forty thousand would have seen Elam and me comfortable for the rest of our days."

"There is one bright side to this unfortunate incident, however," Drudge said. "Death duties were minimal and paid last year when your uncle passed away, so there should be no impediment to drawing on his bequest immediately."

Angus spoke first. "If you have forty thousand from your uncle Arthur, a staggering amount by itself, I can only imagine the value of your grandfather Trefford's estate must be eye-watering."

"Although I don't have access to the current value of Malloray's Eastern and Australasian Shipping Lines," Drudge offered, "I made a quick calculation before I left to come here. I propose the value of the total holdings of the estate, including land, buildings, investments, businesses, and cash at hand to be close to six hundred thousand pounds, one hundred thousand of which will go in death duties."

While his friends exclaimed in variations of shock, surprise, and delight, applauding his good fortune, Lennard was stunned. It was a far vaster sum than he could have imagined. It explained a theory he'd long held, that his uncle Hugh had been mean and spiteful due not to bad character, but a man who lived with an unstable, unrecognised mental impairment. Who else, sitting on a fortune of that size, would seclude themselves in one room of an enormous London house, eating food brought in from inns and bakeries, tupping a ten-shilling whore once a fortnight in a neglected, closed-up house in Soho Square, itself worth thousands?

"There's more," Lennard said.

"More? What more?" Angus asked.

"The reason I gathered you together this morning wasn't solely to inform you of my uncle's untimely demise, nor to reveal with any boastful purpose my change of situation, but to ask your advice and to hear your comments on my ideas for the future. Can I depend upon you to offer me wisdom and your observations in a candid manner, even if you think they may cause me offence?"

Sobered by Lennard's heartfelt entreaty, each of his friends promised to listen to what he had to say and to comment if they felt it necessary.

"The sudden unexpected deaths of my father, my grandfather and my uncles Arthur and Sir Hugh, has focused my mind on the great legacy of the barony, its assets, and its future. Has none of you realised who the next in line to inherit the title will be if something unfortunate should happen to me?"

Slowly, all eyes turned to Robert. "Me?" Robert said, appearing discomforted, blushing mightily.

"You are my first cousin," Lennard said. "Our mothers are sisters of the same blood, and you the eldest male child in the line of succession. Who else could it be, Robbie? As it stands, if you do not marry and produce offspring, after you will follow your younger brother, then his son, Geoffroy."

"Dear God, Lennard, I never—" Robert said.

"Neither did I, Robbie, and that's God's truth. However, I think it's expedient this situation should never be allowed to happen again. So, this is my proposal. I intend to not only embrace the title of eighth Baron Betteridge of Hazlemere, but also everything that the title entails for the benefit of the town, the parish, and for the people who work both in Gresting Hall, and those who work upon the twelve thousand acres upon which it resides. I shall move here, into Birch House, from where—"

"No, Lennard, you simply can't," Angus interrupted. "I'm sorry, but you did ask for our comments. This house is far too small and unimportant for someone in your new position. You must move into Bexford House. It's not far from here, and far more suitable. We'll speak more on this on Wednesday when we meet with the Home Secretary."

"Very well, if you mention the Home Secretary in your rejoinder, then I shall wait to hear reasons and proposals that you obviously feel he might contribute, to add weight to your suggestion," Lennard said.

"It's such a mausoleum, Lennard," Robert said. "What state is it in, do you know?"

"I think it's been closed up, just the same as this house was, isn't that so, Elam?" Lennard said. "You've been there more often. I haven't set foot in the place since the wake for my grandfather's London friends, five years ago."

"I've been there a few times to visit my brother," Elam replied. "Your uncle spent his days in the small sitting room that used to be a sewing room in days gone past. The rest of the house is under sheets.

It's a beautiful dwelling, in my opinion. Hardly a mausoleum, Robert, if I dare venture my own opinion, unless you mean that term for a grand edifice."

"One room, Elam?" Angus asked. "Sir Hugh lived in *one* room?"

"You'd have to ask Miles. I could fetch him if you like. He's gone to fill up the coal scuttle. It's probably time for more tea."

"I don't suppose there's anything stronger?"

"I can check in the cellar if you wish, Sir Angus. It's been many years since I've been in this house, but I do remember Lennard's grandfather ... I'm sorry, I mean the sixth baron ... had some of his best brandy brought down here from Gresting Hall."

"Don't bother, Elam, it can wait," Angus said, checking his timepiece. "I must get back to Whitehall shortly and, with the mood I'm in, I'm likely to quaff a bottle on my own. As I have a meeting with the Prime Minister's personal secretary, with a bottle of Gresting's excellent brandy under my belt, I might be tempted to speak rather too plainly than I might otherwise. What are your thoughts on your new country seat, Lennard?"

"I shall talk of my ideas for the estate shortly, but most important is the continuity and management of the business affairs of Malloray's shipping. Who has been nominally in charge for the past five years since my grandfather, Robert?"

"Mr Rudd has been running things," he replied.

"He's how old now, eighty-two, am I correct?"

"Thereabouts, yes."

"So, in fact, it is you who has been managing the entire business?"

"Sir Hugh gave instructions that the business should continue as it always did, and he only needed to hear of calamities. None ever arose, so he never visited, neither did I have to report to him. We sent weekly accounts and a monthly report."

"It is as I suspected. I suppose he signed a dozen cheques and left them with you to pay bills?"

"No, Lennard, it doesn't work like that," Robert explained. "The business dealings of Malloray's are all in several separate accounts. One for haulage, another for equipment, and so on. Both Mr Rudd and I have chequing accounts for each that we may sign whenever a bill needs paying. The business would never operate in any other way. Sometimes we issue a dozen or more a day from the eight separate accounts Malloray's keeps."

"May I say, Sir Hugh was extremely lucky to have someone like you running his business, Robert," Angus said. "How extremely imprudent to allow an employee access to the company's financial assets."

"Then my proposal is doubly sound," Lennard said. "I propose a change of circumstance for Malloray's. Mr Drudge, I'd like you to take notes on my proposal then advise me on the legality and possibility of my wishes. I have in mind to make the entire shipping concern a private company with two shareholders. There will be neither a public issue of shares nor will the company be listed on the stock exchange. It will be a family business, held by the current Baron Betteridge, myself, and my heir apparent, Robert Fahey. Robert, you will be the manager of the new business. Mr Rudd can be pensioned off into that company cottage he always loved in Penge. Robert and I will hold equal shares in the new enterprise, which I propose to rename as 'Malloray, Beauchamp, and Fahey', as part of the proceeds and eventual inheritance of the company will go to the family of our mothers, who as you may remember were Beauchamp sisters."

Lennard continued, "I also propose that Robert be named publicly as the new owner and manager of the shipping line, I merely being the business partner with no input into the operations. A monthly board meeting in Mr Drudge's chambers to keep myself informed of the affairs of our new company should suffice. As I'd trust Robert with my life, I think it unnecessary to say I'd trust him with our business."

"But, Lenn—"

"I'm not finished yet, Robert. Please hear me out then voice your opinions when I'm done. Gerald?"

"Yes, Lennard?"

"Are you likely to succeed to your uncle's title and estate?"

"As to the title, yes, I'm next in line. I shall one day be the eighth Viscount Bussell of St. Cleer. However, as you know, my uncle is a stranger to me. Since my father's death fifteen years ago, I've not heard a word from him. He didn't even attend the presentation of my medal when I returned from the Crimea."

"And he still …?"

"Gambles, and drinks like a fish. All I shall inherit is a mountain of debt and his title."

"What about the house?"

"The big house was sold years back to pay death duties on my grandfather's estate. My uncle Harold lives in an apartment in Belgravia, living on the kindness of acquaintances and using his title of the seventh Viscount Bussell to move freely in society. If the apartment isn't already promised to someone else when he dies, in lieu of a gambling debt, I suppose those six rooms will come my way … eventually. He may have already sold it and is living there under 'grace and favour'. I'd be the last to know, to be perfectly honest."

"In that case, with no likelihood of a financial inheritance, I should like to offer you the position of estate manager of Gresting. I know you have no knowledge of farming or animal husbandry, but there are people aplenty who work there whom I trust, and who've been managing in Sir Hugh's absence. You can live with me in Bexford House, it that's indeed where I end up taking residence, and you can manage the estate from London."

"From London? But how on earth shall I—?"

"Without difficulty, my friend. The railway service to High Wycombe opened last year and has a regular and quick service, handy to Hazlemere and to the Gresting Estate. You can send a telegram to be picked up at the station when you travel. I'd also like you to manage the various houses and properties that now fall under my ownership in and around London and in Hampshire. I know you were an exemplary officer, despite your reluctance to admit it—everyone I've met who has served with you has been glowing in their praise. I'm more than sure you'll be up to the task, even if it might take you a while to find your feet."

"Lennard, I don't know what to say."

"Then say nothing for the moment but start thinking of what annual income you might need to allow you to lead the life of a gentleman of standing. We can work it out with Drudge. Like Robert, I trust you implicitly, Gerald."

"I'm—"

"Please, I've not yet finished. I shall accompany Robert tomorrow to Malloray's to announce my intentions for the operation of the new business, after which I'll talk to the staff at Bexford House. Perhaps you'd like to accompany us to see what needs to be done. I shall also pay a visit to Gresting Hall at the end of the week and, perhaps, stay for the weekend. If you have no pressing business, I'd like you to come. The staff there will need to be advised of the situation and of your new position. You're welcome to remain for as long as you like, or return with me, as you wish."

"This is amazingly generous of you, Lennard," Angus said.

"Despite what Robert imagined, this is what Elam and I spent many hours discussing this morning. Many of the ideas were his."

"And what will become of Elam?" Robert asked.

"If you'd be so kind to give us a moment, please, Mr Drudge?" Lennard asked.

"Of course, my lord. I shall take a pipe on the back stairs. Fetch me when you're ready."

"We have decided that Elam will continue, as far as the world is concerned, to be my valet and personal manservant," Lennard replied after the solicitor had closed the door behind him. "He may have to learn new skills if I'm to move into society, but that's easily fixed. It's the only way a close relationship such as our own can be carried out in public, as much as it irks me. I also intend to make full private provision for his and for Miles's future."

"Well, Lenn," Robert said, "I can only concur with Angus's statement. You've been very generous. Gerald to take care of the estate and the London assets, and your offer as manager of Malloray's to me, but what does that leave you to do?"

"Ah, I shall continue as a servant of the Crown, happy in the knowledge that you, my true companions, my brothers in all but name, profit from and share my good fortune."

"You've forgotten the fourth of us, Lennard," Robert said.

"Indeed, I have not. For although Angus, a Viscount and son of an Earl, needs none of my wealth and is but the youngest of us all, do any one of you disbelieve that it will be him, manipulating—in the most pleasant sense of the word—everything that any of us says or does for the rest of our lives?"

*****

Lennard was woken by the feeling of someone tweaking his toe. He and Elam had returned to their apartment, tired after a sleepless night, and had shucked off their clothes and stretched out on the bed. Their plan had been to talk over the events of the morning for a short while before closing the shutters of the room, but Lennard had drifted off, almost at the same time as Elam, mid-sentence.

"Hello, Christopher," Lennard said, scrabbling for the coverlet.

"As sweet as two puppies in a pouch," Christopher replied, smiling at Lennard.

Elam was curled under Lennard's arm, one of his own across Lennard's body, a knee laid over his thighs, both of them naked. Lennard continued to pull at the coverlet, but as Elam was lying on it, he sighed and lay his head back against the pillow.

"I've seen you both stripped bare more times than you care to imagine. You have nothing to hide from me."

Elam stirred, nuzzled his chin against Lennard's chest, and then continued to sleep on.

"If you've been spying on us through a peep hole somewhere, there's no need, Christopher," Lennard said, chuckling softly. "You could always come closer for a friendlier inspection."

The coachman laughed. "Thank you kindly for the invitation, but as we've known each other since before we first grew hair between our legs, you know my inclinations lie elsewhere."

Lennard extricated himself from Elam's embrace and, careful not to wake him, got out of bed. "Come, follow me into the other room."

"Our talk won't wake Elam. We can stay here if you wish."

"I'm afraid I need to piss urgently, and the chamber pot is in the sluice cupboard. I forgot to replace it under the bed."

As he led the way, Lennard grabbed his linen drawers from the chair. After he'd passed water, he pulled them on, then returned to the second room of their apartment, which served as a dining and living area, and in which was a small coal stove for heating and for cooking.

"What time is it, Christopher?"

"It's close on seven in the evening. Sir Angus told me he'd revealed my secret to you, Lennard. I'm sorry. I'm aware we've been friends for most of our lives, but I was told that, unless there was a vital need, I should not disclose my position."

"I can't see what any of my family could have done that would merit being shadowed," Lennard said, using the word that intelligencers employed to describe the act of covertly observing the movements of any person of interest.

"When the time is more propitious, I'll tell you all. In your grandfather's case, and in that of your uncle Arthur, it was more to do with where they went and with whom they met, in order to build up a picture of their business dealings. However, with Sir Hugh, it was something altogether different. Something I'm not at liberty to discuss. But don't be surprised if you see me at the meeting with the Home Secretary on Wednesday."

"Now you really have me intrigued. However, I can hear Angus's instruction in your words. Has he ordered you not to explain?"

"Please, Lennard ..."

"Well, from the look on your face and the sound of your voice, I assume that's the case. Very well, I'm not a stranger to waiting for Angus's disclosures. In the meantime, let me congratulate you. As an intelligencer myself, I was mightily surprised when Angus revealed your position within the family ..."

"If you suspected nothing, Lennard, then I consider my job well done."

"Angus told me you'd be dropping something around for me?"

"It's on your table."

"Do you know what it is?"

Christopher smiled, raising an eyebrow. "It's a copy of the partial account of the ship's surgeon aboard the *Sisley* when she and the *Firefly* went down. It's all we have until next Monday when Travis Holland arrives at Greenwich Hospital."

"So … this means you know about The Cargo."

"As I said, Lennard, although I've been forbidden to talk of certain matters, you may make your own inferences."

Lennard opened the packet. In it was the letter and a book, the title of which was new to him: *La Vie Secrète de la Marquise Fonteneau. Mémoires d'une Courtisane.*

"*The Secret Life of the Marchioness Fonteneau. Memoirs of a Courtesan?* This sounds like something more suited to a man of your tastes, rather than mine," Lennard said.

"I think you'll find it's the story of an English lord who disguised himself as a French noblewoman to sleep with the gentlemen belonging to Napoleon Bonaparte's cadre in order to gain information."

"And this has been published?"

"Sir Angus told me it was a private edition."

"I see," Lennard said, although he didn't. His mind was full of imaginings of how a man could successfully deceive male lovers. No doubt, the story itself was not the reason Angus had sent the book, but as a hint that Lennard, although elevated in station in society, would still be able to work for Her Majesty's government. Perhaps his targets might be richer and nobler, but he felt sure when he read the book, he might find that the English *milord* did not always dress as a woman, but also found time to spy among the bourgeoisie and the rabble. Angus never did anything without there being layers of meaning.

"Your stove needed stoking, so I filled up the grate then dampened it down. There's a steak and oyster pie keeping warm in the oven and two bottles of stout in the larder, compliments of Sir Angus."

"Thank you, Christopher. I look forward to spending some time with you quite soon, to discuss how I can help you and your family."

"There's no need, Lennard."

"There's every need. Now go, say hello to your wife and kiss your children for me."

"Thank you … Lord Betteridge."

"I hope you'll still call me Lennard when there's no need for titles and the like and when we're in private."

"Of course. You'll always be Lenn to me, and always have been, even when I've called you Mr Malloray, while in company, just like Elam does."

*****

Elam stirred when Lennard returned to the bedroom. He'd read the letter and a few pages of the introduction of the book, but then decided he was hungry.

He lay down beside Elam, running his hand over his chest and tugging softly at the trail of short hairs that flowed from the base of Elam's neck down to his navel. After no more than a few heartbeats, Elam's hand had found his own and he'd woven his fingers through Lennard's.

"What time is it?" Elam said and, when Lennard turned his face to answer so Elam could read his words, found himself pulled down into a languid, sleepy kiss.

"Christopher's been and gone," he mouthed. "He brought supper."

"Supper can wait, Lennard Malloray. I have more urgent needs than food."

Lennard chuckled, then turned onto his back as Elam rolled onto him.

"You are too handsome for the likes of me, Elam Walters," he whispered into his ear, knowing not a syllable of what he'd said would be heard.

He reached over and turned the wick down on the oil lamp. The room fell into darkness, illuminated only by the glow from the lamp in the room next door, which shone palely over the foot of their bed.

Lennard liked to make love in the semi-darkness, not because he disliked seeing what he and Elam were doing, but merely because he just wanted to concentrate on the feelings and sensations that flowed through his body.

Tonight was one of those times.

3. THE CARGO

On Wednesday morning, Lennard found himself being shown into Angus's office by a new, rather pinched-face young assistant who hadn't introduced himself, but who was painfully obsequious, using both Lennard's title and a plethora of milords rather more frequently than was necessary.

When Lennard had arrived, the young man had informed him that Angus was ready to receive him, and very shortly, they'd be ushered into the Home Secretary's private bureau, which served not only as his office but also as a comfortable meeting room. Lennard was no stranger to it, having sat before the impressive oak desk that had served the seven Home Secretaries under which he'd worked more times than Angus's new assistant had probably passed water since the new year began.

"Good morning, Angus," Lennard said, declining an offer of coffee but accepting a splendid cigar after Angus had waved his hand in the direction of an impressive new ivory and silver humidor. It lived on a pedestal beneath a portrait of Angus's father, who seemingly stared down over his son's desk with a disapproving look.

"You're a little early, Lenn, but I don't mind. It gives us a few minutes to chat before we face Sir George."

"Your new man seems rather dour," Lennard said, shaking his friend's hand.

"Yes, I'm trying him out. His first test is to last the week without revealing his name, even if visitors should request it."

"Where do you find such specimens?"

Angus said nothing but glanced at the painting.

Lennard chuckled. "Ah, a paternal suggestion to repay a favour, I imagine."

Angus gave the merest wisp of a smile and his quick glance toward the ceiling hardly merited the description of an eye roll, but his immediate half-snarl seemed to confirm Lennard's suspicion.

"No matter how many times I come into this room and see your father hanging on the wall, I can't help but observe that he looks immeasurably cross."

"He's become less so since my marriage," Angus said, sighing deeply.

"Based on the few occasions I've met Adelia, I rather liked her. I thought that as she's a sapphist, there'd be no unnecessary awkwardness for either of you …?"

"She's a nice enough creature. No, that's a demeaning term. She's a delightful woman. She's intelligent, with beautiful manners, extremely well-read, and knowledgeable about most current affairs. But above all, she possesses the added excellent quality of caring as much for my company in the bedchamber as I do for hers. She has her own lady companion … if that's the term. But Father is insistent on a grandchild or two before we're allowed to move into our own households. So, we're convivial, which isn't hard, mostly sleep in our own beds, but come together when she tells me the time is right. Don't ask me, Lennard, you know I'm basically an innocent when it comes to women."

"Oh!" Lennard said, trying to keep the soft exclamation as neutral as possible. "I thought you said there was to be no intimacy?"

"Twenty thousand pounds for the first child—for each of us, I might add—followed by fifteen for the second and each subsequent grandchild is an adequate stimulus for us to make an effort."

"And how is it progressing?"

"There's been some fumbling and one or two successful connections, but I think she finds the whole business as awkward as I do. We spend a lot of time giggling and losing momentum mid-coitus. I don't dislike it, far from it, but you know where my passions lie."

"And your *amour*? Have you been still managing to meet?"

"Not as often as either of us would like. Clandestinely these days. The gentleman in question is extremely busy and has more than my iron in his fire, if you get my drift. Were either of us placed otherwise ... well, I'm sure you understand. Now, where's Elam? He was to accompany you. I trust nothing is amiss?"

"Nothing at all, Angus. He'll be here presently. He left me downstairs saying he had a charge sheet to deposit. He'll join us in a few minutes."

"Ah, I see ... of course."

"Then perhaps you could enlighten me? In the nearly two decades I've worked on this very floor, I've never heard of a charge sheet. What on earth is it?"

"It's an abbreviation of 'discharge'. If I'm not mistaken, it will be a document signed by Christopher, discharging himself of further intelligence gathering on Sir Hugh and submitting his expense sheet for the month. Christopher can't come up the front stairs, there'd be no end of awkward suppositions, most of them correct, so no doubt he's asked Elam to hand it in for him. If there's to be a meeting, like ours today, he uses the back staircase that leads to the antechamber behind the Home Secretary's office. He's probably there now, waiting to join us—"

"Expense sheet?"

"I told you on Monday while we were in the garden. Bribes to fellow coachmen, other payments of that nature. You know, Lennard, shadows to follow your uncle, that sort of thing."

"Sir Hugh merited that much attention?"

"No, but I did tell you that we were concerned about some of the company he kept. However, more of that later when we're all gathered. There are other things to discuss before we get to that topic."

"One moment, Angus. You either glossed over it rather too glibly or I was distracted … I could have sworn you said 'he's probably there now, waiting to join us'. Were you referring to Christopher? He's joining our meeting?"

"As are Robert and Gerald, who are presently talking with Sir George who, if I'm not mistaken, will already have sworn them to secrecy."

"They're to be brought into the fold?"

"Well, of course they are, Lennard. You are normally the first to see the necessity for things of such a nature."

"Forgive me, Angus. I had a remarkably busy day yesterday. First of all, at Bexford House—thank you for sending your father's architect along with Gerald. The staff were exuberant when I announced I would be taking up residence. There are only six left, did you know? Sir Hugh sent everyone off. I don't know what I shall do. I've never really had staff before, not in that number anyway. Father and mother kept only four when we lived in Marylebone. There's also the matter of arranging for Sir Hugh's body to be sealed in a lead casket to be sent up to Gresting—"

Angus slid a few sheets of paper across the desk.

"What's this? Please don't tell me it's news of some sort of gathering for my uncle. I want there to be no get-togethers, no celebrations, merely a simple interment in the family vault on the estate. He—"

"It's nothing to do with Sir Hugh, Lennard. It's about the staff—a list we've compiled of suitable servants, all carefully chosen and evaluated by the Home Office, valued for discretion and secrecy. You may feel the need to interview them first, but I promise you they have all worked clandestinely in houses up and down the country. Having been in their various locations for too long, they're all in need of moving about. Your new household will need people who already know what to do without being asked and can be relied on for their tact and circumspection. This lad at the top, Clyford Billings, is whom we've decided shall be your private secretary. You'll need one now, and he's eminently qualified … and is one of us."

"One of … *us*?"

"One of us, Lennard. Not only did Sir George place him in the bureau of Baron Hochschild, the former Swedish ambassador, but he's also … well, I don't have to spell it out."

"The name is very familiar …"

"He's the nephew of General Airey. That's how you know his name. You've met him once or twice, obviously, as Gerald was the general's adjutant in the Crimea."

"Ah, yes, of course. Pleasant-faced young man. Extremely good manners and quiet."

"And has an intellect like a finely-honed razor and will mind his business when it comes to what goes on behind bedroom doors."

*****

"My dear Lord Betteridge," Sir George Grey, the Home Secretary said, rising to his feet and moving from behind his desk. After initially taking Lennard's hand, he drew him into a warm embrace.

It was the second time Sir George had occupied the position, having been re-appointed not more than three weeks previously. Lennard had served under him for six years—from 1845 to 1851—and during that time had developed a close, cordial relationship with him. He'd always been kind, avuncular, and affectionate to Lennard—in some ways replacing his grandfather while Lennard was trying to find his feet. With no mentor or father figure to call upon when advice was needed, Lennard could talk to Sir George.

"I'd rather you continue calling me either Lennard, or Malloray, as you used to. As it's so very recent, whenever someone uses my new title, I'm still inclined to look over my shoulder in case my grandfather has risen from the grave and is standing a yard or so behind me."

Lennard took the seat Sir George indicated, on a wide sofa between Robert and Gerald. Christopher and Angus occupied a small *chaise à deux* at their side. He'd barely greeted them when a knock sounded and Elam entered, excusing himself for his tardiness. He made himself comfortable between Gerald and Lennard, apologising to Robert for the tight squeeze.

Sir George Grey was a man known for coming straight to the point. Lennard understood they'd find private time to indulge in social pleasantries, possibly after the meeting. When Elam was seated, the Home Secretary leaned his posterior against the edge of his desk and began to address the six men.

"The death of Hugh Malloray has precipitated events in such a way that Sir Angus and I were forced to come to the conclusion that a meeting with you gentlemen was in order. There is a situation of some long standing and importance that has also come to a head, coincidental to Lennard's and Mr Fahey's good fortune … and to yours as well, Captain Langbourne, if rumour has it true?"

"Indeed, I've been most fortunate in the choice of my friends, Sir George. Lennard has been more than generous."

"And one day it will be his undoing."

Lennard shifted in his chair, understanding the reference Sir George had made was to his disastrous love affair, which, when the relationship had come to a violent, disagreeable end, had consequences for Sir George and his son.

"Before I explain the nature of this situation, one that has been a volcano threatening to erupt for some time, I wish to put before you Angus's and my ideas for a re-arrangement of our intelligencers. I'll ask him to explain."

Angus turned at an angle in his seat to face his friends. "We've been receiving regular reports over the past five years on the way the new intelligence organisation of the Austro-Hungarian Empire has been set up, and we've been monitoring its progress. The *Evidenz-bureau*, as it's called, has developed a system of small groups of intelligencers who are self-reliant, well-known to each other, and led by one person within the bureau itself. They call their groups *cloisons*, a word that we might translate into English as units, or cells, small divisions within a larger structure. We believe that these smaller, tightly-contained *cloisons* are the future of government espionage, and Sir George and I have come to the agreement that for the dossier we call 'The Cargo', we six, with me as the point of contact within the Home Office, should become a *cloison*, directly charged with dealing with all aspects of the case pertaining to activity in London and its immediate surrounds."

"The Cargo?" Robert asked.

"Sir George will explain. But first of all, as you and Gerald are the only two men in the room who are not privy to one of the greatest secrets in the kingdom, I assume that when you first arrived, Sir George asked you to reaffirm your allegiance to the Crown and to the nation. Am I correct?"

While Robert and Gerald assured Angus they had done so, Lennard noticed the slight frown, a small puckering of the flesh between Robert's eyebrows. His cousin was the most timid of The Brothers, and each of the others knew that as brave as a lion when he found himself in any situation which was serious and a decision had to be made that might lead to possible danger, he was otherwise naturally cautious.

It was Sir George who spoke next. "Very well, gentlemen. Between Angus and I, we'll attempt to explain as simply as possible the most outrageous story you are likely ever to have heard, or indeed are likely to hear for the rest of your years. Let me preface my speech by warning you that you will be astounded at the preposterousness of the saga, and you will find it hard to believe that what we are about to tell you is a truth and not some absurd fiction put forward by the writer of some cheap and tawdry 'penny blood', sold for sensationalism and shock to those less educated than yourselves."

"Please feel free to ask questions as we proceed," Angus added. "Lennard and Elam, who have been working on The Cargo dossier for a few years now, will also be able to illuminate aspects of our explanation as it unfolds."

"However irrelevant this may seem," Sir George said, "we need to dwell a little upon the succession of Her Majesty the Queen to the throne of our kingdom. Although you may wonder why, bear with me, for it is important information to understanding what I'm about to reveal to you."

"Please, proceed, Sir George," Gerald said.

"Very well. In my eighteenth year, a terrible blow fell across the land with the death in childbirth of Charlotte, the Princess of Wales. It constituted a crisis in the line of succession. None of the sons of George the Third had legitimate issue, which left no direct successor to the throne after the Prince Regent."

"In that case, we were lucky that the Prince Regent's brother, the Duke of Kent, fathered a daughter shortly before he too died," Angus added. "I'm sure this is old history, but ..."

"There's always a but, isn't there," Gerald observed.

"Yes, you are correct, there is always a but," Sir George said. "I remember well, hearing from my father at the time, that there were many members of the nobility and in parliament who were not as delighted as the old king with the birth of our current monarch. There were murmurings of 'remember Bloody Mary', and 'remember Queen Anne and her favourites'. These men, after it was realised that there would be no further male issue from the Duke of Kent and the Princess Victoria of Saxe-Coburg-Saarfeld, hatched a plan, the embryo of a scheme, that was kept secret for decades. This plan, as heinous and bizarre as it might appear, has lately grown to adulthood, and over recent years has begun to be embraced by certain peers, magnates, and politicians who are unhappy with the current situation. They could tolerate a woman on the throne. However, it appears to them that she is ruled by her husband, a foreigner, whom they believe wishes to sit at her side as king, eventually usurp her power, and rule Britain in her stead."

Both Robert and Gerald chuckled at the idea. Most intelligent people who read well and who were au fait with politics knew those were neither the wishes of Her Majesty nor of her consort, Prince Albert. However, their smiles soon faded when they saw that their companions were not laughing with them.

"Although all of the Home Secretaries have known of this plan since the accession of our queen, each one of us has thought it so beyond the pale that none of us has ever given it more than a dismissive thought. We've treated it as nonsense. Until a few years ago, we thought it had died a natural death. However, we have recently had cause to believe the plan did not indeed fester and die, but has been fomenting quietly in the background for these past nearly forty years."

"There have been rumours," Lennard said. "It's something Elam and I have been investigating since the outbreak of the war in Crimea, an event we all feel may have precipitated the plan being acted upon, rather than remaining a far-fetched idea in the minds of—"

"Sedition!" the Home Secretary interrupted, his normal composure broken by a quick flash of extreme annoyance. "What do you understand by the meaning of the word, Captain Langbourne?"

"It means conduct or words used to bring about subversion and to challenge the authority of the state. But in this case, owing to your allusions, the institution of our monarchy."

"Very good, sir. I had no doubt you understood the meaning of the word, but I want you to keep it in mind while I tell you about The Cargo. It's the very basis and the idea upon which the plan rests. Please, hear me out to the end."

"Very well, I beg you to continue, Sir George," Gerald said.

"In a nutshell, at the time of Queen Victoria's accession, the clique put it about that the Duke of Kent had already entered into a secret marriage before his betrothal to Princess Victoria, Her Majesty's mother. A morganatic marriage born from a lustful affair, later annulled by King George the Third. This fictional marriage, despite its asserted relatively short duration—no more than a matter of a few months—was supposed to have produced a male child, born some ten months after a civil ceremony in Gretna Green. It is this child, this clique says, who is the true male heir to the throne and should rightfully be our King."

"What?" Gerald said, his eyes wide in disbelief. "This is nonsense!"

"Of course it is. It's even more fanciful than one of those German folk tales, full of preposterous suggestions and written for gullible minds."

"Who would believe such an invention?" Robert asked.

"The tale becomes even more fabulous, as hard as that might be to believe."

"I think I might need some fortification," Gerald said.

"Please help yourselves. There are wines, spirits, and drinking vessels in the cabinet under the window."

Lennard turned to Elam and mouthed. "If they are shocked now, I think we might be spending half the evening calming them down when they hear the rest of it."

Elam smiled and gently tapped Lennard's knee with his forefinger. He blushed when he noticed the Home Secretary had not missed the gesture.

Gerald was the only one of them who felt the need of a stiffener. Once he'd returned to his seat, Sir George continued.

"The bride was supposed to have been a Turkish maidservant, going by the name of Zuleikha. However, no reference was found to any such person having worked in the royal household at Kensington Palace. Although we've never laid eyes on any of them, the clique put it about that they had documents and other 'sworn statements' from so-called witnesses who attended the marriage—even though such a marriage certificate has been elusive, and there are no entries in any of the church registers in Gretna Green. If there is a marriage document, like the other supporting evidence, no doubt it is forged. Their argument is that as the child was conceived in a state of legal wedlock, he has a claim to the throne, and one which suits the seditionists in our great union."

It was Robert who first broke the silence. Normally the quieter of the four, he'd become red in the face and jumped to his feet. "I've never heard such a fairy tale, sir. The whole idea is beyond absurdity ... that's bad enough. But that some people as highly placed as you suggested might seriously take it for a truth? Why, the country would never stand for it."

"You and I, and our companions in the room, and educated men of our ilk, or anyone with tuppence worth of reasoning would never stand for it, that's true. But tell me, Mr Fahey, with whom do you think our fair Queen and her foreign-born husband are most unpopular—for they are at the present time, to tell the truth—with which classes and from which parts of the kingdom?"

"Well, sir, if you put the question to me," Robert replied, "it is my experience that people with no education are oft-times like sheep, following mindlessly if someone spouts some nonsense that appears to be to their advantage. And as for the regions where the monarchy is least popular, why, I'd say the industrial north and ..."

His voice faded when he realised the direction in which the Home Secretary's question had led him.

"Yes, Mr Fahey, the land of your father and his ancestors—Ireland."

"The Irish? I must protest, Sir George, not every Irishman is disloyal to the throne. Why—"

"I do not say this out of disrespect for your family," the Home Secretary interrupted, moving forwards to take Robert's hand in his own, "I've known you and your father, even your grandfather, and have always considered your family loyal to the throne and true friends to both myself and to the kingdom. However, we must not forget the Great Famine is but a few years since, and memories are long. The most blamed are not the Irish landlords but the Crown and the British parliament for not coming to the aid of the million and more souls who died of hunger. Please, be seated, there's more to tell, Mr Fahey."

Gerald passed his glass to Robert, who drained it and then apologised for his outburst.

"What I've revealed to you so far is merely the history of the plan. Over the past two years, since our war in the Crimea, we believe the original clique, its members now older in years and with the addition of fresher faces who regret our decision to fight alongside the French, have decided that the time is right to produce their pretender. They fostered a child—a man of some forty years now—with a Turkish mother and an English father. Our intelligence leads us to believe that he was conceived not by the Duke of Kent, but by one of the footmen at the Brighton Pavilion, the only royal residence in which foreign women were employed as novelty servants to present meals and to give the place an air of the exotic. With the plan already hatched, the child and its mother were packed off to Turkey, supported by donations from wealthy Englishmen, and given a refined upbringing with every necessity, bar one—no education in the English language. To our knowledge, he speaks not a word of it."

"Which would make it easier for the clique," Lennard explained. "At the age of forty, he's unlikely to ever have fluency in our language, and therefore remain dependent on his 'advisers'."

"I think I have an inkling of where this might be going …" Gerald said.

"Let me continue if you please, Captain Langbourne," Sir George said, "then you can confirm your suspicions. The child's training was guided by the same association of disillusioned members of parliament and their friends among the disaffected gentry who wish revolution and change in our country. They think that if they produce this pretender with enough support from others in the land, with a promise of a governance of milk and honey, they will endeavour to install him on the throne, manipulating him from behind the scenes so that they will, in fact, rule the land and with the blessing of a puppet king."

"Dear God!" Gerald murmured, turning to Lennard to ascertain what he'd been told was true. Home Secretary or no Home Secretary, the tale was outrageous beyond his experience.

"There's more," Lennard said, returning Gerald's glance with a sad smile.

"When you have had time to reflect, although laughable, there is some method and purpose behind their insanity," Sir George said, noting Gerald and Robert's extreme discomfort.

"How so, sir?"

"Poverty and greed make for exceptional bedfellows, Captain Langbourne. United, two large groups of people, no matter how disparate their social situations, can cause terrible events to unfold. Need I remind you of the occurrences that came to pass in France in 1787? The revolution that overthrew the monarchy and led to bloodshed and the upheaval of the entire nation?"

"You do not, sir," Gerald replied. "My presumption is the clique of which you spoke is presently intending to take advantage of the current unpopularity of Her Majesty and an unwelcome war against a nation with whom we came to be in conflict in order to support our allies in the Ottoman empire. I fear you are about to say they are trying to bring this Turkish pretender to our shores."

"I congratulate you for your perspicacity, Captain. The pretender has gone missing and, although we've had agents looking for him these past two years since the Crimean conflict broke out, there have only been unsubstantiated sightings. He's accompanied by his lifelong bodyguard, a villainous cut-throat, who we only know as Kadir, which means 'powerful' in their language. He's as dangerous as the pretender but in a different way. He's a Turkish-born Russian, from a disenfranchised noble family, a known assassin with a reputation for being cruel and ruthless. Together," Sir George said, retrieving a folder of documents from his desk and holding them up, "they're known by us as The Cargo, and we need not only find them and prevent them from arriving in Great Britain but also to dispatch them with all haste if they do manage to get to our shores."

"But no one knows where they are," Gerald said. Am I correct?"

"You are. Now, if I'm not mistaken, my secretary will be waiting outside with a *table roulante*. I'm fastidious in my timetable, gentlemen, and while there is more to discuss, if I don't take tea at ten o'clock precisely, I'm out of sorts for the entire day."

Sir George rang a small handbell on his desk and Gerald stared at Lennard as the Home Secretary's man rolled in the trolley, upon which sat a splendid set of Worcester china and gleaming silver tea service.

"You've kept this secret for how long, Lenn?" Gerald whispered.

"Far too long, haven't we, Elam," Lennard replied.

"Sometimes it keeps him awake at night."

"I'm sure you have ways of distracting him though, Elam?"

"I could always do with help. He's a handful," Elam replied.

"In that case, I shall make it my mission to call past this evening."

Lennard shook his head, smiling at his friend's gentle banter.

"I'll look forward to that, Gerald. However, I think you're teasing me, as you normally do ..."

"You may not look forward to it when you hear what else is to come, Lenn," Elam said under his breath, refusing to look Lennard's way when asked to explain. He stood, thus avoiding any further conversation, made his way to the tea service, and began to chat with Christopher.

*****

"So, this partial extract sent by the surgeon aboard the *Sisley* is important because it is only he who can verify the identities of the two unknown civilian passengers who were in the longboat when it was struck?"

"Yes, Gerald," Lennard said. "And may I remind you that the last time The Cargo was supposedly seen was on the dock at Varna looking for passage to Greece, the *Sisley*'s first port of call on her way back to our naval base in Gibraltar. However, our agent on the dockside only caught a partial glimpse of one of them, so until we speak with the doctor, we cannot actually substantiate whether it was the men we're looking for or not. It may or may not be The Cargo. We've yet to establish the fact."

They had repaired to Angus's office after tea because Sir George had been summoned to attend the Prime Minister. He'd beckoned Lennard to follow him to the top of the staircase before going down to his carriage, inviting Lennard to sup with him and Angus at the Oriental Club at six o'clock to discuss 'personal matters'.

"What do we know about Mr Travis Holland, Angus? Have you had time to discover anything?"

Angus blinked at Gerald. "Are you being provocative on purpose, Gerald? Or was that a rhetorical question?"

"I'm sorry. I have never known you in your position as personal private secretary to the Home Secretary. Please forgive me. I have to remind myself that you are no longer the fair-haired lad who used to lay by my side in the cornfield near the edge of the alder copse, staring into the sky, distracted by the shapes of the clouds and flocks of whirling birds."

"I am still that person, Gerald. And now I know you are being annoying on purpose. Perhaps when you regain your former carefree ways, you might join me for another such adventure while I lay flat on my back, investigating the heavens above us—"

"Over my shoulder with your knees under my armpits most likely," Gerald quipped, which evoked a change of atmosphere in the room. The tension ebbed away as the men laughed. Even Christopher guffawed.

Angus laid his head on his forearms, resting on the desk. His shoulders shook with suppressed laughter. He had the loudest laugh anyone had heard, and it always caused heads to turn. From the age of sixteen, when his voice had broken, he'd continued to try to stifle his mirth—people who didn't know him always stared.

Lennard reached over Angus's desk and retrieved the dossier. He'd seen it when he'd first arrived earlier that morning and had wondered about the slim pale grey folder with the surgeon's name written on its cover in Angus's neat copperplate.

"Travis Jago Holland, born in Fowey in 1823. His father is the local doctor, under whom he studied before travelling to Scotland to complete his education at the Medical School of Glasgow." Lennard flipped through a few other documents. "Very good reports, excellent examination results, joined the Royal Navy as ship's surgeon in 1847 at the age of twenty-four. Older brother, Percival, lost in the sinking of H.M.S. *Prince* in Balaklava when she went down in a storm last year. Only six survivors. His brother's body, along with hundreds of others, was never found."

Angus, recovered, held his hand out for the folder, which Lennard passed back to him. "There's also a daguerreotype taken two years ago, just before the outbreak of war," Angus said, retrieving the likeness.

"Comely gentleman," Robert remarked as Angus passed him the image. "Wife? Children?"

"He was engaged to be married to his first cousin. However, she contracted cholera and succumbed a month before they were due to be married. He's stayed a bachelor ever since."

"You mentioned that you'd like me to interview him, Angus?" Lennard asked.

"Well, it was my original idea, and I think it a good one. He's due to arrive on Monday. No one knows what his condition is because his injury was rather severe, although not life-threatening. I've already sent word to Greenwich that they should let us know what shape he's in. Perhaps give him a few days to settle. Then, perhaps, it might be good timing for you to pay him a visit."

*****

"You said I might not look forward to a visit from Gerald when I was to hear what was to come. Earlier on, you said it, just before we had tea when you turned your back on me so I could not query your statement further. What on earth was that all about? No one has said anything to me that was even vaguely disturbing."

"Not yet, anyway," Elam replied. "If I were to hazard a guess, I imagine you'll be told about it over dinner this evening."

Lennard hesitated, one foot on the carriage stair and turned back to Elam. "We've never kept secrets, Elam. If you know what it is ..."

"I'm sorry, Lenn. This time, I shall be there for you after you hear of it, but please don't press me."

"Is it something calamitous? Is someone—"

"It's nothing like that. Now, get in the carriage and let's go to Bexford House. By now, the possessions from our two rooms will have been moved and the bedroom you've chosen will have been cleaned, aired, and made ready. An army of workers will arrive while we're away at Gresting Hall at the weekend, and you need to plan how you'll use the house in Clarence Gardens."

"Have you—?"

"Yes, no need to ask. I've had the valet's pantry turned into my bedroom for the few occasions when you banish me from your bed."

"When have I ever done that?"

"Your memory fails you, Lennard. There was that period of time, years ago, when you—"

"Enough, Elam! I've struck that episode from my mind. It never existed, do you hear?"

Elam didn't answer, but turned his face, hoping Lennard wouldn't see the quick anxious look that flew across his face.

4. THE ORIENTAL CLUB

On the occasion of each of their twenty-first birthdays, The Brothers had been introduced as fully paid members of the Oriental Club by Lennard's grandfather, the sixth Baron Betteridge.

He'd been a great friend of the Duke of Wellington, who'd been responsible for setting up the gentlemen's club in Lower Grosvenor Street, and Trefford Malloray had served on the board since its inception, donating a thousand pounds a year.

Lennard was surprised at the soft applause he'd received upon entering the main room, accompanied by a few vigorous handshakes and congratulatory pats on the back. Word had obviously got around of his change of status. No doubt, at some stage during the evening, or within the next few days, he'd be approached by one of the senior members of the club with either a discrete invitation to take his grandfather's seat on the board or an equally oblique enquiry as to the resurrection and continuation of the sixth Baron's generous annual donation.

Sir Hugh had never visited, not once in five years, and on the few occasions any of The Brothers had either lunched or had dinner there, allusions were invariably inserted into conversations mentioning that it was a shame, because much of London's business was conducted over port, cigars, or boiled mutton and cabbage. The food was, and always had been, atrocious, but much to the taste of those who were members.

Robert went under sufferance, and only very rarely. Lennard, Angus, and Gerald were from notable families. Robert was Lennard's cousin—with a French mother and an Irish father—and mostly invisible to those gentlemen who frequented the Oriental Club. He loathed the forced smiles and indifference to his presence.

It was with no small amount of pleasure that Lennard observed one or two gentlemen, half-frozen, wondering whether they'd slighted his friend in the past when he announced that Robert, now a man with a fortune of his own, would be in charge of Malloray's—the most important shipping business in the city.

As he made his way to the private room, Lennard promised himself that he and Robert would attend the club together quite soon and "hold court" as his grandfather used to call it, deciding who among the suitors would receive the most favourable prices and schedules for the shipping of their wares to all parts of the globe.

*****

"This is a very civilised way of eating," Lennard said, his eyes wide at the beautifully presented salmon-trout with Dutch sauce the footman placed on the table before him. "And quite unlike what I might have expected at the Oriental Club."

He'd learned that it would be *service à la russe*, still considered novel among some members of society, who preferred to have all the food laid out before them on the table at once.

"Angus brought his own people. The food, except for the fish, is already prepared and packed in straw," Sir George said. "He knows I abhor what passes for cuisine here."

"It has a very familiar taste and presentation ..." Lennard said.

"That's because it was prepared by Mr Huilot."

"Is he in your employ now, Angus?"

"You obviously have been far too busy to look through the list of suggested household staff that Sir George and I drew up for you, Lennard. You'll notice I've poached him for you from the Countess Watervale."

"That's extraordinary. Why, thank you, Angus."

"Truth be told, he couldn't wait to get out of the place. She has a bill of fare for each day of the week, never varied. On Mondays, there's one menu, repeated every Monday thereafter, and Tuesday has its own, and so on. If there are to be guests, they get what she normally eats on that same day for breakfast, luncheon, and dinner. She won't try anything new. He almost did somersaults when I fetched him away this morning."

"This morning? Before you even showed me the list?"

"*Je te connais trop bien, mon cher*," Angus replied with a smile.

"You may know me too well, Angus, but what if I'd already had someone up my sleeve?"

"If you'd had someone up your sleeve, Lennard, you wouldn't have been hiding him up there for his cuisine."

The conversation turned to other matters while the food was being served and between courses. A magnificent *Filet de Boeuf à la Périgord* followed the fish, after which cheese was presented, as was the continental fashion. Finally, a raspberry ice cream smothered in fresh berries.

"Raspberries? And in March?" Lennard exclaimed.

"That's due to my greenhouse manager, Lennard," Angus replied. "And you're *not* getting him, I promise you."

*****

"What shall you do about your aunt, the Baroness Winchester, Lennard?" Sir George asked after the table had been cleared and coffee was being prepared.

"What do you mean, Sir George, what shall I do about my great-aunt Caroline?"

"It may have escaped your notice in the upheaval of Sir Hugh's sudden death and news of your inheritance, but as the senior male of the Malloray family, then it falls to you to be her guardian."

"Guardian? My aunt is twenty-five years my senior, wealthy in her own right with an enormous estate in Hampshire. The Baron Winchester left her a fortune."

"Which she can't lay hands on, Lennard. Did no one tell you that? She had to apply to Sir Hugh when he was alive for every penny she needed. Women aren't their own masters if there's a man as head of the family, no matter what his age—or hers, for that matter."

"I've never heard of such a thing."

"You can blame her late husband. He didn't become a magnate in iron and steel by being generous with his money. It was a provision in his will, in order to stop her marrying again and her new husband taking the estate and his fortune."

Lennard was taken aback, and unable to hide it.

"You should visit her and set up some new arrangement," Angus suggested. "The railway service to Basingstoke is very comfortable and not more than an hour and a half. Perhaps you could write to her and suggest a social call from her favourite nephew. Foxley Manor is just outside Nutley, is it not? No more than five or six miles from the railway station."

"I'll write to her tomorrow, after we've seen off Hugh's casket on the early train. I intend to visit Gresting on Friday, returning on Monday morning. Perhaps they've already heard the news, but I feel it should come from my lips."

"I think the arrival of a lead casket bearing your uncle's body the day before you arrive might give most of them the slightest clue," Sir George said, drily, although with the hint of a smile at the corner of his mouth.

Lennard demurred when the footman enquired whether he'd partake of coffee.

"Is he one of ours?" he asked after the man had left the room and closed the service door after him.

"Merrill will be one of yours, Lennard. He's top of the list for first footman. Tall, well-groomed, and comely."

"Miles will have to approve."

"Miles?"

"Yes, I've a mind to appoint Miles as butler at Bexford House. He deserves it after making do for Hugh for five years. Anyway, my grandfather always had it in mind to have it so."

"I suppose you were wondering why I invited Robert and Gerald to become members of The Cargo *cloison* this morning?"

"No, Sir George. Once Angus disclosed to me that they were already in your bureau when I arrived, it made sense. Robert, because you'd already heard from Angus that I'd asked him to take management of Malloray's shipping, and Gerald because of his military connections and friendship with General Airey."

"Her Majesty's government will approach you both shortly regarding Malloray's. There may be an offer of a contract to convey canned beef, soup, and other preserved foodstuffs to our supply depots in the Mediterranean. It could be worth ten thousand a year ..."

"For which we would?"

"Nothing in particular, Lennard, merely a favour or two ... if required."

Lennard smiled. In any other conversation, it might be described as smuggling or dealing in illicit wares hidden among the canned goods, barrels of cod, and preserved herring. He hadn't missed the slight hesitation in the Home Secretary's sentence. Bribery it certainly was, without a doubt.

"As for Captain Langbourne, there's a new dossier upon which we'd like you and him to cooperate."

"Someone military I suppose?"

"No, Lennard. Not quite."

Sir George turned to Angus. "If you'd be so kind?"

Angus produced a slim folder from his leather document case. Lennard had seen the portfolio at his side when he'd arrived and knew that, at some stage during the evening, something would be produced from it that had to do with him.

"The Grand Duke Vassili Vadimovich Kosorukov?"

"Yes, Lennard. He's lived here for the past ten years. Married to Frances, the daughter of the Earl of Twinton. She married for the title of Grand Duchess, he married because his father was a drunkard, gambler, and womaniser, who not only lost the family lands and fortune, but also destroyed his family's reputation at the Czar's court."

"I don't know the Twintons," Lennard replied. "I suppose she brought a huge dowry."

"So he thought, but here's a bit of advice, Lennard," Sir George said. "Sign in haste and repent at leisure. He's on an allowance, one within which he struggles to survive, until a son is born."

"This sounds terribly familiar, don't you think, Angus?"

Angus kicked Lennard's foot under the table, but a smile hovered at the corner of his lips.

"If you read the dossier, Lennard, you'll find an assessment that he's quite likely approachable for intelligence."

"If he's lived here for ten years, what possible intelligence could he have that's of value to the current situation?"

"Who sleeps with whom, for starters. Then there are the peccadillos, the weaknesses and vulnerabilities of the Russian generals and admirals, all of those things you already know are facets of a man's character that we might exploit."

"I see ..." Lennard said, his voice trailing off. At the bottom of the final page was a list of known places of visitation. The majority of the locations a man of his station might be fit to be seen, but the final four were in the three-letter code intelligencers used to denote less salubrious establishments. Lennard read the initials, filling in the details in his mind.

1. TQH stood for The Queen's Head—a tavern near Rotten Row, known to be filled with young guardsmen who would go with a gentleman for a crown.
2. TLH was an acronym for The Lion's Heart—another tavern, not far from Birch House, frequented by Irish navvies and men who worked hard labour. A shilling could buy a connection with a man after a few mugs of ale, especially if he looked down at heel.
3. TSM—The Methodist Seamen's Mission near the New London Docks. Infamous for out of work seamen happy to do anything for a few shillings in a carriage with the blinds drawn.

4. BST—the abbreviation of the Broad Street Terminus. The mustering place for manual labourers wishing to work on the railway at night. It was always packed with men eager for work, and those who were not picked often could not afford to return home to feed their families. There were dark alleyways and empty doorways aplenty in the streets nearby. A penny for a lad to keep his eye out, and the gentleman and the labourer in the shadows with their waistbands sitting on the tops of their shoes.

Lennard raised his eyes slowly from the page and looked to Angus, who shrugged, then said, "*Il les aime musclés, sans cervelle, et bien bénis, mon cher.*"

Sir George smiled faintly, pretending not to understand what Angus had said, that the grand duke liked them *burly, brainless, and blessed*—the latter word used by those who preferred companions of the same gender to describe a man with a large member.

"Would anyone else like coffee?" Lennard said, moving to the service sideboard with his cup. The coffee pot was kept warm over a small spirit flame. He didn't really want any, but he did want to turn his back on Sir George and Angus while he processed what he'd read. Robert would be useful to enquire tactfully of those men who worked for Malloray's and who stayed from time to time at The Seamen's Mission. Gerald could easily enquire at The Queens Head from fellow soldiers.

That left Elam and Lennard to investigate the other two locations the grand duke frequented. They were no strangers to those two places; men of quality or those middle-class men with money, fond of other men's embraces, and who were surveilled by intelligencers, favoured both The Lion's Heart and the marshalling yard because they could find someone attractive or willing without stepping down from their carriages. In both places, lower-class men willing to offer themselves loitered in the gloom where gas lights were dimmed and along streets that attracted little traffic at night.

From time to time, Lennard and Elam employed a few strapping, good looking men, willing and able—for payment—to engage in further assignations with men of interest to the intelligencers of the Home Office. Businessmen, gentlemen of quality, middle-class merchants, all of whom merited a mention in a dossier. Blackmail—or *chantage*, the French term used by Angus's underlings mainly because the English word sounded so vulgar—was used as a last resort. The men upon whom they gathered information seldom were targets themselves but were connected to bigger fish. Spratlings to catch mackerels: thus it was in intelligence gathering agencies across Europe and had been since the days of the Borgias.

"This explains why you sent me the copy of *La Vie Secrète de la Marquise Fonteneau*, doesn't it, Angus? The story of a gentleman who was a nobleman by day and a courtesan by night?"

"You said how you obtained information was your own business. Courtesan is such a specific word. It pertains someone who consorts intimately with men of means and the nobility, whereas we've never had you enquire after those sorts of gentlemen now, have we?"

"Touché," Lennard said.

Sir George had taken Kosorukov's dossier and pretended to be studying it. He knew exactly what went on in his department, but had to be able to say that "he'd never heard of it" if he was ever charged directly by another member of parliament.

"According to the report, it's believed Kosorukov might be willing to share information. I suppose you'd like me to sound him out?"

"Yes. However, you can't meet him somewhere like here. Although he's married to the daughter of an earl, he's still a Russian. Tolerated in society because of his family connections, but ..."

"As you've suggested I travel to visit my aunt, perhaps I might suggest the first-class dining room at Paddington station before I catch my train? How long do I have?"

"As much time as you need, Lennard," Sir George replied.

"No, before I'm recognised as the Baron Betteridge. How long can I spend time incognito, moving in lower-class circles, like the inns and other places from which we normally source our information."

"As long as you don't cause a sensation of your own making, there's no time limit. Of course, you'd have to be careful not to go anywhere the upper classes might wander and recognise you. I ran across you once when you were in disguise. Do you remember? You importuned me, holding out a tin mug, rattling it around, asking for a few coppers for your starving children. I didn't guess it was you until you began to laugh. I'd know that insolent chuckle anywhere. How long, you asked, can you last *à l'abri*? Why we have one intelligencer who's been living two lives for the best part of ten years without drawing attention to—"

"I'm sure Lennard understands, Sir George," Angus interrupted.

Lennard smiled. The less any intelligencer knew about any of the others, the better.

"Very well," he said. "As soon as Travis Holland is fit enough to answer a few questions, and after I've spoken with him, I'll contact this grand duke to—"

"There'll be no need, Lennard. Twinton and his family will call upon you. Given a week after Sir Hugh's interment, calling cards will start arriving at Bexford House from all those in society who count. The new, handsome, Lord Betteridge? Why, you'll be the talk of the town and be invited everywhere, even in full mourning. The Earl of Twinton does a lot of business through Malloray's, and he'll be sure to bring his family once you send back an at-home note. Then it's just a matter of asking Kosorukov if he'd like to give you advice on the refurbishment of the house."

"Advice on the refurbishment of my house?"

"That's what he does, Lennard. Read the dossier more clearly. He has an eye for acquisitions and appointments, both interior and exterior. He never asks for money, that would be far too ill-mannered. He usually requests an open account and purchases one or two things for himself, which he moves on to other buyers."

"So, while I'm showing him around, that's when I should suggest a private talk."

"Yes, see how much he's prepared to share and ask for some gesture of goodwill so we may establish a scale of how much we're prepared to pay."

Lennard sat back in his chair, stroking his chin. "There's something else, isn't there? And I'll hazard a guess that it's something I shan't like, shall I?" he said, daring Angus to speak.

Angus glanced nervously at Sir George, who sighed heavily before speaking. "There's something else about Kosorukov that also has to do with Sir Hugh … in a fashion, but not directly."

"Oh, for heaven's sake, if you're going to tell me Sir Hugh was entertaining an aristocratic Russian catamite at the same time as his ten-shilling whores, then I—"

"No, it's nothing of that nature. But it has to do with someone else who has met with the Russian four times since February."

"When you say someone, I'm going to find this disagreeable, aren't I?"

"It's Astley, Lennard. Terrence Astley."

*****

Terrence Maonaigh Astley, the sixth Baronet Killcaire, inheritor of Killcaire's Irish Trading Company, was a scoundrel, a liar, an arch-manipulator, and the man who'd broken Lennard's heart.

Could it only have been five years ago, at the time of his grandfather's funeral that Astley had sought out his company with a handshake and direct gaze into Lennard's eyes at the London church at which his uncle Arthur had delivered a moving, eloquent eulogy?

Flattered and cajoled, the intelligencer had failed in his first major duty—to investigate whatever or whomever might seem to be too good to be true.

His pale complexion, black hair, and beautiful, long-fingered hands had mesmerised Lennard. He then beguiled him with love poems and ultimately with the longest seduction possible, culminating in a series of tentative, unfulfilled connections. Each time, Lennard almost past the point of being to control himself, abruptly interrupted by Terrence's avowals of not being sure with protestations of never having been intimate before, and too shy to be seen completely naked.

It had been a plan. One long in the making. Terrence Astley had cultivated Lennard's affections, had teased out their trysts, withholding all but a complete surrender, until the Irishman had felt he'd played with the trout long enough, and had reeled in his catch.

One night of unparalleled, mindless, physical intimacy had Lennard putty in his hands thereafter. He'd not thought to question

Astley's expertise at the time. Had he dwelled upon it, it would no doubt have appeared peculiar. Someone who'd avowed more than once that he'd never engaged in intimate acts before, and yet had seemed so knowledgeable of the art of making love, and certainly might not have been willing, unflinching, and wanton as Astley had been, lying on his back with his knees splayed, begging Lennard to possess him, panting with artfully contrived lust.

Lennard had never been played before. Had it not been Sir George who'd invited him for a private chat, it might have been a very long time before he'd discovered the true nature of Astley's deception.

They'd been discreet in their meetings, not even the other Brothers had been aware of the clandestine relationship. Elam, however, as Lennard's most intimate confidante, had broken a promise to keep it secret, and had reported the nature of Lennard's and Astley's connection to the Home Secretary. Unlike Lennard, Elam knew a scoundrel when he saw one.

Sir George revealed to Lennard that he had a man secreted in Astley's household: one who reported on the Irish baron's dealings with insurrectionists in his own country, and who passed on other information, sometimes more interesting.

When Lennard had enquired why Sir George had hidden an intelligencer to spy on Astley, the Home Secretary had explained that his son, George Henry, was infatuated with Astley's ward, Neasa, and Astley kept refusing to entertain his son's proposals without some sort of financial "arrangement". Sir George had felt it wise to infiltrate someone within Astley's household to gather information, to discover why he seemed so reluctant to allow the match—a connection of marriage into the Home Secretary's family was unheard of for a minor, though wealthy, Irish baronet.

The intelligencer, two months before his death from smallpox, suspected Astley was smuggling arms to Ireland from La Corunna, and was also engaged in direct dealings with the prime minister of Spain, Leopoldo O'Donnell, with whom he shared ancestry in Tyrconnell.

Sir George's most alarming revelation was not Astley's suspected disloyalty to Great Britain, but one of a more personal nature. It was something that Sir George had imparted with no small amount of paternal solemnity and care. The Irishman was not only married and the father of four children, but he also kept a pair of former Irish travelling play-actors as lovers, so similar in looks they may have been twins. Conall and Colleen—they shared his bed in London—his wife and children kept locked away in the family house on the west coast of Ireland.

"But why?" Lennard had cried, the words tearing at his soul.

It was then Sir George had proposed his suggestion: Lennard's connection to Malloray's shipping, which had recently come to Sir Hugh after his grandfather's death, and which Astley hoped to buy cheaply, thinking Hugh would not be up to the task of managing the business.

Lennard had felt used and dirty. He'd been wooed with avowals of love and affection by Astley, but had been shocked to learn he'd merely been cultivated for financial reasons. He'd felt nauseated when he'd been told that, at the same time as playing with his affections, Sir Terrence had not only been living in a *ménage à trois*, but also had another more alarming secret—he'd been long married with a wife and four children.

After leaving Sir George's office, Lennard had started to make discreet enquiries. Not that he'd disbelieved Sir George, but he'd wanted to know for himself, to hear from men's lips, and to see documentary evidence of the extent of Astley's duplicity. Over time, with each new revelation and affirmation of the truth, Lennard's hopes that it might all have been a mistake had been sadly shattered.

The first meeting with Astley thereafter had evoked false rage, repudiating Lennard's "ridiculous" accusations, bringing forth disavowals, downright lies, and the absolute denial of the existence of a wife, children, or live-in lovers.

He'd learned a great lesson, one over which he'd more than once shaken his head when observing the follies of others carried away by mad, unbridled passion. He hated himself for being so deceived, but not as much as he hated Terrence Maonaigh Astley, the sixth Baronet Killcaire.

*****

Leaving the Oriental Club, Lennard asked the door footman to call for a boy to fetch him a hackney carriage.

When one of the new hansom cabs arrived, he directed the man to take him to the turning circle in the middle of Regent's Park. When they arrived, Lennard gave him a shilling and told him to drive to Bexford House with a message for Christopher: bring Elam, Robert, and Gerald to the Green Man tavern on the Euston Road, and to meet him there an hour later, at nine in the evening with a change of clothing suitable for a public house.

Lennard wanted an hour to himself, to walk slowly through the park to calm his mind, after which he intended to meet up with his friends and get so barrelled they'd have to carry him home.

The park was invariably quiet at that time of the evening; he felt he could easily have been at home at Gresting with his parents. His father used to take him into the fields after supper and sit with him on the grassy mound that overlooked the lily lake, pointing out stars, encouraging Lennard to listen to the sounds of the night.

Tonight was one such similar evening: calm, no breeze, the heavens shining brightly above, and the soft sounds of insects and other creatures occasionally moving in bushes and trees.

How he'd wished his father was here, or his grandfather, or his beloved Uncle Arthur.

The connection between the Grand Duke Kosorukov and Astley was, at that point unknown, but they'd been seen together more than once. It had been reported as being peculiar, mainly because Astley, being Irish, was perceived to be as much the enemy as Kosorukov was. As such, they'd be expected to stay shy of each other for fear of rumours that they might be plotting something.

However, Sir George had revealed that Christopher had reported three meetings between Sir Hugh and Astley, one not more than a week ago. The Home Secretary had advised Lennard to gain some composure in case the meeting with Sir Hugh had been about making another offer for Malloray's, and that he should steel himself in case the Irishman came to talk business with the new Baron Betteridge.

5. GRESTING

Lennard sat in the rearmost leather sofa of the carriage, reading the *London Illustrated News.*

The front page contained a report of the eighth Baron Betteridge bidding farewell to the casket of the seventh baron on the platform of Paddington station yesterday. There was a short article and a lithographic illustration of Lennard standing outside the carriage of the Great Western Railway funeral coach of the specially routed train that would proceed directly from London to High Wycombe. Normally, a change of platforms and trains was required at Beaconsfield. However, one of the privileges of his new position allowed a direct connection to be ordered a day in advance.

Both the Baron Betteridge and the Viscount Quaisey, whose estate was a little further up the line at Hughenden, were able to have their own private carriages attached to regular services. They'd both contributed heavily to the spur line that passed by both their country holdings. At one stage in his life, Lennard had thought it a little embarrassing, his grandfather flaunting his wealth and station while entering the special carriage on such occasions, surrounded on the platform by less privileged folk.

However, this morning, he'd been touched by the removal of hats and gentle, softly-spoken words of sympathy from total strangers as he and his party had made their way to the reserved carriage. There was quite a crowd waiting to board the train; word had got around the service would be direct to High Wycombe and many travellers had bought tickets, anxious to avoid a change of platform and a forty-minute wait at Beaconsfield.

What had originally been planned as a weekend visit by him, Gerald, and Elam had apparently turned into a minor expedition. That's why he'd asked for the special carriage. In order to have someone with him who not only understood farm and household management but also someone he implicitly trusted, Gerald had asked if he might invite his own family's former estate manager to accompany them. The man had been let go when the large family house had been sold, and now ran a small victualling supply shop in Praed Street, not far from the Great Western Railway hub. Lennard had happily acquiesced, agreeing that someone with a new eye for Gresting and experience in farm management would be an invaluable asset on their first visit.

At the last moment, Robert had also decided he'd like to join them, having left instructions with Mr Rudd to prepare a report on parts of the business with which Robert had never had any direct import, ready for him to peruse when he returned after the weekend away.

Then, yesterday afternoon—and quite unexpectedly—Lennard's new private secretary had appeared at Bexford House with his trunk and his man, ready to start work.

Clyford had expressed his delight at having been chosen for his new position, even though Lennard had suspected he'd had no choice. The final member of the party was Simeon Drudge. His presence had been suggested by Miles, who knew there were mountains of important documents and letters as yet unopened in Sir Hugh's study, not only in Bexford House but also piled up and accumulating dust at Gresting Hall.

What Lennard had initially intended to be a quiet weekend away, had turned into something he felt was along the lines of a state visit. Clyford had been extremely efficient, sending telegrams to all points, arranging carriages to meet the party at High Wycombe, informing the staff of how many bedrooms would be needed, and arranging meetings with the estate workers and the house servants in advance.

Sir George and Angus had chosen wisely. They might have been used to a personal secretary, but it was something completely new for Lennard. However, now that he had finally realised how difficult it would have been to manage the various aspects of his new life without help, Clyford's arrival and assistance had already proved invaluable.

"It's a very good likeness," Gerald said, referring to the front page of the *London Illustrated News* while taking the armchair opposite Lennard and removing his shoes. "The artist was most kind, having drawn your likeness showing your left profile, and the journalist too timid to ask ..."

Lennard pinched Gerald's toe, his friend's stockinged feet crossed casually, resting on the seat at Lennard's side. He glanced at his reflection in the carriage window. The bruise around his eye was spectacular. Clyford had put it about that due to his recent occupation of Bexford House, that Lennard, unfamiliar with his surroundings, had walked into a door in the darkness.

"I think a black eye actually suits you, Lenn," Gerald said, barely able to contain his mirth.

"I'm never going to live that one down, am I?"

"You used to be quicker on your feet."

"You ducked far too rapidly for me to see what was happening. I suppose it isn't the first time I've taken a punch meant for you. I hope it was worth it."

Gerald winked then, after a moment staring out the window, rubbed Lennard's knee with his stockinged foot.

"You were dreadfully drunk by the time we got back to Bexford, you know ..."

Lennard peered down the carriage, where the rest of his friends were engaged in conversation. His new secretary smiled brightly at him and he returned the smile with one of his own, and a slight tilt of his head as acknowledgment.

"Was I very noisy?" he asked Gerald.

"Enough to wake the dead, Lenn. But I'm not complaining," Gerald replied, turning to look up the carriage to see who Lennard had been smiling at.

"Dear God, I hope Clyford didn't hear. What must he think of me?"

"Clyford is a gentleman. Even if he had heard anything, he'd never say a word. Pity he's not for changing."

"Changing? I was led to believe that—"

"He's of our persuasion, yes. But despite my ardent attentions over the years, he insists he doesn't want to muddy the waters by mixing business with pleasure."

"Is that difficult for you?"

"Not difficult, Lenn. I've always felt a strong attraction to him. He's not what one might describe as handsome, but he's capable, intelligent, has wit and charm aplenty—"

"Sounds like you're a little infatuated."

"Perhaps so, and I suppose I do pine a little and engage in bouts of wistful thinking. However, that didn't prevent me from thoroughly enjoying myself with you and Elam—even as drunk as you were. It's been such a long time, and not for wanting either. I've been extremely busy since returning from the Crimea, trying to find my feet after being a soldier, and also trying to find something to keep me busy and out of the poorhouse."

"Angus would ever have allowed that to happen, Gerald. I'm sure you know that. He loves you too dearly. Anyway, now you have not only a roof over your head for as long as you want it at Bexford, but also a secure income that will keep you in the state of comfort that someone as dear to me should expect. I only regret one thing ..."

"And that is?"

"I was so drunk I don't remember one moment of what happened on Wednesday evening. Throwing me around on the bed? I'm sure that's a figure of speech."

Gerald laughed. "Well, after last Wednesday you might find me a more frequent visitor, especially as we're occupying the same dwelling. I'm sure we'd all be very happy to recreate the evening for you, this time with no alcohol-fuelled excesses to drive your unfettered lust."

"Was I truly that uninhibited?"

"No more than usual."

Lennard leaned forward and playfully attempted to cuff Gerald's ear.

"Lenn, you must tell me if I'm interfering," Gerald said.

"Interfering with what?"

"You and Elam. None of us truly knows what's going on between you two."

"We are the closest of companions and the dearest of friends, Gerald. He's an extraordinary man, and what we have is the best we can do. Master and servant to the world, intimates in private."

"Very well, but do let me know if I ever intrude. Shall I wait for an invitation?"

"Most times we curl up and go to sleep—just like every other couple, I suppose. However, a little spice, by the addition of your unannounced and unexpected presence, might be well received. I can only speak for myself, of course."

"I shall be tactful, I promise you."

"And I promise you there's no need."

"There's also something I've been meaning to ask you, Lenn … about your work. Until our meeting with Sir George, I'd always believed you were his third secretary."

"And that is my masquerade, yes. But if there's anything you wanted to know about the department, why haven't you asked Angus? He's your cousin."

"He either changed the subject whenever I asked, or gave me one of those vague smiles of his—you know the ones? Irritatingly bemused with his chin down, smiling from under his eyebrows."

Lennard laughed. "Yes, I know them only too well. Your question?"

"Are all intelligencers … you know?"

"Of our kind?"

Gerald nodded.

"Ah no, not at all. Until now, Elam and I have been the only two in permanent employ, and I can't think of a time when we've actually been asked to … well, you know. There are two other men who are paid piecework when there's a need for bedroom activity, but the majority of us are men and women from all classes. I've met a few of them during the course of our work on several dossiers over the years. Apart from the two pieceworkers, I know of three fellows who will cross the line, if necessary. However, you mustn't get the wrong impression. It's not a brothel. And when it comes to Elam and me sleeping with someone for information, that's best left to the professionals—the men we hire. Most of the work we do is collecting information."

"So, you and Elam have never …?"

"Gerald, I may love you as dearly as a brother but there are some things …"

Gerald laughed, then changed the subject. "I confess that I'm rather nervous, Lenn, about Gresting and my role there."

"Nervous? You, the Crimean war veteran who took a bullet to the chest to save the life of General Airey?"

"The last time I was at Gresting was the Christmas before your grandfather died. I got uproariously drunk and spent most of the evening sitting on your uncle Arthur's knee, do you remember?"

"He never forgot, you know."

"What? Me sitting on his knee, drunk as a lord?"

"We shared everything, Gerald. He was more than a father to me, he was a friend. And the first to know of my secret life. He confessed that connections of the body did not interest him, neither with a woman, nor with a man. However, he said that if he ever felt like straying into a different field, and to fall in love with someone, it would be with you."

"Good Lord, Lenn! I never suspected."

"And he'd have been mortified if you had. Of all of us, it was you whom he adored the most. Perhaps it's because you and he were so alike. Sometimes, if the light is poor, I catch glimpses of his eyes in yours."

Gerald was left open-mouthed, about to speak but interrupted by Robert, who'd come to announce that the train was about to arrive at High Wycombe.

*****

Lennard asked the coachman to stop a quarter mile from the avenue that led to Gresting Hall, the great house of the estate. He wanted to walk through the dense planting of beeches—still holding their brown and copper leaves, yet to be forced off branches by the first buds of spring—to the edge of the wood and to look at the house from afar.

It wasn't the grandest of houses, like some of the other Palladian mansions in the county, but it had a certain style that made it the most attractive of dwellings. Built of red-brown brick with white arched windows along the façade, the house boasted six reception rooms and a ballroom on the first floor, twelve bedrooms, some day rooms on the floor above that, and right at the top of the house, the servants' quarters in the attic.

From where he stood, Lennard thought it could do with a good brush up—it looked a little neglected. He was about to return to the coach when he heard movement behind him. It was, as he suspected, Elam come to join him.

"Are there cuckoos, Lenn?"

"A few weeks off yet. Why do you ask?"

Elam tilted his head and smiled.

Lennard remembered, ashamed that he hadn't reacted immediately to Elam's question. He and Miles had arrived at Gresting when he still had some remnants of his hearing, and Lennard had christened his friend "cuckoo" because that day he'd heard the first cuckoo of the year. Elam had remarked, sadly, that he thought it might be the last he ever heard.

"Are you happy to be back, Lenn?"

"I shall be. Just now, my heart is full of sadness with memories of my grandfather, my parents, and my brother and sister. And, of course, Arthur."

Elam said nothing, but drew Lennard into his arms, nuzzling his cheek with the side of his head.

"You are far too good for the likes of me, Elam Walters," Lennard murmured as he kissed Elam's ear.

"What did you say?" Elam asked drawing back.

"Nothing."

"I felt the vibrations of your voice in your chest."

"I said nothing, my friend. I was purring with the comfort of your embrace."

*****

Lennard stood on the small podium at one end of the ballroom. The room was packed with over a hundred faces: some new, many acquaintances of decades. All of them smiling, eyes bright, having learned that Lennard would not only take up the reins of his grandfather's legacy but also intended to restore the estate to its former glory.

Unlike in the days of his grandfather, when Lennard had arrived under the portico in front of Gresting Hall, there'd been no line-up of smartly liveried footmen and maids in freshly starched aprons and caps, waiting to bow and curtsey to him. Lennard had grown up with most of them; they'd been friends. To everyone on the estate, he'd been known as "Master Lennard", and there were no end of wet eyes—including his own—accompanying the three cheers and a loud huzzah after he'd stood in the carriage and greeted them as they'd crowded around.

"Furthermore, I've decided that the oversight of the estate should fall to my dear friend, whom a lot of you will remember as a lanky sixteen-year-old when he first arrived, all tallow hair and blushes, Captain Gerald Langbourne, the future eighth Viscount Bussell of St. Cleer, war hero, and not eight months returned from the Crimea."

There was loud applause together with gasps of delight. The Brothers had been much beloved by everyone at Gresting, and after Sir Hugh's five-year absence, there was joy in their faces at the news that there'd be another Baron Betteridge at the helm, bringing with him the friends of his youth: men of vision and capability.

Within half an hour, trestle tables had appeared and were put up on the wide terrace outside the ballroom, which overlooked the park behind the house. Jugs of ale and cider, bread, meats, and cheeses all came from nowhere to make an impromptu feast.

"Here's to Black-Eye!" became the toast of the morning, much to Lennard's mock dismay, and the amusement of his friends. No doubt, the soubriquet would follow him for months, if not years.

The house had been mostly locked up, Mrs Bayton, the housekeeper explained. "After your grandfather passed away, Sir Hugh never returned. Your uncle Arthur used to visit every few months to keep an eye on things, but when we realised the new baron intended to live in the city, we closed up the bedrooms and reception rooms."

"What happened to the house staff, Felicity?" Lennard asked. Although thirty years his senior, she'd dandled him on her lap as a child and had always been called by her Christian name by his parents, his grandfather, and his uncle Arthur.

"A lot of them moved to other households ... the men mostly. A few married and settled on the estate, learning new trades. We have a whole collection of very well-mannered and well-spoken shepherds—former footmen and houseboys—now carpenters and farmers, all courtesy of Sir Hugh's continuing payment of their salaries. We had to find something for them to do. With no guests, they all began to get bored."

"I have an idea, if you'll hear me out," Lennard said. "Once Captain Langbourne has had a chance to discuss the condition of the estate with those who've been working it, I've a mind, seeing as I'll be visiting once a month if I can, to keep those who were once in house service at their new occupations. When, given notice of my arrival or of my guests, we contrive a way they might come back inside and resume their duties for however long the house is occupied. Unless it's a ball or a hunt, we'd never need a full household, but enough footmen and maids to cover a small to medium size party. What do you think?"

"Well, Lennard, I think it's an unusual idea. What will fine ladies think of footmen serving at table with tanned faces, broad in the shoulder from their manual labour, and perhaps a little rusty at service?"

"I think both you and I know that Gresting Hall will quickly gain the reputation of the country house in Buckinghamshire that's a must to visit. The way you describe them, most of the footmen will have the ladies of fashion swooning into their soup."

*****

Chester was the most magnificent of animals. Not more than seven years old and only two at the time of his grandfather's passing, the horse had been his grandfather Trefford's passion, a flame now re-awakened in Lennard's breast.

He and Gerald had gone riding, ostensibly to examine parts of the estate, but in reality to escape the house for an hour and to swim. Lennard had left word for Elam to join them at the old lake near the southern border of the land, which was kept topped up by a channel joined into the River Misbourne. William Drake, a member of parliament in the previous century, had been a close friend of the fourth baron, Lennard's great, great-grandfather, and they'd shared construction costs of twin lakes, fed by the river that separated their lands, one on "Shardeloes", Drake's estate, and the other on Gresting.

"He loves you," Gerald remarked, chuckling as Lennard gently urged the white gelding into the shallows of the lake, until the horse was up to his flanks in the water.

"Who loves me?"

"The horse, Lenn. Chester. I'm not sure an animal I rode for the very first time would allow me such liberties."

"I think he remembers me, even if it is five years since I last rode him. I was with my grandfather when this young fellow tumbled from his mother into the straw, all wet and slippery. I broke his birth sac, and had my hands on him even before my grandfather, despite the protestations of his mother, my uncle Arthur's mare. Perhaps the smell of my person is one of his early memories? I'm not entirely sure why, but he's excessively gentle under my hands."

"As we all are, Lenn," Gerald said with a smile as he dismounted the mare he'd been riding. He began to unsaddle her.

"What are you doing?" Lennard asked, urging Chester back to the shoreline.

"I'm taking off her tack, after which I'll do the same. I fancy a swim aback a horse. I've such fond memories of the first year I was here, when Angus and I arrived before going up to Cambridge. Our naked swims, playing that new game … what was it? Ah yes, water polo. But improvised, on horseback, with a pig's bladder as our ball and canoe paddles for our mallets …"

"Are you encouraging me to throw my clothes off … again?"

Lennard said, already shucking off his shirt. They'd both ridden out barefoot, in shirtsleeves and work breeches.

"Since when have you needed encouragement, Malloray?"

With Chester leading, the mare Gerald had ridden seemed calm enough and followed as they made their way slowly through a narrow section of reeds, before the bed of the lake fell away and the water was deep enough for the horses to swim.

"I've a mind to take him back to London with us," Lennard said, one arm around Chester's neck, paddling with the other.

"What would you do with a horse in London?"

"Exercise, Gerald. Regent's Park is no more than a few hundred yards from Clarence Gardens, and there's Primrose Hill to the north if I wanted to stretch his legs and have a gallop. I might even take to riding him around the city to my various engagements."

"Riding horseback in London, Lennard? It's entirely out of fashion. You'd be thought of as eccentric, at the very least."

"Perhaps that's exactly what I intend, Gerald. I may have been born into an aristocratic family, but I wasn't brought up to behave like one. I'd like there to be something that signalled my humble beginnings, and that my parents were merchants—family merchants, but merchants nonetheless."

"Humble beginnings?" Gerald said, barely able to conceal his mirth. "Brought up on an estate of twelve thousand acres, with servants running aplenty, tending to your every need—"

Lennard splashed water over Gerald, grinning broadly. "You tease so easily, and I love it immensely. It's one of your greatest assets," he said. He hoisted himself onto Chester's back then leaned over the space between the horses and pulled Gerald's head to his own, kissing him softly.

"And there I was thinking I had other, more tangible assets you cared about, Lennard Malloray."

"Lennard Malloray still cares about those, my friend."

A loud whistle from the edge of the lake signalled that Elam had arrived in a pony trap. He was hastily removing his own clothes and, after less than a minute, leapt into the water and swam toward them with broad, powerful strokes.

"He's a man of great beauty, Lennard," Gerald said, as they floated together, one arm around each other's shoulders, and the other grasping the manes of their horses.

"Sometimes I wish I could—"

"Perhaps you will, Lenn. Time heals all wounds. In your case, you were sorely used. Perhaps that's why you can't allow yourself to draw closer to him."

Lennard didn't answer at first, but merely half-raised an eyebrow and snorted very softly. "Is that your solution, Gerald? Time?"

"My solution is that you need to give yourself permission to love him, and that permission will come when the time is right and your heart has recovered."

"I think I need to commit murder, to be honest, Gerald. It may be the only way I ever find myself free of the past."

"If you're talking about strangling Astley, I'll put my hand up to assist, if that's of any help."

Lennard chuckled, moved his hand from Gerald's shoulder and ran it through his friend's hair, tousling it affectionately.

*****

"You want me to make enquiries at The Queen's Head for this Kasuro …" Gerald stumbled over the word.

"*Kosorukov*, Vassili Vadimovich," Lennard said.

"I have no ear for Russian names. We gave them all soubriquets in the Crimea. Pustule-face, Fat-arse, Pickle-prick. I relied on Clyford to remember their names."

"Clyford was with you in the Crimea?"

"Yes, he was my lieutenant-orderly, didn't you know that?"

"While you were the adjutant to his uncle, General Airey?"

"I was still an officer, Lennard. I merited my own orderly. So, he was busy looking after me, while I looked after the general."

"I shall never understand the military. Go on, you were about to say something. I saw it in your eyes. Please, continue."

"Well, about The Queen's Head. You know it's a place for dragoons and members of the Coldstream guard when they're off duty. I've never been myself, but I've always been a little more than interested. If I do go, I'd have to keep in the background. The unwanted attention after my award for bravery makes public taverns no longer places of refuge, especially if they're frequented by recently returned members of Her Majesty's regiments."

"Is there anyone you could take with you?"

"I've a mind to take Clyford with me, and offer a comely soldier a guinea to partake in a menage with us. It may be the only way I get to bed him."

Lennard laughed along with Gerald, Elam merely rolling his eyes and sighing with feigned exasperation. Both men knew there was a hint of truth in Gerald's proposal, despite his attempt at levity.

"Who was speaking to me of patience not twenty minutes hitherto?" Lennard asked, referring to Gerald's mention of allowing time to pass, to be able to move forward.

"What's this all about?" Elam asked.

"Gerald's penchant for my new private secretary, unrequited and a matter of personal disquiet."

"I think he's fond of you enough, Gerald," Elam said. "Just because I can't always hear what people say, I've learned to read their faces as well as their lips. Perhaps what Lenn said is correct, maybe it's a matter of time. If it ever comes to pass, I should let him come to you, as hard as that may be."

"Like you let Lennard come to you, Elam?"

"I have to fight to keep him away."

"You do?" Lennard said, only to be drawn into an embrace.

Gerald felt that it was only these two, the closest of his friends, who did not understand the true nature of the friendship between them. For, despite their avowals that there was no great love between them, they were as close as two human beings could ever be. Had he not loved both of them as deeply as he did—and his feelings returned by both men—he'd have been sorely jealous of such a connection. One that came along to most men but once in their lifetimes.

6. TRAVIS JAGO HOLLAND

Lennard had never visited a hospital. People who could afford treatment at home did so. His grandfather had employed a physician to look after the workers on the estate and also retained a private doctor in London to look after his needs.

He'd known Greenwich Hospital had a history for treating and recuperating men who'd been injured while serving in Her Majesty's navy, but until this recent war in the Levant and in the Crimea, it had mainly housed veterans. It was a sad fact that, although conditions were poor, the men might otherwise have been forced to fend for themselves on the streets.

On Monday evening, after returning from Gresting, Lennard received word from Sir George that Travis Holland had arrived back in the country and was being treated at the hospital. Although his wounds had begun to heal, the surgeon still needed bed-rest. The Home Secretary's note, accompanied by a copy of Holland's full account to the Admiralty of the sinking of his recollection of the loss of the *Firefly* and the *Sisley*, suggested that Lennard give the man a few days to recover from his voyage from Gibraltar.

On Thursday morning, Christopher drew the carriage to a halt under the entrance portico of the hospital. An elderly porter enquired the nature of Lennard's visit and, after taking his card, disappeared into the building, telling Lennard to wait until the hospital administrator came to greet him.

Fifteen minutes later, no one had exited the building and Lennard, long since having abandoned the comfort of his barouche, started on his second cheroot. Having just lit it, a red-faced man in an ill-fitting jacket and grubby trousers issued from the building and hurried down the stairs to greet him.

"I'm sorry to keep you waiting, my lord. Word came that you arrived, but it was only when I realised you were the gentleman sent by the Home Secretary that I understood my tardiness was inexcusable. His letter seemed to have gone astray and it took me ages to find it and then put two and two together. In my defence, your card said Lennard Malloray, and the Home Secretary's letter, the Baron Betteridge."

The man had not given his name and seemed unusually flustered. Lennard held his temper. "So, you were prepared to leave the man who owns the company that victuals your hospital waiting, yet you run obsequiously at the realisation the same man is not only a baron but is also about Her Majesty's business? Who is in charge here?"

Lennard was inwardly mortified at his own behaviour, but he'd spent most of his life dealing with the upper classes and had seen how those in ranks below them hurried to be of service when spoken to gruffly or dismissively. Christopher's barely concealed smirk signalled that he'd acted appropriately, although completely out of character.

"The hospital supervisor is currently indisposed, my lord. However, I'm completely at your service. How can I be of help?"

"First of all, you can give me your name, sir, then you can lead me to Travis Holland, who arrived on Monday from Gibraltar."

"Holland, you say? I'm afraid I don't deal with patients. I'm the supervisor of the wardsmen. I can get one of them to help you. I'll send him directly."

Lennard was left open-mouthed as he watched the unnamed man quickly turn his back, then scuttle up the stairs behind the carriage portico, disappearing behind a stout, twin-doored entrance.

"Well done, *Lord* Betteridge," Christopher said from behind him.

"Did you see that? The man didn't even give me his name, even when I'd asked him for it to his face?"

"If he has no name, you can't report him to anyone, Lenn."

"Dear God. Did I truly behave like Sir Hugh? I never thought I'd live to see the day that—"

"Sir Hugh would probably have taken to him with his cane, Lenn. Don't be so harsh on yourself by behaving the way that's expected of you. Had you been less so, the man would have reported you as being a milk-sop."

"My grandfather—"

"Your grandfather had an established reputation, Lenn. Your family name is all you have for the nonce. If you want my advice, you should behave as you're expected to, otherwise you'll be taken for a man without a spine, and not worthy of your grandfather's title."

What Christopher said was a simple truth. Lennard may not like what he'd heard but he recognised the advice was well-founded, as distasteful as he felt the resultant behaviour might require. "Very well, then. If I'm to be a man of standing, I shall act as one," he said, pulling down the peaks of his waistcoat to straighten it across his torso. He tapped his top hat into place firmly then strode up the stairs, pushing the doors open with both hands.

A startled boy took two paces backward and gaped at him. "Here boy," he said, giving the lad a penny. "Fetch me a porter and be quick about it."

A man arrived within the space of a few moments, wiping his hands on his dirty apron, a garment that Lennard noticed was blood-stained, barely any of its white linen unsmeared.

"I beg your pardon … sir. How may I help you?"

"Your name?"

"Grofner."

"Grofner, *my lord*," Lennard snapped. If he was going to play the part, he would. He was not unused to the ways powerful men treated their underlings. "I'm here to visit Travis Holland, arrived this Monday from Gibraltar. Can you show me to his room?"

"Room? He'd be in the large ward on the first floor with those just come from there."

"My lord!"

Grofner quickly added the correct form of address, colouring spectacularly, when Lennard asked to be taken to the ship's surgeon.

The place was a nightmare. While following Grofner, he had time to wonder whether all the employees "scuttled"—a rapid gait with a short stride and a slightly hunched back—like the man who'd come to his carriage and had fled up the stairs. He'd imagined a hospital to be a place of treatment, of rest and recuperation, with light and air, not this sequence of squalid narrow corridors off which issued small rooms packed with a dozen or so men on stretchers. Not infrequently, cries of pain or calls of help issued from the rooms as he passed by.

It stank of unwashed bodies, excrement, and a festering bitter and acrid smell that he had no name for.

"Why is the place so dismal, Grofner?" he asked as they proceeded down corridors and through open rooms, equally as densely packed with men, all coughing or weeping, lying on small closely spaced cots.

"We're told to keep the gas low, my lord. Due to the cost, sir."

Lennard trod on something wet and soft. He dared not look to see what it was. He was not unused to squalor; in their trade as intelligencers, he and Elam spent much of their time mixing with the great unwashed in the poorer parts of London. What he'd not been prepared for was to see the filth and dreadful conditions transported to a place of supposed healing and convalescence.

"Here you are, sir," Grofner said, opening the door of a large room, more open than any he'd seen so far. "Last bed on the left, if you please. Near the window."

Lennard pressed sixpence into the man's hand. "Bring tea for us, Grofner. Mind you wash the cups beforehand, and in clean water. You might wish to change your apron and tidy your hair before you return."

"Tea?"

"It's a beverage taken by everyone in the kingdom, man," Lennard said, more drily than he intended.

"Oh yes, of course, I know what it is, my lord. Right away, yes—"

"And you can get a boy to send up my carriage driver. Mr Hoskins is his name. Ask him to wait twenty minutes and to find a bath chair in the meantime."

"A bath chair?"

"If you think I'm leaving a man so important to Her Majesty's government in such a foul place as this, you're sorely mistaken."

Lennard had already decided that Holland, no matter his worth, was a man from a good background. He'd studied the dossier. A man who'd served under Great Britain's flag and had been the sole survivor of a catastrophic naval disaster did not deserve to be "looked after" in such a cesspit.

He was filled with much sadness as he made his way slowly to the end of the room; the men in their cots on either side of the central alleyway, most of them bandaged and lying recumbent, were barely covered by the dirty, torn sheets and bed linen.

"Mr Holland?" he asked quietly, crouching at the side of the last cot on the left.

The man was lying on his side, facing away from him, Lennard not entirely sure whether he was either insensible or asleep.

"Who wishes to know, sir?"

"Good morning, Mr Holland. My name is Lennard Malloray. I'm the Baron Betteridge of Hazlemere and I'm here on behalf of Sir George Grey, the Home Secretary, to enquire about your well-being."

"Dear God," the man said, sitting up so quickly he nearly knocked Lennard off balance, his elbow striking Lennard's as he turned in his cot. "Please forgive me, my lord. I thought it was one of those hideous creatures who calls himself a physician."

Lennard chuckled and held out his hand. Travis Holland regarded it for a moment then shook it firmly. "You look surprised, Lord Betteridge," Holland said.

"You are quite unlike your daguerreotype, sir, and I'd prefer it if you called me by my Christian name, Lennard, or Malloray if that familiarity feels uncomfortable. I'm not more than a week ennobled after the death of my uncle, and the use of my title, as useful as it has seemed today, is still quite foreign to me."

"Very well, Mr Malloray. If you wish to call me Travis, I shall have no objection, although having served in Her Majesty's navy for eight years, I'm afraid that the use of rank and deference has become part of my very being, and I shall find it hard to form such a familiarity upon new acquaintance with a member of the aristocracy."

He said it with such charm that Lennard could not help but smile. The man was truly delightful, far more than comely than his daguerreotype had seemed to show, and rather cheeky-faced, with bright, intelligent eyes, and a prominent chin, broad and powerful—something that only added to the impression of a man with thoughts of his own and no small amount of confidence.

"This place is truly disgraceful, Mr Holland. How you can appear so cheerful is beyond me. It's a hell-hole."

"Perhaps if you are, as you say, so well placed with Sir George Grey, you might get him to have a word with the Admiralty. This place suffers greatly from the lack of funds. Unsanitary conditions are the least of the problems. Inadequate and poorly-trained staff, so-called doctors who are but barber-surgeons, assisted by men who have evaded the workhouse seem to be those who run this institution—for want of a better name for this 'hell-hole' as you call it. I've been a surgeon aboard ships in naval battles, Mr Malloray. I've treated casualties as you might never have seen in your life, but still those under my care have never suffered conditions such as these."

"Are you permitted to smoke, sir?" Lennard asked, as a way of avoiding a direct comment on the doctor's impassioned diatribe. "A pipe perhaps?"

"I'm not one for loose tobacco, sir."

"In that case, you are a man after my own heart. Such a messy business packing a pipe and cleaning it afterwards. You are in luck, sir. I have either cheroots, or very fine hand-rolled cigarillos from Spain."

"In that case, I should be delighted to accept your offer of either. The smell of a fine cigarette will help mask the stench of the room. I wish there was more I could do for the others around me."

"You already have, Mr Holland. I shall make it my duty to say the right words to the right people. Heaven knows if it will achieve anything, but there are ears that will listen to me, mainly due my affairs in the transport of goods across the globe—"

"Malloray! That's it. I've been wondering why the name should sound so familiar."

"Indeed, I confess, Malloray's Eastern and Australian Shipping Line is a family company."

"Of which you are now the owner, I presume?"

"Part owner. I've just divided the business between my first cousin and myself."

"Then it's an extraordinary pleasure to make your acquaintance, sir. Malloray's is as famous a name in shipping as any in the world."

"The pleasure is mine, Travis," Lennard said, noticing with some pleasure the smile on the doctor's face at the use of his Christian name. He leaned forward to strike a sulphur match to light the cigarillo Holland had chosen.

"My brother, Percival, learned his seafaring as a guard aboard one of your company's vessels, Mr Malloray. The *Argus*, out of Fowey. Do you know it by chance?"

"She's the brigantine who plies our route to Rabat. I know her by name only. I've never been part of the business that deals directly with the crew, so I have to admit I've no knowledge of your brother, other than he served on the *Prince*."

"I have every hope in my heart that he has survived, Mr Malloray. I've been at my wits' end with worry about his fate—"

"I've already made enquiries for any news on your behalf, sir. However, if anything was known, I give you fair warning that I should feel it my duty to impart it to you. Protection from sad news is no man's duty. I consider it cruel and inappropriate. When it comes to kin, dissembling is a disservice as far as I'm concerned."

"I imagine from the earnest tone of your voice that you are no stranger to loss, Mr Malloray."

Lennard was saved from further conversation on the topic by the reappearance of Grofner, wearing a clean white apron, his hair now slicked down, carrying a large cane tea tray, upon it three cups, a teapot, and a sugar basin.

"Three cups, Grofner?" Lennard asked.

"Your coachman said he'd join you, my lord."

"This offer of tea was probably ill-advised now that I've seen the condition of your surroundings, Travis," Lennard said, once Grofner had placed the tray on the foot of the cot and then disappeared. "The men around you must be feeling desperate, even for a sip of our tea."

"I fear you do not understand men who come from humble backgrounds, sir," Travis replied. "It is the lot of men not born to privilege, such as these around me, to observe the behaviour of those who have it with neither comment nor desire for such things. It is what it is, if I might be so bold as to say."

Lennard felt embarrassed to be put so well in his place, but without a hint of censure. It was, as the doctor had said, what it is. Those in need did not expect those who had what they did not to share. It was the way of the world, as sad as it made him feel.

"It may be as you say, Mr Holland, but it gives me no comfort."

"You've already said you'll speak about what goes on here. That shows your concern and the type of gentleman you are."

"The type of gentleman I hope to be, Travis. As I've already mentioned, my title is very new."

"But gentlemen are bred and taught to be what they are, sir. It's clear you've been a gentleman all your life. The ability to listen is something that can't be turned on, like the steam pipe of a locomotive. It's something that's schooled over years from early childhood."

Lennard found himself staring at his teacup, wondering whether he should fill it or not. Averting his gaze was a device to avoid showing sadness at the loss of the men who'd taught him to be a gentleman. His father, his grandfather, and his uncle Arthur: men who'd moulded him into the man he'd become. How he still loved them, despite their passing, and missed them in some way each and every day.

"Mr Malloray, there's a gentleman standing in the doorway looking in our direction," Travis said.

"Ah, that's my carriage driver, Christopher. I see he has a bath chair for you."

"A bath chair? For me?"

"I haven't explained why I'm here, Travis, and to your credit you haven't asked. As I said, I'm here on behalf of the Home Secretary. There are a few things I'd like to discuss with you, but on no account may I allow you to stay here for another moment—"

"Please, Mr Malloray, my family—"

"Is in Cornwall. And word has reached them with a telegram advising that you will be well looked after, something I sincerely doubt will happen here. I hope you won't object if I invite you to be my guest until you are back on your feet. We can discuss what the Home Secretary sent me here for after we've seen you bathed, in a clean set of clothing and with some decent food under your belt. How does that sound?"

"I could never repay such a thing, sir. Why I'd feel in your debt for the rest of my days."

"What utter nonsense, Travis. I'll hear no such talk. Why, the Crown is in your debt for your service in the Crimea. Besides, I should never rest easy if I were to leave you here, and if you don't want Sir George to arrive in person and have you carted away, you'd do best to come with me. The company of affable men, much of your own age, in a large light-filled house in Clarence Gardens, near to Regent's Park. Does it sound like something you wouldn't like? Oh, and may I add I have a French chef, who is the talk of society."

"Well, sir—"

"Christopher and I are strong enough to pick you up and carry you off if we must. Besides, a few days in our care will see you better to be able to think about your future."

"I really must decline—"

"You have no choice," Lennard said, knowing it had been a refusal made from politeness rather than desire. "I shall be mortally offended if you refuse my offer of hospitality, Mr Holland."

"In that case, let me meet your man, have our tea, and then I shall be at your service, my Lord Betteridge."

Lennard smiled at the cheeky wink that accompanied the doctor's quiet, acquiescent reply.

*****

"Please, Mr Holland, don't feel compelled to eat everything," Gerald said.

"It is the most agreeable food I've ever eaten in my life, Captain Langbourne," Travis replied, feeling awkward at how little he'd consumed. "But as a military man yourself, may I remind you of the staple foods we are used to? Eight years of sea rations and meagre meals ashore on infrequent revictualling stops in foreign ports have made me cautious about overindulgences. This is far too delicious to leave, but I'm fearful for the condition of my chamber pot in the early hours of the morning ... oh, pardon me. As you can tell, I'm likely too used to conversation among fellow sailors and rough talk at sea, not careful repartee among gentlemen of quality."

Lennard had tried to stifle his mirth by pressing his table napkin to his mouth, but to no avail. He guffawed, slapping the table with one hand, delighted to see his guest was not at all like the family physician, Dr Hallstrom.

"Please, Travis, you've said nothing that one of us might not have uttered himself, were we not with a new acquaintance. Our speech is oft-times coarse and vulgar, a remnant of our years as lads."

"Then I should have been more circumspect, now you admit I'm new to your company as well."

"Nonsense, sir. It gives me a great deal of satisfaction to believe you find yourself at ease in our company," Lennard said. "Eat as little or as much as you like, Travis. If there is something particularly to your liking, feel free to send a note to the kitchen. Mr Huilot likes nothing better than to please those he cooks for."

Eight hours after they'd returned to Bexford House, Travis Holland had appeared for an evening meal, having avowed that he was too tired and probably would not eat with Lennard, Gerald, Robert, and Clyford. However, after a bath, which Miles and Elam had prepared and helped him in and out of, a change of clothing, and a good six hours of uninterrupted sleep in clean, starched linen bedding, he'd sent word that he'd like to join the other gentlemen for dinner.

To his credit, Travis had not remarked on the fact that Lennard's valet, Elam, sat down to dinner with the gentlemen. It was hardly a formal affair, although conducted in the dining room, the men appearing in shirtsleeves without neckerchiefs, exchanging noisy banter across the table as they helped themselves from a bounteous selection of covered chafing dishes. Perhaps he'd never lived with servants, Lennard had thought, or perhaps growing up in a household as a doctor's son in Fowey allowed the entire household to sup together, masters and servants both.

"You did an excellent job on my hair, Elam," Travis said, then stopped when Lennard nudged Elam's elbow and nodded in Travis's direction.

"I beg your pardon, Mr Holland?"

"I said I was grateful for your tonsorial abilities. My hair has never sat so well upon my head. Normally, no matter who attends to it, it remains unruly. But you, sir, are a true artist … and as for the shave, why, I can't thank you enough."

"It was my honour, Mr Holland. I am at your service whenever you need attention."

Travis noticed that Elam seemed fixated on his mouth whenever he spoke. He realised there must be a problem with his hearing. However, as he spoke so clearly and his words were carefully enunciated, he postulated that perhaps he was just a little hard of hearing. Nothing unusual with men of his age. Most likely a build-up of wax in the ear canals, he thought. Something easily fixed.

*****

Eventually, Travis Holland became aware that the other gentlemen had made excuses, leaving him alone with Lennard and Elam. "I imagine you might be on the point of broaching the reason you came to visit me on behalf of the Home Secretary. Am I correct?"

"Not necessarily," Lennard replied. "I don't want you to think my kindness could be construed as anything but a genuine wish to save you from that awful place."

"However—"

"It can wait. I must admit that there is a little urgency behind Sir George's wish that I put certain questions to you, but a day won't make much difference."

Travis Holland tapped his finger on the surface of the polished mahogany table, inspecting Elam's face. He was no fool. For years at sea, he'd served among men confined in close quarters for months on end. He made no judgements when it came to such matters. He was not of the persuasion himself and felt no unease in the presence of men who were.

"Ask your question, Lennard. I slept for half the day and am not yet tired."

"Does your leg pain you?"

"Grievously. I thank you for your query, however, I think that is not what interests Sir George. What is it that he wishes to know?"

"It has to do with the *Sisley* and the *Firefly*, Travis."

From the look on Travis's face and utterances he made at the ships' names, it was obvious to Lennard that the topic of the catastrophic loss of both vessels was a complete surprise. "If you'd prefer not to ..."

"Perhaps Sir George is unaware of the full report I submitted to the Admiralty, and—"

"Yes, he's read it, and I have also. It made for very fine reading, Travis. I congratulate you on your keen eye, your memory, and your ability to write informatively, yet in a smooth, flowing style."

"You said you read it?"

Lennard nodded.

"I swear, I left nothing out."

"And yet you did, Travis."

"I'm not quite sure what you could be referring to."

"Sir George is intensely interested in the two civilian passengers who drowned when the longboat crossing between the *Sisley* and the *Firefly* was hit by a shell."

For a moment, Lennard thought Travis would not speak. The doctor coloured deeply and stared at his hands for an inordinate amount of time.

"I would not only be betraying a confidence, but also reliving one of the greatest tragedies of my life, Lennard."

"Names do not matter. I do not wish to labour the point, but … can you at least assure me the two passengers were not a short, rotund man of some forty years, accompanied by a taller, moustachioed companion of a similar age, brawny, and taciturn?"

Travis's eyebrows shot up, his eyes wide.

"Good grief, no, sir. At least I can swear to that."

Lennard glanced at Elam who sighed, rubbing his forehead with two fingers.

"The news disappoints you?"

"Alarmingly so, Travis."

"Perhaps you could explain the reason?"

"You must permit me to keep my confidences too, Travis. I am not at liberty to discuss why the identity of the two passengers is so important to the nation—"

"To the nation, my lord? Good heavens! Could such a thing as two civilian passengers be of such vital interest? Please disillusion me that you thought us complicit in some way in some heinous endeavour. I swear to you by all that's dear to me—"

"Please, Travis. Don't distress yourself. We thought that the two civilians were gentlemen we have been trying to find some two years now … and I've said too much already."

"We have been trying to find? You said 'we', Lennard."

"Tell him, Lenn," Elam said.

"Tell me what?"

"I have not deceived you, Travis. I am indeed the new Baron Betteridge of Hazlemere and, with Robert, owner of Malloray's Eastern and Australian Shipping Line. I am also third secretary to Sir George Grey. That's the official description of my position, sir. However, I have reason to trust you and hopefully, in time you will find that I am not duplicitous with men such as yourself, except when I am gathering intelligence in the name of Her Majesty. I am a servant of the Crown, as are Elam, Robert, Gerald, and Clyford."

"Gathering intelligence?"

"It is the duty of everyone in the Home Office to assist the Home Secretary by providing information that may be of interest to the Crown. There are subversives aplenty afoot in all levels of society."

"It sounds very much like spying, if you'll forgive my bluntness. Surely confidences should be kept."

"And if the Admiralty had known of the incipient interception of the *Sisley* and the *Firefly* by the Russians, sir? Such a tragedy might have been avoided. Or do you believe the enemy came across your vessels by chance? No, I hate to disillusion you of such a fortuitous encounter, they must have been observing you for some time, as we do with our enemies, both at sea and on land. Imagine what might not have happened had we previous cognisance of the vessel that opened fire on you, having obtained it covertly and not reported it due to some misguided perception of keeping confidences."

Travis adjusted the base of his wineglass, from which he'd drunk very little. "I feel suitably chastened," he said, his eyes still lowered, colour rising over his neck and cheeks.

"Chastisement was not my intention, sir, and if I have offended you then I beg you to forgive me. As you are a lieutenant-surgeon in Her Majesty's navy, I merely impressed upon you the need for every vital snippet of information that might help turn this dreadful war to be considered, weighed, after which, if found to be of value, to be acted upon."

"My information, about the civilian passengers, was that, too, something to do with the war against the Russians?"

"Not directly. It was something of far greater importance, something that could possibly change all our lives in this great nation did it ever come to pass. Now, as I said previously, that's the limit of what I'm allowed to reveal."

For one brief moment, Travis held Lennard's gaze, quickly flicking to Elam's eyes. Neither man showed the least sign of duplicity. "Then I shall enquire no further, as alarmed as your pronouncement has left me. May I propose a toast to intelligence gathering?"

"To intelligence gathering," Lennard and Elam said in unison raising their glasses.

"And now, Travis. Let's talk of other things, unless you're anxious to get more rest?"

"Indeed not. What would you like to discuss?"

It was Elam who replied. "I'm very interested to know what your future plans might be, Mr Holland."

Travis leaned back in his chair, steepling his fingers under his chin while he tried to formulate what had been mulling in the back of his mind ever since he awoke in Gibraltar with the news that due to his injury, he would be discharged as a ship's surgeon, and would need to find another metier. He'd never walk without a severe limp for the rest of his days. His life as a ship's surgeon had come to an end.

7. FRIENDS, FOES, AND FAMILY

"You are convinced, Lennard?"

"I am, Sir George. The man was astounded when I enquired whether the two civilian passengers fitted the description of The Cargo. I will admit, a moment of alarm fell across his features, but it was more reminiscent of tragedy and sadness than deceit."

"That's extremely unfortunate. And he was not forthcoming with the identities of the civilians?"

"He was not and, before you ask, I did not explain why the question of their identities had been put to him."

"I've always thought it extremely imprudent to carry civilian passengers aboard battle ships during time of war. One only has to think of that barge, the *Heraklion*, in 1798. Went down in the Nile Delta, laden with British citizens trying to escape the French bombardment of Abukir ..."

"Well before my time."

"And mine, Lennard, no need to provoke."

"I was jesting, sir. Affectionately, of course."

Sir George smiled. He'd understood. "How is he faring?"

"He's a man of great good temper. I'm not sure I could remain as cheerful as he, especially under the circumstances. A man of barely thirty-two years finding himself surplus to Her Majesty's needs. A man with undoubted talents. On Tuesday morning, I took the liberty of visiting the naval surgeon who'd trained him. From all accounts, Holland is a skilled physician, surgeon, and a remarkable diagnostician."

"Hmm ..."

"I know those ruminative sounds, Sir George. You've had an idea?"

"You know, Lennard, sometimes the stars align in a propitious manner and one door closes while another opens. Old Mr Hallstrom passed away not two weeks ago. Did you know that?"

"I'm fortunate in not having had need of a physician for the past ten years or so, and I've no idea what happened to him after my grandfather died."

"He was my doctor too, I bet you didn't know that either. Well, it seems to me that Mr Holland, should he wish it, and with the skills and reputation as you describe them, could become a popular society doctor, especially with his youthful, good looks."

"He's from a humble background, Sir George."

"Yes, but he's skilled, and his reputation as being the sole survivor of the naval battle of Varna will be the talking point of London once it gets about."

"And ...?"

"And how much is he worth, have you any idea?"

"Four hundred a year, I think."

"Not really enough to buy premises of his own. However, there's a dwelling sitting empty, newly inherited by the eighth Baron Betteridge ..."

"What? You mean Birch House?"

"What else are you going to do with it? You have a staff now, with all their associated ills, and you're no longer a youth yourself. Sickness and injury come to us all. You could offer him the house at say, twenty pounds a year, and negotiate some sort of arrangement for treatment for you, your friends, and your servants in exchange for such a small rental fee. Just think about it."

"This has nothing to do with the passing of Mr Hallstrom, I suppose?"

"Peripherally, Lennard. There's any number of people of quality now in need of good care. Hallstrom, despite his dour nature, was the first port of call to those who lived close to Soho. My wife, the Quaiseys—your neighbours in Buckinghamshire whose city mansion is but a stone's throw from Birch House—not to mention your great-aunt, the Baroness Winchester, who always visited Hallstrom when she came up from the country. Not only for her own treatment but also for her late husband who, as you will remember, suffered greatly from gout. Although I'll admit she's as hale and hearty as any woman of her age I know, but occasionally she must still require medical advice from time to time?"

"Hmm ..."

"Do I detect my own rumination echoed back at me, Lennard?"

"How long have I known you, sir? Can it be seventeen years now since I first came to work at the Home Office?"

"You've known me far longer, young man, and well you know it. I sat you on my knee in your earliest years when I used to visit Gresting, and when you lived there with your parents."

"There is more to this unexpected stroke of inspiration, am I wrong? I'm sure there is another agenda to having a physician who deals with the intimate ailments of the aristocracy and the well-to-do."

"The Huskersons, Lennard."

"Mark and Eugénie Huskerson, who used to be my parents' housekeepers when we lived at Marylebone?"

"The very same couple."

"What about them, Sir George? I'm afraid I don't understand their connection to Travis Holland and Birch House. Is that not what we were discussing?"

"Indeed, we were. Now, hear me out and you'll discover my seemingly abrupt mention of their names. Their time has come to an end as servants to the Dowager Duchess of Maitland. They've provided much information to the department over the past twenty or more years and she's not long for this world."

"Now I see, sir. Your suggestion is that they become housekeepers at Birch House, look after Mr Holland—if he agrees to this insane proposal—and keep their eyes and ears open for any information that might come their way 'by accident' when patients come to a capable new face for treatment."

"Ah, you've seen through my deceit, Lennard."

"Blind Freddy could see through such an obvious strategy, Sir George. The doctor with 'youthful, good looks' gave it away. Ladies love to gossip and perhaps share intimacies with their doctors. What do you imagine might happen? That the Huskersons stand outside the closed door with an ear trumpet to it, listening to consultations and treatments of Mr Holland's patients and report back on overheard indiscretions?"

"Now there's an idea ..."

"Oh, for heaven's sake," Lennard said, then began to laugh. It wasn't such a bad idea, but for the deceit on Travis Holland—which did not sit well in his mind. It was no worse than any of the agents the intelligencers used when gathering information, but somehow it felt wrong.

"Scruples, scruples, Lennard," the Home Secretary said.

"Let me think on your proposal, sir. I need to make peace with my misgivings."

"Your misgivings are unrealistic, Lennard, if I may be so bold to venture. The Huskersons would not be there to report on Travis Holland, but upon his patients."

"Still, it is the betrayal of trust that discomforts me, sir. The sharing of secrets between doctor and patient ..."

"I fear that were you not quite so taken by the man, and if it was any other physician in the country, you'd have no such hesitation."

"And of course, you are right, Sir George. It would be as if I'd placed someone within your household to listen through the door at what went on with you and Lady Anna in the privacy of your bedchamber."

"If you haven't already, shame on you, Lennard. Any good intelligencer would find it his duty to gather as much as he could about the man who was his immediate superior."

"Sir George!"

The Home Secretary laughed at Lennard's faux outrage and placed his arm around his shoulder. "Besides, these days, anyone so placed would hear naught but snores and grunts accompanying the aches of stiff joints as each of us turned over in our sleep."

*****

Lennard was a little more than surprised to see his new first footman running after his carriage as it turned into Albany Street. The man leaped onto the running board, calling out to Christopher to pull up the horses.

"What on earth is it, Merrill?" Lennard asked, relieved he'd remembered the name of the recently arrived young man.

"Sir, there's been a disturbance."

"Has anyone been injured?"

"Miles, sir, but it's not serious."

"Then please tell me what is so urgent you feel need to intercept my carriage that couldn't wait until I got home?"

"Elam sent me to watch out for you. We had to lock him in the coal cellar passage, he's in such a rage."

"Get in the coach," Lennard said, then told Christopher to drive on, but to direct the carriage through the stable entrance which issued out of Clarence Gardens and not to draw up at the front elevation of the house in Albany Street.

"Now tell me in as few words as possible what has happened that's caused you to restrain Elam."

"The gentleman struck Miles such a blow to his face with his riding crop that it cut through to his teeth."

Lennard stood in the coach and yelled at Christopher to give the pair their reins. Falling back in his seat, he asked, "Which gentleman?"

"Sir Terrence Astley, my lord. He refused to leave after presenting his card, even when Miles told him you were abroad. He forced his way into the library, shoving Miles aside who called out for help. When I arrived, Miles was on his knees holding his face, blood everywhere over your new carpet. Why, sir—"

"The new carpet be damned. Astley? Did Elam try to intercede?"

"Yes sir, that's when Sir Terrace produced his pistol."

"How long ago did this happen, Merrill?"

"Not more than fifteen minutes ago, sir. We'd have sent one of the lads on horseback, but there's mayhem in the stables and the grooms seemed hard-pressed to calm the horses after the shot."

"The shot?"

"Yes, my lord, in order to force Elam to stand back, Sir Terrence discharged his pistol through the library window."

Lennard felt a cold anger rising in his belly. Despite his years of unwelcomed thoughts, dreams, and nightmares playing out scenes of vengeance upon Sir Terrence Astley, the sixth Baronet Killcaire, Lennard knew a show of bluster, anger, and lack of self-restraint would afford his former Irish lover enormous satisfaction. He'd often called Lennard a petulant child to his face in the most heated of arguments.

As the carriage drew up in the stable yard, Lennard told Merrill to go straight to the kitchen and ask for tea to be prepared. When it was ready, he was to take it up to Astley, informing him that Lennard had returned and would join him presently.

"What are your plans, sir? Shall I need to fetch help?"

"No, Merrill. I'll speak with Christopher first, then we'll release Elam and try to get him to calm down. Nothing will come of further violence."

"Very well, my lord, I'll see to your orders at once."

"What do you wish me to do?" Christopher asked.

"Once Elam's in a fit state to be civil, I'll ask him to be at my side when I speak to Astley."

"Are you sure you don't want me there too? Astley has already discharged his pistol once."

"No, nothing will be gained by treating this as anything unexpected. It will unnerve him to see us calm when we enter the room. However, I'd like you to wait outside the library door with my riding coat, boots, and equipage, as if I'm about to take a turn on Chester in Regent's Park.

"Your equipage? You're really going riding?"

"No, of course not. But, please, do as I ask. And have two of the burliest stable lads standing at hand too, and out of direct sight of the library. It might be prudent if things do indeed get out of hand."

*****

"What's that you're reading, Astley?" Lennard asked, entering the room. He was in his shirtsleeves, his neckerchief undone and hanging loosely around his neck.

Terrence Astley turned the book over and inspected its spine. "Something foreign," he said, before throwing the book onto one of the low tables in front of the large, leather Chesterfield on which he was semi-recumbent.

"I've asked for tea to be sent up."

"Very kind, Malloray."

"Betteridge, Terrence."

"Ah! We're playing that game, are we?"

"It's not a game, as well you know. I'd hate it to get around that you called to see me without notice during deep mourning and addressed me inappropriately. As you know, due to the change in my circumstances, I have the prerogative of calling you by your Christian name, whereas you do not mine."

Astley snorted softly, stretched back on the Chesterfield, crossing his ankles. "I suppose you wonder why I'm here, unannounced."

Lennard drew up a library chair, not replying, barely turning his head when Merrill arrived with the tea service. He was followed by Elam, who did not sit but leaned against one of the library's four enormous breakfront bookcases with his arms folded across his chest. Astley glanced at him briefly but did not acknowledge his presence.

Waiting until Merrill had poured tea and passed him a cup, Astley raised it to his lips, but then abruptly changed his mind, placed the cup on the floor, not bothering to swivel from his prone position on the sofa.

"I'm sorry to hear about Sir Hugh," he said.

"No, you're not," Lennard said.

"No, you're correct, I'm not. He was a fool and a wastrel."

"Wastrel? My uncle was anything but, as well you know. He was a miser, disturbed in his manner, rude and petulant in his behaviour."

"I've come on business, Lennard," he announced, sitting up on the sofa, pulling on his riding boots, which he'd taken off and left next to the arm of the Chesterfield. "I'm aware I should have delayed this visit, but I've waited long enough. I'd like you to honour your uncle's agreement with me."

"First off, Terrence, not only do you continue to insult me by referring to me in an overfamiliar manner, but you'd also like me to hear you out and grant you a favour?"

"It's no favour. It's a gentleman's agreement. The purchase of Malloray's Eastern and Australian. I made your uncle an exceptionally good offer."

"And the agreement? What form did it take?"

"A handshake."

"Nothing in writing?"

"No, an agreement in writing had not yet been prepared before his untimely passing. Twenty-five thousand in gold bullion was my offer."

"Your witness to this 'gentleman's agreement'?"

"My word should suffice."

"Your word, Terrence? Which particular word are you referring to? Is it liar? Perhaps cheat, perhaps blackguard, perhaps whore—?"

Lennard stopped himself. He'd forgotten he'd promised to keep calm and under control, and now he found himself beginning to lose his temper. The soft smirk on Astley's face alerted him to the fact that he'd once more played into the Irishman's hands.

"Surely you can think of more words ... Betteridge."

"Indeed, I can. However, I've forgotten myself. Several years have passed since we last spoke and, in that time, much has changed within me. Alas, I fear your sudden, unannounced arrival, the mistreatment of one of my servants, blood on one of my best Turkish carpets, and a bullet hole in my library window seem to indicate that nothing much has changed within you. Unless you can provide me with a legal document, signed by my uncle, witnessed in accordance with the law, I'm afraid I cannot entertain the notion that such an agreement actually took place. And certainly, even if it were a handshake, the agreement can no longer stand with Sir Hugh. He's dead and I am the owner of the shipping business. Twenty-five thousand? Had you said one hundred and twenty-five, close to the current value of the enterprise, I might have believed you that some such conversation had taken place."

Astley stood, red-faced with anger. "You seem to find it easy to call me a liar."

"Only because it's not the first time I've had occasion to. Now is there anything else?"

"Nothing," Sir Terrence replied, reaching into the fob pocket of his waistcoat, he retrieved a crown piece and threw it onto the table on which the tea service sat. "This is for the window. Send me a receipt for the replacement of your rug."

"Fetch Christopher, if you please, Elam," Lennard said.

"What? Are you going to have me manhandled out the door?"

"No, Terrence. Christopher is waiting for me with my riding equipage. I was about to exercise my horse and I shall do so once I've seen to Miles. You've paid me for the destruction of my window and given me a promise for the carpet, but surely you realise you owe me for the mistreatment of my butler?"

"You can't be serious, Lennard. We're talking about chattel here. Servants are no different from your carpet or your *priceless* window. He'll recover. A quick slash across the chops is a lesser thing than one of my own servants might have received had one of them tried to grapple with me. How dare he touch a person of—"

Lennard strode quickly to Astley and grabbed the fronts of his jacket.

"Let me tell you this. Although I said I've changed, my hate for you still burns in my chest. How dare you stride into my house, abuse my servants, and feel free to do whatever you like. Remember this before you leave. One word from me to the right person and you'll find yourself gasping for air as you descend to the depths of the Thames, your arms bound behind your back, and your feet chained to an anchor. You'd just disappear. Like that!" Lennard snapped his fingers next to Astley's ear.

"Have care to whom you make threats, Lennard. I'm too valuable to the Prime Minister. I still hold a seat and a loyal group of Irish lords who keep him in power."

"Threats against other men interest me not, sir. I wish to have nothing ever to do with you from this day henceforth … not ever. Do you understand?"

"You're making a big mistake."

"Not so big a one as you made by appearing at my door and forcing your way into my house."

"I shall take my leave of you. But don't think this is over. I'll put it about that you dishonoured your uncle's word."

"Do what you feel best, sir. But, by now, my coachman will have arrived with my riding gear and is waiting outside the door. If I were you, I'd leave this very moment before I grab my whip and thrash the living daylights out of you. You can apologise to Elam on your way out for injuring his brother."

"Apologise? Why, I—"

"Oh, and Astley?" Lennard added, interrupting the man by violently releasing his jacket and pushing him backward, his knees hitting the edge of the Chesterfield. "Putting it about that I dishonoured your agreement with my uncle? Well, two can play at that game. It would not be hard to start a rumour that you've dealt with your ward, Neasa, inappropriately, and that's the reason you're so reluctant to allow her to marry into one of the most noble families in the land."

"No one would believe that for one moment."

"People have been wondering about your reluctance these past four or five years, ever since Sir George's son first approached you. However, now, with my new title, I will have the ears of not only the leading members of society, but also those close to the throne. An innuendo is as good as an oath, don't you think? Even Irish baronets who hold some sway in parliament are not immune to gossip. You'd not be invited anywhere, whether the slander is proved or not. Everyone knows Sir Hugh was not a businessman, and although the sum you offered would make you out to be a villain at the best, the premature plucking of a tender blossom before its time ... why, Her Majesty would send someone banging at your door."

*****

Lennard nearly vomited when he eventually found Miles sitting patiently in the servants' dining room and Travis perched on the edge of the large, scrubbed-pine dining table, which had been drawn close, stitching the gash in Miles' cheek.

It wasn't from revulsion, or from the sight of blood soaked through Miles's shirt that he felt sick to his stomach. It was more a feeling that came over him of how much worse it could have been had Elam intercepted the bullet that had shattered the library window when he'd come to the aid of his brother. At his side, Lennard felt Elam trembling slightly and, concealed from the doctor's line of sight, drew Elam's hand into his own, squeezing it gently while passing him a grim smile.

"Fear not, Lennard. Miles will be as good as new," Travis said, directing his speech over his shoulder. "I must admit, I've not seen such fine thread and so strong. Although there will be a scar, it will lend an air of insouciance. You can put it about it's the legacy of a duel, Miles. What do you think of that? No, don't smile! Not yet, you'll pull your stitches too tight."

"Is the light strong enough for you, Mr Holland?" Elam asked, making his way to his brother and winding one arm around his waist so he could observe the doctor's reply.

"I must admit I'd have wished a thousand times for the brilliance of these new gas mantles, Elam," Travis replied with a friendly smile. "And the luxury of stitching wounds with gossamer-thin silken strands and a steady floor under my feet, it's as good as a naval surgeon could ever wish it. There now, all done," he added, standing back and turning Miles's face back and forth in his hand.

"Thank you, Mr Holland," Miles said casting his eyes in Lennard's direction, about to speak.

"If you apologise for doing your duty, I shall cut the other side of your face," Lennard said cheekily. "I'm in agreement with Doctor

Holland, the surgery is as neat as anything I've seen. And your 'duelling scar' will make you an object of admiration by all the young ladies."

Elam's quick, unvoiced "thank you" to Lennard did not go missed by the surgeon. He, however, lowered his head quickly and began to wash his hands in the basin at his side.

"I'll kill him," Elam said, against his brother's neck.

"Not before I do," Miles answered.

"You shall both have to wait in line," Lennard added. He was about to ask Miles to explain what had happened when Merrill clattered noisily down the servants' stairs.

"I beg your pardon, my lord. But there's another visitor arrived."

"*Another* visitor? Does the world not understand the rules of deep mourning? Cards after ten days, then at home cards sent out for visits a month after. Tell them I'm not at home, whomever they may be."

"But, sir, it's—"

"I don't care who it is," Lennard said angrily.

A woman's voice echoed down the stairway from behind Merrill.

"Not even your dear aunt Caroline, come all the way from Hampshire to clutch her dearest nephew to her breast?"

"Not a word of Astley, my friends, please," Lennard whispered urgently. "We'll talk of what happened after my aunt has gone. Agreed?"

The men readily acquiesced to his plea, all except Travis who nodded, but sat still, rigid, desperate to know what to do, because it was obvious that a lady of quality seemed insistent on descending the stairs into the servants' hall and he was perched on the edge of their dining table in his nightgown—a short one, which only covered his thighs halfway to his knees.

However, when the lady swept past Merrill, raising one edge of her full skirt to pass him on the stairs, she headed toward Miles, her gloved hands to her mouth, eyes wide and threatening tears.

"Miles, what on earth has happened to you?"

"It's nothing, Lady C. A scratch."

She took his hand in hers and peered closely at his face, turning his cheek into the brightest part of the light that issued from the gas lamp on the wall behind him. She sensed that something untoward had brought this about, but also realised that the men would not readily talk about it in front of her. Men: so fragile when it came to women's sensibilities, she thought.

"Are you responsible for this delicate needlework, sir?" she asked of Travis, who had crossed his knees and was pulling down his nightshirt as far as it would go.

"This is Travis Holland, Aunt," Lennard said. "A doctor, as you can see, of some skill who's staying with us for a short time while he recuperates from his own injuries. Lieutenant-surgeon Travis Holland, this is my great-aunt the Lady Winchester, sister of my late grandfather, the sixth Baron Betteridge."

"I'm delighted, my lady, although mortified you catch me in a state of undress."

"Ah, Mr Holland, may I call you that? My nephew, Miles, and his brother Elam ran through my brother's house in their stockinged feet—and sometimes less—when they were in their 'teen years. You are considerably more well-covered than they were on many occasions."

"Aunt Caroline, you're embarrassing me," Lennard said, moving into his aunt's proffered embrace, kissing her, French-style three times, on alternate cheeks.

"Come, please," she said, after releasing Lennard and beckoning Elam for a tender embrace. "This one is my favourite," she said to Travis, over Elam's shoulder. "He was the tempering iron in the fire of all of their youthful exuberances."

"He was?" Miles asked.

"My dear boy, you know he was. The most vulnerable and yet the strongest of you all. Now, where are Gerald and Robert? Is Angus to arrive this evening by chance? I'm longing to see all you boys together."

"Robert is—"

"I know he's living here, and so is Gerald, and Clyford Billings, General Airey's nephew … why, Lennard, of course, I knew. And I knew Lieutenant-surgeon Holland was here too."

"Aunt Caroline, he arrived but yesterday."

"Yes, you brought him directly from Greenwich Hospital. Don't look at me like that. Why do you think I'm here? How long do you think the penny post takes to arrive from one part of the country to the other? Lady Grey wrote to me yesterday, the letter was delivered last evening, and I decided that I'd come up to London this morning. My house in Bedford Square is being readied, and although it's only March, I thought I'd stay for the spring season, catch up with my favourite nephew and his companions, help you sort out your social life, now that you're the handsomest and most eligible wealthy bachelor in the city, and direct you to the best catches in the kingdom."

"But—"

"I'll hear no buts. Now, if you please, I'd like to be shown around the house. It's more than five years since I last was here, and already I've seen how spruce and orderly the hallways are. I'd like to take tea in the morning room. You'll send someone to fetch Robert and Gerald won't you, Lennard? Oh, and don't forget Angus. Affairs of state can wait. I need my boys around me."

Before he could say another word, she kissed Lennard's cheek then gestured at Elam to offer his arm, both of them disappearing up the servants' staircase, their faces wreathed in smiles. Elam loved her as much as she cared for him, Lennard observed. She'd always been the same, favouring and fussing over them in equal measure, despite Elam's and Miles's position as servants. She'd hidden away secret treats for all of them, spoiling Robert, Gerald, and Angus—notwithstanding his grandfather's admonitions they lead a relatively spartan life, free of overindulgences, ready for society and the lives of men of character.

As for Lennard, there'd always been a special bond between him and his aunt, strengthened after the loss of his family. She'd told him, when he was no more than sixteen, that the title would come to him after Sir Hugh and then his uncle Arthur. He'd protested, saying his uncle was still young, and there was plenty of time for him to marry and to have his own children. In that case, the title would skip him completely. However, she'd expressed her opinion that his uncle Arthur was not the marrying type. Far too shy around women to make an effort and happy to spend his days with pugilism, riding, at hunt, and attending lectures at the geographical societies around the city.

It was after her first confidences that led Lennard to wonder whether his uncle Arthur, despite his protestations to the contrary, had a hidden preference, but as he'd never seen any evidence of it, assumed that like a myriad of other unmarried men, his uncle simply preferred his own company.

*****

It was later that evening, after dinner and when the company had adjourned to the drawing room, that Lennard realised how artfully they'd been played.

He'd been well aware that his aunt had realised something was amiss: Miles's injury had been no mere scratch but evidence of something more serious. She'd hustled and bustled them about, giving none of them time to dwell on Astley's importunate arrival, in order to provide them with an excuse to talk later, when tempers had cooled and more reasonable heads could prevail.

Mr Huilot had provided an extravagance of simple, yet tasty dishes for Lennard's guests, the first formal dining occasion in Bexford House since Lennard had become its owner. His Aunt had returned with her former husband's niece, Miss Peters, and Angus had arrived with his wife, Adelia, whom he had just been accompanying on the pianoforte while she'd entertained the assembled company with a very accomplished rendition of "Scenes that are the Brightest", from Wallace's opera *Maritana*.

"How wonderful," Lady Winchester said, applauding softly, her face glowing with pleasure.

"They make an extraordinary couple, don't they," Travis remarked, sitting carefully on a rattan recliner, its back in an upright position and his injured leg stretched out on its front extension.

"Someday, I wish to have Lennard so suitably matched," she replied, extending her hand for Angus's kiss as he returned to take up his place between her and Lennard on the chaise.

"What were you saying, madam?"

"Please, Angus. Do as you men did when you were lads, and call me 'Lady C'. I adored it so."

"It's entirely inappropriate."

"Perhaps, but it's the least of our worries when among friends of long-standing."

"Very well, Lady C. Now please, will you share what you were discussing when I interrupted you?"

"I was merely remarking that my nephew should be lucky to marry a woman such as your wife, Angus. She's a delight."

"I concur, a woman such as my wife is probably the only choice for a man like my friend Lennard."

Lennard's wry smile was hidden as he lowered his head, pretending to inspect his wine glass. A sapphist wife, like Angus's, would certainly be the only choice for him should he ever find himself compelled to marry. However, he was truly content, Elam at his side, their lengthy relationship a comfort in itself. How he wished they could exist on an equal level and yet consort together in public. Only as master and servant was that possible, and they'd long grown used to the pretence; so much so that it seldom bothered either of them much.

"And you, Mr Holland? Is there no one close to your heart?" Lady Winchester asked.

"There was, madam, but alas cholera claimed her before I could."

"Oh dear, I'm terribly sorry. It has oft been my wont to speak when I perhaps should have trodden more carefully."

"It's of no matter, madam, and I thank you for your kind solicitation. Alas, it was not to be, and I've made my life caring for others these days."

"Speaking of which, what do you propose to do in the future? Surely a life at sea would prove troublesome, unless your injury proves to be a hindrance rather than an exclusion to Her Majesty's service."

"I've had a few thoughts on the matter, madam. I'm a man of a small income, but I'll probably look around for rooms and start a private practice."

"That's a wonderful idea, Mr Holland. Your surgical skills, as I've seen with my own eyes ... in fact, our old physician, Doctor Hallstrom, recently passed away and now neither I nor members of my set have someone close at hand. It's been a sore topic of conversation for some two weeks now."

Lennard's ears shot up.

"What about Birch House, Lennard?" she said, turning to him. "It's standing empty. What plans do you have for it? Why, just last week I had a letter from the Huskersons. You remember them, they used to be housekeepers for your parents when you were a child. The poor Dowager Duchess of Maitland is letting her staff go and they wrote asking if I had placement for them. Indeed, you could put them up in Birch House to look after our new friend, Mr Holland. The three rooms on the western side of the house on the ground floor would be perfect for a doctor's study, a consulting room, and a surgery, don't you think?"

It was at that moment, Lennard realised he was but a wheel in the great machinery of State. No doubt the letter to his aunt from the Home Secretary's wife may have included instructions about subjects he'd only heard of himself earlier that very morning. It took little imagining to suspect that his aunt had also received a visit from Sir George after she'd left Bexford House and had returned to her house in Bedford Square.

There could be no doubt that his morning's earlier, casual conversation with Sir George had been something planned, likely a day or two in advance. In his mind, he congratulated his superior on his feigned nonchalance, as if the ideas had come spontaneously to him, passed off in a way a normal conversation might have unfolded. Lennard admitted to himself that he still had much to learn about the art of contrivance.

It was clever, he owned. Were the idea of letting Birch House to have come from his aunt, staffed by suggestions of her own, then the Home Secretary had provided a future disavowal for Lennard, should he be accused of complicity in the architecture of the scheme. "When one locks one door, one must be sure there is an avenue of escape." It was one of the first lessons he'd learned from Sir George.

"Birch House?" Travis asked.

"It's in Soho Square, not far from here," Lennard explained. "One of my grandfather's purchases. I'll take you there."

"Soho Square, Lennard? You forget my circumstances, and the depth of my purse."

"Lennard's grandfather, my brother, kept Dr Hallstrom on a retainer, Mr Holland," Lady Winchester said, "ready to treat members of his household, both masters and servants. I'm sure my nephew would be accommodating when it came to a rental agreement if the same arrangement could be put in place. Isn't that so, Lennard?"

Lennard noticed the slightest narrowing of his aunt's eyes as she regarded him. No doubt, she'd been well-coached to direct the conversation to Sir George's ends. "It's something worth thinking about, of course. I'll speak with Travis on the subject when he's feeling better. He's just arrived here, aunt."

"How are you feeling, Mr Holland? You look well enough?" she asked, turning away from Lennard.

"Exceptionally well, my lady. My leg hurts, but it's healing. I'll never walk straight without a limp again, nor shall I be able to run. But presently I'm more tired than anything."

"Please send a card, sir, when you're ready to start accepting patients. My niece suffers far too frequently from the vapours, and I have a bunion that needs looking at—"

"And my wife will have need of care, should our expectations prove true and she is indeed *enceinte* ..." Angus added.

"Wait, Adelia is with child?" Lady Winchester clapped her hands in delight.

"We're not sure," Angus replied. "But we live in hope."

"Oh, my dear boy. Surely this calls for celebration!"

"Let's not swallow gudgeons 'ere they're catch'd ..."

"Nor count our chickens before they're hatched," Lennard's aunt added, finishing the old saying, smiling greatly. "Agreed, sir. But I hope I shall be among the first to know."

"I'll be well enough in a few days from now to attend to a few consultations," Travis said, "but not too many. I'm aware that fatigue is the greatest hindrance to recuperation, and of course, it will entirely depend on the good will of Lennard to allow me to use one of his rooms here for the purpose."

Lennard gestured around the room. "There are dozens of empty spaces in this great edifice, Travis. I'll make sure you're not overtaxed, but may I suggest you give yourself more than a few days. Perhaps a week? How would you like to spend some time at my country house, Gresting Hall? There'd be peace and quiet, and fresh food of the most excellent quality. The air would certainly do you a world of good."

"What a wonderful idea, Lennard," his aunt said. "I should have thought of it myself. However, let's take Dr Holland to see Birch House first, shall we? You two men can talk business in the meantime and I'm sure you can have the dwelling appointed to Dr Holland's taste, ready for his return from Hazlemere."

"My dear Lady Winchester," Travis said, blushing lightly. "You seem the master of organisation on my behalf."

"She does that," Lennard said. "Take care she doesn't have you married with a family of five before you know what's happened to you."

His aunt's soft smile made him take her hand and kiss it. Her remedy for every unmarried man's ills was a wife.

8. THE RUSSIAN CONNECTION

By Wednesday, the 27th of March, a week after he'd visited Travis Holland in Greenwich Hospital and Terrence Astley had made his importunate visit to Bexford House, Lennard was starting to realise the weight of his new position and the responsibilities it entailed.

Calling cards had been arriving by the dozen, many from people he didn't even know. But thanks to his aunt Caroline's knowledge of society, he soon learned most of them had been former friends of his grandfather. Business cards, of which there had been plenty, were fewer in number, but of urgency, usually accompanied by short notes requesting meetings. The dealings of Malloray's had been well looked after by Robert and Mr Rudd, who—anxious to take up the offer of the cottage in Penge—seemed reluctant to make any decisions and encouraged Lennard to attend all new discussions with former clients of the shipping business.

Lennard had to remind himself that it had been over five years since anyone had dealt directly with a member of the Malloray family, and realised it was expedient that he made himself available as each client presented himself to discuss future dealings. Each meeting was also an opportunity to reinforce Robert's new position as manager, director, and co-owner.

After church on Sunday, he'd visited Birch House in company with his aunt Caroline and Travis, to show him the dwelling and to talk about a possible rental proposal, within reach of the doctor's purse, yet agreeable to them both. The following morning, he'd accompanied the doctor to Paddington station, Miles as Travis's travelling companion, both to spend a week at Gresting recuperating.

And now, a few days later, he was on his way to the offices of the recently renamed shipping company: Malloray, Beauchamp, and Fahey. New signs, the lettering outlined in gold glittering in the sunlight as his carriage drew up outside the long, imposing main warehouse that housed the administrative offices of the company.

Today, he was to meet with the Earl of Twinton. As the major importer in the country of the finest teas from India and Ceylon, he was one of the shipping company's most important clients. The meeting had been arranged to reassure the earl that their business dealings would continue as they always had done, and to guarantee future trade prices. Lennard had never met Twinton; he'd been a friend of his grandfather. Five years ago, when the sixth Baron Betteridge had died, Lennard was still a distant relative, unlikely to inherit the title during the lifetime of the earl.

Twinton was one of those old-fashioned aristocrats, born to a notion of superiority and strict observance of rank. He'd already arrived and was waiting by the time Lennard entered the room. He neither stood from his chair to greet him nor responded to Lennard's proffered handshake.

"Betteridge," the earl said, in not an unfriendly manner.

"Twinton," Lennard replied, torn between using the man's title and a "my lord"—he opted for the easiest and least offensive mode of address. He'd forgotten one of the first major rules when conducting business with wealthy men of station and with titles: handshakes from gentlemen such as Twinton came at the end of a negotiation, to seal it, not beforehand.

His grandfather had always referred to him as "Blister Barrington", the earl's family name, preceded by a soubriquet that described the gentleman's complexion. From youth, the earl had suffered from an inflammation of the skin of his face, stretching it taut and bestowing it with a pale, yellowish hue.

"You've already met my cousin, Robert Fahey?" Lennard asked.

"Mr Fahey has been my 'port of call' these past five years, since the death of your grandfather. May I offer my condolences on the passing of your uncle."

"Thank you, my lord," Lennard said, then waited to be introduced to the tall, dark-haired man who stood quietly behind the earl, and who'd been observing their conversation.

"May I present my son-in-law, the Grand Duke Vassili Vadimovich Kosorukov, whom I've invited this morning to observe how business is done."

"Grand Duke," Lennard said, bowing in deference to the man's rank.

"Baron," came the polite reply, accompanied by a smile that barely passed for one.

It soon became apparent that the grand duke was not in the slightest bit interested in affairs of business. He seemed distracted, glancing around the room while seated in a library chair, one ankle crossed over the knee of the opposite leg, inspecting his nails from time to time. Once or twice, he threw a watery smile in Lennard's direction, before glancing away quickly.

Contracts were eventually produced and signed, after which tea appeared, brought in by Robert's nephew—recently arrived from Lyon, sent to learn English like Robert had been, twenty-five years ago, and, like his uncle, to be brought up in the ways and manners of the greatest trading nation on earth. Robert, at least, had the advantage of an Irish father and had spoken not only the language of his father's country but was also fluent in good, barely accented English when he'd arrived.

"Tout va bien, Geoffroy?" Lennard asked, reaching out to help the young man. He was slight of build and a few weeks shy of his tenth birthday. The tray was enormous in comparison.

"Tout va bien, monsieur le baron. Merci bien," the lad said, allowing Robert to help him place the tray on the large office desk.

"You speak French?" the grand duke asked Lennard, in the same language.

"Yes, Mr Fahey and I are first cousins," Lennard explained, also in French. "And our mothers were French sisters from Lyon."

"Come here," Kosorukov said to Geoffroy, standing from his chair and squatting down so that his face was at the same level as the boy's. "Here, take this," he said, handing the boy a gold guinea. "Keep it safe somewhere and remember the day a cousin of the Czar of all the Russias gave it to you."

The boy turned to Robert, as if to ask permission. Then, when it was given with a smile and a nod, he gingerly took the coin and placed it in his pocket, thanking the grand duke while shaking the Russian's hand and bowing deeply at the waist.

"Your French is exemplary, grand duke," Robert said after his nephew had left.

"It's the court language at St. Petersburg. I learned it before I did Russian, which is not considered a suitable language for the nobility in my country."

Lennard was rather puzzled. After reading Kosorukov's dossier—which revealed the man's forays into the most undesirable parts of the city in the search for male companionship, and his apparent willingness to offer secrets of his own country to the British—he'd expected someone quite different. He'd expected the grand duke to be aloof, as he'd appeared to be when Lennard first arrived, and somewhat haughty, not a man who'd stoop to be kind to a lad and to give him a keepsake he might treasure as a memento of meeting someone with such an illustrious pedigree.

"That was extremely generous, sir, if you'll permit me to comment," Lennard said.

"I adore children, Betteridge. There's little artifice when it comes to those of his age, so unlike dealing with adults. Now, if the business that remains does not require your presence, I'd be grateful if you would show me around the wharves, and perhaps tell me a little of how this enterprise of yours functions."

Lennard quickly realised the invitation was to give the Russian an excuse to leave the room and to avoid pretending to be fascinated by things he found tiresome.

"If you'll excuse us, my lord?" Lennard asked of Twinton, reverting to English.

"Yes, of course, Betteridge. I shall discuss the finer points of our shipping arrangements with Mr Fahey. You can sign the rest of the documents when you return."

*****

"I'll have you know, I understand little of the management and operations of the shipping business, grand duke," Lennard said.

"I'm aware of that, sir. I'm also aware that you are newly elevated to your title and have worked for some time as third secretary to Sir George Grey."

"Indeed, that is correct."

"This came to me last night," Kosorukov said, switching back to French when two dockhands passed them close by, each doffing their caps and murmuring "good morning" while studiously avoiding eye contact.

"Good morning, gentlemen," Lennard said, stopping briefly to raise his hat. He was rewarded with bright smiles from the two men. "What came to you last night, sir?" he asked, returning his attention to his companion.

Kosorukov handed Lennard a small square of folded paper, a gold-headed pin inserted diagonally between two of its corners. There were two groups of three letters, placed horizontally on the front of the square, in small, but neat writing:

V.V.K.

T.Q.H.

The gold pin through a folded square of paper, with two sets of initials on its face, was a device that only Sir George used to pass on information to his intelligencers.

"It was delivered to me last evening with the message that I should give it to you today."

"Delivered by a man in uniform at an ale house in which someone of your standing should not frequent, sir?"

Kosorukov shrugged and let forth a soft snort. "I'm not sure how you know where I was, Betteridge. But there's nothing inside the note, in case you were wondering."

"This message was meant for me, not for you, even though it's marked with your initials and to be delivered to you at The Queen's Head in Knightsbridge."

"Do I have your confidence, Lennard?"

Lennard smiled. The use of his Christian name was telling, unexpected, and very intimate. It was obviously done in an attempt to disarm him. However, he was used to these sorts of games, so replied, equally as informally. "Indeed, Vassili Vadimovich. Perhaps I should reveal to you that this meeting was not unexpected."

"I see. So, business can be conducted?"

"Perhaps it could be, yes."

"Discreetly?"

"Sir, I have not been employed by the Home Office for nigh on twenty years because of my inability to keep confidences. In this instance, I would be acting as a courier, a go-between, not an agent of my own employ. If there's something that needs to be passed on, it will be me who does that, and I would be that same person who arranges some consideration for the level of your ..."

"Information?"

"You may use whatever word you wish, grand duke," Lennard said.

"You said you were expecting such an approach from me?"

"Either that or an opportunity for me to mention that I'd been sent to see whether you might be amenable to share ... information."

"The messenger last evening?"

Lennard shook his head. "He may be one of ours, he may be just a man in need of coin."

"Is it that well-known? Where I go and what I do?"

"You have no reason to fear that you will be exposed, sir, if that's what's on your mind. But yes, one or two people are aware of your ... nocturnal meanderings."

"And you disapprove?"

"Good heavens, sir. It's none of my business what you do. Although, I'd offer you some advice to perhaps find some regular companionship and consort with them somewhere more discreet."

"Are you familiar with …?"

"The variations of connections between or across the sexes are not unknown to me, grand duke. I've observed most everything you could possibly imagine, and I promise you, I make no judgement. It is of my opinion that, conducted with care and discretion, ladies and gentlemen should take solace in the arms of whomever can provide them succour."

"A regular companion or two would be ideal, as you suggest. However, my father-in-law keeps me on a short chain. It's only after the house has retired that I can escape his eternal vigilance. I'm unlikely to be recognised in the places I frequent. And I prefer the lower classes, the rougher the better, as they're the types who are unlikely to frequent any of the establishments in which I might be seen during the normal course of my day, and who are equally as unlikely to be literate, and therefore able to read news pamphlets and perhaps recognise me by description."

"I do suggest you act with caution, grand duke," Lennard said. "Such creatures as you describe could turn violent."

The grand duke turned to face Lennard. They'd been leaning on a railing at the edge of the dockside. "As long as my face bears no bruises, perhaps I'm amenable to such treatment … if the companion has other, irresistible attractions."

Lennard blushed, despite himself, much to the amusement of the Russian. Angus's description of Kosorukov's preferences when it came to male companions as "brawny, brainless, and blessed" had come to mind, unbidden.

"We should return to the office, sir," Lennard said. "But before we do, perhaps you could offer something of value as a token. Something for which we may judge the level of compensation for your … information."

"Give me your arm, Lennard," he said. "Let's promenade along the wharf, and when we get to that vessel flying the gryphon as its pennant on the mainmast, we'll stop. You'll point out the banner, as if explaining what it means, and I'll give you something that may curl your toes."

"In exchange for?"

"Your good will. The understanding that I'm not about playing games. And, in return, something of no great value to you, but something which might in the future prove valuable to me."

"And that is, sir?"

"An introduction to Arnott and Evelyn Simperknell."

"Viscount Quaisey and his wife? Why can't you arrange it with your father-in-law?"

"My dear Betteridge, the Quaiseys are considered *parvenus* in society. He's thought of as a bore, and she bumbling. They aren't the type that my in-laws would even acknowledge in public, except as convention requires it should they meet by chance. However, I've heard she's looking for someone to provide advice to refurbish her enormous London house."

"And you'd like to offer your services?"

"No, sir. I'd like you to arrange an introduction and to mention to Lady Quaisey beforehand that I'm a person of quality, with a reputation for taste and eye for all things fashionable, decorative, and of the highest standard. Suitable for another person of quality wishing to advance his or her standing in society."

"Advance their standing in society? He's wealthy enough, why—"

"It's obvious you don't know something about Lady Quaisey, sir. Her grandfather was an ironmonger from Sheffield, and her mother was a lady's maid in a large house who married the elderly cotton baron who owned it. She gave birth to a daughter shortly before his death. Evelyn Simperknell inherited a fortune and married for a title with her enormous dowry. She's ever since been trying to climb the social ladder, hoping that her natural lack of taste and awkward manners might carry her through society because of her husband's name and title."

*****

Lennard arrived, slightly out of breath, after hurrying up the four broad flights of stairs that led to the floor on which Sir George's office was situated.

The Home Secretary had been in his office with Angus, piles of documents spread over Sir George's desk and were passing letters and plans to each other when Lennard was shown into the room.

"My dear boy! I wasn't expecting you."

"Indeed, I rather think you were, sir."

The Home Secretary smiled, then spoke Kosorukov's name under his breath to Angus, who let out a soft sigh with a nod.

"There's no need to whisper, gentlemen," Lennard said. "It's obvious that you both knew what came to pass this morning at Malloray's."

"I have no idea, Lennard," Angus said, before glancing at Sir George.

"I may have omitted to tell Angus about your impromptu meeting, Lennard. You mustn't blame him. Now, please, take off your jacket and sit for a moment. We're right in the middle of something that needs our attention, and while we're at it, perhaps you could think of the best way of explaining what it is that has you so agitated."

"I'm agitated because I've been running ragged all morning. You ambushed me, sir. I was totally unprepared to deal with Kosorukov."

"It's when you do your best work, Lennard, when you are taken by surprise. Help yourself to a glass of whatever you like, you know where to find everything."

Lennard checked his pocket watch. It was half past eleven and far too early for anything fortified so he poured himself a glass of water, drank it down quickly, then replenished his glass. Sir George and Angus continued to mutter to each other softly, signing one document after the other. Bored after a few minutes of watching them, he wandered to the large, leaded diamond-paned window of Sir George's study that looked out over the back of Whitehall and over the Thames.

He'd been in such a flurry of activity after bidding farewell to Twinton and Kosorukov that he'd hardly had time to draw breath. These few minutes as he waited gave him time to reflect and to draw the threads of his thoughts together. Standing calmly, observing movement in the courtyard far below, his gaze shifted over the tops of the buildings behind. Every few seconds, from his vantage point, he caught glimpses of dusky red sails as river barges and packets moved back and forth along the Thames.

Almost at the same time that Sir George rang his handbell for his assistant, Angus arrived at Lennard's side. "Have you recovered from Astley?" he whispered.

"Does Sir George know?"

"No, Lennard. I haven't said a word, and you didn't tell me much about it either."

"It was neither the time nor the place, Angus, over dinner and with your wife and Lady C at table."

"You would have sought me out had it been difficult, I hope?"

Lennard patted Angus's hand, which his friend had placed on his shoulder. "I've survived worse, Angus. Anyway, you'll hear all about it this morning, I promise you."

"All?"

"Well, enough for Sir George's ears, and I'll tell you the rest when we have time alone together."

"Secrets, gentlemen?" the Home Secretary called out across the room, smiling as both Lennard and Angus turned to face him.

"Secrets are the stuff of our business, sir, if you'll forgive me quoting your own words back at you."

Sir George laughed, moving to the cabinet that held his refreshments and poured himself a rather large glass of something of a deep red colour, holding the decanter up as if to ask whether Angus would like a glass of the same.

"No thank you, Sir George."

"It's not what you think it is, Lennard," the Home Secretary said. "It's some sort of berry cordial my wife's maid makes, and which I've promised to drink instead of wine when I'm not eating."

"Lady Anna is persuasive, sir," Lennard replied.

"More so than most people realise. Now, gentlemen, please be seated. I'm sorry to have kept you waiting, Lennard, but truthfully, I did not expect you this morning. As you're here, I can only imagine what I thought might be an opportunity to make an assignation has turned out to be more than that."

Lennard sat quietly for a moment before speaking. "How did you arrange for Kosorukov to be at The Queen's Head last night?"

"After church on Sunday, a regimental lieutenant—whose name

you need not know—may have suggested he drank there sometimes on Tuesday evenings."

"A real regimental lieutenant, Sir George?"

The Home Secretary's reply was a smile; nothing more. Lennard read into it that the gentlemen, whether an officer or not, had been the man who'd been in charge of assessing the Russian's willingness to "come across", as the intelligencers called it.

"So, that was well played, Sir George. A note delivered to Kosorukov, in a place he should not have been, with a whispered admonition to accompany his father-in-law when he visited Malloray's this morning, and to find an opportunity to speak with me at my place of business. I thought you told me to wait for Twinton to come to my house?"

"The earl and countess were dinner guests at Downing Street on Saturday evening, Lennard. He mentioned he'd made an appointment and was intending to visit Malloray's this morning. Heaven knows when he might have eventually come to your house. It could have been months in the future. I seized the opportunity, that's all."

"Well, it worked to our advantage, sir."

"Then you managed to make an assignation in order to judge the quality of his information?"

"I had no need, Sir George. Of his own volition, he shared the most astounding secret, right then, while walking along the dock."

"That was unexpected. I scarce believe it? You must have been quite shocked."

"I was, sir. Not only because the information he shared, but also because he revealed matters of a personal nature, which were also quite unexpected and exceedingly frank."

"Good gracious! I can only imagine that must be a Russian thing. Your assessment of the man, before you share what he told you?"

"To be frank, Sir George, despite his supremely indifferent nature, I believe the man is dangerous."

"Dangerous? In what manner, Lennard?"

"He's duplicitous. He hides it behind a veneer of hauteur, and uses his title of grand duke as a way of distancing himself from those in ranks below his, even though his station counts for naught in any country but his own. But he's avaricious, the mark of a man who shows the desperation of living in restrained circumstances, no doubt married reluctantly, and with a seemingly voracious sexual appetite, sated by connections with men he considers inferiors of the basest quality. No doubt, those men do not merit the term, and neither you nor I would refer to them as such, but rough, physical types, who probably carry out the frustration of their own meagre circumstances and poverty by abusing his body, and by treating someone of the upper classes roughly."

Sir George coloured, lost for words.

"And you garnered this impression from observing the man for how long, while you walked on the dockside?" Angus asked.

"No, I garnered it from his words, Angus. As I told you both, he shared personal information of the most intimate nature, and without provocation or enticement on my behalf. He showed great delight in telling me that he liked his men base, uncouth, illiterate, and violent, and was happy to be slapped about by them, as long as there was no visible bruising he could not explain."

"Dear God," the Home Secretary said.

Angus said nothing but raised an eyebrow. "The man's a fool to speak so frankly upon first meeting. Perhaps he did it to test the depth of your waters, Lennard. To see whether you might be amenable to a possible connection."

"I promise you I gave no indication of any interest, Angus. Neither did I react, despite my wish at the time to draw back in amazement."

"Very well, Lennard," Sir George said, anxious to change the subject. "You mentioned he offered you a 'most astounding secret', if I remember your precise words."

"Yes, he offered us something of great value to prove his value to the Crown. What he told me was of such magnitude that I could not in due conscience accept it without the promise of enticement to share future, equally as informative intelligence. I've guaranteed him ten guineas, even though the information was freely given."

"Ten guineas? Have you lost your mind, Lennard? Why, I can't—"

"Admiral Oblensky," Lennard said. "He's Kosorukov's cousin by marriage."

"Oblensky? The commander of the second Black Sea fleet?" Sir George sat up in his chair, his interest piqued.

"He writes to his mistress every week."

"So? When I'm away, I write to my wife every day," Sir George said.

"But, sir, you don't send your letters from the thick of the Crimean war to your mistress in Paris, full of information about where you will be for the following weeks, replete with news of how the war is proceeding from the Russian point of view, while describing the cleverness of your future plans."

"Indiscreet indeed."

"His mistress, sir, is what makes the whole affair prodigiously interesting."

"Please, Lennard, proceed."

"She's the niece of the erstwhile Princess Charlotte of Prussia."

"*That* Princess Charlotte? There can't be any other. Dear God! Do you mean his mistress is the niece of the Czarina of Russia?"

"It's a huge secret and her father would lock her up in a convent were he to find out. It would cause an enormous scandal, not only in the Russian court, but all over Europe."

"So, you're thinking that, with encouragement, his mistress might be prepared to share some of Oblensky's indiscrete missives?"

"You've read my mind, Sir George."

"I have to say this is a stroke of fortune. Now, how to go about it is our next problem."

"That's already attended to, sir. It's one of the reasons I arrived here two hours after my meeting with Kosorukov and in such ill-temper. I spent the morning rushing from pillar to post to put measures into place. I've sent Clyford."

"Sent Clyford where?"

"To Paris of course. Malloray's sends packets to France on every outgoing tide. It's an eighteen-hour crossing by sail. However, I've sent my new private secretary on one of our compact steamers. In that way, we didn't have to wait for the tide. He'll arrive in perhaps half that time, all being well. He can travel by train to Paris, visit the Gräfin Mecklenburg-Strelitz, have a pleasant chat with her, then return with copies of one or two of Oblensky's recent letters."

"If these letters prove to be informative, they could be of interest, Lennard. However, I think that by the time it takes for them to travel from the Crimea to Paris, the information in them might be out of date. Peripheral information may be of use, but current military strategies would be long past."

"Perhaps so, sir. Those were my thoughts too. However, if the letters are as detailed and informative as Kosorukov asserts, intentions can be drawn from his writings about events that have already come to pass, and therefore may perhaps prove to our advantage. Besides, his letters often reach both Paris and London within a week."

"Only government missives arrive that quickly, Lennard."

"Or those brought in the hands of returning military men. A gold coin to bring a sealed letter to a 'relative' would twist any poor man's arm to the task. How often do you suppose we return fighting men, injured or otherwise?"

"Why, there's a constant flow back and forth, both military and ..."

"Yes, sir. Via civilian victualling supply ships of nations other than our own. It's no more than ten days by sail and rather less by steamer or paddle-wheeler from the Crimea to Le Havre or La Rochelle."

"But what I don't understand is how a Russian admiral would be able to give his letter to a member of the enemy, in order to have it delivered once he'd returned to France?"

"You forget, sir, the war is not being conducted on the sovereign territory of either the Russians—although they claim it to be—or of the British, or French. As you are well aware, we've had problems with the Turks supplying goods to both sides, even though they're supposed to be fighting alongside us. And, as for other nations in the area, we rely on their local supplies just as much as the Russians do. How easy do you think it would be for a merchant from the Levant to cross easily from one side to the other? I'd propose it was a simple thing and performed regularly with no great trouble."

"You seem particularly well-informed on the matter, Lennard."

"Only because I posed the same questions to our Russian, Sir George, and I am merely repeating his answers to me."

"When will Clyford return?"

"Within a week, Sir George."

"So long?"

"I've entrusted him with a second mission while he's there, and also sent him to visit one or two establishments."

"A second mission?"

"Sir, you are nothing but questions this morning."

"Do forgive me, Lennard. I'm sure I'm a thorn of irritation in the sea of your calm."

Lennard smiled at the Home Secretary's stiffened jibe. "Kosorukov has a brother in Paris. I'll wager you didn't know that."

"Indeed, I did not."

"He asked me whether his brother, wife, and their newly-born child, could be the recipients of any future dealings he might have with Her Majesty's government. I've directed Clyford to find out all he can about them. And, while he's at it, to order some jewellery from Rothschild's for my aunt Caroline for her forthcoming birthday."

"That's surprising. Not the jewellery for your aunt, but that he's prepared to pass on anything he earns from us to his family in Paris."

"It seems they're extremely poor, Sir George. He is godfather to his nephew. You may find this as strange as I did, had I not seen it with my own eyes, but he adores children. I watch him give Geoffroy, Robert's nephew, a gold coin, crouching down at eye-level and smiling brightly as he did so. His interest was genuine."

"If he's to pass over funds to his family in Paris, then what will he gain for himself out of our association, Lennard?"

"Ah, that, sir. I was coming to that. I need your wife, Lady Anna to meet with Evelyn Simperknell."

"My wife will kill me. She hates that woman."

"Very well, then perhaps you could ask your good consort if she will visit my aunt. When she arrives, she'll find that it's been arranged for Lady Quaisey to have been invited as well."

"My wife? Lady Quaisey? Your aunt Caroline, Lennard? How do these ladies connect with Kosorukov?"

"Kosorukov wants me to suggest that he'd be perfect to refurbish the Quaisey's mansion. I can't approach her directly as I'm still in mourning. I would need Lady Anna to make some remark to my aunt that I'd mentioned to you that I'd heard, after my meeting with the Earl of Twinton, that Kosorukov was a man who understands fashion, furniture, and refinement, and who'd greatly enhanced the embellishment of the Twinton mansion in Mayfair."

"Have a care that Lady Quaisey doesn't ferret out a different truth, Lennard."

"There is no different truth, sir. Twinton actually said to me, as I accompanied him to his carriage, that he wishes he was as delighted with his son-in-law as the Countess Twinton was. When I asked him to explain, he told me she'd given him free rein and now their London residence was a site of pilgrimage in the smart set because of Kosorukov's eye for appointments."

"And the reason that my wife needs to be at this meeting, Lennard?"

"You will brief her in advance to agree with my aunt—who will have already been prepared by me—when she suggests to Lady Quaisey that perhaps Kosorukov would be the perfect man to engage."

"Engage? Like a tradesman? Good heavens, he can't ask for a fee, Lennard. That would be more than vulgar."

"No, Sir George, but he can ask her to open an account, from which he'll make his purchases, and most likely fleece her for thousands at the same time by selling items superfluous to his needs to others."

"And you think Lady Quaisey will follow your bait and swim into your net?"

"Do you know her, Sir George? Just ask Angus what he thinks."

The Home Secretary turned to his personal private secretary.

"Evelyn Simperknell would wet her drawers over the prospect of having any connection to the Earl of Twinton, even obliquely, by means of his son-in-law. She cares nothing for wars, enemies, and foes. Her greatest endeavour is to advance her own social standing, whether directly, or by association with other members of the peerage."

"Wet her drawers, Angus? How uncouth."

"And yet you smirk, sir."

"I do so because propriety demands it. To laugh would be unseemly. Why, look at Lennard. He's as stony-faced as the marble bust behind my desk."

"That's only because the visual image of Lady Quaisey peeing herself with glee is irrevocably burned into my mind," Lennard replied.

A knock at the door, in two repetitions of three, caused Sir George to call for his assistant to enter. The man handed the Home Secretary a large document, which he took to his desk and signed, whispering to him for a few moments after he'd done so.

"Will you have some lunch with me, Lennard?" Sir George asked. "Or are you in a hurry to get away?"

"Lunch, Sir George? I have much more to tell you sir, and I'd rather do it here before venturing out to your club."

"We'll eat here, in my private dining room."

"Your private dining room, sir? I've worked in this department for seventeen years and this is the first time I've heard of a private dining room. I thought you went out every day."

"There's a suite of rooms, accessed by a panelled door behind my desk. It's hard to see, I grant you, but behind it there's a small water closet, newly installed, a bathroom, a dining room and a small room with a cot. Shall we eat? It may be early, but I'm rather hungry."

"Lead on, sir," Angus said. "Lennard can wait here if he'd rather, but I'm happy to lunch with you."

Sir George spoke quickly to his man, who bowed, then opened the door to the private dining room before exiting through it.

"I've just sent word there'll be three for lunch. Heaven knows how, but there's always ample sufficiency for unexpected guests. It shan't be long, and perhaps we can have something to wet our whistles before we eat, then talk business in a civilised manner with something under our belts."

"May I observe, Sir George, that you are a veritable cornucopia of aphorisms this morning."

"I'll give you aphorisms, you cheeky pup," the Home Secretary said with the most enormous grin of satisfaction. He loved to be called out on his abundant use of them. "And, as quick as boiled asparagus, too, my lad."

*****

Lamb chops with bread sauce, tiny potatoes with fresh peas—and in March too. A delicious cabinet pudding, with thick cream to follow, all made Lennard wonder how Sir George remained so slim. Were he to eat so fulsomely every day, Lennard thought he'd no longer fit into his clothes after a week. He ate well at breakfast and in the evening, but barely ate during the day. Bread and cheese, with some relish or quince paste and a mug of ale, was his habitual fare for luncheon.

"I'd have horsewhipped Astley, were I in your place, Lennard," Sir George said, throwing his linen table napkin angrily onto the table. "However, you've played him well. Sometimes an untruth, launched as a threat, is as good a threat as a cocked pistol. Damn his hide!"

"I hope that what happened has not affected your son, Sir George. I wouldn't put it past Astley to ruin his chances, merely as an opportunity to put it about that it was my fault in some way."

"Well, Lennard, you might be rather astounded to know that yesterday an invitation arrived for both Lady Grey and me, together with our son, George Henry, to accompany Astley and his ward, Neasa, for a carriage perambulation around Hyde Park this coming Sunday after church."

"Really?"

"Now that you've explained what happened, I can only imagine your threat was seen as a distinct possibility, and perhaps he's finally realised that there can be no reason for his own status not to be elevated, were his niece to be married into our family."

"Neasa is his niece?" Lennard asked. "I knew she was his ward."

"I think he hoped to profit from the association. You know he asked me for ten thousand to allow my son to marry her?"

"He asked you? I'm confused. Surely, it's the young woman who brings the dowry, not the man."

"The softening in his attitude to my boy leaves me in a predicament, Lennard."

"How so, Sir George?"

"As I told you at the Oriental Club, the intelligencer whom I had hidden in Astley's household reported to me, some time before he died, that he believed Sir Terrence was bringing in arms from La Corunna with the help of his fellow countryman, the prime minister of Spain."

"But you had no evidence."

"Not at the time. But yesterday, Lord Palmerston gave me a name."

"Our Prime Minister gave you a name, sir?"

"Yes, Lennard. A name not of a person, but of a vessel: *Pendragon*. Do you know it?"

"The *Pendragon*? Yes sir. I believe that's the ship we hire from Astley's company to import goods from the Spanish colonies. Malloray's does not have trading rights with the Spanish Caribbean nations, so we purchase goods in—"

"La Corunna, which are then unloaded in Falmouth. Yes, the *Pendragon* runs the route from northern Spain to Cornwall, thence to Ireland."

"You think that whenever the vessel is hired to bring cargo to England, Astley is also smuggling armaments?"

"Your family company need no customs inspection at Falmouth, Lennard. Malloray's has had an exemption for decades because it's in that port your company unloads goods from Spain that we find hard to procure ourselves without exorbitant tariffs. I think you'll find the *Pendragon* sails on to Wexford after Falmouth, carrying Astley's declared 'cigars, sugar, and tobacco', on which he pays duty in advance, but which are placenames for other, illicit goods."

"But, as you said, you have no proof, and yet the Prime Minister has passed on the name of the vessel."

"He did not explain, nor did I ask, Lennard. It was done in the House during a meal break. A slip of paper inside a document passed over the table for me to read. When I raised an eyebrow, he glanced across the dining room at Astley, who was dining with the Secretary of State for the Colonies. 'Get Betteridge on to it,' he whispered."

Lennard leaned back in his chair for a moment, staring at the wall behind the Home Secretary while he digested the information. "I shall get on to it, as the Prime Minister advised you, Sir George. Consider it done."

"Now, I'm sure you are aware you have an epithet here in the office, Lennard?"

"I believe I'm called 'the Terrier' behind my back, sir."

"Indeed, you are the finest of our rat catchers. It's one of your greatest qualities, did you know that? Your ability to ferret out rodents of all sorts as they try to hide, concealed in the depths of their burrows, dragging them out into the light of discovery."

"It's not a metaphor that I'd use myself, but I understand perseverance is one of the things that drives me. In that you are correct."

"And, since you arrived this morning, I haven't failed to notice that my Terrier smells a rat … or two."

Lennard laughed. "Am I that transparent?"

"Indeed not," Angus said. "Certainly not in my case, for I've no idea what Sir George means."

"Tell him what I suspect is gnawing away, Lennard. I hope my suspicions are correct," Sir George said.

"Indeed, you are indeed correct in your assumptions that I've been puzzling over a connection. A connection that will not form in my mind, yet one of which I am certain exists, even though it's evasive at the moment."

"And it is …?" Angus asked.

"What is the link that connects a Russian nobleman, an Irish baronet, and a Turkish pretender, Angus?"

"What? You think they're connected?" Angus was astonished, turning to Sir George to judge his reaction to the statement, only to be greeted by a softly-raised eyebrow and a faint smile.

"These were my thoughts, too, Angus. And, like Lennard, I've been struggling to make a connection of my own. However, I know Lennard well. I fear he has some thoughts on the matter he'd like to share."

"Perhaps by voicing my postulations, Sir George, it may clarify some of my suspicions?" Lennard said. "What could possibly connect Astley to The Cargo? Here's my idea, and it's a tenuous link, but if you remember the day that Sir George brought Gerald and Robert into our *cloison*, it was he who led Robert to the conclusion that the fellow countrymen of his father were most likely involved in the plot to replace our good Queen with a Turkish pretender. As for Kosorukov? Well, that connection is even more fragile. We know the bodyguard, Kadir, is a Turkish-born Russian. There's been a large Russian community in Constantinople for centuries. If there's to be some connection between him and the bodyguard, it's probably through them. As I said, the supposed link is gossamer-thin. However, it's my immediate thought."

"And the link between Kosorukov and Astley?"

"I can think of none for the moment, Sir George. However, that does not mean there could not possibly be one. But there's another thing that might link Astley to The Cargo and it's just come to mind."

"What is it?"

"If The Cargo were to arrive on our shores via Ireland, who best to provide transport, from, say, Morocco?"

"Ah, that's something that did not cross my mind, Lennard," Sir George said.

"Astley has trading rights in Rabat," Lennard explained. "It's the only port in which his company and ours shares facilities, other than Falmouth."

"It's a gruesome thought, Lennard, that Astley could be involved so deeply in such a dastardly scheme."

"Indeed, it is, Home Secretary. We'd best get someone following both Astley and Kosorukov, in case we've missed something they have in common. Perhaps it could also prove valuable to discover whether they've spent time anywhere together over the past few years—at least since the war in the Crimea broke out. Are there any places in which both of them might meet that we don't know of? I can guarantee that Astley wouldn't be seen dead at The Queen's Head, The Lion's Heart, the Methodist Seamen's Mission, or Broad Street Terminus, the four places Kosorukov is known to procure his bedfellows."

Sir George rang his handbell and, within a minute or two, his assistant arrived.

"The taupe sharkskin folder in the top drawer of my desk. Would you fetch it please?"

After his assistant had returned with the folder, Sir George waited until he'd left the room before speaking. "We've been keeping our eyes on Kosorukov for some time before his dossier came your way. Apart from those four establishments, there are some places he goes where our usual shadows were unable, or at least unwilling, to follow him. Perhaps one of these establishments might be somewhere they could arrange a clandestine meeting."

Sir George passed the folder across the table to Lennard. In it, was one page with the names of three establishments.

"Any of those familiar, Lennard?" Sir George asked.

Lennard smiled. "None of them is unfamiliar, sir."

"And you know what goes on inside each of them."

"Oh, yes, sir. Indeed, I do."

"You shouldn't look so pleased, Lennard," Angus said. "Unless a penny has dropped, and you've realised something we should know."

"I tell you what, Angus. How about Elam and I take you to them, one at a time. You'd find each of the three … interesting, to say the least. The sort of interesting that you swear no longer interests you."

"Really, Lennard? How can you think such a thing? I'm a married man."

Even Sir George rolled his eyes.

"Again, Terrence Astley would not go to any of these three establishments, even if his life depended on it. However, it's interesting that Kosorukov does … Home Secretary?"

"Yes, Lennard, what is it?"

"If you've had someone following Kosorukov for some time, enough time to know he visits these places, then there is obviously more to the man than you've disclosed to me. Did you know about this, Angus?"

"No, I didn't," Angus said with some surprise.

"Then, if your personal private secretary was unaware, then you're certain he's up to something duplicitous. Am I correct?"

"You are, of course, correct, Lennard. For some time, we've had reason to believe that someone in London has been passing information to the Russians. We don't know how, but there have been far too many coincidences for us to believe anything but. Spies will always exist. We have our own in St. Petersburg, so obviously they have their own here."

"And you suspect, Kosorukov of …"

"Suspicion is too strong a word, my boy … it was a thought, that's it."

"In the years I've known you, Sir George, you rarely have 'just a thought'."

"Well, from the look in your eye, Lennard, I see that you've already come up with a few ideas yourself. Would you care to share?"

Lennard stood from the table, wiped his hands on his linen table napkin, then leaned on the back of the chair in which he'd been sitting.

"While you and Angus were signing your papers, Sir George, I happened to catch glimpses of the masts and sails of the river barges as they sailed up and down the Thames. It made me think of their shallow keels."

"Shallow keels, Lennard?"

"Deeper keels, where the river runs shallower than in the port, would make traversing this part of the river challenging, because of the strong undercurrents associated with the outgoing tide."

"You're beginning to sound like Sir Angus, Lennard. All riddles, convoluted language, and illusions."

"Undercurrents, Sir George. Things that flow below the surface, seemingly hidden because of a more prominent assumption. The moment you mentioned you suspected someone in London could be passing information to the Russians, it came to me that Kosorukov was well placed to learn certain things that could be of value to his former countrymen. Perhaps, if he was, he could be augmenting his brother's income in the same way that he intends to when we pay him for secretes. Payment to Paris, and his hands apparently unsullied here in London."

"What sorts of things, Lennard?"

"Who are the types of men he consorts with, sir? Soldiers and navvies in the taverns, seamen and labourers at the mission, and at the railway assembly yard. Each one perhaps with a sentence of no importance to their own minds, but perhaps of value to the enemy. Let me outline my thoughts as points in a list."

Lennard proceeded to point out each of the four meeting places they knew Kosorukov met his partners, and the reasons why he thought each could be, in certain circumstances, a mine of information for anyone trying to gather intelligence:

- The Queen's Head—a meeting place full of grenadiers, cavalry officers, soldiers in the marine forces, many of whom, with a belly full of grog and unguarded in the company of an attentive handsome gentleman with a large purse, might let slip when and where they would next be deployed, or even when their friends might be disembarking.
- The Lion's Heart—Irish navvies and men who worked on the docks. Information for a coin about the lading of any vessel, and where she might be headed.
- The Methodist Seamen's Mission—sailors waiting for embarkation, rife with gossip from fellow seamen about trade through the Mediterranean, warships, and their sailing schedules.
- Finally, the Broad Street Terminus—packed with poor men, anxious to feed their families, men who oft-times were employed for a few days at a time on the railway lines from the north. Those very railway lines brought in regiments of men to be shipped off overseas. If they worked often enough, they always knew what was coming in and when. The movement of troops and materiel, even in a home country, far from the battleground, could prove useful to enemies.

"Kosorukov is in a position to gather information that would be otherwise impossible to garner among his usual social circles. Poor men might have no conscience when it comes to the choice between a half-crown for the treatment of a sick child, or a month's rent, or food on the table for a family of ten. Although it irks me, I can understand what a man in such reduced circumstances might disclose, especially after an intimate act, and with a shilling over the agreed price in exchange for information. We call it 'two pillow talk', Sir George."

"The sharing of post-coital confidences. I assume that's what you mean," the Home Secretary said.

"Although I think many of Kosorukov's connections are carried out in less comfortable places than a bed, Sir George," Angus added.

"Still," Lennard said, "if he is passing information to his fellow countrymen, how does he do so?"

"Ah, Lennard, you disarm me with your question."

"Have I fallen into another of your traps, Sir George? Have you planned this entire meeting in advance to bring me to some inescapable conclusion?"

"Planned? How could I plan such a thing, Lennard? You arrived without appointment. I merely led to you discover conclusions of your own. All I did was show you the way."

"You want me to focus on Kosorukov?"

"I merely wish you to arrange it that he's one of your priorities, Lennard. The Cargo is still our major interest. However, should there be some connection between the two that would be a bonus, don't you agree?"

Lennard turned with amazement to Angus, who merely shrugged and let out three short barks. "Sic him, Lenn. There's a good boy!" he said, then ducked when Lennard threw his table napkin at him.

9. TARTS, TRYSTS, TREASON, AND TURKS

The first establishment on Sir George's list of places Kosorukov visited, but whose intelligencers had been loath to enter, was a poxy dosshouse, with doorless rooms on the upper floors, each containing a paillasse or two, little lighting, and unfettered public connections of all sorts. No one had wished to speak with them, covering their faces and scuttling away into the darkness, even with the offer of two crowns and the promise of confidentiality.

It seemed merely a shell of a building that provided spaces for all comers; casual releases for men who could wander in off the streets and indulge in the basest of lewd behaviour. Lennard and Elam couldn't get out of it quickly enough. They'd seen it from the outside and had known its reputation, but until yesterday, had never set foot inside. Elam suggested they might send one of their pieceworkers—a lad who worked in Spitalfields as a warehouse labourer—to see if he could discover anything.

The second location, Hedger's Molly House, owned by Mary Wilson, was situated in Cowcross Street, Farrington, and was a different proposition altogether. It was a well-kept, handsome, three-storied house at the end of a quiet street, with a tidy, narrow front garden. Although Lennard and Elam had known Mary for years, her establishment was unlike other molly houses, mainly due to its refinement of appointment, tasteful decoration, and elegantly and expensively dressed gentlemen companions. Its discreet and cultured atmosphere was one of the first things he'd noticed on his earliest visit, years back, while investigating a former government minister—a man who had been suspected by the Home Secretary of the time, of selling cabinet secrets to the shadow treasurer, his counterpart on the other side of the house.

It was far enough from fashionable areas of the city, but close enough for clandestine visits both during the day and of an evening by gentlemen of the law, the cloth, and of commerce. "A hop, step, and a jump from Chancery Lane, St. Paul's, and the Bank of England. The perfect refuge for wigs, vestments, and money changers," Mrs Wilson would say with enormous charm to newcomers who'd been introduced by gentlemen who were regular clients.

Hedger's was renowned for its discreet hire of rooms by the hour, and also for its merchandise: the type of men so liked by those for whom Kosorukov had a penchant—muscled, masculine, and handsomely endowed. Its owner was renowned for her willingness to bend the rules of discretion for Lennard, who'd known her when he was a lad of twenty, shortly after he'd started working as an embryonic intelligencer, and when Mary Wilson was then a Martin, not a Mary.

With the patronage of wealthy gentlemen and an eye for business, Martin—at the age of thirty and no longer the object of desire of his former admirers—decided to set up his own house, designed to cater specifically for men of substance who wanted a bit of "rough" but without the hazard of frequenting places where it was usually available.

There was only one problem. Molly houses had never been run by men. For some reason, gentlemen were cautious, preferring an establishment run by a member of the fairer sex. Almost overnight, Martin became Mary, after which his house thrived.

"I must say, nobility suits you well, Lennard," Martin said. "And you too, Elam. So finely fitted out and, if I'm not mistaken, bearing the hallmark of the excellent craftsmanship of Poole's. Am I correct?"

"Indeed, you are," Lennard replied. "My grandfather's tailor was one of our first visitors, even before Sir Hugh was laid to rest. Angus—you remember him, I'm sure—pointed out that clothing maketh the man, and we've had new wardrobes designed, cut and delivered by an army of tailors and seamstresses."

"Beautiful."

"Do you …?"

"Yes, I have not only my own gentleman's attire made there too, but also that of the gentlemen's companions who work for me. Normally, during the day, I go about my business as a man. In the evenings, however, it's tresses not trousers. It seems to put the visitors' minds at ease to see a charming woman greet them when they arrive."

Lennard smiled. Although slender, Martin had neither been petite in stature nor feminine in manner. In fact, he'd been a strong market boy at Covent Garden, later an adolescent at Billingsgate, lugging around enormous weights either in his arms or towering baskets balanced on his head. No one had been more surprised than Lennard when Martin had revealed his dreams for his future life as the owner of a molly house. "If that's the case, may I ask why you've come to meet us in a beautiful gown and wearing a bonnet of the latest fashion?"

"Because, at two o'clock this afternoon, after we've lunched, I'm to meet with a certain peer of the realm, who's enquired whether he might take the entire house for an evening."

"The whole establishment?"

"For him and six of his gentlemen friends who will disrobe when they arrive and spend the entire evening completely naked, wearing nothing but harlequin eye-masks to disguise their identities."

"I'll offer you five guineas for their names," Lennard said, with a wink.

"If there were to be some advantage to you to know their names, it would be given freely," Martin said, playfully tapping Lennard's hand with his fan. "Otherwise, if you really want to know who they are, perhaps I could entice you to offer yourself to the room as an amuse-bouche before the evening starts?"

"You are such a tart," Lennard said, delighted to hear Martin's saucy rejoinder.

"It goes with the nature of my business," Martin replied, then glanced across the dining room of Trapper's, the elegant eating house to which Lennard had invited him, and smiled at the owner, who'd been hovering.

"You know Stanley?" Lennard asked, catching the glance.

"Know him? I've *had* him, Lennard. And more than once."

"I'm confused. Had him … how?"

"Oh, Lennard, you're such an innocent for such a man of the world."

"Perhaps you'd explain, Martin? Although, I believe you secretly think I'm a degenerate, skilled in every carnal vice that exists, I can assure you, my tastes are … simple."

Elam rolled his eyes so theatrically that even Lennard smiled.

"Stanley?" he asked again, indicating the proprietor, who was making his way across the room to them, accompanied by a smart, well-dressed waiter.

"Really, Lennard? Well, let me tell you there's many a pillar of society, or a businessman with a wife and children—such as the owner of this establishment—who likes nothing better than to be tupped by a man wearing a corset and half-crinoline, and blessed with a member twice the length and girth of his own."

Lennard, eyes wide, stifled his laughter. Elam, however, chortled into his handkerchief, his eyes wet with suppressed mirth.

*****

"So, Martin recognised him from the daguerreotype?" Christopher asked, having returned after conducting Mary Wilson to her meeting. Lennard had offered his coach as a courtesy.

"Yes, regular as clockwork twice a month, on the first and on the fifteenth, two hours in the same room with another man who arrives at about the same time. Frequently, after the companion has left, Kosorukov sends for 'Ladley', one of her stable, and he'll spend another hour with him too."

"Have you arranged to speak with this Ladley lad?"

"Not yet, but Elam and I know who he is—and he's not a lad either, but a strapping man of some twenty-seven years. He's one of the longshoremen who work at St. Katharine Docks during the day. You must remember him, surely, Christopher. His real name is Arthur, same as my uncle."

"Arthur Pencott? The man who used to work for Malloray's, and who had a falling out with Robert and went to work as a navvy? He's a molly boy?"

"He's like a lot of working men who ply the same trade, Christopher," Lennard explained. "Navvies and the such by day, and gentlemen's companions at night. Molly houses aren't all youngsters in corsets with powdered faces and arses like peaches these days. There are plenty of gentlemen who like the companionship of muscular men from the lower classes with hair on their chests."

"Did you at least find out the name of the man he meets here every two weeks?" Christopher asked.

"No, but we intend to. Martin told us Arthur finishes work at about six at this time of year, when it begins to get too dark to work without it becoming dangerous. He's not normally due to arrive at Mrs Hedger's until nine, so we'll intercept him on his way home before he heads off to Farrington."

*****

A plate of steak and kidney pudding and two jars of ale finally allowed Arthur Pencott to relax.

Lennard had been observing him while they ate, his initial reluctance to talk eventually faded when Lennard explained that his sudden interception in Cartwright Lane had not been for any other reason than the offer of food for some information, and perhaps a guinea for his time.

"I've already explained to you, sir, that the reason for my leaving Malloray's was nothing to do with your friend, Mr Fahey, but because Mr Rudd would not stand for me constantly pressing him to be included on the roster of those who worked at night-time. He told me that it was dangerous, not only to myself, but to those around me, if I was to work from six in the morning until midnight."

"Well, he had good reason, Arthur," Lennard said, the use of the man's name feeling at once strange in his mouth and yet somewhat comforting. He could not help but equate the name with his uncle, especially since the stevedore was equally as tall, strong of features, and as broad across the chest. Alarmingly, his infrequent smile, showing a sliver of his upper teeth and no more, was the same smile as his dear uncle's. "Extreme fatigue is one of the reasons that accidents happen. You look as strong as an ox. Why on earth would you want to flog yourself into a state of exhaustion? You surely understand more than any other man what incredibly hard work on the docks requires."

"I wanted more for myself, Mr Malloray, and an extra shilling a week would have made all the difference. Is it a bad thing for a man to wish to rise above an impoverished position, to want something better in life?"

"No, of course not, Arthur. Do you have a family? Is that the reason?"

"No, sir. It's for the want of knowledge. Your grandfather, God rest his soul, would do his rounds every morning, bringing a few treats for us young ones. While he was at it, he'd teach us boys a few letters a day—to understand what appeared to us to be scrawlings and scribbles on the sides of crates, so we could know what we were unloading and have a care to the contents. Most of the lads got to recognise the shapes, but I learned my letters, sir, and I taught myself to read. It opened my eyes to the world, and I understood that, for the likes of me, education and reading could lead to a life that did not chain me to breaking my back for the rest of my life."

"Sir, you have much moved me," Lennard said, quickly wiping his eyes with his shirtsleeve. "You have reminded me of the loss of a man who was generous to all, no matter what station in life. I've never heard that story before, but it's so like a thing he would have done, I can't but thank you for sharing such a tender tale."

Lennard caught Elam's quick glance from the corner of his eye.

"Your grandfather was much loved by everyone, as I am sure you will be yourself one day. Among those of us who worked at Malloray's, you and Mr Fahey were always considered gentlemen of kindness and generosity of spirit."

"Mr Fahey is to take over the business, Arthur. Perhaps we could tempt you to return to our employ?"

"I earn well where I am, sir."

"How well do you read, Arthur?" Lennard asked.

"I can read the news sheets people throw away in the streets, and the few books I bought for a ha'penny each from a barrow in Cheapside. Walter Scott has a fine way with words."

"Indeed, he does, my friend. A fine way with words ..."

"And the words you've been waiting to ask me all evening, sir? I may be a working man, but I know when someone else wants something from me."

Lennard chuckled. "Before I get to that, I fear I must own a minor deceit."

Pencott raised an eyebrow and sat back, leaning against the wall. He took out his pipe and began to clean it with a spill he'd retrieved from his pocket. "I'm listening, sir."

"Both Elam and I have known Mrs Hedger very well for some fifteen years."

"Ah ..."

"But it's not for reasons of her business that I wanted to meet you."

"You mentioned you wanted to know something. Something that was worth a decent meal and a gold guinea."

"It would not compromise you, Arthur."

"And yet, at first, I had the feeling that it would, sir, if I may be so bold to say."

"You say at first? And now?"

"Mr Malloray, had I not worked in Mrs Hedger's house for the past five years, I might have thought something questionable was afoot. However, I cannot bring myself to believe you'd bring your lover to a meeting where there was to be some unpleasantness."

"Is it that obvious, Mr Pencott?" Elam asked, much amused.

"No, it's the lack of obvious that gave it away, Mr Walters. The closeness you sit to each other and the deference each of you give to the other's speech. However, the most obvious is the way that you cannot keep your eyes from Mr Malloray's lips when he speaks."

"That's because I'm stone deaf, sir."

Arthur Pencott sat upright, startled. "I'm so dreadfully sorry—"

Elam laughed and patted the back of the man's forearm. "There's no need. I frequently watch his lips for reasons other than his speech."

Further conversation was halted by the arrival of the innkeeper's boy, who removed their plates and enquired whether they would like another mug of ale each.

"I think I've had enough," Arthur said. "I need to go home and get cleaned up."

"As you wish, Mr Pencott," Lennard said. "However, tarry a while longer. Another for each of us, lad."

"Mr Malloray, Mrs Hedger will tan my hide if I'm late."

"Not this evening, Arthur. Your evening is mine. Mrs Hedger will hand over your earnings tomorrow evening when you go to work. I paid for your time in advance. Elam and I are your gentlemen companions for the entire evening."

Pencott looked between Lennard and Elam.

"Do you mean …?"

Lennard chuckled, shaking his head. "No, sir. As tempting as the idea might be, I'd like to ask you one or two questions. Then, depending on your answer, perhaps make you an offer that might assist in your endeavour to better your lot in life."

*****

"He's German, or something foreign. I've never asked."

"He doesn't speak when he's with you?"

Arthur Pencott smiled. "He's often unable to."

Lennard, much amused, raised his eyebrows but said nothing.

"And it's always after his companion has left?" Elam asked.

"Yes, they meet regularly on the first and the fifteenth of the month. I'd say once a month, perhaps less frequently, I'm engaged for an hour after the companion has left."

"I know this will sound peculiar, but are you sure they meet to …"

"Meet to what, Mr Malloray? It's a bawdy house, sir. Of course they … have … I'm not quite sure what the polite term is, sir, forgive me."

"Mr Pencott, you may say the words," Elam said. "Both Mr Malloray and I have heard such turns of phrase. We were never so pure of speech from the day we met until the present time, when we both can curse like stevedores and navvies."

"I suppose then, Mr Walters, what you would like to know is whether they fuck."

Lennard smiled. "I'm curious. Two hours seems a long time a-fucking," he remarked.

Arthur Pencott laughed. "Not for some, sir," he said with a wink. "I think they thrash about on the bed for the first hour then talk for the second."

"About?"

"No idea. They're always yakking in something foreign if I'm ever asked to join."

"Wait. They ask you to join them?"

"Occasionally. The gentleman in the daguerreotype likes to play 'piggie-in-the-middle'. Karl and I change positions once or twice, but that's not a regular—"

"Karl? You know the man's name?"

"Yes, of course I do. He's my only gentleman friend away from Mrs Hedger's."

"And he's …"

"Blond, handsome, very attentive and cares for my wishes more than his own. That's why I continue to see him."

"How often do you see him?" Lennard asked, curious, yet unwilling to admit his suspicions.

"Twice a month, after he gets paid. No fixed days but usually every fortnight or so … you won't tell Mrs Hedger, will you? I'm not supposed to—"

"This Karl, you don't know anything more about him, do you?"

"I think I've said enough, to be honest, Mr Malloray."

"We'll find out, you know—with or without your help. So, if there's anything you'd like to tell us, to make our investigation easier …?"

"Investigation?"

"Arthur, do you remember that I said I'd like to help you advance your wishes for a better life? How much do you earn at the moment at St. Katharine's Dock?"

"Over the year, around thirty pounds sir."

"That's a pittance, if I may say so."

"To you, it may be, Mr Malloray. But those of us who work with our hands, and who are lucky enough to find regular work, consider ourselves blessed. There are many who go without food on a daily basis."

"My offer, Arthur is a choice of two. I promise you they will both allow you to keep working at Mrs Hedger's, but with an income of at least sixty a year, perhaps more, no matter which you chose."

"I'm listening, sir, but I hope you're not going to offer me a position similar to my evening occupation. There's only so much—"

"Steam in the boiler?" Lennard said, with a chuckle. "Yes, I understand, and no. Even my companion here, with his limitless libido, has his limits."

Both Elam and Arthur smiled, both realising it was a jest; one which was meant to break the formality of their conversation and elicit a more relaxed, friendlier engagement.

"Neither position would require anything like that," Lennard continued. "Let me ask one thing. If you can read Walter Scott, you can read the manifest of goods to be loaded and unloaded from a vessel, and the instructions on where to store them, am I correct?"

"Yes, sir, easily."

"Then these are the positions I can offer you: the first will be a loading supervisor at Malloray's. The second is working as an assistant to Mr Fahey, who desperately needs someone who knows the docks and who can convey orders, and help supervise the rostering of reliable staff. I'm sure you also know every man who comes looking for extra work when we need it."

"Mr Malloray—"

"The name of your friend. If he's done nothing wrong, I promise you no harm will come to him. We merely wish to ask him some questions, as we have done with you."

"His name is Karl Paulsson. He's a guard at the former Swedish ambassador's residence. He's a nice man, Mr Malloray. Please, you promised, no harm … you said so."

"Yes, I did, and I'm a man of my word, Arthur. I'll state it once more to reassure you that it was no mistake: no harm will come to him, if he's done nothing wrong. Now, this Karl Paulsson of yours, tell me, what's he like?"

"What's he like? Like as in what does he like to do, or like as in his physical appearance?"

"His physical appearance."

"Why would you want to know that, Mr Malloray?"

"If I may be so bold to say, Arthur, you're a very handsome man, strongly built, with an open and friendly countenance. A man most likely well sought after at Mrs Hedger's, and it intrigues me to know why you'd want to meet up with only one private client, when you've stated you need money? There must be something special about him."

Elam was used to this game: Lennard reeling in the catch. He sat back and watched as Arthur revealed that his Swedish lover was just that—a lover. Someone who offered him affection along with sex. A tall, blond man, with bright clear blue eyes, a penchant for drinking too much. Strong, broad in the chest, but with little belief in his own good looks.

"He sounds god-like, the way you describe him," Lennard said, feeling a little uncomfortable because that's exactly how he felt about Elam sometimes—that his companion deserved someone far more attractive than Lennard believed himself to be.

"He's very handsome, Mr Malloray, but aloof with it. He can't get past his birthmark."

"On his face?"

"No sir, below the ear on the right-hand side. It flows down over his shoulder, and all he can see when he looks in the glass is that fault."

"I think it's time you confess that you don't meet up with him for the money, am I correct?"

"Yes, you are correct, and I tell him to keep his coin, but he gives it just the same. I've worked for Mrs Hedger for five years and in that time, I've realised some men can only make peace with their inner demons when they feel they have to pay for something that, with the right person, could be given freely."

*****

The following morning, not long before noon, Christopher dropped Lennard and Elam off in King William Street, near the northern approach to the New London Bridge. "What time shall I come back, Lenn?" he asked.

"Two o'clock should see us done. Park the carriage in Newcomen Street at around half past one, in case we get away sooner."

Christopher tipped his hat and Lennard and Elam watched him drive off.

"Ready for this, Elam?" Lennard asked.

"As ready as ever, and thankful this is the third and last den of thieves on Sir George's list."

"I've been here twice, for Home Office reasons. You were invited, if you remember."

"I do remember. And both times I told you that, despite your lurid descriptions of comely naked men by the dozen, I'd rather eat burned toast than boil my nuggets off in a hot room, choking on steam."

"The men of the middle east love their hammams, Elam."

"Maybe so, but how you expect me to read men's mouths when I'm not able to see my hand in front of my face, I'll never know."

"It's not as bad as all that, you'll see."

*****

The Sultan of Khartoum was one of the most popular gathering places for the Turkish community in London. Built at the back of a maze of alleyways, mostly without names, it had an unprepossessing entrance, with no indication of what lay on the other side of its bland, red-brick façade.

However, behind the entrance doorway was a suite of first-class, velvet-draped private rooms, serviced by smartly liveried attendants, separated by a central corridor from another section of spartan wooden cubicles for those who could only afford second-class booths in which to undress.

Out in the public areas of the twisting complex, classes were forgotten. Men—either naked or loosely draped in white sheets—lost the identity of the class their habitual clothing might have signalled and became just men. Different shapes and sizes, but outwardly with no indication of their status or situation.

The two occasions that Lennard had visited had been after receiving information that suggested there may have been something linking Kadir—the bodyguard of the Turkish pretender—and a Turkish importer of brassware and carpets who owned an emporium in Wapping. It had been rumoured they were cousins, albeit distant. However, after a few months of having the man followed, culminating in Lennard's two visits to the steam closets of the Sultan of Khartoum, where the oriental purveyor seemed to do nothing but play chess with fellow Turks, the Home Secretary had become convinced the informer's implied connection had been nothing but a fabrication.

Lennard and Elam were shown into a white-tiled private room to one side of the main bathing area of the complex. There was a chaise longue in one corner, but they eschewed it in favour of the long, low, tiled bench that ran across the back wall of the room. It was pleasingly cool to their bare buttocks through the thin linen sheets they'd wound around their waists. After about ten minutes of peering through the beaded curtain of the doorway, Elam decided to fasten it back against the wall. As he returned to Lennard's side, he discarded his linen wrap and threw it onto the chaise.

"You're naked," Lennard said.

"As are more than half the rest of the men in this establishment, Lenn. It's unlike you to keep your clothes on when there's so much nudity about you."

Lennard laughed, pinching Elam's knee in good humour. "I shan't rise to your provocation, Elam Walters," he said cheekily.

"I assume you already have, and that's why you're still covered."

Lennard lifted his sheet, briefly exposing his lower body.

"Ah, as I thought, Lennard Malloray. You are so predictable."

"Seeing you standing naked in a public place aroused me far more than I thought it might have."

"Even after all these years?"

"The day I stop finding you irresistible will be the day I go to meet my maker, Elam."

"You shouldn't jest about such things, Lennard, as appreciative as I am of the sentiment."

"Father always said something similar to mother, right back as far as I can remember. He had no qualms about asking her for a kiss, no matter what she was doing, and she'd invariably say, 'Really, Faris? I hardly look at my best', before winking at us children and turning into his arms."

"Is that where you learned your flirtatious ways to make me acquiescent to your desires."

"I think you have the shoe on the wrong foot, my friend. My recollection of our life together has been you drawing me away from whatever I've been about for a stolen kiss in some dark corner."

"If that's a complaint, I shall cease from this day forth."

Lennard laughed, then quickly ran his hand behind Elam's neck, squeezing it affectionately.

"It's quite pleasant here," Elam said. "Much more salubrious than you described it."

"That's because the man I was shadowing always arrived late in the evening when the place was crawling with all sorts, some of them fornicating out in the open, with no regard to propriety. Rather like that dosshouse in Cheapside we went to on Thursday last, but cleaner, with tiles on the floor, and better lighting."

"You didn't explain why this particular time of day is important."

"Do you see that dusky skinned gentleman, perhaps the same age as us? Sitting on the bench opposite, on the other side of the bathing pool."

"I haven't been able to stop looking. He's been there for the past fifteen minutes, hugging one knee allowing his sheet to gape open, pretending that he's not interested in us."

"Are you sure?"

"Just half-close your eyes and lean your head against the wall. Throw off your sheet and watch his reaction through slitted eyes."

Lennard did so. The dusky man's gaze moved down from Lennard's chest. He suppressed a chuckle and turned to Elam. "He's quite shameless, indeed. I swear he licked his lips."

"I shouldn't get too worried, Lenn. It's not just us. We're merely easily observable from where he's sitting. Just watch him for a minute. He can't stop staring at the assets of every man that passes."

"Don't you think he's strikingly good looking?"

"Well, of course, Lennard, but—"

"He's a man we believe Kosorukov meets when he comes here. I enquired when we arrived, and the attendant pointed him out while you were changing. Don't worry, his palm was well-greased to ensure his silence. The man's name is Hakan Zeybeck, and he's the captain's steward aboard the *Koniah*, which arrived this morning on the first tide. She's here for three days. Hakan makes a beeline to this establishment and spends his two days of shore leave in this hammam, never leaving its walls until it's time to set sail back to Constantinople. Coincidentally, those are the same dates Sir George's shadowers noted that Kosorukov invariably comes here."

"Ah, and as our grand duke can only evade his vigilant father-in-law in the evening, you thought we'd come here during the day, as an expedition of sorts."

"Yes, to see whom he meets, what he does."

"He seems very interested in us, Lenn. If you glance discretely right now, you'll see he's allowed his sheet to fall open and his hand has wandered. I caught his eye by chance, and he smiled. Is that what you want? Do you want to lure him in here and sweet talk him … or perhaps more?"

"I'm not sure, Elam. It's not that he's unattractive, but in a public place like this? I think if anything were to happen, it should take place somewhere private. And, to be honest, before anything untoward was to take place, I'd like to know a lot more about Hakan Zeybeck. He could be anyone."

"I love you for your reliability, Lenn," Elam said with a chuckle. "I knew that would be your answer. I merely wanted to see how you'd react if I were to suggest a casual encounter with a handsome stranger. It's never been something you've been interested in. You're far too cautious about your encounters."

"Unlike you, you mean?"

"Lennard Malloray, I'll have you know it's only ever been in the line of duty—"

"I know, I know. I was just teasing."

"By the way, how did you know he'd be here today? You didn't mention anything last night?"

"Angus sent around a note early this morning. It was delivered while I was out exercising Chester."

"You were out and about that early? I thought you'd slept through, just like I had."

Lennard chuckled. "Up at five or thereabouts. Christopher and I rode up to Primrose Hill and gave our horses free rein for half an hour. When I came back, I found Angus's note waiting, then climbed back into bed with you."

"And woke me in the most delicious way possible. Thank you, Lenn." Elam chuckled and began to blush.

"What's wrong, Elam?"

"Our Turk's sheet is now draped around his neck and he's making no pretence of not looking our way."

"Is he …?"

"Upright? Yes, and mightily so."

"I think it best we avoid direct contact. Pillow talk might be profitable, or it might scare him off. Besides, I'm not sure I have the energy after this morning."

"You're getting old, Lennard Malloray," Elam said. "Wait, he just stood up and refastened his sheet around his waist. I thought he might be coming over to talk to us, but it appears he's seen someone."

"Tell me what's going on. I'll keep my head down, I don't want to draw any more attention to us than we already have."

"He's beckoning to someone. I can see his reflection in the pool but the doorway is blocking my view of who it …"

"Elam? What's wrong?"

"You won't believe this, Lennard, but he'd dropped his sheet and is embracing another totally naked man."

"I told you men misbehaved here, although I thought it was only at night. The Turks frown on public behaviour of that sort in—"

"It's him."

"Who?"

"Karl Paulsson. Arthur Pencott's Swedish guard."

"Are you sure?"

"They're talking in English."

"What are they saying, Elam? Can you read their speech without it seeming too obvious?"

"You can take a quick glance if you like. They're sitting on the bench side-by-side facing each other. Neither is looking over here."

Lennard turned his head quickly. There was no doubt about it: the tall blond man with sharp, fine features, was unmistakeably the same man Kosorukov met twice a month at Martin Wilson's establishment. There couldn't be two men of the same colouring, bearing the tell-tale brown birthmark that flowed from under his right ear and over the shoulder of the same arm.

"They're talking about his voyage, when he arrived, how long he will be here. Now there's some smutty talk about what the Turk wants to do to the Swede ... someone else has arrived ... damnation! Quick! Hide yourself."

"What do you mean hide myself?" Lennard said, having pulled on Elam's shoulder to make him look at him.

"Flatten yourself against the wall next to the doorway, out of sight. I think Kosorukov has come to join them."

"Dear God, Elam. He can't see me here."

"Leave it to me, give me a moment to think."

"What will you do?"

"Provide enough distraction for you to get out of here. None of them knows me, but you're right, Kosorukov can't see you here. It would create enormous complications. I'll see you at home later. Don't worry," Elam said.

"Don't worry? For heaven's sake, Elam ..." Lennard said, but then realised Elam had not read his words, because he'd moved into the doorway, blocking it.

Lennard watched as Elam languidly stretched, arching his back, before retrieving his sheet from the chaise longue where he'd thrown it.

How he wished Elam might hear his whispered admonition to go cautiously, but knew it was futile. Elam had moved out of sight, so Lennard angled himself in the room—out of the line of sight of Kosorukov and his two friends—watching Elam move around the pool until he stood in front of the men, blocking their view. Lennard seized the moment and made his way out through the bathing area, his sheet draped over his head, blotting his face with the edge of it, in order to hide his features, on the merest chance that one of the trio may have looked his way.

*****

It was nearly nine in the evening before Elam arrived back at Bexford House.

Lennard had eaten supper, a little listless but not overly worried, wondering what had happened and what was taking Elam so long. He'd just stretched out on the Chesterfield in the sitting room and had started to read a new translation of Tolstoy's latest novel, *Boyhood*, which had arrived by post earlier that day, when Elam sailed through the door, throwing his hat onto a chaise and sitting down at Lennard's feet. He exhaled deeply then leaned forward to kiss Lennard's knee.

"Good evening, Lenn," he said, winking cheekily.

"Well then, the hunter home from the hunt."

"I must say, I've never witnessed so many copulations in succession."

"How many times?" he asked.

Elam smiled, then held up three fingers, extending a fourth quickly after Lennard's look of surprise. "Both the Swede and the Turk have unlimited reserves, Lenn, and the Russian? Well, let me just say he's a cuspidor of sorts, and greedy with it, too."

"That's an awful word to describe someone, Elam."

"You'd have to have been there."

"And you …?"

"Intact and unspent."

"Really?"

"I admitted to them I was profoundly deaf and had never participated, but was interested to observe as I had little knowledge and wanted to know what went on. I accepted a little fondling and some very expert osculation, performed by both the Swede and the Turk, but firmly refused anything more intimate than their extremely voluptuous kisses. They seemed to enjoy me watching."

"Was it arousing?"

Elam smiled and nodded, his eyes slightly narrowed. "Very. Reminiscent of the early days when we five lads first discovered our members were made for other things than passing water. Had Kosorukov not been there, then perhaps ..."

"And yet you stayed for the duration of four couplings?"

"I hoped to understand more of their conversation, Lennard. The longer I was with them, the more relaxed they became in my presence and the looser their tongues."

"Very well then. What did you learn?"

"Kosorukov and Karl spoke in a foreign language, as did Kosorukov and the Turk. They didn't appear to be the same languages, however, as the mouth shapes between the pairs were distinctly different. It was only Karl Nilsson and the Turk who spoke to each other in English."

"And?"

"I think our new friend, Arthur Pencott, will be very disappointed to learn that his Swedish guard is playing fast and loose with the emotions of men other than himself."

"What makes you think that?"

"He has an ability to be very amorous, in a way that's suggestive of more than a carnal connection, Lennard. He behaved as if he was torn between two lovers, lavishing affection on both the Turk and Kosorukov. I could see the desire in their eyes, and yet when he kissed me so ardently it took my breath away, I felt the artifice. It was almost as if I could hear his thoughts, as if he'd managed to congratulate himself on the belief he'd made me fall under his spell."

"But yet you didn't?"

"He's talented with the use of all parts of his body, Lennard. Lascivious without being debauched. His lovemaking is unfettered, enthusiastic, and he's willing to do anything. With you I can hold nothing back, you know that, so I'd be lying if I didn't admit that I was sorely tempted, and more than once. It was a struggle not to let myself go and to join in."

"Perhaps they saw your inner battle as an affirmation of your reluctance to partake as a truth, Elam. It would make sense for a man who was interested, and yet undecided. Maybe that's why they relaxed in your presence. Did you learn anything?"

"I learned that Vassili Vadimovich Kosorukov is sorely interested in my company."

"Really?"

"When the other two left us to cool off in the centre pool, he confessed that he'd love to be the man who was my 'first'. He offered me fifteen guineas. Can you imagine that? Anyway, I told him I was a domestic servant, a bee-keeper come down for a week to look after the hives on the roof of my master's London house and that I'd be returning to Hampshire tomorrow."

"That's a complication we could have done without, Elam. It means you can never be with me in any place that Kosorukov might be."

"Ah, but I have a twin brother who's a valet and factotum to a gentleman of quality—a gentleman unnamed, I hasten to add."

Lennard laughed. "Oh dear, that old chestnut? That ruse is as old as the hills."

"Perhaps, but he seemed to accept it, especially when I started to press him as to his own identity. He changed the subject quicker than a dog let out of a hutch. If we do meet again, while I'm at your side, I shall avoid any eye contact with him, and you can call me by my real name in his presence. I introduced myself to him as 'Paul', the hastily-invented name of my 'twin brother'. He's scarcely going to seek me out at a social occasion when I'm there with you to find out when my invented identical sibling will next come up to London."

"This makes me nervous, Elam—"

"What would have been worse, Lennard? Kosorukov discovering you in a place such as that with me at your side? You and your servant both naked in a place of assignation? Such a thing would ruin any further investigation into his possible treason or connection with The Cargo. He'd have a hold over you. I had to do something, and it was the first thing I could think of."

"But why didn't you just come away quickly and join me. A momentary distraction, followed by an excuse that another time would suit you better."

"Because, Lenn. When I arrived and before I greeted them, I saw the Turk ask his friends in English, 'Have either of you met with the Irishman of late?'"

10. CONNECTIONS, BOTH AT HOME AND ABROAD

On Wednesday morning, two days after his visit with Elam to the Sultan of Khartoum, Lennard found himself standing dockside at Malloray, Beauchamp, and Fahey's receiving wharf. Arthur Pencott was at his side, waiting for the steam packet from France to draw close to its berth.

He checked his pocket watch. "Five minutes, give or take, Arthur?"

"Most likely another ten, if not fifteen, Mr Malloray. She'll have to heave to, to allow our wool clipper, the *Faithful Lass*, to pass by first. The tide's running out and she can't afford to lose a minute."

"The clipper's a fine vessel, isn't she?" Lennard said. "She'll be back before we know it with five thousand bales of the finest merino wool from Port Melbourne."

A double ringing of the wharf's docking bell announced that the clipper had cleared the channel and the mail packet was about to make her approach to the wharf.

"I haven't thanked you for your kindness, Mr Malloray. I'm very grateful to be here and to back working for your company."

"I congratulate you on the swiftness of your decision to act upon my offer. It shows, I think, that you were ready for a change, and perhaps you missed this place?"

"I did indeed, Mr Malloray. And I would think myself a fool were I not aware that your offer was more than generous and provided an advancement in my standing. Thank you very much."

"You made an impression, Arthur. For that, there is no need for thanks. I know this is only your fourth day back, but do you think you'll enjoy your new position? You could have taken the offer to become Mr Fahey's assistant?"

"The position of loading supervisor is all I could ever wish for, sir. I get to work out in the open air, among the ships that I love, and go home at the same time every evening with the thought of more than twice the money in my pocket that I earned at St. Katharine's dock—and without the aching muscles and stiffness in my back. And, to be honest, to have the joy of reading every day, even if it is bills of lading and work rosters. It makes me feel I should be paying you, sir, not the other way around."

Lennard patted his shoulder. "Tell me, Arthur. On Sunday night, did—"

"Yes, Karl came and met your gentleman. It was the first of the month, so they were expected. It was odd really ..."

"What was odd?"

"Normally they have a room for two hours. They paid for it, but only stayed for an hour."

"Did you ...?"

"Yes, I was summoned to join them about fifteen minutes after they closed the door to their room. Mrs Hedger fetched me, telling me they wanted me from the start, but she'd explained that as I had another gentleman before them, who'd left as they arrived, I needed to take a few minutes to clean up and to catch my breath."

"I don't know how you do it."

"Much like you and your Mr Walters, I imagine, Mr Malloray."

Lennard chuckled.

"I know what you mean, sir. My remark was a jest. Most of it is play-acting. What's not seen can be interpreted as having happened."

"I'm sorry, I don't follow you, Arthur."

"Well, let me put it this way, sir. No one knows what the mole is doing when he's down deep in his burrow. He could be unloading his burden, or merely rearranging the furniture, and no one would ever know."

Lennard felt the blush before he could react. However, it didn't stop him from guffawing. A few of the dockhands glanced his way and smiled.

"As I said, Mr Malloray, more often than not it's play-acting. The right grunting and groaning, eyes rolling back in their sockets, and vigorous thrusting, culminating in a dramatic, pretend sigh of release at the same time as the gentleman beneath me has earned a gratuity more than once."

"I'm intrigued, and I suppose if a gentleman requires you to, well, you know ..."

"Gentlemen who require a man to roll onto his back or lie face down don't come to Mrs Hedger's. We're renowned for assets other than our arses, there's plenty all over town give theirs away for free."

*****

Lennard was still smiling five minutes later when the mail packet docked and Clyford made his way down the gangplank. "How was Paris?" he asked.

"Splendid, my lord."

"Good news, I hope?"

"The very best. Are we straight home?"

"No. Sir Angus and Sir George are waiting for us at the Oriental Club. I thought you might be hungry and, although it's nearly nine, I haven't breakfasted yet either. Robert and Gerald will join us."

"To hear about Paris?"

"Not only Paris, Clyford, but there have also been developments here, too. I thought it best to reveal my latest discoveries, not only to the other members of The Cargo *cloison*, but to both Sir George and Angus at the same time."

"Have you been concealing information from them?" Clyford asked with a small smile. "Tsk, tsk."

"No more than they do from us, Mr Billings. Now, let's find Elam and Robert. Christopher has the carriage waiting for us, and Mr Huilot is already at the Oriental. He thinks English chefs can't cook."

"I'm rather inclined to agree, my lord. But there are very few I'd admit that to, especially after ten days of extraordinary cuisine at the Maison Crillon. The Hôtel was exceptionally well-appointed and the staff extremely attentive. How did you know of such a place?"

Lennard tapped the side of his nose. "My grandfather's portfolio was far more extensive than most people know. Malloray's has a large investment in the establishment."

"I should put my hand up, and with great fervour, for any future assignments there, my lord, if that's the level of luxury I could expect."

"I look forward to hearing all about it. I've never been there, but it's not improbable we might spend some time there once the crisis in the Crimea has settled. Now, let me find a porter. We need to get moving. I don't know about you, but I'm famished."

"Indeed, sir, so am I. I'm so hungry I could eat a horse behind the saddle."

*****

Lennard, Elam, Robert, and Clyford arrived at the same time as Gerald, who'd alighted from a handsome cab as Lennard stepped from his landau. Sir George and Angus drew up in the Home Secretary's barouche immediately after, and the seven made their way into the Oriental Club.

Lennard had sent Christopher back to Bexford House, telling him they'd take a public conveyance home, and asked him to enquire after Mr Holland, who'd returned from Gresting the day before with Miles, to see whether he needed conveyance to attend to purchases for the fitting of his new consulting rooms in Birch House.

Mr Huilot, as was his wont, had prepared food for twenty, rather than the seven men who sat around the dining table. "More lamb chops, Sir George?" Merrill asked. Lennard had been quite unsurprised to see his first footman in attendance when they'd entered the room. Mr Huilot had always believed in appropriating staff for his own use whenever he thought it necessary, rarely having sought permission beforehand.

"No, thank you, Merrill, as delicious as they were."

"There's a dozen or more of Mr Huilot's very fine hand-rolled sausages, if you'd rather?"

"I'll have some more," Clyford said, "and a pair of poached eggs if you please."

"Honestly, I don't know where you put it," Sir George said, patting his tummy with one hand as he wiped his moustaches on his linen table napkin with the other.

Lennard smiled, then turned his head to make sure Merrill had closed the serving room door behind him. He wasn't concerned for his footman, but for the sommelier who might overhear something not meant for his ears. "Whatever my private secretary has to report will be new to me too, gentlemen. We talked of other things in the coach on the way here. So, Clyford ... about Paris. Do tell."

Clyford Billings was one of those bright young men, as depicted by Gainsborough in his paintings, with a complexion ubiquitous to gentlemen of his age. Peaches and cream, they called it, and Lennard was convinced that many a young lady was envious of his pale skin and the slight blush of his cheeks. However, unlike the young ladies, Lennard was aware that Clyford had been trained to shoot, fence, and use his fists. As a result, his speech and manner could often be more forthright than some gentlemen might expect, given the fine nature of his build and facial structure. Blunt, some called it, although always couched in the most civil of terms.

"The Countess Mecklenburg-Strelitz declined to see me when I arrived, unannounced, at her apartment in the Rue des Enfants-Rouges," Clyford said. "But, eventually, I 'persuaded' her *majordome* to escort me to her salon."

"I shall reimburse you any expenditure, of course, Clyford," Lennard said.

"My pistol was an adequate encouragement, my lord. The man refused my *pourboire*."

"A French servant refusing a tip?" Angus said, looking mildly amused. "That would be unimaginable in our country."

"When I announced that I'd come to speak with the countess about something unsuitable for the ears of her major-domo or her servant, she refused to look at me. That was until I explained the nature of my visit in her native language."

"You speak German, Clyford?" Sir George had a reputation for being astonished that any language existed other than English. To him, foreign languages were an obstacle constructed by people who wished to thwart his comprehension.

"Indeed, sir, I do … and Russian too. She informed me neither of her servants spoke German, so directed them to sit to one side in French, before our conversation started in earnest in her native tongue."

"But eventually, you …?"

"Left with six of Admiral Oblensky's latest missives, and a promise that every new one would be copied and sent to my … I mean, our … agent in Paris and forwarded onto us."

"The threat of scandal and her association with the Czarina must have shaken her sorely," Sir George said.

"No, sir. She brazened it out. It was only when I mentioned that, as the French are our allies in this war against Russia, it could be seen as treasonous if it were discovered she was corresponding regularly with a leading member of the enemy's military establishment."

"And her response?"

"She stared at me coldly for such a long time that I thought it prudent to play my trump card, Sir George."

"Your trump card?"

"I remarked what a long fine neck she had, sir, adding that when it came to the execution of members of her sex or rank for treason, the French held no qualms. They'd had a lot of practice, not sixty years since, with *Madame La Guillotine*."

*****

"Karl Paulsson?" Clyford exclaimed the moment Lennard mentioned the Swedish guard's name in connection with Kosorukov.

"You know this man?" Sir George asked, his eyes wide.

"Well of course I know him, sir. It was you who sent me to work for the Baron Hochschild, the Swedish *chargé d'affaires*. Karl Paulsson is the most trusted guard at the former embassy. He's a lapdog for the baron, Home Secretary. Does errands for him around town … wait, you said he and Kosorukov seemed to speak in one language to each other, and Kosorukov and the Turk in another, Elam?"

"Yes, that's what it appeared to me."

Clyford stood from the table and pace for a minute or two, deep in thought.

"Ah yes, that's it!" he said, his face flushed in excitement. "I was trying to remember, and now I have. Paulsson's mother was born in Russian-speaking Finland, and his sister is married to … oh, dear …"

"What is it Clyford?"

"His sister is married to a member of the Russian embassy staff in Stockholm."

Sir George began to suck on his cheeks, inhaling noisily through tight lips.

Clyford turned to Lennard. "When did you say he meets with Kosorukov at the molly house, my lord?"

"On the first and the fifteenth of every month."

"And which is the only country with whom we share diplomatic relations that has a Russian embassy, Sir George?"

"Why—"

"Yes, sir. It's Sweden. Any negotiation we make with the Russians is through their embassy in Stockholm, via the Swedes, am I correct?"

"Yes, Clyford, you are."

"And do you know when the mail packet from London to Stockholm departs, gentlemen? On the third of the month and on the seventeenth! Two days after every meeting between Kosorukov and Paulsson at Mrs Hedger's."

One by one, the members of the room realised the implication of what they'd just heard.

Lennard rose. Could it be that simple and yet so horrendous? Could Kosorukov be using Paulsson to send information to his countrymen via the Russian embassy in Stockholm—most likely in a letter? Perhaps it was clutching at straws to imagine such a thing, but their regular meetings at Mrs Hedger's, followed two days later by the mail packet to Sweden seemed too much of a coincidence to dismiss the notion out of hand.

"I believe Kosorukov was speaking to the Turk in French," Clyford explained to Elam, "and conversing with the Swede in Russian, the native language of his mother. The reason you understood it when the Swede spoke with the Turk is that they share no common language but English. I know Paulsson speaks no French, because he used to stand by, perplexed, when official diplomatic business was discussed in his presence. As we all know, French is the language of diplomacy for every civilised nation in the world."

Lennard was about to speak when Merrill knocked at the door to politely enquire whether any of the gentlemen would like more breakfast. Mr Huilot was anxious to get home to start thinking about food for the rest of the day. For the briefest moment, Lennard thought Clyford might ask for more sausage and eggs, but when he said nothing, Lennard thanked Merrill and told him that would be all and that they'd see him back at Bexford House.

"I'll visit Hochschild," Lennard said after his footman had left them.

"I can do it," Angus said.

"Leave it to me, Angus. He was a very dear friend to my grandfather and used to visit often when I was a child. Do you know he courted my aunt Caroline before she married? It broke his heart when she said she'd prefer it if he didn't visit her father, my great-grandfather, to ask permission to pay her court. Nonetheless, he was a frequent visitor to Gresting and was particularly fond of Robert and of me—and especially of our mothers—the Beauchamp sisters. I think this needs to be handled cautiously. Are you in agreement, gentlemen?"

"Of course, you're correct, Lennard," Sir George said. "I'm sure what you suggest is the wisest course of action under the circumstances."

Lennard noticed Clyford stifling a yawn. He'd not done the Channel crossing for more than ten years but remembered how tiring it could be if there was even the slightest swell. It had been windy last night. Frequent travellers to France had told him that under such circumstances the sea was choppy and sleep nigh impossible.

"Gerald," he said. "I wonder if you'd be so kind to see whether Merrill and Mr Huilot are still here. If they haven't left yet, perhaps you could accompany them and take Clyford back to Bexford House and see him comfortable. Christopher will have provided one of our carriages, and I've more to speak upon with Angus and Sir George. Don't worry, I'm not hiding anything. I'll tell you when we return, around lunchtime."

"I can manage—" Clyford started to say.

"Please, Clyford, for once let Gerald look after you. You're no good to anyone in the state you're in. A tummy full of food on top of a sleepless night. You and I will convene later in the day to catch up."

"Very well, my lord. Thank you, Gerald. It will be good to spend some time with the man who saved my uncle's life. We seem to have had such little opportunity."

Gerald's fleeting look of gratitude made Lennard smile. He, for one, saw no problem if his private secretary and one of his best friends were to find solace in each other's arms at some point in the future.

*****

"You look tired, Lennard," Sir George remarked after Clyford and Gerald had left.

"I must confess, sir, I had no idea of the responsibilities and travail involved in the change of station from your third secretary to the position in which I now find myself. I can scarce believe it's not yet four weeks since Sir Hugh took his calamitous tumble down the stairs at Birch House. There don't seem to be enough hours in the day to attend to what needs to be done."

"May I suggest that it will not always be so, my dear boy? The unfortunate coincidence of this latest business with The Cargo, Travis Holland's unexpected arrival, then the hideous affair with—"

"Astley is the least of my worries, Sir George. I have something he wants, over and above his preposterous offer on our shipping business, which he wouldn't jeopardise by doing anything foolish. He's proud, without doubt, and has proved to be sorely aggravated if he doesn't get his own way. Tell me, sir, how did he behave during your carriage perambulation this Sunday last?"

"He was cool but affable, comfortable in conversation with Lady Grey, but rarely addressed me unless I spoke to him first. He even allowed George Henry to walk with Neasa and to speak with her privately under the avenue of Linden trees, within sight of his carriage."

"That is surprising."

"You mentioned you have something he desires?"

"Yes, sir. I'll let Robert explain as he was instrumental to the plan."

Robert cleared his throat then glanced quickly at Lennard before speaking. "To tell the truth, sir, this is a business secret that would be awkward, to say the least, were anyone outside this circle to learn of it too soon. With Sir Hugh absent and unconcerned in the affairs of Malloray, it was left to me to carry on one of the greatest schemes of the sixth Baron Betteridge: the acquisition of the main wharves in the southern colonies."

"I take it you mean the Australian colonies, Mr Fahey?"

"Quite so, sir. It's not common knowledge just yet. However, Malloray, Beauchamp, and Fahey have recently acquired cargo rights for the main wharves in both the Port of Melbourne and in Sydney Cove. All vessels from other companies will have to negotiate a tariff for the use of our facilities. As well as that, I received a letter yesterday advising me that our tender to connect Melbourne Town to the goldfields in the State of Victoria and Sydney to the mining towns in the west by telegraph has been granted, and very soon, we will control the passage through both ports of not only wool and grain, but also gold and first-class passenger transport to destinations in the East, South Africa, thence to London and Liverpool."

"Good heavens! That's a remarkable achievement."

"And an expensive one, Sir George. The licensing fees to the colonial governments were well over ten thousand pounds."

Angus and Sir George exchanged quick glances.

"That's a fabulous sum, if I may say so," the Home Secretary remarked.

"It's about what we expect to earn in added revenue within two years, sir," Robert explained. "After that, as the business grows and the volume of goods through our warehouses increases, we predict an annual extra income of perhaps almost that initial licensing fee, per annum."

"Dear heavens," Sir George said. "Is it too early for whisky?"

Lennard laughed. "Expenses will come from that sum, sir. There will be new ships to be built, crews to be hired, and expansion of our docks here in London."

"There's not much room on either side of your current location."

"We're looking somewhere as yet undeveloped, to the east, sir. A location easily reached by a new connection from Fenchurch Street station. Less than a mile from a newly-built railway station."

Angus knew where it was. Lennard could see by the look on his face. It was immensely risky to share commercial confidences such as he had, but he trusted the other men in the room with his life.

"And this thing Astley desires has something to do with Australia? Or is it your new proposed wharf development to the east of the city?"

"Neither, Sir George. Terrence Astley owns two shipping companies, both registered in Ireland. The first is the company that sails between the south of France, Northern Spain, and Morocco, to the south of England, thence Wexford. That's the company we lease vessels from, or cargo space, to import out goods purchased from the Spanish colonies in the Caribbean. His second company trades in furs, bone, and whale oil from Nova Scotia, Newfoundland, and the Danish colonies in Greenland."

"So ..."

"He has no commerce with the rest of the Mediterranean, usually conducting trade in that region by hiring cargo space from us. However, due to the necessity to rearrange our fleet to cater for our new connections in Australia, there's a rumour been put abroad among the trading companies that we are, perhaps, interested in leasing warehouse and docking space at our wharves in Genoa, Naples, and Messina in Italy."

"It's the first I've heard of it," Sir George said.

"Ah, that's because it isn't true, sir."

"I'm sorry, I don't understand."

"What is my position in your employ, sir?"

"You are an intelligencer in my bureau, Lennard."

"And one of our most successful lures when trying to catch 'big fishes'?"

"I fear you are quoting me, sir."

"Indeed, Sir George. It was you who taught me that a near untruth, with the pedigree of probable verisimilitude, spread as gossip, might reel in the biggest catches with the biggest hunger."

"And this is what you think will keep Terrence Astley at bay?"

"He didn't hate the fact I stood up for myself. In fact, I think he rather liked it. But being humiliated and threatened to be horse-whipped in front of my servants and to be escorted from my house by my coachmen and two of my burly stablemen? Well, no doubt revenge burns bright in his breast. But while a business advantage could be in the offing, he'll stay his hand. He has a few of his Irish vessels tied up in Warrenpoint, which was recently connected by rail through Newry to Belfast. Those three ships of his would be perfect if he could negotiate a new trading route from the east of Ireland to the Italian peninsula. So, in the hope of tendering a successful bid, if such a thing was ever floated, he'll do nothing to aggravate the situation between him and me."

"You don't think that after his last visit, he'd dare—"

"No, he wouldn't dare approach me in public again, unless it was in a social situation that neither of us could avoid. He'll do it through someone else. A third person who'll be acting as his agent. Some duped fool who thinks he'll gain an advantage for himself while he's about Astley's business then overplay his hand. It's his way. He chooses his agents unwisely."

"The mark of a man with supreme self-confidence."

"Over-confidence, Sir George. He's convinced of his supremacy in everything, which blinds him to the weaknesses of others in his employ."

Lennard was suddenly overtaken with emotion, forced to grit his teeth and turn his head. Anger, hurt, despair? He wasn't sure which, or whence it came, but he'd nearly allowed his true hate of Astley to pour forth in an inappropriate manner, in a situation that did not merit such a display of emotion.

"Lennard—" Elam said and moved to his side, but Lennard quickly excused himself, and left the room through the door that led to the gentlemen's retiring room.

"Astley is such a blackguard," Angus said. "I wish—"

"Things are in hand to bring him down a notch, Sir Angus," Elam said, vacillating between staying where he was and following after Lennard. "You may ask Sir George, he'll explain," he added.

The Home Secretary looked puzzled. "I will?"

"Lennard will surely tell you when he returns, but may I venture to mention, in confidence, that the *Pendragon* affair is in hand?"

*****

"All this in the space of nine days, Lennard?"

"Yes, Sir George. Eight to be precise. Robert and I organised it the day after my first meeting with Kosorukov on Tuesday of last week—the day I came to your bureau in a clear state of agitation, and when you first mentioned the *Pendragon* to me."

Lennard had returned from the gentlemen's retiring room calmer, his face splashed with cool water from a basin the attendant had filled for him. The man had stood by while Lennard had peed noisily into a chamber pot. He'd clenched and unclenched his buttocks at the end, emptying his bladder with three final aggressive spurts. "Take that, Terrence Astley," he'd said to himself, imagining them to be rapier thrusts to his former lover's breast.

"You have a man aboard the *Pendragon* already?"

"Not yet, sir, but all being well, we will. In ten days from now, on the fifteenth of April, the ship will leave La Corunna en route for Falmouth with our cargo of walnut timber, destined for Gillow and Company. It came to both Robert and me that rifles and the such, being long and narrow, could easily be stacked in flat pine crates underneath our shipment of timber, which is fastened in tall, long pallets. It was merely fortuitous we'd already leased space aboard the vessel when you mentioned her name. Then it was only a matter of sending one of our Spanish-speaking Irishmen to enquire about passage back to Falmouth aboard her."

"You have a Spanish-speaking Irishman so readily at hand, Lennard?" Sir George asked.

"You'd be surprised who we have at hand, sir."

"I seriously doubt that. But your plan?"

"I'll let Robert explain, as it was he who directed our man in their own language," Lennard said.

"I'm sorry, you've simply lost me. Was there a specific need to speak in Irish?"

"May I remind you, Sir George, of the hole that exists in our knowledge of what passed between Kosorukov and the Turk, and between Kosorukov and the Swedish guard. There are eavesdroppers aplenty, even in the sanctity of private spaces, sir, and it's better to be safe than to be sorry."

"Of course, a wise precaution. Although one I might have never considered. If you please, Mr Fahey, the plan?"

"Our man speaks working-class English, Sir George. He's Irish-born with fluent Gaelic from his father and Spanish from his mother, a Castilian emigrant. Brought up in Hackney, he works for us mainly dealing with our Spanish exporters. However, unless there are unforeseen circumstances, he should already have registered as a stevedore at La Corunna and will have obtained a signed preference, in advance, for work aboard a British vessel, so he'll labour in exchange for passage back to England. We gave him coin to grease enough palms to have his name placed close to the top of the list for the *Pendragon.*"

"You must explain seafaring, sir. Doesn't the ship have its own crew?"

"It has a basic crew, Sir George. They invariably lose members at every port for variable reasons. Merchant sailors aren't press-ganged. There are always locals looking for work, and most vessels pick up a handful of men who are happy to work in exchange for passage to a new place. Or, as it will seem in our man's case, work in exchange for a passage back to his homeland."

"I worry too much, Mr Fahey. This is new territory to me, please excuse my inquisitive nature. Please, continue."

"The plan is for our man to investigate the nature of any other cargo other than our walnut once the ship is at sea. We have leased the entire cargo space, so anything other than crates of lengths of timber will be obvious. When the *Pendragon* is approaching the dock in Cornwall, our man will stand on the quarter-deck smoking his pipe. A customs officer will observe him through a glass from the upper-storey window of the government warehouse on shore. If our agent has a red kerchief around his neck, the vessel contains nothing but our cargo. However, if it's blue or green, that's the signal to the customs officers to make an unexpected inspection."

"Won't that make Astley suspicious?"

"Not at all. You don't think he doesn't line the pockets of some of the customs officers of Her Majesty's government do you, sir? Our ships oft-times have a customs official or two come aboard before unloading begins, even though we have an exemption. They usually share a glass of port with the captain and move no further than the interior of his cabin before signing papers then disembarking. However, from this Saturday forward, there will be a change of customs staff—a rotation of duty—and, if the ship is carrying contraband, our man will be arrested along with the rest of the *Pendragon* crew to avoid any unnecessary suspicion."

"Curious that there will be a change of staff in a few days. Good timing, I suppose, Mr Fahey?"

"Greased palms work both ways, sir, and the less you know the better. To all appearances, it will seem like happenstance. Astley will curse his bad luck, and we shall have clean hands. The penalty, although great for some other shipowners, will merely be a thorn in his side and inflame his urgency to obtain trading rights through our ports in Italy."

"Again, I don't understand," Sir George said.

"In cases such as this, although Astley will swear the captain of his vessel is responsible and he had no knowledge of contraband, should it indeed be aboard the *Pendragon*. The vessel and his warehouses at Falmouth will be seized by the Crown. He'll lose the ship, and most likely his licence to deal in the south of England. We'll arrange something new—perhaps his next ships out of La Corunna will be forced to use our London docks. No one else but us will touch his business," Robert said.

"That would play to our advantage," Lennard added. "Falmouth is in the country, he could be unloading other contraband offshore, but here, in the capital, we could keep a strict eye on everything. And when I say 'we', I don't necessarily mean Malloray's, but also Her Majesty's government."

"Besides, sir," Robert explained, "all the customs officers in the Port of London are aware they are scrutinised and kept under government observation. Bribes that are commonplace in regional ports are impossible in the nation's capital these days."

"It peeves me to think that such corruption should exist among officials of the government, Mr Fahey. However, I'm not naïve enough to refute the existence of such irregularities. It may be eighteen fifty-five, and we may believe we live in more structured and regulated times, but I'm no longer surprised to hear frequent reports of graft and the molestation of the law for the purposes of unlawful benefit to men of business and of standing."

"It's corruption that propels the need for intelligencers, Sir George," Lennard said. "Whether it be financial or moral corruption, it's what we do, sir. Fighting corruption of one sort of another is what those of us who work for Sir Angus spend our time doing. And, as his superior and the head of the department under whom he travails, it's also what we do for you, sir."

Sir George passed a reluctant smile at Lennard, owning the truth of his words. It was a particular smile Lennard recognised: one with a hint of sourness, as if acknowledging some bitter truth and unable to refute it. The Home Secretary must have realised that he was the last man to pass judgement if some bureaucratic manoeuvring within Her Majesty's customs service exposed the illegal import of guns meant to arm Irish insurrectionists—even if it did entail the exchange of money.

*****

"We still don't know the reason for Kosorukov's meeting with the Turkish sailor, Lennard," Sir George said. They'd tarried a moment in the dining room after the other men had left.

"Perhaps he's a courier, Sir George. Perhaps this is how Kosorukov learns of what the Russians are planning in the Crimea. The Turk has left now, and he won't return for another six weeks, according to the sailing manifests. I did check. My suspicions are that Kosorukov receives broader information from the Turk but sends regular news to his fellow countrymen through the Swede in his letters to his sister."

"But do you think this has anything to do with The Cargo?"

"What Robert didn't tell you is that we have just placed someone aboard the *Koniah*, the Turk's vessel, in case that's the way they intend to smuggle the pretender to our shores. He can also spy on Hakan Zeybeck in Constantinople."

"Excellent work, Lennard. Now, about the most disturbing part of your report of what happened in the Sultan of Khartoum. The mention of 'the Irishman' …"

"Do I think it's Astley? I can't be sure. There's simply no other connection between him and Kosorukov that we know of—yet. Despite his insurrectionist sentiments, he's hardly an iconoclast, sir. He may wish for independence, but I can't bring myself, as much as I loathe the man, to believe he'd wish to be part of a plot to overthrow Her Majesty and plant an unknown despot in her place. It could well prove to lead to greater suppression and more violence against his countrymen. The Ottoman Turks tended to rule with blood, not by politics."

The Home Secretary sighed deeply. "Then, in many ways, we are no further advanced with the question of The Cargo than we have been for months."

"Until we question Karl Paulsson, Sir George."

"Isn't that precipitous, Lennard? No one has any proof that he's involved in any way."

"I'll wait until I have my skittles lined up, sir. First off, tomorrow I shall pay a visit to my dear friend, the Baron Hochschild."

"Can you do that, out of the blue, while you're still in deep mourning?"

"I shall take Mr Holland with me, sir."

"Mr Holland?"

"The baron has had an untreatable ulcer just above his right ankle.

Mr Holland is a specialist in such maladies, having served for two years aboard the *Vincent* in the tropics."

"So, your gesture of goodwill will entail a private word with the former Swedish ambassador?"

"Indeed, Sir George. And, mindful that Her Majesty's government is due to sign a treaty with the King of Sweden at the end of the year, he'll more than likely be amenable to any conversation about his favourite guard, whether it means breaking confidences or not."

"Fine work, Lennard. Fine work indeed."

11. THE SWEDISH QUESTION

Chester hated London; he shied at every corner. At heart, he was a country horse, still not used to the hustle and bustle of a busy city at mid-morning.

Lennard had decided to take Geoffroy to Birch House to meet the Huskersons and to give him some practice with more people of Lennard's acquaintance who were French by birth, but who spoke English fluently. He didn't believe in the immersion nonsense that was the rage these days, especially with young, sensitive lads like Robert's nephew, who was still all eyes and ears to the sights and sounds of a huge metropolis.

This morning, Lennard had donned his new riding outfit, delivered five days ago, the morning after Clyford had returned from Paris. Pale fawn breeches, knee length boots, a stylish cutaway tailcoat in charcoal-grey fine wool, finished off with a matching top hat of the same shade in beaver. The glorious feature of his outfit was a lemon-yellow embroidered waistcoat, sitting fashionably over a white linen stock, which Elam had tied artfully for him this morning while they'd dressed each other. He looked every inch a man of fashion and of refinement, constantly tipping his hat to those who touched theirs as he rode past them, and to ladies who cast smiles in his direction. Geoffroy sat forward in the saddle, grasping its pommel, touching his sailor's cap at the same time as Lennard tipped the brim of his stovepipe.

It must have made a fine sight, he thought. A youngish, well-dressed man riding a spirited white stallion through the city, unusual in itself these days, with a lad—possibly his son—seated in the saddle with him. It explained the smiles and hat doffs from those they passed. He could almost hear the word "charming" repeated over and over as he and Geoffroy acknowledged each salutation.

Chester had been very cranky. He'd tossed his head and had neighed so loudly when Lennard had ridden out though Albany Street and had not turned into the direction of Regent's Park that Lennard had been forced to dismount and stroke his muzzle, whispering calming words against the side of the horse's head. However, a circuitous route through the various leafy, quiet squares that linked Bexford House to Soho Square had calmed Chester, and he'd nudged Lennard's shoulder after they'd dismounted in front of Birch House, as if to say "is that all?"

"*Il n'est pas encore habitué* … he's not used to it yet, my lord," Geoffroy said, as Lennard crouched down in front of the lad, in order to adjust his coat and to help him put on his gloves, which he'd refused to wear when they'd left Bexford House. "There are too many carriages, carts, colours, shapes, and movements for a country boy like him."

"Are you talking about Chester, or about yourself, *mon brave*?"

"Phht!" the boy answered. "I've been travelling in the carriage every morning with my uncle to the docks. I won't say I'm used to it, but I feel safe with him … and with you."

"You don't otherwise feel in any danger, do you?"

"No, sir. What I meant is that if I got lost, I wouldn't know what to do. My English is still not good enough. But you, and the other gentlemen, are exceedingly kind—even the men who work on the wharves are very friendly and help me with my words."

"Let's go inside, shall we? Mr and Mrs Huskerson arrived yesterday, and I haven't had much time to spend with them before Mr Holland moves in tomorrow. I thought it would be nice for you to meet them, and we can speak in French all morning. I know how tiring it can be to concentrate so hard all day in a foreign language."

"Pay no heed to me, my lord. I must learn English and the best way is to speak it as much as possible."

"Very well, I'll leave it up to you. We can speak both, as I've always done with them. Now, let's see to Chester."

"Are there no stables here at Birch House, sir?"

"There are, but they've been closed up for many years now. Perhaps, when Mr Holland can afford a coach of his own and a groom, I'll attend to their refurbishment. In the meantime, he intends to use a public carriage if he needs to go anywhere."

"What will you do with your horse while we're inside? Will you leave him to graze in the garden?"

"No, Geoffroy, I'll find the … ah, there he is." Lennard called out to the penny-stableboy who patrolled back and forth across the northern end of the Soho Square. "There's a carriage house around the back for public use. They'll look after him there."

"Will he be all right, my lord?"

"I'm sure he'll be spoiled and reluctant to carry us home when it's time to take our leave."

It was mostly carriages these days; there was little call for taking care of the needs of solitary horseback riders, apart from the occasional itinerant land-purveyor or government official with a message. But the stableboy was already used to Lennard's frequent visits in order to make sure the house was ready for Travis and knew that the handsome gentleman with the ready smile and a twinkle in his eye always paid with an extra half-penny.

"Will you take my hand, Geoffroy, or are you too old for such a thing?"

"I'd prefer your arm around my shoulder, my lord. It's how my father walks with me."

"Do you miss him?"

"Don't you miss yours?"

Lennard smiled but said nothing. He pushed open the black iron entrance gate of Birch House and gestured to Geoffroy to precede him.

"Let's go in the back door, shall we?" he said. "The garden is looking beautiful. I employed a man to work it about three weeks ago and I'd like to see what he's done with the vegetable garden."

"You don't have a vegetable garden at Bexford House, sir. It's something I noticed almost right away."

"There's a Portuguese family who calls past every morning. Mr Huilot organised it. They have a farm in Islington and bring fruit and vegetables by cart to the large houses in the area."

"It seems odd to not have a vegetable garden, if you don't mind me saying so, sir."

"We can find some space at Bexford House and make one for you, if that's what you'd like, Geoffroy."

"Thank you, sir, but no. I'm afraid I'm far too busy helping my uncle. One day, perhaps, when I'm old, like you, then ..."

"I'll give you 'old like me', you scamp," Lennard said, laughing as he chased after the boy, who'd dangled a bait Lennard had found impossible to resist. Like Robert and Lennard, he'd inherited the Beauchamp family trait: teasing, and at every opportunity.

*****

"Hello?" Lennard called out into the hallway that led off the basement kitchen. "There's no one here," he added, beckoning Geoffroy to follow.

"Oh, yes there is," the lad said, making his way past Lennard down the back stairs that led from the garden into the house.

Lennard smiled. On the end of the kitchen table sat an enormous white cat, who meowed softly when Geoffroy extended his hand and began to stroke it. "*Monsieur le chaton, tu es le plus gros chat que j'aie jamais vu*," the boy said, leaning over and nuzzling the cat's fur with his chin.

"He might be the biggest cat you have ever seen, but just be careful he doesn't claw you," a voice said from the other side of the room.

"Ah, Mrs Huskerson. There you are. We let ourselves in by the back door," Lennard said.

"It's your house, sir, and Mr Huskerson and I saw you both running down the side garden from upstairs, *monsieur le baron*," she replied, moving into the room, and performing a quick half-curtsey. "And who is this?"

"This is Geoffroy, he's Robert's brother's son. He has come to London to learn business and to master English."

"Then he's your second cousin, Lennard?"

"Yes, Eugénie."

She smiled at Geoffroy, who'd eased the cat into his arms and held him against his chest. The cat was so big, his back legs dangled almost down to the boy's knees. "What's his name?"

"Champignon, Geoffroy," Mrs Huskerson replied, "and you'll never believe it, but when he came to us, he was so tiny he looked like a field mushroom, all clean and white, yet to open—a mere button. He fitted into the palm of my hand."

*****

"How was the visit?" Travis asked.

"Excellent, my friend," Lennard replied, "although there's something I need to ask you. The Huskersons have brought their cat. I hope you don't mind?"

"A cat? How excellent. The ship's cat aboard the *Sisley* slept between my knees in my hammock more nights than I'd care to mention. It will be exceedingly welcome to have an animal, even if it is someone else's pet. I've been wondering if you had any objection to a dog at some point in the future, Lennard?"

"No, of course not. Why do you need to ask? You're renting the premises."

"It's your garden, my friend."

"Dogs dig when they're lonely. That's been my experience anyway. I'm sure a friendly dog sitting at your feet at night will be a great consolation, not to mention the calming effect on any children who might come with their parents for treatment."

"My father had a hunting dog, a spaniel. The patients adored him."

"Then it's settled, you may do whatever you like as far as I'm concerned. Now, have you seen Elam?"

"He's gone to sign some documents at Mr Drudge's chambers,

after which he had a list of things to do for you. He said he'd be back in time for dinner this evening."

"He's gone to Drudge's because I've made proviso for both him and Miles, merely as a precaution in case anything untoward happens to me or I get too old and forget. I'd not wish the nightmare of my uncles' failures to leave wills on anyone."

"Are we still to visit the Baron Hochschild this afternoon?"

"At three o'clock."

"I've spent the morning going through my texts on tropical ulcers. I hope you don't mind but I asked Christopher to stop at the apothecary in Tottenham Court Road on his way home from taking Robert to Malloray's this morning. I was low on my supply of *flores sulphuris* with which to prepare a topical ointment, should the baron's ulcer be the type that responds to such a treatment."

"Shall I open an account there for you, Travis? It will be easily done for me, without you having to provide credentials and to find business acquaintances to recommend you. London isn't like a provincial town, you know. Name is everything, and with mine alongside yours on the account, you merely need to send around a note and they'll deliver it. You can order whatever you like, and I'll send you the monthly bill after I've paid it."

"I already—"

"If you say the word 'owe' I shall spank your backside—bad leg, or no bad leg. Do you hear me? It's what friends do for each other."

"Well, I'm incredibly touched, and I accept your kind offer. I'm not used to such largesse."

"Kindness bears its own rewards, Mr Holland. I may have not been discerning enough in the past with some of my kindnesses, but on the whole, I've been amply rewarded by those to whom I've extended some generosity. I think of it as if planting a seed. The seed may take time to grow and mature, but perhaps that seed might turn into a tree—a tree which might provide shade, or fruit, or some other benefit. And if not? Then the effort of planting it is still of value because that act has provided a moment of pleasure to my heart."

Travis closed the book he'd been reading and lay it on his lap, his hands folded over its cover. "Such a wonderful philosophy, if I may call it that, Lennard. It's no wonder you are so loved by all those around you."

Lennard snorted. "I think you mean respected, Travis, not loved."

"And I think you need your eyes checked, Lord Betteridge. It's apparent that you don't have as much care for yourself as the men around you, who not only count you as their friend, but who love you as dearly as one man might another."

Lennard was aware that he'd coloured profoundly, such was the burning in his face, but smiled at Travis, who shook his head slowly, deeply amused at Lennard's embarrassment.

"What's to become of you, Lennard Malloray? I fear my compliment and simple observations of the truth seem to have undone you."

"I've always found it difficult to speak on matters of such intimacy, Travis."

"Even to Elam?" the doctor asked, over the top of his book, which he'd retrieved from his lap and had re-opened. He lowered his head and pretended to be busy reading, to allow Lennard the luxury of not having to reply.

*****

Lennard was at work at his desk when the note arrived. Robert had sent one of his assistants from Malloray's and the letter was in a simple code. In essence, it said a message had arrived by mail packet that their man had obtained passage aboard Astley's vessel, the *Pendragon*, which was due to sail on Sunday the fifteenth, four days hence. She would arrive in Falmouth on the Saturday or Sunday a week later.

Lennard tipped the man and told him to ask Christopher to get someone to take him back to the office, because hackney carriages were few and far between in this area of London. Christopher's new groom could use the opportunity to become acquainted with their brougham, which had been stored away, unused for five years, and which had recently been spruced up and repainted.

After the man had left, Lennard scribbled a letter to the manager of their warehouses and receiving station at Falmouth, advising him to organise the arrival of the *Pendragon* with the customs officers, reminding him of their planned course of action. He addressed the envelope and rang for Merrill.

"Please pass this to the postman when he comes to deliver the second post."

"Certainly, my lord. It's half past two and Mr Holland is ready and waiting, sir. Shall I send one of the lads to get Christopher to fetch the carriage around?"

"There's no need, Merrill, but thank you. Christopher is punctual and will have the landau drawn up at quarter to the hour, as we arranged this morning. Do you know if Robert's man was seen off successfully?"

"Yes, I watched them drive off through the library window. The brougham looks splendid. Now, will you change, sir? I can help you if you wish, seeing as Elam is abroad."

"No, I rather like this riding outfit and it's quite suitable for an afternoon visit."

"Well, if I may observe, my lord, it is very beautifully cut, and you look like a modern-day Beau Brummell."

"Good grief, Merrill. I don't want to look too well-outfitted. You must tell me if I—"

"What you are wearing is both à la mode and extremely stylish, sir. I've dressed many noblemen during my time when footmen are required to act as valets on weekend house parties, and I know what suits and what doesn't. You'll do just fine, sir, if you'll forgive me saying. However ..."

"However?"

"A walking cane, baron. The height of fashion. There's a basket of them in the cloak closet downstairs. Shall I choose one for you?"

"Thank you. Now, please inform Mr Holland that I'll be with him shortly."

"Of course, my lord."

Lennard checked his pocket watch. He had ten minutes, not nearly long enough to write to his aunt. Perhaps he'd just take a chance and assume she'd fit in with his plans. Tomorrow would see the end of his deep mourning and the time it would be expected for him to return to society. He intended to host a dinner at Bexford House on Saturday. Perhaps it would be late for invitations, but Angus had assured him that even if those invited were already engaged, they'd shift around their plans for a chance to dine with the new Baron Betteridge, a man of great fortune and new to the world of society.

The newness of his arrival would guarantee their attendance, for—among the wealthy circle in which Lennard was destined to move—novelty was everything. He'd invite twenty-four, with the hope that sixteen might reply with affirmative responses. As a bachelor, his aunt Caroline would be expected to act as the lady of the house for the evening, even though he hadn't yet asked her.

He planned to call in to see her, with Mr Holland, after they'd visited the Swedish attaché, in the hope she'd be at home and would receive them, both to extend his invitation and to ask her if she would stand at his side to greet the guests, and also to take care of the ladies for the evening. He walked to his study door, opened it calling out for Merrill, whom he hoped was still within earshot.

"Mr Thompson is downstairs in the cloak closet, my lord. Shall I fetch him?" asked Stephen, one of the under-footmen, in answer to Lennard's call.

"No, Stephen. Fetch your jacket if you please. I'd like you to accompany us to the Baron Hochschild's residence, after which Christopher will take you to Lady Winchester's house in Bedford Square. You're to ask her housekeeper to enquire whether my aunt will be at home at around six in the evening, as I'd like to call past for a short visit on my way home."

"Of course, sir. Wouldn't you prefer to write a note I could deliver?"

"That won't be necessary and I don't have time. Please, grab your jacket and wait for Mr Holland and me outside. You can sit up front in the landau next to Christopher."

"Very good sir. Right away."

He wanted to discuss the etiquette of such an occasion. He'd never hosted a grand dinner before, and indeed had never had cause to be invited to one. Third secretaries who were not expected to inherit a title at any time soon were considered, at the best, merely as last-minute fillers at minor events and only then if someone grander had been unable to attend at the last moment. However, his station in life had changed considerably and he was expected to entertain in style. Therefore, who better to ask than his aunt.

The dinner would serve two purposes. First, as his introduction to society, second as an excuse to include some guests who might be not only surprised by his invitation, but also eager to attend, especially when they found out that Angus's secret beau—Prince Christian Jost Saxe-Meiningen, cousin to Prince Albert, her majesty's consort—had already promised to attend.

Dinner was never simply dinner on occasions such as these. Much would be done after the ladies retired and left the gentlemen to their port and cigars. He planned to lay a few traps, to set plans into motion through a few subtle, but well thought-through "accidental" revelations, mentioned off-hand during casual, but artfully contrived, conversations.

It would be amusing to see Kosorukov and Terrence Astley at his table, and to have Elam at hand, watching through the dining room spyhole to read their speech when they sat side-by-side over dinner.

*****

Lennard had not seen Travis at work before, other than stitching Miles's cheek, so it was somewhat surprising to notice the care and attention the doctor paid to the Baron Hochschild's ulcerated leg.

For such a strong man with large hands, his touch appeared gentle and his voice calm and soothing, showing no reaction after peeling back the last layer of bandage covering the open sore. The stench, as it was finally uncovered, made Lennard so fearful that he almost recoiled. However, Travis's sigh of relief and assertation that the ulcer was not as bad as it looked, stayed his reaction.

"This is a dry ulcer, baron," Travis said, gently turning the leg in his lap. He'd crouched on the floor, sitting on his heels, to better observe the injury. "You have it continually covered I see."

"It weeps rather badly, Mr Holland, and I can't bear the smell, let alone think of the revulsion of my staff and any visitors may have with such a strong odour."

"The smell, sir, is caused by the wetness. How often do you change the bandages?"

"My manservant does them once a week, doctor."

"Could you fetch him here, sir? And your cook, if you please?"

"My cook?"

"Yes, I'll give your manservant instructions on how your leg is to be treated, and I'll give your cook a recipe for poultices. There'll be two a day, I'm sorry to inform you, but each will only remain on your leg for an hour at a time. The rest of the day, you'll have a light dressing of boiled muslin, loosely tied over the ulcer."

"For how long, sir? I mean, how long will this treatment last?"

"The initial stage will last about twelve days, after which the pain will have gone completely. After that, we'll institute a different treatment, one which will preclude air from the skin and will involve a tightly-fitted stocking—one perhaps two sizes smaller than you normally wear."

"This seems extraordinary, Mr Holland, if you'll allow me to make an observation. Two different regimes of treatment for the same wound?"

"The first stage, baron, is to heal the ulcerated flesh, to take away the pain, and to prevent the ulcer from becoming aggressive again. I've seen this type of abscess before many times. I can promise you that, if you follow my directions to the letter, you'll suffer a complete cure in about three to four months."

"Three to four months? Can this really be true? The physician who has been treating me for the past four years since it first came about told me that I'd suffer it for the rest of my days."

"With respect to a fellow medical practitioner, my lord, the only thing you'll have to suffer for the rest of your days is a fool of a doctor who has no speciality in diseases of the skin."

For a moment, Lennard thought Travis may have spoken in too forthright a manner, but gradually, the Swedish attaché's features softened, and he laughed, reaching forward to pat Travis's shoulder.

"I appreciate plain speech, sir," he said. "And I rather hope I may call upon you in the future for any further ailments."

"Of course, baron. You may either visit me at my new lodgings or send one of your men with a note and I'll come to you as soon as I am able to."

"Wonderful! And where shall I find you?"

"At Birch House, baron," Lennard explained. "Mr Holland will take up residence tomorrow."

The baron's manservant and chef arrived quickly, escorted by two guards, one of whom was exceedingly familiar to Lennard. When Travis had asked why such an assembly was necessary, the baron explained that as his personal manservant was nigh on seventy years old, it sometimes fell to one of two house guards to stand in for him. They aided him into and out of his hip bath, and sometimes, if the pain in his leg was severe, in and out of his carriage and up and down the stairs in his residence.

Karl Paulsson was much finer of feature than Lennard had been able to observe from the dimness of the room in which he and Elam had sat at the Sultan of Khartoum, and from the distance at which he'd observed him. There could be no doubt of the man's physical attraction; Lennard had noticed his firm musculature when he'd observed him standing first, and again later, sitting with Hakan Zeybeck, both of them completely naked. It rather irked him to see that the guard seemed genuinely concerned for the attaché's condition. What Lennard had to discuss with Baron Hochschild about his guard made the task a little disagreeable, if indeed there was some fondness between the two men.

"Green tea, doctor?" the cook asked.

"Yes, madam, green tea. Both India and China teas are fermented—you'll have to source it from an importer if you have none in the house. You'll need to add a half-gill of boiling water to one ounce of tea, let it steep for perhaps a minute, no longer, then strain it. When it's cool to the touch, you shall pack the leaves in boiled muslin, washing your hands beforehand, after which the baron's valet of one of his other servants can bind it firmly over the ulcer, where it will remain for one hour, no more."

"And this is in the evening?"

"Yes, madam. In the morning he's to have two ounces of softened willow bark prepared the same way and packed in clean, previously boiled muslin, to be left on the ulcer for an hour. It must not be left for longer, do you hear?" Travis said to the valet and to the two guards, who nodded in reply to his admonition. "Willow bark, if not used with caution, can cause problems when applied topically and left directly in contact with the skin for too long."

"Where shall I procure these items, sir?" the cook asked.

"I'll send them around, tomorrow morning," Lennard said. "I'll have a few pounds of the Earl of Twinton's finest green tea from Ceylon packed and delivered. I'll get my under-footman to purchase the willow bark from the apothecary on his way back from our warehouse."

"Send me an invoice, Lennard, if you please. Thank you very much for your consideration."

"Invoices are for customers, baron, not for friends. Now, when Mr Holland has finished with your leg, I wonder if I might have a word with you in private? I'm afraid I'm also here on Her Majesty's business."

"Then I am your humble servant, Lennard. You will have my full attention for the next hour."

"I assure you, I won't need that long, sir."

*****

"He what?"

"Please, baron, I've known you since I was a child. It's the reason I'm here and not the Home Secretary. In view of the negotiations between His Majesty, King Oscar and Her Majesty's government, I suggested a personal visit."

"I can hardly believe it, Lennard."

"Well, sir. You've no need to believe anything yet. However, Karl Paulsson has been seen keeping company with people of interest to the Home Secretary's department. I thought I should head it off, so if there is any fire beneath the smoke, it should not be seen that you had any hand in fanning the flames."

"Well then, Lennard. Since you call upon our long acquaintance and have taken the time to introduce me to your excellent new physician—"

"Which has nothing to do with the reason for this private conversation. Let me be frank, sir. Travis Holland is a man of great care and talent, and I'd like him to succeed. Introductions to members of society, such as yourself, will help his practice thrive and in the doing of it provide me with a trustworthy and reliable tenant for Birch House. Besides, I like him."

"And I like Paulsson, Lennard. Let's be mindful of that while you explain."

"Very well, sir. Perhaps I may broach the subject by enquiring whether you know if he corresponds regularly with his sister."

"With Brita? Yes, he writes to her twice a month."

"I'm curious to know how you are aware of such regular correspondence, sir?"

"His letters go in the diplomatic bag on the mail packet to Sweden. They're very fond of each other."

"And she's married to a man who works at the Russian embassy in Stockholm."

"I'm not sure how you know this, Lennard. But yes, that's correct, he's an undersecretary to ..."

"I see you're beginning to understand why the Home Office is so interested."

The Baron Hochschild coloured deeply, unable to speak for a minute or two. "Why, Lennard, if this is true, even suspected, it could compromise our whole mission here in London. The very thought of one word getting out—"

"You have my assurances, baron, as a friend of long standing, that nothing will pass that could be associated with you."

"I'll do whatever I can, as long as there is no breaking of confidences."

"Unfortunately, sir, diplomacy, as you are aware, defines 'confidences' in a manner that the rest of mankind might find difficult to associate with their more common definition. It's all in the perception of confidence versus advantage, is it not?"

"Lennard, you should have been a diplomat."

Lennard laughed and held out his hand. The baron regarded it for a moment, before taking it and returning Lennard's proffered handshake.

"I'm offering you a gentleman's agreement that whatever transpires between us will neither compromise you, nor the Kingdoms of Norway and Sweden. A handshake before a deal has been struck is my guarantee that you will not be ill-used."

"Very well, the thrust of your interest?"

"This Saturday, the fourteenth of the month, I'm to host a private gathering, to herald the end of my period of deep mourning. There will be twenty-four guests at table, after which the gentlemen will retire to my library, as is the custom, to play billiards, to drink port, to smoke cigars, and to—"

"Talk business."

"Precisely, baron. During the course of the conversation, something will be mentioned. I ask you to do one thing."

"You want me to attend?"

"No sir, I think it best that, on this occasion, you do not. Merely to avoid any connection with the matter. I merely wish you to read Paulsson's letter to his sister after it's been placed in the diplomatic pouch and before it's sent on the packet to Sweden on the seventeenth of this month."

"Well, Lennard, I'm not sure that—"

"I don't want a word-by-word report, nor do I want a copy. I want you to look for the word Caroline. Then, if you find it, tell me the context in which it is mentioned. That's all. I don't wish to hear personal details, simply Caroline and the sentence or paragraph in which it occurs. If there is nothing, then our matter is at an end and I shall bother you no more."

"Caroline? Not Caroline, the Baroness Winchester, your aunt?"

"No, sir. The *Caroline* is the name of one of our vessels."

*****

"What on earth are you doing here, Clyford?" Lennard exclaimed when he stepped up into his barouche. He'd been busy chatting to Travis and hadn't noticed the sole passenger already seated when the coach drew up under the baron's portico.

"I've come to warn you, my lord."

"Warn me? And where's Stephen? He was supposed to bring me news."

"Alas, sir, it fell to me to bring you news."

"I'm not sure I'm ready for anything calamitous. You'd best explain."

"When Stephen delivered your message to Lady Winchester, she was intrigued. So much so that there's been a constant traffic of riders with notes back and forth between Bedford Square and Clarence Gardens all afternoon."

"What is it about a simple query as to whether she'd be at home at six this evening that has my aunt so intrigued, Clyford?"

"Her first note came to me, sir. I'm your private secretary and your business is my own, if I may be so bold to say so directly. Lady Winchester had another engagement at the time you mentioned you might call, and, as you'd taken the trouble to advise her of your visit, queried me as to the urgency of your unexpected request."

"And your reply?"

"I wrote back simply, my lord. Please don't be annoyed, but I may have mentioned that the purpose of your visit was to talk about your planned dinner this coming Saturday evening. To cut to the chase, sir, after several exchanges of notes, your aunt has taken charge of the whole affair and she and I, along with Gerald, have been at work all afternoon planning the dinner."

"What do you mean? You, Gerald, and my aunt have been at work planning *my* dinner?"

"If I may speak plainly, baron, you are new to your position. It is for you to give orders, and for us to carry them out. The baroness was fit to be tied when I mentioned Prince Christian Jost Saxe-Meiningen and his sister, first cousins to Prince Albert, were to be among your guests, along with the Prime Minister, the Foreign Secretary, and the Home Secretary and their wives."

"Fit to be tied?"

"I fear that wheels have been put in motion, my lord, that require you to observe, and perhaps comment, but at a distance."

"Dear Lord, is my house not to be my own?" Lennard said to Travis, who'd been smiling mightily while observing the exchange.

"Don't ask me, Lennard. I'm sure your private secretary will explain."

"Clyford?" Lennard asked, trying to look annoyed, but failing, mainly due to the rather timid look on his secretary's face. "Oh, for heaven's sake, you're a man of action, Clyford. Out with it!"

"Well, in this particular case, my lord, with a Crown Prince and Princess, two Earls of the Realm, one of whom is the Foreign Secretary, the Prime Minister, a Russian grand duke, and two Viscounts, I'm afraid the matter is out of your hands. Your aunt has already sent a telegram to Gresting Hall."

"Gresting Hall? Whatever for?"

"The family plate, the Gresting service, which apparently was purchased by the third Baron Betteridge for a state visit by George the Second in 1758, Mrs Bayton the housekeeper, twelve of Sir Hugh's former footmen with their house livery, and Mr Hungerford, your grandfather's former butler."

"Hungerford? Dammit, Clyford. Miles is my butler."

"Miles, sir, has no experience with dining on this scale. Mr Hungerford will arrive tomorrow and start to train the staff. Besides, Miles declined the offer of taking charge of the dining room, my lord, on account of his scar, which still bears stitches. He's fearful on account the ladies might find his disfigurement, unhealed as it is, gruesome, rather than as Mr Holland's suggested badge of honour—a duelling scar."

"I see. And what is there for me to do, Clyford? And you may stop smiling this moment, do you hear me?"

"Ah, my lord, I'd rather not be in your shoes when it comes to discussing the guest list with your aunt."

"My guest list?"

"To quote her ladyship, 'There are too many men! We must lose two!'"

"Well, that's one argument my good aunt will not win, Clyford."

"And why is that a problem, Lennard?" Travis asked.

"Because it's imperative that two of my male guests sit side-by-side over dinner, Travis, and if we were to lose two men in favour of two ladies, that positioning around the table would not be to my advantage."

"Affairs of state, I suppose? I'm rather intrigued."

"Well, you'll have a beautiful young woman on your arm, so you'll be oblivious of any behind the scenes machinations. I'm sure your attention will be completely taken."

"Me? I can't possibly attend, Lennard. I have nothing to wear ... wait! Which beautiful young woman will completely take my attention?"

"Mr Tavernier will call on you in the morning, Mr Holland," Clyford said before Lennard could answer him. "It seems you, sir, Mr Fahey, and Lord Betteridge are to be outfitted in the latest evening wear. The prince will be wearing it and therefore it would be considered déclassé if you three were not also to dress similarly for the occasion."

"Latest evening wear?"

"It's a smart outfit, my lord. Cutaway black tailcoat over black military-style trousers, side-seamed in black satin, with a white silk waistcoat, linen shirt, and stock of the same colour. Very elegant."

"I'm not sure I can—" Travis started to say.

"Your attire is a gift from Lady Winchester, Mr Holland."

"A gift from Lady Winchester? Why would she be so generous?"

"Well, sir, you're hardly going to be able to partner her niece, and his lordship's cousin by marriage, Miss Peters, in your old frock coat now, are you, sir? And, as you're no longer a naval officer, you can't wear your dress uniform, like Gerald and I shall. No, her ladyship was correct, her niece, Philomena, must take the arm of a man as smartly attired as any other in the room."

"Then I should prove churlish to decline her ladyship's very generous offer."

"You're blushing, Travis," Lennard said.

"It's warm, Lennard."

"Nothing to do with my cousin, Philomena, on your arm?

"Nothing at all, Lennard. Nothing."

"Well, let's take you home first, Travis. After that, I'll go to Bedford Square to face my aunt. I hope she has some decent scotch whisky at hand."

"Ah, I can guarantee you she has, my lord," Clyford said with a broad grin. "It's your very own, and she's holding court in your sitting room at Bexford House awaiting your return, no doubt with a list as long as your arm of suitable, unmarried, young heiresses not only to replace the two gentlemen she considers surplus to your dinner arrangements, but also as eligible marriage prospects for the continuity of the barony."

12. LENNARD ALEXANDRE MALLORAY, THE EIGHT BARON BETTERIDGE OF HAZLEMERE

"I'm absolutely convinced you've taken leave of your senses, Lenn," Elam said as he stretched out beside him in the grass. They were lying near the copse of whitebeams at the top of Primrose Hill, their horses tethered on loose rein nearby, grazing on the sweet, new growth of spring.

"I wanted to get you out here, away from the house, just you and me."

"Why?"

"Because there's something I've been meaning to tell you, and I thought here was the perfect place."

"I'm watching. Say what's on your mind. Although I can't think why it couldn't wait, Lenn, it's barely quarter past five in the morning."

"Because the morning, at the break of day, is the best time to talk of affairs of the heart."

"Ah, you own that you have one, do you?"

Lennard chuckled, winding his fingers through the back of Elam's hair. "I was jealous."

"Jealous of what?"

"Jealous of you and Paulsson and Hakan Zeybeck."

"What about Kosorukov?"

"You said he didn't touch you."

"He fondled me for a bit, but when he realised I wasn't interested in anything more, his attention turned elsewhere."

"It was the kissing, Elam. That's what made me jealous. You said their osculations were expert, and that you shared 'extremely voluptuous kisses'."

"That's the case, but no more voluptuous than your own, Lenn. Are you saying that you were jealous of me and wanted to be in my place, or jealous of them, for sharing their lips and tongues with me?"

"The latter, Elam. It's an odd thing that I should have been thinking of it, because you and I have consorted over the years with Gerald, and sometimes Angus, in threes, at other times all four of us together. At times, we've even shared ourselves with one or two others outside The Brothers."

"But?"

"But, since I've acceded to the barony, something has changed. Our roles as master and servant have become far more strictly defined. It's no longer Lenn and Elam in our two rooms in Jermyn Street, but the two of us living in a huge house, surrounded by servants, and defined by our divergent roles within the house. You're my valet, that's one thing, but now I see you thrust into a subservient role against my wishes, and yet there's nothing I can do about it."

Elam rolled onto his side, winding an arm over Lennard's chest and kissed him. "Once more, Malloray," he ordered, "and this time voluptuous, if you please."

Lennard obliged.

"Yours are far better than theirs, Lenn, because you kiss me with passion, not with lust in your heart."

"I do that sometimes," Lennard protested weakly.

Elam chuckled. "But you didn't just then. Now, jealousy. Let's talk of it."

"It was when I realised you couldn't be in the room this coming Saturday evening. Because of Kosorukov. I'll have to hide you away, as if I am ashamed of our relationship."

"It's for the greater good, Lenn. What else would be possible?"

"What else? If I had my way to change the world, you are the dearest person to me in my life and I'd choose to have you at my side forever, out in the open, unabashed of our friendship."

"Friendship?"

"I dare not speak the other word, Elam. Every other person in my life for whom I've expressed that affection has been taken from me. Without you, what would the point be?"

Elam was so moved, he rolled onto his back, gritting his teeth while staring into the sky. Despite their adventures with other men, he loved no one like he did Lennard, yet was fearful of saying the words too, so afraid was the man at his side of hearing them used in connection to himself.

"The next few days will be dreadfully busy, Elam. That's why I wanted to speak what was on my chest. We'll probably only see each other in bed, at night, or when we're changing clothing during the day. I'm not ashamed of feeling jealous, it's helped me realise how much I care for you."

"We could always visit Mrs Hedger's together, Lenn. Drag Karl Paulsson into a private room with one of Martin's other gentlemen consorts and taste fruit from a different tree."

"Different? What do you mean, different?"

"Because I have a hankering to lay back and let them do what they like to me while you watch. I rather like the way jealousy sits on you, Lennard, if it causes you to talk of deeper things."

"I'm not sure I could cope with that, Elam."

"Cope with what? Jealousy?"

"No, the sight of you being taken by two other men."

"There's a shape in your britches telling me something quite different, Lennard Malloray."

*****

They'd bathed together before breakfast, luxuriating in the newly installed bathtub, in what had originally been a wig and powder chamber attached to Lennard's bedroom. Finished not four days previously, all the new bathrooms in Bexford House were provided with hot water from a boiler system in the basement. To have a special room, dedicated solely to bathing, was the newest of fashionable modifications all over London and because of that, and with the enticement to spread the word among the gentry, the installation costs had been minimal, but still only afforded by the very wealthy.

"A house with six bathrooms and as many water closets!" Lennard had exclaimed after the pipe workers and the boilermaker had finished.

"It is easy, my lord, in old houses such as yours. There are cavities between every wall and there are passageways behind most of them so the servants can move about and not be seen," the man had said. "No need to rip up walls and replaster to run the pipes throughout this building. The tiler will be here for two days from tomorrow and after he's finished, you'll be as clean as Her Majesty, every day of the year."

Lennard had no idea how the man had any idea of the ablutions of the nation's sovereign, but he had paid him his invoice on the spot, something obviously exceedingly unusual because the workman's eyes bulged. Lennard was doubtful he'd ever seen a twenty-pound note before.

"Gerald spent nearly an hour in his bath yesterday," Elam said, as he towelled Lennard dry.

"How do you know that?"

"I think he was rather hoping Clyford might come looking for him."

"I think that's a lost cause, to be honest, Elam."

"Why?"

"Because, although I think Clyford finds him attractive, there seems to be no 'spark', from his side, in any case."

"Spark?"

"He smiles and blushes, but his eyes don't follow Gerald around the room when no one's looking."

Elam smiled. "Like yours do me, you mean?"

Lennard chuckled and began to finish drying Elam.

"What are your plans for today, Lenn? Or should I negotiate your movements with Clyford?"

"Mr Tavernier from Poole's will be here this morning to bring fabric samples for our evening wear. While he's here, I shall have you fitted for a new travelling outfit, a new set of clothes for the evening, and another for when you accompany me on social visits as my personal manservant—dear God, I hate that term."

"It is what it is. And after Tavernier?"

"I said I'd help Travis. He's to move into Birch House today and I'd like you to come with me, if you don't mind. When my aunt was here last evening, Clyford alerted me to the fact that Sir Hugh's estate had seen probate, and at the same time, the Solicitor-General has sent the petition for my title to Her Majesty. She will sign it tomorrow, most likely, so it will be gazetted on Saturday, just in time for my official coming out into society that same evening. I'll have to call in to see Drudge this afternoon, to deal with that matter and another I've arranged with my aunt"—a knock at the door caused Lennard to pause—"who is it?" he called out.

"It's me," Gerald replied, entering the bathroom without waiting for an invitation. "I hope I caught you *in delicto*," he said with a very cheeky grin.

"Too late for that, Gerald," Lennard answered. "You needed to be on Primrose Hill this morning at sunrise ... and good morning to you."

"Good morning," Gerald said. "I'm off now. I thought I'd let you know that if I don't manage to catch the last train this evening, I'll be back first thing tomorrow."

"Off? Where to?"

"To Gresting Hall, of course. Now I'm the estate manager, it's fallen to me to arrange the transport of the 'great service' as your aunt calls it, the family plate, most of the table linen, pick out which of the lads are still able to perform table service, and, while I'm at it, make sure they haven't outgrown their uniforms. They'll arrive with Hungerford tomorrow morning. Christopher is taking me to Paddington station to greet Mrs Bayton, who will arrive this morning. Once the compartments have been cleaned, I'll be taking the same train back to High Wycombe. Christopher will bring Mrs Bayton here."

"Wait, Gerald. Felicity Bayton arrives this morning? It was only last evening that my aunt spoke of the details."

"Did you not wonder what had happened to Stephen yesterday, Lennard? He was supposed to come back from Bedford Gardens, and yet you found Clyford waiting in your coach when you left Baron Hochschild's residence."

"He was sent to Gresting?"

Gerald nodded. "Now, are you two going to put some clothes on or stand there flaunting your nudity in front of a man who's running late to catch his train?"

"We could bend you over the bathtub for a quick one, if you wish, Gerald," Lennard said with a wink.

"Lennard, the barony has done something to your mind. You never used to speak so saucily. Power, that's what's done it!"

Lennard laughed. "You know I was joking. However, if you arrive home when we're already in bed, you know how to wake us."

"I shall thump you with my night-stick, like the Peelers do."

"Oh, so you've been practising with the constabulary, have you?

"You'd be the first to know. Both of you."

Lennard and Elam looked at each other and in unison, said, "I doubt it."

*****

Lennard had just finished dressing when Merrill arrived to tell him the dining room and public rooms were ready for his inspection, and that Hungerford was waiting downstairs for him.

For two days, the house had been so packed with people running from room to room that he'd kept right out of the way, deciding that morning to visit Travis with Elam, and to take the doctor to lunch. After, they'd attended an exhibition in Piccadilly. When he and Elam had returned a little after half past five, they'd taken the servants' back stairs to Lennard's room and had bathed before Lennard had started to dress for dinner.

"Please, my lord, I hope you'll like what has been done," Hungerford said, opening the dining room door.

Lennard almost gasped, and might have, had not his grin been so broad that he'd been unable to. The room looked magnificent. Two newly installed gasoliers illuminated the dining table, set regimentally with rows of perfectly placed cutlery, glasses, and table decorations. In the soft yellow light from above, everything either glowed or sparkled, enhanced by the highly polished reflective surface of the mahogany table.

"It's spectacular, Hungerford. I've never seen such a beautiful thing in my life."

"Thank you, my lord. I'll make sure to send word to Mrs Bayton and I'll thank the staff on your behalf."

"No, no, Hungerford. It's something I'll do myself. I'm aware of protocol, but you forget that I knew many of them when they were but boys and young lasses, now men and women in their twenties and thirties. I know it's not a thing to be encouraged, but I'd like you to bring all the staff up here—those who aren't busy about other things. It will only take a few minutes, but I'd like them to see the result of their efforts, and to give some words of encouragement. It's a new start for us all and, as the first Baron Betteridge to host a grand dinner in Bexford House since the celebration of the engagement of my dear aunt, Lady Winchester, over forty years ago, I think a few words are in order."

"Ah, that was a splendid evening, Lennard … I mean, my lord—"

Lennard chuckled. "Please, when we are in private, it's acceptable to call me by the name you always have. It's only our second meeting since I've become the master of the house, you are forgiven."

"It won't happen again, sir."

"Please, Hungerford, if indeed you can't bring yourself to continue to call me by my Christian name when in private, I should consider it an honour for you to call me 'Master Lennard' as you used to when I was a lad. I shan't be offended and it would afford me a great deal of pleasure."

Hungerford smiled, dropping his head a little, no doubt to hide his emotions. "Very well, my lord. But forgive me if I might find that difficult at times. Respect for titles and standing is bred into such men as me: those who serve ladies and gentlemen of quality."

"Now, you attended my aunt's engagement party?"

"Yes, my lord. At the time, I was under-butler and sometimes valet to your great-great-grandfather, but I stood at service during the evening. There were sixty at table then."

"Sixty? At this table?"

"Yes sir, the spare leaves for its extension are still stored in the attic, should your lordship wish to hold a more substantial formal dinner."

"And I was worried about seating twenty-six," Lennard said. Despite his assumptions that no more than twelve, perhaps sixteen, of the guests he'd invited would accept, all twenty-four had sent prompt replies. "Tonight's dinner must seem a trifle compared to a party of sixty, Hungerford."

"Were it for four, my lord, it would still get the same care and attention, I promise you."

"What was it like, my great-aunt's engagement party?"

"It was in 1813, a few days after the great battle of Salamanca, during the Peninsula Wars. The house was filled with friends of your great-grandfather. Some of them, now long gone, refugees from France who'd fled from the revolution twenty years beforehand. You've never seen so many jewels and decorations worn by people who depended on the charity of others."

"I can understand, Hungerford. Perhaps that's all they had left of their lives in the *Ancien Régime*, like me and my farm breeches."

"Your farm breeches?"

"Don't you remember when I was ill with scarlatina and I stayed under Uncle Arthur's care? It seemed to be months that I was sick—"

"Now I remember, my lord. On the first day you were allowed out of bed, you pulled on a pair of old rags, ran outside and rolled in the mud at the back of the stables before we could stop you."

"It itched so much, Hungerford. Something inside me told me it was the best thing to do, and when Uncle Arthur told me that he'd thrown those breeches into the midden, I ran back outside to retrieve them. They reminded me of how close I came to dying. I've kept them all these years."

"Why on earth would you keep something like that?"

"Because they'd been my father's, Hungerford. He'd been intent on becoming a farmer, remember? How he used to get out and get dirty in the harvest, me on his back?"

Hungerford said nothing, but grunted a little, unwilling to meet

Lennard's eye. He placed his hand gently on Lennard's shoulder. "I'll summon the staff, my lord."

"Before you go, Hungerford. Captain Langbourne told me he was bringing the table linen from Gresting Hall, and yet I see the table is uncovered?"

"Ah, if I may explain. Only the wealthiest of houses dine without a cloth. It's a signal they can have the table re-lacquered and polished, and not worry about the cost. Besides, this table was the pride and joy of the fourth Baron Betteridge. It was made entirely from one enormous tree over one hundred and twenty years ago. It has the most beautiful patina, my lord. It seemed such a shame to hide it in light of these beautiful surroundings."

"Is everything about money, Hungerford?"

"No, my lord. Sometimes showing wealth in a quiet, understated manner is about status. Everyone will talk about the quality of your dining room after this evening. It is one of the things upon which every gentleman or lady of quality is judged by their peers—their ability to entertain in style."

Hungerford bowed then left, leaving Lennard to wander around the dining room, marvelling at how wonderfully it had been decorated for the evening. The entire house was filled with boughs of greenery and early flowering bushes, all brought down by rail from Gresting. Every corner of every room seemed to be filled with tall vases of flowers on plinths, burdened with cherry blossom, mimosa, tall lilies, racemes of winter holly, still bright and berried. No doubt the cost of the additional out-of-season flowers from the Charter Market would be eye-watering, but that was only if he thought of it in terms of his former life. This morning, he'd written cheques for hundreds, a drop in the ocean for his current account.

He was admiring the arrayed silver and crystal vases on the table, spilling over with bright blooms and ferns, which would be removed before food was served, when Merrill knocked at the door and asked whether it would be timely to admit the staff, who'd assembled in the hallway.

"Please, Merrill. Tell them not to be shy. I only wish to say a few words."

Quietly, one by one, the dining room filled: those who worked in Bexford House, including twelve footmen from Gresting, hastily refitted into the formal house livery by an army of seamstresses Mr Tavernier had produced, seemingly out of thin air, four stable footmen, loaned by Angus to greet guests on the stairs as they arrived in their coaches, and a small army of kitchen workers, all nervously inspecting their surroundings as they filed into the room.

"I've never felt so nervous in my life," Lennard said, then joined in with the unexpected laughter of the nearly forty other souls in the room. "It should have been my dear Uncle Arthur standing here this evening. Had it not been him, then my beloved father, sadly taken well before his time … which leaves me, the forgotten son of the brother of the brother of the heir to the estate, the man who eschewed the life of a titled family in favour of working in an office on behalf of Crown and country."

Lennard continued. "However, if I've learned anything during my years, it is the unexpected nature of the turn of events. Within a heartbeat a life can be taken, and from that last heartbeat onwards, the duty of maintaining the lifeblood of a family or dynasty falls into another man's chest, whether he wants it or not."

There were many murmurings of shared sadness. His grandfather, his uncle Arthur, and his own father had been much beloved by everyone at Gresting.

"I didn't expect to make a maudlin speech, but it seems my heart has led me to fields other than those I thought I might be harvesting this evening. It does one good to look around oneself for a few moments and to enjoy what we have now. It's the reason I asked you upstairs this evening, to see the fruits of your labours, for it is you who have done this, not me. It is as much yours as it is mine, and I'm eternally grateful for the love imbued in the positioning of every glass on this magnificent table, on the spotless cleanliness of every utensil and plate, the gleam of the floors, the care and attention to every aspect of this beautiful, but long-neglected house."

Lennard couldn't help but be moved by the wide smiles and soft, almost-whispered acknowledgments in response to his words. Nevertheless, he cleared his throat and continued.

"Please, I hope you will share my pride when I welcome some of the most important ladies and gentlemen in the land at table this evening. I thank you, in advance, on behalf of the Prime Minister, the Foreign Secretary, and the Home Secretary. Their greatest compliment will be if they say nothing, but simply thank me for the evening when they leave, for it is then that I'll know that *we* have succeeded."

*****

"How do you feel, Lennard?" his aunt asked.

She'd arrived nearly half an hour earlier than expected, and after having given her seal of approval to the public rooms and the dining room, had taken his place in the entrance hall of Bexford House in order to greet his guests as they arrived.

"Extremely nervous, aunt," he replied. "I'm not sure how I should behave. Is it full bows, or head bows? I've never been at the head of a receiving queue before."

"I shall give you a clue. Hungerford will announce each guest as they arrive. If I clear my throat once, it's a head-bow. Twice, and it's a full bow. If I say nothing at all, it's a handshake, understood? I shall ask you to lend me your arm when the Crown Prince and his sister are presented, as I shall be forced to perform a full curtsey, something not easily accomplished at my age."

Lennard chuckled and kissed her cheek. "I'm still nervous though, aunt."

"You've no reason to be so, my dear. The house is magnificent. The appointments you've made in such a short period of time are extraordinary. And may I remind you that, after our business arrangement and your visit to Simeon Drudge two days ago, you are now the wealthiest man in the room by far, and no doubt they'll all have heard of it."

"They will?"

"It does nothing to hide the wealth of the barony behind the veil of minor aristocracy, Lennard. Now you have my estate as part of your personal fortune, you could easily purchase an hereditary duchy from your petty cash book and not notice the balance substantially reduced. I've made sure news has been circulated."

Lennard smiled at her exaggerated turn of phrase. However, there had been some truth in it. It had been his aunt Caroline's idea to divest herself of what she considered a millstone around her neck. She'd decided to pass on her entire fortune to Lennard, who would eventually have been her heir in any case. In exchange, the Gresting Estate was to manage her country house, Foxley Manor, and her London House in Bedford Square. She'd also have an open checking account, drawing on Lennard's personal holdings, and receive a monthly allowance of one thousand pounds, more money than anyone could spend, no matter how hard they tried.

"Now I shall be free to accept suitors," she'd said to Lennard at Drudge's chambers, while perusing the document. "With no fortune to steal, the only thing they could take would be my heart."

"Aunt Caroline!" Lennard had replied, in mock shock.

"Line them up, I say!" she'd added, before signing the document.

He was immensely mindful of that rejoinder as they stood passing small talk while they waited for his guests. He had noticed immediately, the moment Merrill had taken her cloak, how beautifully attired she was. He'd entrusted the family parure to her, to use until his own marriage—a never-to-be occurrence as far as he was concerned, but his vague assurance had pacified her.

She had her own jewellery, soon to be augmented by his purchase from Rothschild's for her birthday, but the Betteridge diamonds and rubies were outstanding. He did not doubt for one moment that she was still a great beauty, despite her sixty years, and was about to comment on the fact when he was interrupted.

"The first carriages are arriving, my lord," Merrill announced.

Even though it was mid-April and the weather comparatively warm, his aunt had insisted that the fire in the entrance hall be lit. It was a signal to the guests that their welcome would also be warm—he had so much to learn, he'd thought when she'd explained the reason, but now with the fire adding a bright glow to the foyer and issuing the soft scent of imported firewood from the east, he understood that, for the aristocracy, there were symbols in everything.

"Ah, here we are," his aunt said. "No need for throat clearing. Half bow to the Home Secretary, who is a baronet. Although being your senior in the civil service, he is a guest in your house and you outrank him. He will bow his head and you should take his hand and shake it. Lady Grey looks magnificent, and the family sapphires too! What beautiful jewellery …"

His aunt's voice faded into the background as Lennard concentrated on what he should say and to whom. But then, Sir George's bright smile and glowing appraisal of the entrance hall as he accompanied his wife to greet Lennard and Lady Winchester made him forget his nerves. He even managed a smile at Lady Anna's quick curtsey as he kissed the back of her gloved wrist.

*****

Lennard need not have worried. For although he'd never attended a formal dinner of such prominence before, even as a guest, everything was strictly choreographed by Hungerford, who ruled over the room like a major-domo, despite his nearly eighty years.

Soupes, Poissons, Entrées, Relevés, Rôtis, Salade, Entremets, and finally, a *Bonne Bouche*, all served *service à la russe*, each course carefully presented then whisked away silently by the small army of sixteen footmen who waited on table.

Mr Huilot had been beside himself when he'd heard the guests of honour were cousins of Prince Albert. He'd organised his *brigade de cuisine* in such an efficient manner that, to the delight of Lennard's guests, they'd been offered a choice of dishes for each of the courses. It was something practically unheard of, mainly because of the enormous cost. However, what was not eaten at table would not go to waste, as Lennard had promised what had not been consumed as a great feast for all his staff in the downstairs servant's hall at the end of the meal, after his guests had gathered in the drawing room.

While the roasts were being prepared on the sideboard, Lennard had arranged for Merrill to speak to him over his shoulder, and he'd excused himself to his guests momentarily, making his way to the servant's corridor that ran behind the northern wall of the dining room, in which Elam had been observing, through a spy hole, Kosorukov and Astley seated side-by-side.

"Anything?" Lennard had said.

"Kiss first, Lenn." Lennard obliged. "Oh, my, you taste of goose liver!"

"Mr Huilot isn't paid enough, Elam. That ragoût of foie gras in pastry was so delicious I could have eaten just that for every course. Don't worry, I've made sure there's plenty for you."

"They've chatted briefly, Lenn. Nothing important has passed between them, except …"

"Except what?"

"They're obviously very well-acquainted. Their conversation is not one of a grand duke meeting an Irish baronet for the first time—there's a great deal of familiarity in their choice of words. There's only been one thing and I missed the end of it because Astley dipped his head halfway through the sentence and blotted his lips with his table napkin, hiding what he was saying."

"Which was?"

"Kosorukov asked, 'Have you heard anything I should know of?' To which, Astley replied, 'not yet, but hopefully next—' and that was all."

"I'll have to return, sorry. Everything is in place for later, after we join the ladies in the drawing room. I'll keep you informed as much as I'm able to."

"Enjoy yourself, Lenn."

"I would a lot more if you were sitting at my side."

*****

Lennard returned, apologising for his sudden absence, in time for champagne and dessert.

As glasses were filled, he rose to his feet and proposed a toast to their Royal Highnesses, the Prince and Princess Saxe-Meiningen, his distinguished guests, and finally to Her Majesty the Queen.

During his speech, which as the host of the dinner was expected of him, he noted that while all the guests regarded him with respect, if not affection, it was Kosorukov alone who kept his eyes on the table. Beside him, Astley sat, his eyes narrowed, inspecting Lennard as he spoke. Lennard recognised that look and it made him extremely uneasy. There was no mistaking it. Astley could not have signalled lustful thoughts more clearly had he licked his lips.

No doubt at the end of the following week, lustful thoughts would be forgotten. The *Pendragon* was due to set sail from La Corunna on the morrow, and seven days after his attendance at Lennard's dinner, Astley's vessel would either be sailing to Ireland, having imported no contraband, or it would be impounded by Her Majesty's customs officers, to be offered up for sale to the person who offered the highest sealed tender. Lennard intended to be that person, although perhaps in the acquisition of the *Pendragon*, he might thus unavoidably disclose his hand in the whole affair.

At the end of his speech, he turned to Angus and announced to his guests that his close boyhood friend, the Viscount Fallerton, had asked Lennard's permission to make an announcement.

Rising to his feet, Angus took his wife's hand across the table, leaned over and kissed it. "After a visit to our estimable new friend, Dr Travis Holland, yesterday, I'm delighted to announce that my good lady wife and I will be expecting our first child before Christmas."

Lennard noticed nothing but happiness and excitement from his guests as a toast was called, accompanied by clapping and words of congratulation and delight. There was only one man whose face did not show pleasure. He made a show of it, but Terrence Astley seemed to disclose a hint of malicious enjoyment. Lennard could not understand why his former lover should appear to relish some sardonic pleasure upon hearing news of such importance to Angus, who—as far as Lennard knew—was a relative stranger to Astley.

*****

News of the acquisition of his aunt's business interests, estates, and fortune, formerly managed by her late husband's bankers, had reached the ears of all the gentlemen, and toasts were offered again to Lennard's great good fortune.

The Prime Minister played billiards with Sir George, while Christian

Jost, the Prince Saxe-Meiningen, chatted with Angus and Robert, Kosorukov, and Travis. The Marquess of Twinton sat with George Henry, Sir George's son, on a chaise, laughing at something, while Lennard, Gerald, and Clyford sat at a small table playing a few hands of whist. Hungerford moved among the gentlemen, a cut-crystal carafe in his hand filled with Lennard's grandfather's best port, the third bottle of which had just been strained and decanted.

"Another five minutes, my lord," Hungerford said after Lennard had declined a refill of his glass.

"Very good, Hungerford. I'll depend on you to rally us gentlemen when it's time to return to the ladies."

"The new evening wear from Poole's is extraordinarily fetching on you, Lennard," Gerald said after Hungerford had moved on.

"As it is on Mr Holland and on Robert, I'm sure, Gerald. But nothing compares to how splendid you two are, decked out in your military finery. I'm sure I could buy a new ship with the bullion that went to make your epaulettes, ropes, and frogging."

"Surely you've seen us in uniform before, Lennard?"

"No, I haven't. Not this uniform at least."

"They're our regimental formal dress uniforms. Only trotted out for best. Now, why are we here at a card table when you should be mingling, doing business deals, and seeing to your guests?"

"I shall do that once we join the ladies for there are plans afoot. Clyford has said nothing?"

Gerald shook his head.

"Well done then, Clyford," Lennard said, turning to him. "You've been remarkably busy this past week, Gerald, and I'll enlighten you either after the guests have left tonight or in the morning. But I wanted to ask you to help Clyford, should he require it. During the evening, while Astley is keeping his eye on his niece and George Henry, I'd like to make it impossible for Kosorukov to sit anywhere but in that double-backed chaise in the salon."

"The one with seats on either side and a shared back?"

"Indeed. We must make sure that no one who speaks French is able to sit next to him."

"Why?"

"Because Robert and I intend to have a moment pretending to talk about the reason I was fetched away during dinner, and we will converse in French, loudly enough that Kosorukov, seated behind us will overhear."

"Ah!"

"I thought it wise to ask you now. Clyford, Robert, Sir George, Angus, and Lord Palmerston are aware of the plan, but you may be needed."

"The Prime Minister is involved?"

"And I hadn't told you earlier, Gerald, because it's taken some organising to make sure everything is ready. Clyford?"

"Yes, my lord?"

"Would you mind talking to the Foreign Secretary for a moment, he seems to be looking for something on the bookshelves."

"Immediately, sir."

"What was that all about, Lennard? Getting rid of Clyford like that?"

"You don't know Astley, do you?"

"I've met him once or twice. Why?"

"There was a look on his face when Angus announced that Adelia was with child that I can't put my finger on. However, would you mind spending a few moments being convivial with him later this evening, mention Angus's good news, and judge his reaction? It may be nothing, but I trust your senses. You have a gift, Gerald, an ability to see into men's hearts by the looks in their eyes."

"Then why am I so unlucky in love, Lennard?"

"Because, my dear friend, you spend too much time looking for lust, not for love."

*****

Angus and the prince had just finished playing a piano duet allowing Angus, finally, time to speak to Lennard alone.

"Congratulations, Angus. You managed the accolades of impending fatherhood with great aplomb," Lennard said.

"Far easier than the copulations that have brought about such happy news."

Lennard chuckled. "And now?"

"And now, I shall be free to sleep with whomever I wish, until it's time for another infant."

"Such an inaccurate turn of phrase when it comes to you, Angus."

"What is?"

"The word 'sleep' generally refers to connections in a bed."

Angus laughed heartily, unable to stifle it. Most of the guests were aware of his loud guffaw and merely raised their eyebrows and smiled.

"Tell me something. Do you know Astley?"

"Know him? I've had little to do with him, Lennard. I read reports of him and I greet him at social functions, or if we ever cross paths in the house when I'm visiting Sir George. Why do you ask?"

"It's nothing …"

"I hope you didn't mean know him *biblically*, Lennard?"

"No, of course not. Not even you would stoop so low, Angus."

Angus managed to bite the back of his wrist this time, to stop his loud chortle before it escaped his lips. "Is everything in place?"

"Yes, Angus. It's all been worked out step by step. The moment your wife moves to the pianoforte, my aunt will hand over my cousin, Philomena, to the care of Travis, who will lead her to the lover's seat on the far side of the room. That's my cue to take my place on this side of the double chaise, and for the Prime Minister to ask Kosorukov to join him on the other side. Of course, the moment Adelia starts to play, they'll have to stop chatting and that's when Robert will join me."

"Won't it appear ill-mannered for you to speak while my wife is playing?"

"It's not a concert, Angus. The Prime Minister told me it's not unusual for people who are far enough away from the performer to continue conversations. It's no disrespect to the performer."

"Well, you'd best hurry, Lennard, for I see Adelia is rising from her seat, and the very perambulations are starting to unfold before my eyes. Good luck."

*****

There's a certain posture, a slight rigidity to the position of the head on its neck, that Lennard recognised as an attempt by someone who wanted to appear to be absorbed in something else, but who was concentrating on another thing altogether.

Such was Kosorukov's apparent indifference semaphored to Lennard almost the moment Robert sat down beside him and asked, in French, why Lennard had been drawn away from the table in the middle of dinner.

"It was a message from the wharf," Lennard explained, leaning close to Robert, directly behind Kosorukov's head. He could not have avoided hearing what they were discussing.

"Surely they could have pulled me away?"

"Far easier for me, as the host, to attend to matters of extreme importance, Robert."

"What was the problem?"

"Those huge guns."

"Which huge guns?"

"The shipment being loaded onto the *Caroline*, Robert. How many guns do we ship for the War Office? The cargo load is too heavy so I've ordered the shipment of Irish corned beef to be unloaded and sent on Friday this week onboard the *Princess Henriette*. Those bombards have to go at the bottom of the hold, such is their weight, and the dockmaster wanted permission to unload everything then redistribute the placement of everything else before she sails on Monday."

"Thank you for taking care of it, Lennard. I'm quite grateful I wasn't pulled away at that precise moment. I was enjoying a wonderful conversation with the Grand Duchess Kosorukova. She's a delight."

"As is her husband," Lennard added, smothering a smirk. "Anyway, you'll get to meet them again, socially, at my aunt's house in Bedford Square."

"I will?"

"Yes, it's been rather delayed, but my aunt is intending to introduce the grand duke and duchess to the Quaiseys sometime toward the end of the month."

"The Quaiseys?"

"Yes, I believe they have someone in common."

"Who? Explain yourself, Lennard."

"Why, the grand duke and Lady Evelyn of course. She's in need of help with the refurbishment of their London house and the grand duke is the paragon of fashion. I believe she wishes to ask his advice."

Lennard could not help but notice the ever so slight twitch at the corner of the grand duke's mouth, who'd turned his head ever so slightly to better hear the conversation.

"And why me?"

"Well, as you're now a fabulously wealthy bachelor, I imagine it's the first of such introductions into society, Robert. My aunt believes no man should be without a wife."

*****

When Lennard eventually staggered into his bedroom, Elam was sitting up eating fruitcake with a bottle of sherry next to the bed. "How was it?"

"Exhausting," Lennard replied, throwing himself face down onto the bed.

"The plan?"

"Executed flawlessly."

"So now it's just a matter of waiting."

"Kosorukov and Paulsson are due to have their regular meeting tomorrow at Mrs Hedger's. The packet to Sweden sails two days after that. Baron Hochschild will read Paulsson's letter to his sister and then we'll know one way or another whether Kosorukov is sending information to his former compatriots."

"Have you had any thoughts on Kosorukov and Astley, regarding their strange conversation, Lenn?"

"None. I think it might be wise to interview everyone who's ever been assigned to shadow either of them, to find out how and where they might have met in the past."

"Do you think they're …"

"Fucking?

"Lennard Malloray, that's such an explosive word to use to a man like me. A man who's sensitive to—"

"Gutter talk?" Elam laughed and got out of bed, hauling Lennard to his feet.

"Let's get you undressed and into bed. Then we can discuss gutter talk for as long as you like."

"No more than five minutes is your usual limit, Elam—"

"Why did you stop just now? Did you hear something?"

"I think it's Gerald knocking softly at our door. Do you ...?"

"I fancy watching you and him for a while, before I—"

"Come in!" Lennard called out loudly, interrupting Elam's words.

"I'm drunk," Gerald said from the doorway.

"Too drunk?" Elam asked over Lennard's shoulder.

"Never that drunk, Elam."

"Then you'd best get yourself in here, Captain Langbourne."

Gerald performed a tipsy salute and, after closing the door behind him, ran across the room and jumped, landing on his back on the bed with a loud "Huzzah!"

Lennard smiled; his hands clasped in the small of Elam's back. "What shall we do with him, Elam?"

"I know what I'm going to do, Lennard. The question is what are *you* going to do while I'm about it?"

13. TWO CAN PLAY AT THAT GAME

Early on Wednesday, not long after Lennard had begun to discuss the business of the day with Clyford, Merrill interrupted them.

"I beg your pardon, my lord, but a letter has just arrived, and the courier is waiting for a reply."

"Courier?"

"He's from a poste dispatch service, my lord."

"Give it here then, Merrill," Lennard replied.

Poste dispatch services were only used by the wealthy who did not wish their missives to be recognised by the livery of the person delivering them, or by the face of the man who brought the letter to the door.

"Fetch my coat, if you please, Merrill, and send word that I'll ride out on Chester."

"Immediately, my lord."

"What on earth has you in such a fluster?" Clyford asked immediately the footman had left to attend to Lennard's orders.

"It's from the Baron Hochschild."

"He has news?"

"He doesn't say, but what he does say is that he's visiting Travis at ten in the morning, and he'd like me to show him around the garden. Obviously, he wants to meet with me and seemingly by chance. If I were to go to his house or he to come here ..."

"So he thinks he's being shadowed?"

"Have you heard anything from the office?"

"Not at all. Mind you, I'm not as au fait as you are. Surely, you'd have heard something?"

"Not a whisper. I'll write out a very quick response to the baron saying I was intending to be there to speak with the Huskersons at the same time as his appointment with Travis and I'd be delighted to talk roses to him ... although I know some of the names, I'm sure I'm as in the dark about them as he most likely is."

"A wise precaution, in case someone else might read your note."

"I'll ask you to give it to the courier then make haste to the Home Office and ask Angus whether there's any ongoing surveillance on the baron. If there is none, and the Swedish attaché believes there is, then a third party is involved and Her Majesty's government needs to know who it is."

"Shall I come to Birch House directly after?"

"Yes, but back here first. I'd like you to bring Miles. Travis was to have visited later this afternoon to remove the stitches from his cheek. It will provide an excuse for you to be there, so your arrival doesn't look contrived."

"I'm starting to believe you think the baron isn't the only one who might be under surveillance, my lord. Do you suspect that someone is keeping an eye on your movements?"

"I have the greatest faith that my dear friend, Angus Spratt, has one or two shadowers of his own keeping watch on all his friends. Not for any other reason than care for our well-being. However, until I speak with Baron Hochschild this is all conjecture. Now, let me write him a quick letter and we'll get about our business."

*****

"I'm still shaking, Lennard. Lend me your arm, please."

"Of course, baron. Is it your leg? I thought by now that—"

"My leg is painless thanks to your good friend, Dr Holland. It's the pain in my heart, Lennard. I loved that boy like he was my own. Such treachery, and under my own roof."

"Here, sir. I see Mr Huskerson has replaced the garden seat against the east-facing wall of the garden. We can sit in the morning sun and you can let loose your ire to your heart's content. I'm a good listener."

Lennard glanced up in time to see Clyford and Miles walking up the pathway to the front door of Birch House. Clyford quickly shook his head. The news from the Home Office must have proved negative. If the Baron Hochschild was being watched, it had not been ordered by Sir George, or anyone else in the department.

"It was but three lines, Lennard. If not for those, I'd not be in such a state of distress."

"Perhaps, when you find a moment, you might share them with me?"

"Just let me quash the violent rage within my breast. Ah, damme!"

"What is it baron?"

"That I be taken for such a fool, Lennard."

"No one has taken you for a fool, sir, if you'll allow me to comment. Karl Paulsson has not deceived you, except by omission. He has not lied to you, has he?"

"No, he has not. But—"

"But nothing, sir. You are vexed because he has, apparently, committed an act of treason within your establishment that might be linked to you, ruin your reputation, and what is worse, perhaps jeopardise the forthcoming November Treaty. Am I correct?"

"Is that Elam I see at the back of the house, Lennard?"

"Like us, he's sitting in the sun, absorbing the warmth and, from what I can see at this distance, tamping his pipe."

"I wonder if you'd be good enough to ask him to enquire whether Mr Huskerson might bring me a glass of brandy, Lennard."

"There's no need, I'll do it myself, sir. Leave Elam to his sunshine."

"You must not spoil your servants, Lennard, if I may be so bold to say. There's no need to be rude or dismissive of them, but it's their position, to look after their masters."

"Indeed, baron. But you forget that Elam is my valet, not my manservant as such. Were there a footman abroad, then perhaps I'd fetch him. But, seeing that Elam is not only my friend from childhood but also my confidant, then allow me the pleasure of fetching a brandy ... for the three of us."

The baron raised his eyebrows, but then shrugged. "Bring the bottle, if there is one. I'll send around a replacement."

"There's no need, baron. It's my cellar, to which Mr Holland has free access as part of his lease on the house."

"Good heavens, perhaps I should procure a room here myself!"

Lennard chuckled, lit a cheroot, then stood, about to head toward the back of Birch House, but hesitated. "Why did you want to meet here, baron? Do you think someone might be eavesdropping on your private conversations?"

"No, it's absolutely nothing like that, Lennard. I was so distressed after reading Karl's letter yesterday that I couldn't sleep. Everyone was aware of my agitation and had I sent a note to ask you to come to my house, people may have wondered why. If anything comes of this dreadful situation, I can't afford to have anyone put two and two together. I was merely being cautious."

Lennard was somewhat relieved at the baron's sensible precaution. "We'd erroneously jumped to the conclusion that you thought you may have been being spied upon."

"Dear heavens, Lennard! Am I?"

"Not by us, my friend ... tell me, your reaction just then. You seemed rather startled."

"I hadn't thought about it much until just then when you posited the suggestion. But there's been a man ..."

"A man?"

"Yes, in the alleyway behind my house. You know, at the side elevation, where there's a passage runs alongside the wall. From my study, I sometimes notice a man, quite distinctly dressed, who leans against the brick wall on the other side of the alleyway. He's always there, most days, between four and five when I'm having tea. I often drink it while standing to get away from my desk and I like to observe the comings and goings down in the street."

"Distinctly dressed you said?"

"Yes, he wears a square-cut coat, open at the front, a waistcoat, trousers, and a round brimmed hat."

"That's hardly distinctive, sir."

"I was getting to that, Lennard. The edges of both of his coat fronts have a row of large pearl buttons from the neckline to the hem and around the sides."

"Does he smoke a clay pipe? Long, very long, with a curve near the bowl that tilts the end?"

"Why, how did you know? Are you acquainted with this gentleman?"

"No, not personally, sir, but I can tell you he's a costermonger, and how you describe him is their habitual dress."

"But he has no barrow, Lennard. None that I can see."

"Four to five you said?"

"Yes."

"I shouldn't worry about it. I'll see that it's taken care of."

"'Taken care of' sounds so ominous, Lennard."

"Nothing like that, sir. I'll have someone from the Home Office have a word with him this afternoon and we'll find out why he's there. Now, brandy. Are you still thirsting for a drop?"

"Indeed, I am, thank you."

"Then I'll see to it. I'll send Elam over on my way into the house. He's very educated, I'm sure you'll find him charming, even if he is just my valet."

*****

"Caroline Bombadera, the woman I've had my eye on, left London this morning and my heart is broken. It's a heavy weight on my heart, but she says her life will be happier. Her beefy friend, the noble Henriette, will follow fully laden on the twenty-first."

Lennard turned to the Home Secretary after he read out the translation of what the Baron Hochschild had discovered in Karl Paulsson's letter—the three sentences that had broken the attaché's heart.

"Caroline Bombadera is hardly deep code. Why did he bother?" Sir

George asked, his brow furrowed. Lennard recognised the look as one of annoyance mixed with confusion.

"And the mention that the *Princess Henriette* will be transporting Irish beef? Why was that included? Although it's a truth, I added it to my conversation to give it colour and credence."

"I've heard rumour the Russians are finding it difficult to victual some of their garrisons, Lennard. How much beef are we talking about?"

"Twelve hundred tons, Sir George."

"Dear God, I had no idea."

"The *Faithful Lass*, our newest wool clipper, which sailed for Australia but two weeks ago, can carry close on two thousand tons, with plans for larger, steam-powered vessels able to carry nearly three thousand, yet to come."

"You have no fears for your vessels, Lennard?"

"None whatsoever, Sir George."

"I suppose you have arranged for a naval escort?"

"A naval escort would signal that the cargo was of some value, don't you think? I believe something like that might reveal our hand—that is, if you want to keep your options open."

"What makes you think I have other options, cards as yet unplayed?"

"Seventeen years and more of your cognisance, sir, many of those working under your aegis. I think you'd prefer to protect the channel that's been feeding information to the Russians for our own use. Revealing his messages had been intercepted would not be advisable, in my opinion."

Sir George smiled. Of course, Lennard had worked out that Karl Paulsson would become an extremely useful conduit through which to funnel misinformation. Once exposed, with the threat of execution over his head and the possible repercussions afforded his sister in Stockholm, the guard would feed the Russians whatever the Home Secretary or the Prime Minister wished them to hear. As for Kosorukov? Well, Sir George knew that, no doubt, Lennard had also worked out how that relationship, now discovered, might prove to the advantage of Her Majesty's government.

"I suppose there will be a change of vessels?" Angus asked.

"Yes, Angus. The *Caroline* is carrying cannon, but not destined for the Crimea. She has twenty-two large artillery pieces aboard destined to reinforce our defences in Gibraltar. After they're unloaded, she'll take on oil and provisions for the colony at Cape Town before returning to London, laden with palm oil products. If anyone cares to check the bill of lading, either here or in Gibraltar, they will see that is exactly what's written on our original manifest. As for the *Princess Henriette*, her beef is intended for the various navies of the Italian states. Her final destination will be Malta, before she sails on to Rabat to pick up cargo for her return. In my conversation with Robert, which Kosorukov overheard, the destination of neither vessel was mentioned."

"However, the illusion, because of your contracts with the Royal Navy and the War Office, would make him believe that the guns and the beef were headed for the Crimea."

"Indeed. And it appears that our hook was swallowed whole."

"Well done, Lennard," Sir George said. "Now, I also have news for you. News that not even Angus is aware of because it arrived by despatch not ten minutes before you walked in. There's been a confirmed sighting."

"A sighting of what, or of whom, Sir George?" Angus asked.

"Of The Cargo."

Both Lennard and Angus were taken completely by surprise.

"Where and by whom?"

"Five weeks ago, in a port city that our contact called Arsenaria in his missive."

"That's the ancient Roman name for the modern harbour city of Arzew Le Port, in Algeria," Angus explained.

"I see you remember your Pliny," Sir George remarked.

"It's a French town now," Lennard added. "We sometimes have a few ships trade there, once or twice every few months. Why would The Cargo risk being seen in a French colonial port in North Africa? I don't understand."

"Well, Lennard, the message that arrived this morning said the

Pretender and Kadir are staying in a villa just outside the town and have not moved outside its walls since they arrived on the tenth of March."

"They're waiting for something," Lennard said.

"Obviously, but what?"

"Transport, surely. I'd have to check with Robert, but I think that, other than us, there's only a French trading company out of Marseilles that services the population. The agreements of the local traders, again I'd have to check, are limited to coastal vessels which ply the seas to Ottoman Tunisia, Egypt, and to Greece. Malloray's and the French company are the only foreign trading companies with contracts to ship into and out of that port."

"This leaves us in a difficult situation, Sir George," Angus said. "If The Cargo were to leave Arzew Le Port, how would we know where they'd gone?"

"How long ago was this missive written?" Lennard asked.

"Fifteen days ago."

"Then the message has come by sail. I can get a steamship there in six, maybe seven days. Perhaps I can arrange for there to be an unexpected problem with the engine, such that our vessel needs to heave to in Arzew Le Port. Repairs can take as long as they need—steam engines can be temperamental beasts. Do we have any Arab-speaking contacts we could send? As soon as The Cargo leaves the town, we must know where they are headed, and with one of Malloray's fastest vessels is in port, we shall have an advantage, either to follow after them or to bring back word with haste of their intended destination."

"You'd do this, Lennard?"

"My life is Her Majesty's, Sir George, as is my fortune."

The Home Secretary did something he'd never done before. He drew Lennard into his arms and hugged him, contrary to all notions of propriety. "I do hope my George Henry becomes a man with your convictions and strength of character, Lennard."

"From what I have seen on him, he already has achieved that, sir. You should be enormously proud of him indeed."

"I thank you from the bottom of my heart, Lennard. Now, back to business momentarily. What shall you do with Karl Paulsson?"

"I believe he's due for a rendezvous with someone I know this evening. I shall arrange a surprise for when he arrives and we shall have a very frank discussion, after which, at a later time, you and the Prime Minister can decide what should be fed to the Russians in his next letter to his sister."

"And Kosorukov?"

"I would suggest nothing, for the time being, sir. I believe it wise to wait until we have the best opportunity to use him to our advantage. For the moment, his information, although not of enormous importance, has been prodigious, and for that reason, we should keep him under observation, yet easily detained should the need arise. I intend to play Paulsson as a double agent, except that he will be passing on things we want the Russians to hear, not what Kosorukov is feeding him. And, if I may add, by playing the Swedish guard thus, we may learn where Kosorukov is gathering his information. A spider web catches more than midges, if you'll excuse my clumsy metaphor. What I'm hoping is that one of the larger creatures may entrap themselves. It could be the beginning of discovering a whole circle of seditious monsters if we can get but one caught up in our sticky threads, then use persuasion to get him to betray his circle of vipers."

"It is precisely as I would have done, Lennard. Well done!"

"And now I shall leave you, sir. Please make haste to find suitable men to send to Algeria. I'll speak with Robert to find out where the *Cutler's Edge* is, sir. She's our fastest steam-powered vessel and one of the first we've built with a screw propeller. Not three months from the shipyards, but I vow she's the fastest anywhere in the nation."

"Is she far abroad, Lennard? Time might be of the essence?"

"I have no precise idea but, from memory, Robert told me she was running to Danzig and back. Her journey is a matter of days. So, if she's on her way back, packed with Prussian furs, timbers, ores, and amber, she'll be ready to steam off to the Mediterranean by the weekend. If not, it will be a few days after."

"Before you leave, Lennard. I did so want to iterate my pleasure at your 'coming out' dinner on Saturday evening last. And, as much as I know how much you loathe Astley, I'm forever in your debt for inviting him. George Henry has been floating on air ever since."

"It was my great delight, Sir George, and hopefully it won't be the last of such celebrations. My aunt is already talking of a summer ball at Gresting."

*****

"Merrill, do you have any idea where Gerald is?" Lennard asked as he handed his hat to his footman then turned to be helped out of his overcoat.

"He's with Elam, my lord. They're in the morning room, I believe."

"What ho, Lennard," Gerald said when Lennard entered the room.

"What are you two up to?"

"I was asking Elam's advice. Do you remember the river sluice that fills up the lake?"

"Where, Gerald? Which lake?"

"The Misbourne, Lennard ... what's wrong? You seem agitated."

"Let me take off my boots and I'll tell you about my morning, after which I'm all ears about the river sluice at Gresting."

Lennard sat on the sofa, pulled off his boots, and began to relate the events at Birch House with the Baron Hochschild to Gerald, then his later meeting with Angus and Sir George.

"Arthur Pencott? Do I know him?" Gerald asked.

"No, but I think you'd rather like to," Elam said after Lennard had explained his plans for the interception of Karl Paulsson that evening.

"Oh, really? Why, Elam?"

"First of all, he's a man, Gerald. Isn't that enough?"

The three men laughed, interrupted when Merrill enquired whether they'd take lunch in the morning room or in the dining room.

"Is Clyford here?"

"Yes, my lord," Merrill replied.

"Perhaps you could fetch him in half an hour and we will eat in here. There are matters still to discuss so we'll retire to my study so as to not be in your way if you need to set anything up here."

"We could have talked about anything in front of Merrill, Lennard," Gerald said, once they were comfortably seated in Lennard's office. "He's one of Angus's choices and has worked for the Home Office for years. That's what I was led to believe, anyway."

"Of course we could have talked in front of him, Gerald," Lennard replied. "However, the first rule of intelligence is to keep your circle of knowledge close and small."

"Very well, I understand. Now, why do you want me to be there this evening?"

"Elam, Arthur, and I will wait in the room in which they always meet. You're to stand by, out of sight, in the corridor, in case Paulsson takes scared and tries to flee. He's a tall, strong lad, but no more than you, Gerald. I don't think it will come to that, but we need to make sure this goes smoothly."

"That's not all now, is it, Lenn? I know you well. There's something else."

Lennard smiled. "Do you have anyone you might take with you this afternoon to have a gentle conversation with a tradesman?"

"A gentle conversation?"

"There's a costermonger, loitering in the alleyway next to the Baron Hochschild's residence. He's been seen there every afternoon between four and five," Lennard explained. "Perhaps he's hanging around for another reason, but it's a very strange part of London for a man such as himself to be spending time. Leans against the wall, smokes a pipe. Go lightly, just in case it's nothing untoward."

"And if it is?"

"Find out first, then decide. If he's up to no good, take him somewhere and send word to me. If there's nothing to it, tell him the Peelers have got their eye on him and perhaps he could find a less salubrious part of London in which to pass an hour smoking his pipe."

"And that's it?"

"No, my friends. While I was with Sir George and Angus, I learned something extraordinary. I went straight to Malloray's after I'd heard it."

"Something to do with Kosorukov?"

"No, Gerald. There's been a verified sighting of The Cargo."

*****

At six that evening, Lennard watched—with no small amount of amusement—as Gerald shook hands with Arthur Pencott. They locked eyes for a little longer than might normally have been expected, especially notable because of the difference in their classes. It was Arthur's shy smile that caught Lennard's attention. He hadn't expected someone who slept with men for money to show such polite, yet obvious attraction.

Of course, Arthur had been astounded when Lennard had arrived at his lodgings with Elam and Gerald, and even more so when he'd been informed of the reason they'd come.

"What time are you due at Mrs Hedger's?" Lennard had asked. "I know this news must come as a terrific shock to you, Arthur, and I'm more than happy to send word to Cowcross Street that you're unable to work this evening. Christopher can deliver it for me. Mrs Wilson will understand if it comes from me."

"I don't work on Wednesdays or Sunday evenings, Mr Malloray, unless either of those days fall on the first or the fifteenth, when your foreign gentleman requests my presence. If that's the case, Mrs Wilson allows me another evening off work."

"Why do you need to work there at all, now you're employed by Mr Fahey as his dock supervisor at Malloray's?" Gerald asked. "I'm sorry. You're quite welcome to tell me to mind my own business, if you wish. I shan't take offence."

"I'm trying to save, Captain Langbourne. For the first time in my life, I'm in a position to put a few shillings aside every week and I'd like to move somewhere more comfortable than this room. Besides, I've gone without for so long in my life, I'd also to treat myself once in a while."

"Treat yourself?"

"Books, sir. And lessons in writing, geography, and the sciences. I can't have both new lodgings and those other things, even with my generous increase in salary since I moved back to Malloray's."

"You astonish me, Arthur."

"Is it such a bad thing to make a better life for oneself, sir?"

"No, please, don't misinterpret my astonishment. It was born from admiration, not from any other emotion."

"Thank you, Captain. But to answer your question about work at Mrs Hedger's, it's not all that bad and it gives me company of an evening. The other men who work there are all sorts. We play cards and have a laugh. Mrs Wilson always has a plate for each of us when we arrive and is generous about sharing tips. Most evenings, early in the week, it's fairly quiet. I have a few regular gentlemen. Other than that, perhaps a request from someone new a few times a week. The work is not onerous, and …"

"And?"

"I dare say, Captain Langbourne, you are extremely inquisitive," Arthur said, laughing.

"I beg your pardon, Mr Pencott. As Lennard and Elam will tell you, having known me for close to twenty years, it's in my nature to be forthright."

"What you really need is a patron, Arthur," Elam said. Then, ignoring Lennard's slight head shake, continued, "A gentleman who might help you find somewhere comfortable to live, spend time enjoying your company, keep you in books and help you with your studies, in exchange for—"

"Elam! Really!" Lennard said, laughing despite himself.

"Stop pretending to be so righteous, Lenn," Elam replied. "There's plenty that enjoy that sort of arrangement, no matter whether their companion is a lady or a gentleman."

"I'm afraid that casual encounters for money are one thing, but if I were to venture into such an arrangement with a sponsor, it would have to be because I really liked him," Arthur said.

Gerald checked his timepiece, his head lowered, briefly catching Lennard's eye, who smiled at his friend's deep blush.

*****

When the time came, Karl Paulsson could not have looked more shocked. He entered the upstairs room in the inn and looked at Arthur then quickly at Elam, who he recognised immediately. Confused, he turned to Lennard, who greeted him with a raised pistol.

"Not so fast," Gerald said, from behind him, blocking the doorway as Paulsson took a step or two backward.

"What's going on, Arthur? Who are these gentlemen, and what are you doing here, Paul?"

"I'm sorry, Karl," Elam replied. "But my name is not Paul, and I'm the valet of the gentleman with the pistol in his hand."

Paulsson stared at Lennard, bravely enough for a man who had a firearm pointed at his breast.

"I'm not sure what's happening here, but I'll have you know that I'm a guard at the Swedish embassy and there will be—"

"The Baron Hochschild is one of my oldest friends, Karl. Surely you haven't forgotten my visit to him Tuesday last with my friend, Dr Holland, to treat his ulcer?"

"*Herregud!* Of course! I'm sorry, my lord. I was so completely distracted by the sight of the gun aimed in my direction that I didn't recognise you, sir. Yes, of course I remember you. But my lord, what's the meaning of—"

"Please, Karl, we mean you no harm," Lennard said, passing his pistol to Elam. "The weapon was merely a show of arms, to make you think twice about fleeing. Now, if you'd be so kind as to take a seat at the table, we can discuss the reason we've been waiting for you."

The room was one of the better ones for an inn in a backstreet behind the Strand. A large, canopied bed took up most of the space, but there was still enough space for a sofa and a table with four chairs around it.

Karl pulled out one of the chairs and sat, joined by Lennard, Elam, and Arthur. Gerald perched on the side of the bed, positioned so he'd be able to stop Paulsson quickly if he made an unexpected bolt for the door.

Lennard retrieved a slip of paper from his pocket and referred to it. "Forgive my dreadful Swedish, Karl. But, '*Caroline Bombadera, kvinnan som jag har haft mina ögon på, lämnade London i morse och mitt hjärta är i bitar*—'"

"Stop!"

"You wrote this to your sister."

"It's what I was told to write."

"Told to write?"

"You don't understand."

"No, I don't understand, Karl. Perhaps you'd like to enlighten me."

"I don't know what business it is of yours—"

"That's where you're wrong, Karl. Not only am I the Baron Betteridge of Hazlemere, but I've also worked for the Home Office for seventeen years. Do you know what this is?" Lennard asked, holding up the note. "This is a very short step away from the gallows for both you and your sister."

"No! She has nothing—"

"If you say she has nothing to do with it, I won't believe you. She's married to an attaché at the Russian embassy in Stockholm. Do you know what your king will do when he finds out one of his guards is sending secret information to the Russians while he's trying to negotiate a treaty with the British? Don't you understand the magnitude of the act you've committed? It's treason, no matter in which language you care to spell it out."

"He makes me do it."

"Who, Kosorukov? Is that while you're servicing his rump or after? The fact he pays you adds to the charge, Karl. You are a traitor to the Baron Hochschild, a man who thinks of you as his son."

Paulsson gasped. "He knows?"

"How do you think I know what you wrote?"

"Arthur," he said, turning to Pencott, "did you …?"

"I knew nothing until an hour ago, Karl."

"But I—"

"But you what? You care for me? Is that what you were going to say?" Arthur Pencott said, his face red with anger. "Almost at the same time I learned of your treachery to my country, I learned of your treachery to me. Your avowals of affection, of how much I meant to you? Is that what you said to the costermonger who loiters in the alleyway outside the Baron's house every afternoon waiting for you to couple with him in the back of the public stables? Don't deny it! He was interrogated by the Home Office this afternoon and confessed everything to them."

"Well, to be totally honest, he confessed to me," Lennard said. "The Baron Hochschild asked me to find out who he was. If you're going to dally with more than one lover, Karl, I suggest you keep your men well apart and out of sight of each other."

Paulsson fiddled with the cuff of his coat sleeve for a short while, deep in thought, before speaking. "What do you want, sir?"

"Ah, now that's the question a wise man would ask in your situation."

"If I was to be hanged, I'd be in some cell already. It doesn't take a genius to realise you want something from me."

"Indeed, there is, Karl. However, there are three things I need you to do," Lennard explained. "What I want from you is tied up in all three. I suggest that if you wish to keep your neck, and that of your sister's, free of the hangman's rope you should attend to my requests."

"And they are?"

"The first of them is merely that you're to go on as usual, to visit Mrs Hedger's and meet with Kosorukov as you normally do, twice a month. You're also to meet with him and Hakan Zeybeck at the Sultan of Khartoum whenever the *Koniah* is in port. However, here's the catch. You're going to tell us in detail every word that passes between the three of you, and you're going to recount every word that that was spoken during Zeybeck's last visit, when Elam was with you, on the second of April."

"And after that?"

"The second thing you will do is to return to the former embassy and grovel on your knees for forgiveness from the Baron Hochschild. I've known him for years and I can't believe he would place his trust and affection in a man who was rotten to the core. Am I correct in guessing that Kosorukov has uttered a threat about the safety of your sister in Stockholm if you don't write what he tells you to?"

"Yes, our entire family is under the risk of death if I don't pass on his messages, or if I were to go to the authorities here."

"Then your secret is safe, Karl. No one other than a very select few will learn what you are up to. You are simply too valuable to Her Majesty's government."

"Valuable?"

"You don't think you're going to get off that easily, do you? That the sharing confidences of your meetings with Kosorukov and Hakan Zeybeck is enough to exonerate yourself from the betrayal of trust implicit in the wearing of your uniform and the oath you swore when you were first given it? No, Karl, a confession of your misdeeds is simply not enough."

"I suppose you're going to tell me about punishment, are you? Disgrace? The loss of my position at the attaché's side, stripped of my rank, and drummed out of the military?"

"No, Karl. I haven't yet told you of my third request. On the second and the sixteenth of the month, the day after your regular meetings with our mutual friend, the Russian grand duke, at nine in the morning you're to wait for a carriage at the back entrance of The Lion's Heart in Tottenham Court Road, from where you'll be taken to a secure, private place and spend time with Sir Angus Spratt, the personal private secretary of the Home Secretary. You'll tell him everything that occurred on the previous evening with Kosorukov, and I mean *everything*. He'll then direct you what to write to your sister. Do you hear me? You'll write some of what Kosorukov tells you so there's no undue suspicion roused, but mainly you'll be used as a vessel to channel to the Russians what we want them to know. Understood?"

Paulsson nodded dumbly, glancing sadly at Arthur, who averted his gaze.

"What about when the Russian nobleman wants Arthur to join us?"

"As far as Kosorukov is concerned, Mrs Wilson will inform him that Arthur has found a gentleman of quality who has agreed to become his permanent sponsor."

"So, we won't—"

Arthur Pencott rose to his feet abruptly, his face red with anger.

"Not if you were the last man alive, Karl. Now, I'm sorry, if you don't require my presence any longer, I need to get some air."

"I'll accompany you," Gerald said. "If you need me, I'll be outside with Arthur in the courtyard, Lennard. If I hear gunshots, I'll take my time, shall I?"

"Thank you, Gerald. I'm sure violence won't be necessary, will it Karl?"

The guard shook his head.

"I'd be grateful if you could ask the landlord to send up a large jug of ale and some mugs. You drink beer, don't you, Karl?"

The guard nodded and then winced as Arthur walked past him, knocking his shoulder with his hip "by accident" as he left the room.

14. THE *PENDRAGON* AND CONSEQUENCES

Sir Terrence Astley, the sixth Baronet Killcaire, stretched out on a chaise in the dressing room of his Bayswater house. Conall, one of his "twins", at his feet, massaging his toes.

Astley was furious. A telegram had arrived at two in the afternoon informing him of the boarding of the *Pendragon* and the discovery of arms in her hold, hidden underneath Malloray's shipment of walnut. The ship had been seized, as had his warehouse on the dock, and the lock-up house across the bay at St. Just in Roseland.

"Have a care, you lout!" he said, pulling his foot from the man's grasp.

"Your feet are a dreadful ball of muscle," Conall said. "I've never known anyone hold their tension in their extremities in quite the same way you do."

"You could always suck my toes," Astley said.

"What makes you think you deserve such a thing?"

Terrence Astley smiled. This lad was the only person he'd allow such intimacies. Over the years, it had served him well—the push and pull of power between landed gentleman and peasant, each serving the other roughly. Conall was a constant reminder of the wild years when his father had still been alive, and when he'd had no responsibilities, spending whatever he wished, and consorting with people far below his class, and long before he'd been forced to marry.

Nearly fifteen years ago, not a year before his father had died and he'd acceded to the baronetcy, he'd paid well for the comely Irish lad and his "sister". They weren't kin, but they looked so alike they could easily have passed for twins. Former travelling play-actors, they'd been lucky to find work in an upper-class bawdyhouse in Kerry when their troupe had been disbanded. That's where he'd found them one drunken night with a taste in his belly for a man and woman whore at the same time. So many others of their countrymen had either emigrated to countries on the other side of the globe or had simply succumbed to starvation during and after the Great Famine. Conall and Colleen were their Christian names. If they'd had surnames, he hadn't bothered enquiring at the time; instead, he'd handed over his hundred and twenty guineas to the bawdyhouse keeper and had signed a receipt using a false name. They'd brought many talents with them: nimble fingers for pickpocketing and easy impersonations were but a few, and he'd had recourse more than once to employ them to use those well.

However, their greatest gift to him was their free and easy acceptance of his body's needs. He looked after them well; their accommodation was luxurious, their purses were never empty, and they had whatever else they desired. For that, they were always happy to repay his investment in his bed, either in turn, or together. Tonight, he'd been in the mood for Conall, who'd pushed him onto his face, used him roughly, and who'd been more than willing to satisfy the fire in Astley's belly afterwards with his mouth.

"It's your own fault, you know."

"Who asked you, Conall?"

"No one. But you were warned. I was there when Fetcher told you to hold off the shipment. You knew at the time the change of customs officers might prove risky."

"Talking of Fetcher, where is he?"

"He said he'd gone to meet with the two men and the woman he employs to keep eyes on Lennard Malloray. After which, he had an assignation with the prince. What time is it now?"

"I've no idea. My timepiece is in the bedroom, or you can check the mantle clock."

"I can't be bothered getting off my knees. I heard the half hour chime not long ago, so I expect it's half past five."

"If you had an idea of the time, why did you ask?"

"To annoy you," Conall said, before sinking his teeth into Astley's knee cap.

"Ow, damnit, Conall! What on earth are you up to?"

"If you're going to sit naked, stretched out in front of me, your prick directly before my eyes, you deserve a good bite."

Astley laughed. Why on earth he'd taken to such a rough, coarse-mouthed, irreverent creature he still didn't understand. He knew in his heart the lad cared nothing for him and was simply interested in the comfort of a lifestyle afforded by looking after the needs of Astley's flesh. They sparred, like pugilists, but with words. That was the profit in their relationship. That, and the rough, violent coupling they both liked so much, and which few other of their partners could provide so readily, and without recoil.

"Do you trust Fetcher?" Astley asked.

"That's an odd question."

"Somehow, the whole idea of a double agent makes me uncomfortable, even after the length of time he's been working for me."

"Does Spratt know you're aware that Fetcher is one of his men?"

"No. It works better that way. I tell Fetcher what's safe to report on, but I promise you, Conall, I get the better end of the deal. He brings back more information that I give him to disburse."

"That will change quick smart if Spratt ever gets wind that Fetcher's in bed with his prince."

"It serves the prince very well that Angus Spratt never learns that Fetcher is one of his stable of extras. He won't be discovered. He uses a perfect disguise when he visits."

"You've never told me."

"Nor should I. Why do you want to know, Conall?"

"I'm not particularly interested in what Fetcher does with the prince. Most likely, it's the same he does with me when you're not around."

Astley leaned forward and cuffed Conall's ear playfully. "Is it any different from what you do while I'm watching you both?"

"You like that, don't you?"

"I'd like it a lot more if Fetcher wasn't too dangerous to play with. I'm sure much of what you both say and do is for my benefit."

Conall laughed. "I'd like you to join in, you know."

"You'd like it if I joined you with half of London, you trollop!"

"You should be careful who you start calling a trollop, Terrence. May I remind you of days past, in the back rooms of halfpenny-a-glass slop houses on the docks at Dundalk, when you'd get so drunk, you'd fall on your face and take on half the room."

"With you slapping my arse and calling for them to form an orderly line ..."

"You enjoyed that, didn't you?"

"It was long ago, and I was a young man and foolish."

"We could still arrange it one day ..."

Astley ruffled Conall's hair. "You were asking about Fetcher's disguise."

"And you didn't tell me."

"He arrives at Kensington Palace, disguised as a groom and standing on the back of the prince's private secretary's coach. That's all you need to know. Now, your turn. You didn't answer when I asked whether you trust him."

"I trust no man with a prick that big, who's as good looking and strong as Fetcher."

"And as wanton?"

"He can be. But there's a dark side to him, too. Much like yourself."

"And you ... but no one can hold a candle to my callous soul when I'm stirred."

"Perhaps not, but you don't punish your bedfellows with your pisser in the same way he does sometimes."

"Oh? Now I'm interested."

Conall snorted softly. "Give me your other foot now. If it is half past five, Fetcher will be back soon."

"Why are you smiling?"

"Our talk of smut and Fetcher has loosened your temper, that's all, and has raised something more than your spirits."

Astley looked down, slapping it a few times, then grinned at his companion.

"Despite the stiffness of my member, my temper still rages strong, Conall. Have no fear. If I find there's anything more to the loss of my possessions except a change of customs officers, I'll make whoever responsible pay with the skin on their backs."

"Too good for them."

"What do you suggest?"

"It depends on who it is, but humiliation if they can't be killed without causing trouble, and if not, then you know how craftily disguised I can be and how happy I am to use my dagger."

"You'd do that?"

"You'll never know until you ask me," the Irishman replied, twisting his head to one side. "I think I hear Fetcher coming up the stairs."

Fetcher was tall and strapping, and exceedingly handsome; no longer a lad, but not far from it. Astley had discovered him when the Irishman had come to London to make his fortune. A short time later, Fetcher had fallen under the gaze of Angus Spratt, who'd taken an interest in him, especially when he'd been led to believe that Fetcher had information on some of the insurrectionists in his home country—supplied, of course, by the Baronet Killcaire himself.

Bertram's square jaw, broad shoulders, and white smile coupled with sky-blue eyes had bewitched Angus, who, at the time, had elected not to thoroughly investigate the former Kilkenny farmer's background. However, after checking the veracity of Fetcher's information, Angus had agreed to give him one or two assignments to check the efficacy of a would-be intelligencer who didn't baulk at the idea of sharing the beds of other men in order to discover their secrets.

Fetcher had been Angus's choice after his previous "placement" with Astley had died. A simple letter of introduction written by a compliant Irish earl, a friend of the Home Secretary, had been enough enticement. Had Angus dwelled on the ease of Fetcher's acceptance within Astley's circle, he may have perhaps discovered they were already acquainted.

It hadn't been hard for Astley to recruit Fetcher. Money for his family in Ireland and the release from the tenant-farmership of greedy English landlord and a smallholding of their own as a gift. It had been but a small amount to spend, compared to what their son had later repaid with information on Spratt, as well as the Foreign Secretary, and the Prime Minister, and his associates. The English never seemed to have understood that you should never send an Irishman to work against one of his own kind; a lesson too many had learned to their ultimate chagrin over the course of centuries. Then, there was the matter of Fetcher's penchant for men, and his lack of concern should the man be part of an arrangement or as an assignment. He was exceedingly lustful for his age. Astley had used it to good ends, and in return had supplied Bertram Fetcher with a bottomless purse.

Infiltrating the young man into the bed of the Prince Christian Jost had been simplicity itself—a plan of Astley's devising that he'd been extraordinarily proud of it, delighted by the ease of its execution and the rapidity of its results.

A cheeky smile as the prince rode past Fetcher on his morning ride along Rotten Row, the prince unable to miss the young comely man standing half-hidden behind a horse-chestnut with his lengthy prick hanging out of his unbuttoned breeches, pretending to pass water against the tree trunk. A few mornings, a week apart, and the prince's equerry, his riding companion, was arranging a quiet meeting with His Royal Highness in a pavilion on the Serpentine.

"For God's sake, take your clothes off, man," Astley said after Fetcher had entered the changing room. "Conall and I are both naked and you make me uneasy. Give him a hand, Conall."

"You're the strangest Irishman I've ever met in my life, sir," Fetcher said with a grin, drawing off his trousers while Conall helped him out of his jacket.

"Tired, Bertram?"

"Yes, sir. Extremely. The prince was very demanding."

"How many times?"

"Once only, but nearly thirty minutes in duration. I could barely stand by the time he'd had enough. Even then, he remained sprawled out on his bed, his face in the pillows, begging me for a repeat performance after he'd regained his breath and his stamina."

"And did you?"

"I begged off, Sir Terrence, with the excuse that I would be missed if I stayed longer."

"Did he pay you?"

"Gold coins. Foreign money. It's in my jacket pocket."

Astley snorted softly. "Very well, tell me about your day."

Fetcher sat on the chaise next to Astley, one leg resting on Conall's shoulder, who'd returned to the task of massaging Astley's feet. "I met with my three shadowers, who reported on the comings and goings of Lord Betteridge for the past few days."

"And?"

"Nothing out of the ordinary. Since Thursday he's been back and forth between the Home Office, the shipping yards, and his house in Clarence Gardens. He lunched twice at the Oriental Club, once with Robert Fahey, when they met with the Earl of Clarendon—"

"Malloray and Fahey met with the Foreign Secretary? Have you any idea what they discussed?"

"I have no entrée to that establishment, sir. Find me a peerage or a fortune and I might be able to gain access. As it is, there's no way I can bribe any of the staff, and Lennard Malloray's coachman spent most of his time monopolising the time of the Foreign Secretary's man."

"Are any of the staff of the club … you know?" Conall asked.

"I have no idea. In any case, I couldn't be seen associating with any of them."

Conall chuckled. "I could though. 'Fancy a bit of Irish dick, mate? Or a taste of my mouth or tail?'"

Astley poked Conall's chest with his toe, laughing, before encouraging Fetcher to continue.

"They ate at home on Thursday and Friday evening. Last night they attended a performance of Il Trovatore at the Royal Opera House. Did you know the family has a box of their own? After the opera, they supped at The Carnegie in James Street. This morning, the entire household attended the ten o'clock service at St. Pancras New Church. The lady in my employ sat behind them and overheard Lady Winchester inviting them for supper and cards this evening."

"Sounds very ordinary. So, nothing unusual?"

"I had to pay out ten shillings to the rider at the telegraphic office in Euston, but there have only been normal business communications, and a few sent by Captain Langbourne to Gresting Hall."

"If you're running short, you know to take whatever you need from my cash box. Fill out the book, as you usually do."

"Every penny is accounted for, sir. Even that which I spend on myself."

"Ale and male whores?" Conall asked playfully.

"Why should I spend money on those when Sir Terrence has his own barrels of beer and you are always so lascivious and available?"

"Stop it, you two," Astley said. "Was there any news of Spratt and his friends?"

Conall, still smiling at the exchange, shifted his attention from Astley's feet to Fetcher's.

"As you may be aware, Napoleon the Third is visiting Her Majesty. They attended a performance at the Royal Opera House on Thursday last, and the whole glittery crew, including the Prime Minister, was in attendance. Apart from that, there's to be a State banquet this evening for the King of France, and they've all been invited. Anyway, that's what the prince told me this afternoon."

"It all seems too ordinary, Fetcher."

"In respect of ...?"

"I'm convinced there's more to the seizure of the *Pendragon* than a simple change of customs officers. It's far too convenient. We haven't used the ship for anything but regular goods from Spain for months. And now, all of a sudden on our first import of arms, the ship is boarded? It's far too coincidental."

"The crew have been apprehended?"

Astley nodded, aware that Conall's attention to Fetcher's feet had produced a physical effect on the man sitting at his side.

"None of them are new?"

"No, Fetcher. Not as far as I'm aware."

"Would you like me to travel to Truro to see what I can discover?"

"I'd rather you not, Fetcher. I have someone I can contact in St. Mawes who'll do the digging. I'll write this evening. He should get the letter tomorrow late, or on Tuesday morning. I'd like it spread abroad that I've been in Ireland these past few days. Can you do that, Bertram?"

"Of course. It's an alibi to preclude you from any involvement."

"Yes, the captain already knows what to do in the case a shipment is ever discovered."

"Is it to do with the Spanish prime minister, O'Donnell?"

Astley nodded. "The captain can produce a false manifest, saying the crates arrived at the dock at the last minute from O'Donnell's office, saying it was an urgent delivery to be collected on the wharf at Wexford. He'll show them a bill of lading that states they are millet brooms. The captain and the crew will be interrogated, my property seized, and perhaps questions asked by the Foreign Minister to the Spanish ambassador. However ..."

"The signatures will be aliases?"

"Exactly. I shall still lose the ship, the warehouse, and the lock-up house, but at no cost to my neck or that of the crew."

"I'll be waiting in Rotten Row tomorrow morning with my cock out for Prince Christian Jost," Fetcher said.

"Won't he think that odd, especially after he's seen you for most of the afternoon today?"

"It will give me the opportunity, when he asks why I'm there, to say that you've been away for a few days in Ireland, not expected back until the end of the week, so I've found myself unencumbered."

"That's very good work, Bertram. Thank you."

"Is there anything else you'd like me to do, sir?"

"You can entertain me. Break my mood."

"How?"

"Raise your knees and let Conall take you while I'm sitting close by."

"But sir—"

"Your body betrays your protest, Fetcher. Perhaps it's time Conall had a turn atop?"

"It wouldn't be the first time, sir," Conall said, already on his feet, tumescent, his hands on the backs of Fetcher's ankles, holding the man's legs aloft and spread apart. "Despite what he tells you, he likes it just as rough and wild as both you and I."

*****

"What's this, Lennard?" Sir George Lewis asked.

"It's my tender for the Baronet Killcaire's seized property, sir," Lennard replied.

The Chancellor of the Exchequer was another old friend of his grandfather's and had eagerly invited Lennard into his office, even though he'd arrived without notice, the morning the invitation to submit closed tenders for Astley's confiscated assets had been published in *The Times*, and four days after the seizure of the *Pendragon*.

"But, Lennard, neither is this envelope sealed, nor is there a sum written on your enclosed cheque."

"Lord Palmerston asked me to inform you that you should add two thousand above the highest private tender."

"The Prime Minister requested this? This is highly irregular, Lennard. As much as I like you—"

"It's to avoid an embarrassment, sir, were the ship, the warehouse, the cottage, and its land go to the wrong buyer."

The Right Honourable Sir George Cornewall Lewis, also newly titled, having inherited his father's baronetcy at about the same time as Lennard the Betteridge title, was no fool. He quickly realised the purchase was a political necessity. He inspected the cheque for a moment or two before speaking.

"The company name is one I'm not familiar with, my lord. Is it one of yours?"

"As of yesterday, it is indeed. Elenrob Pty Ltd. It's a contraction of my Christian name combined with the shortened version of two others, who are silent directors. The company will be hard to discover, sir, as it is shelved under one of the steel companies formerly belonging to my aunt's late husband, now in my own portfolio. There are so many levels of evasion that only a wizard will find out who the actual owner is. The company is registered in Besançon, in France, with a poste restante address in London."

"And why are you telling me these details, Lennard, if you are trying to be so secretive about the nature of this new venture?"

"Because, sir, as the Chancellor of the Exchequer, you may be asked to turn a blind eye to some of the business performed by me on behalf of the Home Secretary, the Foreign Secretary, and of course, your benefactor, the Prime Minister. Now, sir, would you and your good wife, Lady Lewis, be so kind as to be my guests for dinner this coming Saturday evening? Shall we say at about six?"

"Of course, we'd be honoured and delighted, Lennard."

"I look forward to seeing you both then, sir."

The Chancellor of the Exchequer shook Lennard's hand warmly. He knew when he'd been played by powers higher than his own and realised that whatever was afoot would ultimately be of benefit not only to the new Lord Betteridge, but also to Her Majesty's government.

*****

In the back of his mind, Lennard had been expecting to hear about an explosion from Astley after the confiscation of his ship, warehouse, and cottage. However, information had reached him that the day after Astley and his niece had been guests at Bexford House, his nemesis had sailed to Ireland, to attend to business, and was not expected to return until the end of the week.

Although there was no direct evidence linking Lennard to the scheme, nevertheless, he and Angus had spent half a day preparing excuses to disavow any involvement on his behalf in the affair, in case Astley had stormed wrathfully into his presence with accusations of malfeasance.

After Lennard's visit to the Chancellor of the Exchequer, his Wednesday morning had been rather uneventful. He'd purchased four newly-bound presentation copies of Walter Scott's novels—including his own favourite, *The Pirate*—and had sought out Gerald afterwards, insisting that his friend should find time to visit Malloray's docks and present the collection to Arthur Pencott, with the excuse than the man needed cheering up after his recent disillusionment. He'd smiled when Gerald had agreed, suggesting that he might help the man with some of the more difficult parts of the text, if Arthur needed help.

He arrived back at Bexford House around noon, prepared to attend to his correspondence. He'd just asked Stephen to fetch some light ale, bread, and cheese to be sent in on a tray for his lunch when Merrill asked if he might speak with him. He mentioned that a letter had been left for him by a gentleman passer-by, who'd been accosted by a lad on the street telling the man he'd found the envelope, addressed to Lennard, laying at the entrance gate of the house.

"A passer-by in Albion Street?" Lennard asked.

"He was well-dressed, my lord. Finely cut clothes that gave the impression of a man of substance. Why he should be perambulating in this area I have no explanation."

"And the lad?"

"He said he looked like one of the neighbouring children, smartly dressed in a sailor suit with a straw hat and had a hoop and stick in his hand."

"Why would a child like that not take the letter to his parent? Or at least bring it to our door. I don't understand. Very well, where is this letter?"

"It's on your desk, my lord, along with this morning's post."

Lennard shuffled through his mail until he came to the letter Merrill had mentioned. Addressed to him in neat copperplate, the envelope was unstamped.

"Merrill!" he shouted but two minutes later, running to his study door, the letter from inside the envelope clutched in his hand.

"Yes, my lord. What is it?"

"Is everyone about the house, or have they been?"

"I'm sorry, sir. I don't understand. What do you mean is everyone about?"

"Clyford? Robert? Geoffroy?"

"Mr Billings left for the Home Office not half an hour ago, sir. Mr Fahey and Geoffroy went in the carriage to Malloray's, as they normally do, at about eight this morning."

"Miles and Elam?"

"Miles is in the drawing room, sir. Shall I fetch him?"

"No, no. But Elam, where is he?"

"He was out in the stable yard talking to Stephen when I last saw him."

"When was that?"

"Not long after Mr Fahey left this morning. Why, what's the matter, my lord? Is something wrong?"

"Quickly, tell Christopher to make all speed to Whitehall to fetch Clyford and Sir Angus. Tell him not to tarry."

Lennard fell onto the chaise in his office, his hand trembling, in it the letter from a person unknown:

> *I have something that belongs to you. You'll get it back in one piece, more or less that is, if you come alone to the old Smither's warehouse at Wapping at eleven this evening.*
>
> *You'll be watched. If there's anyone else other than you and your coachman, what we have will be returned, however in a condition only fit for burial.*
>
> *A friend.*

*****

Whittlechurch Street had been one of the first to trial the new hexagonal-shaped wooden cobblestones. It made for quieter horse and carriage traffic. He'd noticed it the moment the carriage drew to a halt.

As he alighted from his coach, a strange thought came to Lennard, unconnected with his current circumstance. He remembered there'd been a plan to pave the entire area around Buckingham Palace with the same material, to dampen the noise. Prince Albert had been behind the idea; it was he who found it hard to concentrate with external sounds, not Her Majesty. However, the project had come to nothing because granite setts were more popular, cheaper, and easier to lay.

"Lenn?"

"Sorry, Christopher, my mind was wandering."

"Wandering? Wandering where? At a time like this?"

"I'm nervous and afraid, Christopher, and I don't mind admitting it."

"Are you sure you don't want to take a pistol?"

"No, I think that might lead to a more dangerous situation than I believe this may be, if I arrive armed. I've no idea what this 'friend' may want from me, but if I haven't returned in two hours from now, you're to go to the Peeler's lock-up in Clegg Street, tell them who you are, and that you fear I may have suffered a misfortune. I'm not afraid for my own safety, but I smell the stench of Astley behind this. I know his ways well—if there's to be an argument with his agent, whoever this person turns out to be, it won't be over in a hurry. The imperative thing is to recover Elam."

"What do you want me to do in the meantime?"

"Stand at the corner and watch down the street."

"Have a care, Lenn. The fog off the river is thick and there are no gas lights in this laneway."

"I'll take the hand lamp, Christopher. If you hear a blast from my bosun's pipe, come running. Otherwise, wait for me to return."

"Lennard ..."

"I'll go now, Christopher. Stay away, please, unless you hear my whistle blast."

Lennard turned on his heel, snatching the hand lamp and adjusting its wick as he made his way down the laneway, at the end of which was the loading dock entry to Smither's long-abandoned warehouse. Beyond it, the wharf itself.

This area of the docks had been partially destroyed by fire in 1849 and, despite promises to rebuild, the consortium of shipping agents who owned the various buildings had prevaricated to such an extent that many of the structures were simply fit only for demolition. On one side, overhanging first floors of ancient boarded-up houses jutted over the laneway. Lennard glanced up as he passed beneath them. Last night was the first quarter of the moon and the night was cloudy, making it very dark. Because of the dim light and the fog, he seemed to stumble frequently over obstacles in the gloom. Not once or twice he cursed softly as he trod on something soft that gave way under his foot, causing him nearly to fall as he recoiled in disgust. There were few sounds, other than the occasional unseen creature scuttling in the shadows. Other than that, a dog barked somewhere in the distance, its yelps matching the rhythm of the strong thumping of his heart.

Drawing closer to the end of the laneway, Lennard gradually became aware of another lamp. As he came closer, he saw it to be held by a man, his face half-covered in an Italian *commedia dell'arte* mask, wearing a black hat, the brim of which was pulled down over his forehead, his body swathed in a full-length cloak.

"In there," the man grunted, gesturing at a short flight of wooden stairs that led up to the deck of the loading dock. At its end was an open door. "Wait inside," the man said. "Someone will come."

Before Lennard could speak, the man disappeared around the corner of the building. He took a few deep breaths in order to settle his nerves then made his way cautiously into the building.

It was a gloomy, cavernous space, smelling of tar and something sour … rat piss and pigeon droppings he realised after a moment or two. It was whisper quiet, even the distant dog bark was now inaudible. His footsteps echoed as he made his way across the floorboards toward the centre of the empty warehouse. He stood for a while, listening keenly, but all he could hear was the very faint sound of water lapping somewhere beneath the end of the building closest to the dockside.

A soft whistle made him turn. About thirty yards away from where he stood was a man, holding a candle in one hand, sheltering its flame with the other. "Down here," he said.

"Who are you?" Lennard called out.

"No harm will come to you, Lennard Malloray. But if you wish to get back what is yours, you'll do as I say."

"Where is he?" Lennard shouted.

"Enough! Come now, or you'll never find out."

By the time he'd reached the man, Lennard was already starting to feel annoyed. Fear often did that to him.

"Up the stairs. The door at the top," the man said. "I'll follow after you, and don't do anything stupid. Agreed?"

Lennard sighed, determined to play out this charade come what may. All he cared about was Elam's well-being, and being able to return him home.

The door opened into a room lit with two oil lamps, one on a small table near the centre of the room, the other on a stool next to the only other piece of furniture in the room—a wooden bedframe, on it a rough, stained, and lumpy mattress.

Although he felt the chill of it through to his belly, Lennard guessed what was going to happen. "So, it's to be humiliation then, is it?"

The man who'd followed him up the stairs said nothing.

Lennard clenched his jaw, deciding he'd inspect the man's face, in case there was anything recognisable that might lead to his identity at some time in the future. However, there was little to see, apart from the man's thick black eyelashes. They accented his eyes so strongly that Lennard wondered for a moment whether they'd been outlined in kohl, the cosmetic so favoured by both men and women in the Middle East and in North Africa. However, there was enough light to see the exposed skin of the man's face was very pale, even though the lower half of his face was masked by a black bandana.

"You made a very great mistake, Malloray," the man said, after what felt like an interminable length of time.

"You make very free with my surname, sir," Lennard replied. "I assume that, because of the bed, you intend to make free with my body in exchange for my companion, as some sort of a retribution for whatever imagined transgression you believe I may be guilty of?"

"Something like that. A lot of men are without a living, thanks to your spy."

"What spy? I don't know what you're talking about."

"I said you made a very great mistake. Didn't you hear me? Your man may have had a Spanish mother and have been brought up as a cockney, but an Irishman is an Irishman, no matter what language he speaks in or what clothes he wears."

"I have no idea what you're talking about," Lennard said, trying to brave the situation, but internally cursing that his man had been discovered.

"I'm talking about the *Pendragon*, sir. We have cousins and brothers aboard the vessel. Men now locked up at Her Majesty's pleasure, each one of them with wives and children. But now, without their breadwinners, families have nothing and are starving ... thanks to you."

"Me? I really—"

"One of my cousins recognised him. Lots of Irish have worked for Malloray's over the years. He may not have known our kin aboard the ship, but a few of them sure as hell knew who he was, and by whom he is oft employed, doing your dirty work."

"What I heard was the customs officers were the men who discovered contraband aboard the *Pendragon*—"

"No one fucking cares about the cargo, you fool! We care about the livelihoods and the futures of our fellow countrymen."

"Why punish me? I had nothing to do with it."

"You can deny it to the end of your days, my Lord Betteridge. But, it's been decided among us that you and your companion need to pay for the beatings our men had to endure, and the poverty their families will suffer, with no money to pay for rent or for food—"

"This is too much. I tell you, I had nothing—"

"Shut up!" the man said, producing a pistol. "Take off your clothes and lie face down on the bed. There's a tin of grease on the floor next to the bed. Prepare yourself with it, or not, it's up to you whether you want pain or pleasure."

"Pleasure? You damned stupid—"

The man discharged his pistol into the ceiling, causing Lennard to draw back in alarm. The immediate sound of anxious men's voices, their feet slapping against the stairs as they hurried up, made him realise there was more to this plan than this solitary Irishman with dark lashes having his way with Lennard.

"Are you all right?" The first of four men who piled into the room asked of his companion. The faces of all four were partially covered: either by domino masks, or like those of the first man he'd seen in the street, wearing *commedia dell'arte* masks.

"Never better," Dark-lashes replied. "You're just in time to watch our nobleman friend here disrobe."

"I always enjoyed myself more with an audience," Lennard said acidly, not wishing to give them any inkling of the fear he felt in his gut.

"What makes you think they're the audience, Malloray?" the man said, then gestured toward the mattress with his pistol.

*****

Lennard lay on his stomach, his face wet with tears and bile rising in his throat. He'd acquiesced during the ordeal, mainly to avoid injury and also to rob his assailants of any pleasure they may have found had he struggled and screamed in protest.

If humiliation, rather than injury, had been the purpose of their business, they'd succeeded. However, he swore they'd never learn the extent of the mortification he'd felt. He refused to give them that satisfaction—it was the sole positive thought he'd been able to muster during the ordeal.

They told him not to move until he heard their signal: two distant gunshots. Only then did he scream his despair into the rancid mattress.

The last of them to make free with his body had been the dark-lashed man, who'd settled gently onto his body and had used him as he might have done a lover. That was even more revolting than the ferocious and punishing defilements of the four men before him, two of whom had returned for a second, more frenzied assault.

The dark-lashed Irish man's gentle biting of the back of Lennard's neck and soft, caressing of his body had made him want to vomit. That last coupling had been the one truly abusive and most repulsive act of them all, especially when, after he'd finished, he'd turned Lennard onto his back, had one of the men pull back his knees, then had deeply pricked each of Lennard's buttocks with the point of his dagger.

Lennard jumped off the bed and grabbed his waistcoat, the only of his garments the men had left in the room. He raced down the stairway, falling near the bottom in the dark and crashing face first onto the floorboards, cracking his nose. Ignoring the warm taste of blood in his mouth, he ran toward the light of his hand lamp, which he'd been told would be left near the exit to the warehouse.

Once outside, he fumbled in the pocket of his waistcoat. The damned bosun's pipe had fallen from it in the dark. He cursed under his breath, racing up the laneway to the corner where he'd asked Christopher to wait, not far from an empty house in which he'd been told he'd find Elam bound and gagged. He ignored the bumps and scrapes to his feet and shins as he tore down the darkened street, his waistcoat bunched up in one hand and pressed against his groin—not for modesty's sake, but as padding should he collide with something or fall over again, in order to protect the tenderest parts of his body.

"Lennard! Quick, over here!"

Lennard ran toward Christopher, who was hunched down on the edge of the street beside the carriage. He seemed to be struggling with a sack of chaff, or something unwieldy, hanging loosely in his arms, as he tried to pick it up.

"He came tumbling out of the doorway just after I heard the shots—" Christopher started to explain.

"Elam!" Lennard screamed as he recognised the bundle as a man, not an object. He threw himself onto Elam, pushing Christopher aside and howling in fright. Elam was a mass of blood; his eyes swollen shut, lips split, and gore soaked through his clothes.

"Lenn, is that you?" Elam shouted, pulling Lennard into his arms, sobbing loudly.

"Yes, it's me, Elam," Lennard yelled, frustrated that Elam could neither see him nor hear him, but hoping the familiarity of his smell or his embrace would comfort his friend.

"There's no time, Lenn," Christopher said. "We need to get him to a doctor."

"Travis Holland! We'll go to Birch House. Help me put him in the carriage and we'll go straight there ..." Lennard couldn't continue what he'd been about to say. The words dried up in his mouth and he began to dry heave.

"Lennard? What's wrong?"

The enormity of what had happened had finally hit home. Lennard turned his head and vomited onto the roadside, Elam still clutched in his arms. It was the first time since his ordeal began that he'd become truly aware of what had been done to him.

"Lenn, for Christ's sake, where are your clothes? There's blood on your arse and down the back of your legs. Let me see—"

"It's nothing," Lennard shouted through tears. "The blood must be Elam's."

Christopher knew Lennard's lie the moment he heard it. He growled silently, his heart filled with anger, assuming something terrible had happened. But respectful of Lennard's assertion that nothing was wrong, jumped to his feet and opened the carriage door before bending down to help Lennard pick Elam up from the ground.

As he leaped up onto the driver's platform all he could hear from inside the carriage were the sounds of two men calling each other's names, sobbing loudly.

15. HUMILIATION AND RETRIBUTION

Travis had been in bed for ages, but he'd woken with a start, imagining he'd felt the room move beneath his bed. But then realised it had been a dream of being at sea in a rolling swell and his mind had played tricks on him.

Unable to get back to sleep, he'd relit the oil lamp beside his bed and had picked up the novel he'd been reading, *Hide and Seek*, by Wilkie Collins. He'd initially thought it rather trite, but the more he'd been reading it, the more he'd been drawn into the mystery. Lady Spratt had presented it to him, inscribed with thanks for the "kindest physician it has been my privilege to have known". He'd been very touched. She was a delightful creature, oddly ignorant of the duties of her impending motherhood. Still, he reckoned that they were wealthy enough not to have to bother with the actual rearing of their children.

He'd just reached the paragraph in the story in which the hair bracelet is first noticed when he became aware of a noise outside in the street. He glanced at his timepiece, which always remained next to his bed in a holder stand. Half past one? What on earth was going on in Soho Square?

Almost immediately the thought had crossed his mind, he heard loud banging at the front door of the house and the sounds of men's voices shouting below. He threw on his nightshirt—he usually slept naked, even in the middle of winter—and had reached the top of the staircase that led down into the house when Lennard thundered up, stopping on the landing below him, completely naked, his face contorted, and cheeks wet with tears.

"Please, Travis, it's Elam! He's been beaten so severely that he's just fallen unconscious. Dear God, please—"

"Stop, Lennard. Get a hold of yourself and help me down the stairs. I can't manage with my leg. You can howl all you like once I see to your friend."

Lennard jumped up the stairs, stopped, then bent his knees. "Ready?" he asked.

"Ready for what—?"

Travis Holland found himself in a sailor's hoist over Lennard's shoulder, no mean feat as he had at least a stone over Lennard and four inches or more in height. However, Lennard's sure step on the staircase and familiarity with the hold allayed Travis's anxiety that they might slip and both come crashing down.

"He's in here!" Mark Huskerson called out from Travis's consulting room.

"Put something around yourself, Lennard," Travis said. "You can tell me why you're naked and your legs are bloodied after I've seen to Elam. Is the blood his?"

"No, Travis—"

"Have you been injured?"

"I think not, sir. The blood is from two puncture wounds to my arse cheeks."

Travis recoiled momentarily then limped away from Lennard as he moved toward his consulting room. "You can help me while I attend to Elam if you wish, and tell me what happened, and how you came to be wounded. I've never heard of such a thing. Grab one of the tablecloths from the linen cupboard in the dining room to cover yourself. You know where it is."

"I'll be with you directly, Travis. I need to give instruction to Christopher."

"While standing naked in my front doorway for the whole of Soho Square to see?" Travis called out over his shoulder as he disappeared into his room.

"It wouldn't be the first time," Lennard replied, amazed that he was able to be so flippant under these extreme circumstances.

Having sent Christopher back to Bexford House with instructions to wake Gerald and return with him and a set of clothes, Lennard made his way into Travis's consulting room, the damask tablecloth tied loosely around his waist.

"He's no longer unconscious and keeps calling for you," Travis said, the moment Lennard appeared in the doorway.

Lennard moved quickly to Elam's side and took his hand, which Elam pressed to his lips.

"Mark has gone to heat water, Lennard. Make yourself useful and tell me what happened," Travis said, carefully inspecting Elam's face, gentle in his touch as he used two fingers to pry apart the lids of one of Elam's eyes. "Can you see me?" he asked.

"Yes, Travis, I can read your words. Lenn are you there?"

Lennard leaned over into his line of sight. "Can't you feel me holding your hand?"

"Yes, of course I can. I just wanted to know if you are all right?"

"Worry about yourself, Elam," Travis said. "Let me examine you. If anything hurts too ferociously, you have my permission to strike out. Do you understand?"

Elam nodded then felt for Lennard's shirtfront. Finding nothing, he wound his hand behind Lennard's head. "Did they …?"

"Yes, Elam. But I promise you I'm not harmed."

At that moment, Mark Huskerson arrived with a large basin and a jug of hot water.

"Use those towels next to the examining couch, Mark, if you please. Dampen the edge in hot water and carefully clean away the blood on Elam's face—"

"Travis, please—" Lennard started to say.

"There seem to be no broken facial bones, Lennard. He has a gash on his scalp that accounts for the worst of the blood. That, together with a split of his eyebrow and of his lip make it look worse. He's taken a beating, but I need to speak with you. Immediately, and outside in the corridor."

Once outside the room, Travis closed the door. "I've seen hundreds of beatings during my time as a naval surgeon, Lennard. Elam will recover. He'll be bruised and no doubt will be sore for days, but I'd like him to stay here while he recovers. I'm not sure, but I suspect he has a fractured rib. I also need to make sure there's nothing worse, hidden away, as yet undetected. A week at most and you can visit every day. Now, about you."

"Please, don't fuss, there's nothing—"

"Were you violated? Tell me straight. No secrets, no lying. This is important, Lennard. From your conversation, as little as there was with Elam, I need to know whether someone forced themselves upon you without your permission."

"Travis, I—"

"This is no time for prudery or omission, Lennard. I'm no fool. I make no judgement about what men do, especially when I see such happiness that comes from it as I do with you and some of your friends. Now, answer me plain, did someone—"

"Yes! Yes! Five of them, two twice."

"Good God, Lennard! The blood on the backs of your legs, are you sure it's from the puncture wounds. Could you have been torn? Is there any internal pain?"

"No, there's no pain, even when I clench. I fear the puncture wounds, done with the point of a dagger were meant to be a constant reminder to me of the humiliation I was forced to suffer, and that every time I sit down, I shall think of—"

"We can talk of this later. But I need you to wash yourself clean, then use the chamber pot. Before you empty it out, please tell me if there's any blood. If there's just stool and mucous, then you're lucky, but if there's been any internal injury, mark my words, it could be very serious indeed."

"Travis, I—"

"I'm sorry to cut you off, but I must see to Elam. I'll examine you later, after you report to me whether you have passed blood or not."

Travis turned his back abruptly before Lennard could answer, so he did what he was asked, making his way to the sluice room where he found a towel and some soap. Then, after cleaning himself, fetched a chamber pot from the draining shelf and made his way to the earth closet with a candle to light his way.

*****

Gerald arrived in time to see Lennard stretched out over Travis's examination table on his stomach with the doctor crouched down, using a silver-backed lamp for more light, apparently examining Lennard's fundament.

"Dear God, Lenn … what happened?"

Lennard was about to respond when Travis cut him off. "Questions and answers can wait, Gerald. I'm sorry to be so abrupt, but for the moment, please allow me to get about my work. This is most important."

Gerald glanced at Elam, frowning at the pile of blood-stained clothes on the floor next to his cot. But as he seemed to be asleep, he pulled up a chair, sitting at one side of the examination table, his mind reeling, and fear in his belly. Travis did not seem to be inspecting the twin wounds on Lennard's buttocks, but was carefully touching and gently prodding somewhere else.

"There seem to be no tears, Lennard," Travis said. "You were very wise not to resist. I've seen dreadful injuries when men have struggled."

"It made it no less disagreeable."

"I've seen two men die from a perforated bowel, Lennard. Consider yourself watched over by some greater power. I'll give you a lanolin-based ointment to apply three times a day. The bruises around your waist and on your arms will fade and the bites on the back of your neck and your shoulders are skin deep. Were they to have broken the epidermis, I'd be advising salt water. You can use gin if it's from a reliable source. Sometimes that can help with the bruises. Now that Captain

Langbourne has arrived—good evening, Gerald—and while I'm stitching Elam's eyebrow and scalp closed, you can tell me what happened."

"I can tell you parts of it, Travis," Lennard said.

Travis polished his magnifying spectacles, regarding Lennard sternly. "If we're to continue being friends of such closeness, there must come a time when you decide whether I'm a man to be trusted or not, Lennard. I wish to know for no other reason than wondering what other disasters may appear on my doorstep in the depths of the night, and what I shall say if anyone ever asks me difficult questions about them."

"You should have let me come with you, Lennard!" Gerald almost shouted. "You forget you and Elam are as dear to me as you are to each other. Why I allowed you to risk yourselves—"

"They were armed, Gerald. I think us lucky that Elam and I may have been merely injured and not killed."

"Astley is behind it?"

"Indubitably. They said it was for the punishment of their friends about the *Pendragon*, but—"

"What? Stop, the pair of you!" Travis said. "Please don't ignore me. I shan't continue with another stitch until you tell me what this is all about."

Gerald stared at Lennard for a moment. "How many men, Lennard?"

"Five. Two of them twice."

"You were used seven times?"

Lennard nodded, without raising his eyes, the heat of his shame burning up over his chest and neck.

"I shall kill every one of them."

"No, Gerald. That would be of no use. It was done to humiliate me. They knew what they were about. Tempered violence is the way I'd describe it."

"Then we should speak. There's no reason Travis should not know about this episode."

"There are others?" Travis asked.

"All in good time," Lennard said. "But first, sir, I'm anxious to the point of exploding about Elam."

"Exploding will do no one any good. Now tell me everything you can about the *Pendragon* and what it has to do with Sir Terrence Astley and the indignities and injuries both you and Elam have suffered."

*****

Angus arrived at Bexford House at nine the following morning, rushing through the front door and throwing his hat to Merrill without stopping to say a word. He burst into the breakfast room, startling Lennard with the violence of his entry.

"Lennard, are you all right? I had a telegram from Robert saying you and Elam had been hurt. As he gave no details, I came straight here."

"As you can see, although I'm in my dressing gown, I'm sitting up, eating my breakfast, and enjoying every bite. I assure you that I'm not ready for the grave just yet."

"Dear God! I've never seen you look so pale."

"You'll look much the same after I've told you what happened."

"What do you mean?"

Lennard stood and, ignoring the fact that Stephen was standing at service near the credenza, eased his dressing gown from his shoulders and allowed it to fall to the floor. He was naked underneath and his body shades of purple and blue from his shoulders to mid-thigh.

"Was it …?"

"Thank you, Stephen," Lennard said to the under-footman. "That will be all for the moment. I'll ring should I need anything. Will you eat something, Angus?"

"I'll have coffee, if there's any."

"There's tea on the sideboard, but Stephen will bring coffee up for you presently."

"Thank you, Lennard," Angus said, visibly shaken, having slowly run his eyes over the bruises on his friend's shoulders, waist, torso, and buttocks.

"I'm afraid I'm becoming an old hand at telling this story, so forgive me if I start at the beginning and hurry through to the end. Please hear me through then ask your questions afterward."

Angus leaned forward and gingerly laid his hand on Lennard's shoulder. "It can wait if you wish, Lenn. I can see by the pain in your eyes there's more to it than bruises."

*****

Twenty minutes later, Angus sank back in his chair, his head bowed. It was all he could do not to weep. Despite Lennard's protestations of his soul being "untouched", Angus had known him all their shared adult life and recognised the incandescent rage that seethed under Lennard's veneer of self-control.

"I could see to it that Astley suffered an unfortunate accident, Lennard. No one would ever know. Losing an eye, or perhaps a limb?"

Lennard carefully folded his linen table napkin and rang for Stephen to clear the table.

"I have a much better idea, Angus. Would you like to increase your fortune?"

"Is this a rhetorical question? What do you have in mind—robbing Astley's coffers?"

"In a manner of speaking. Now, before we proceed, how is the coffee? Is it to your liking?"

"Indeed, Lennard, it has an excellent taste. Something reminiscent of chocolate lingers on the back of the tongue."

"Stephen," Lennard said to his under-footman when he entered the breakfast room. "Would you please clear the table then ask Miles to bring up another pot of coffee and a new set of cups and saucers, enough for three?"

"Miles?" Angus asked after Stephen had left with the breakfast service.

"Do you remember my conversation with Sir George that day at the Oriental Club? I spoke of the rumour I'd put about that Malloray's intended to offer warehouse space and docking rights at our Italian ports."

"Yes, I do remember, but you told us that it was a fabrication, to keep Astley at bay. Obviously, that hasn't worked."

"Ah yes, but it has, Angus, and too well. The price has been high, and unexpected, but what is that saying about vengeance?"

"Which particular saying?"

"Euripides, from Medea."

"Ah, the one about lovers?"

"Yes, but please don't quote it in Ancient Greek. I know how you love to dazzle me with your brilliance."

Angus chuckled, placing his hand on top of Lennard's. "You can't hide your hate and anger from me of all people, Lennard Alexandre Malloray. Yes, the hate of a lover for a former lover is like none other. The translation is something akin to '*stronger than lover's love is lover's hate. Incurable, in each, the wounds they make*'."

"My hate for Astley is inestimably more profound on account of Elam. Was my defilement not enough? Why did my poor, lovely man have to suffer on my account?"

"Terrence Astley is a wretched creature, Lennard. Who understands a person with such a black heart and a conceit as great as his?"

"I shall ruin him, Angus. I shall bring down his house and his fortune, one brick at a time, a shilling after a shilling. I'll leave him with nothing but a memory of his former comfort and I'll shame his reputation so thoroughly that he'll not only lose his seat in parliament but also so gravely that no person of quality in the land would see him fit to be in their presence. He won't see it coming until the very last minute, when everything is snatched away from him in the blink of an eye."

"I should wait until you've calmed, Lenn. Take time to reflect on such a course of action. Breathe deep. Then, in a week or two, reconsider your plan. You may not feel quite so white-hot as you do now."

"Have you ever known me to be rash or foolish, Angus?"

"No, never. And that's what has me alarmed now, Lennard. Such talk about destroying Astley is surely born as a reflex of last night. Give it time—"

"Give it time? You don't understand, Angus. This is not a plan of my making of the past ten hours. I've been planning my intentions for the past five years, ever since I first learned of his calumny and his betrayal of my trust. Do you think me that precipitous? No, my dearest friend, this last insult is merely the nudge I needed to begin to put my plan into action."

"Well, Lenn. You'd best tell me which seat I'm to occupy in the great steam locomotive of your ferocious revenge."

"Wait until Miles arrives, because he, too, will be a passenger on the same journey."

No more than a pair of minutes later, Miles entered the room carrying his silver butler's tray upon which was an array of pastries, the coffee pot, cups and saucers, and small plates.

"Shall I help you dress later this morning, Lenn?" he asked as he placed the tray on the table and began to set out the china.

"Yes, thank you, Miles, unless you're too busy. Who else has valet training?"

"Stephen helped gentlemen on weekend shooting parties for his former employer."

"Seeing Elam will be away for a week and you have other duties, perhaps we should train both him and also a few of the new footmen. Speaking of Elam, I'm intending to visit him directly I'm dressed. Will you come with me? I'm sure you're anxious to see him."

"Of course, I am. However, you told me last evening, when you returned, that Mr Holland had given him a sleeping draught, otherwise I would have gone there directly you informed me of his condition."

"I asked you to have coffee with us because I have a plan in hand that concerns both you and Elam, and The Brothers. Please, inform Stephen we're not to be disturbed, close the door, and pour yourself a cup. This is family business and I'd like it to remain in the room between us."

"Where is Gerald?" Angus asked.

"I informed him last night of what I'm about to tell you. He's attending to some of the business already. Miles knows a little of the background, but you don't. I believe I've mentioned the carrot we'd dangled before Astley—the Italian trade possibility. You already know that's not a reality. What you don't know, however, is that I have engaged an agent who has been working on behalf of a new company, one which I'd like you to affix your name to as a shareholder. The documents have been signed by the rest of us, yours is the last to be appended."

"Another new company? Sir George told me about Elenrob Pty Ltd."

"This one is called Fratelli Imports and Exports, registered in Messina, with a limit of six shareholders."

"Fratelli? That means 'brothers' in Italian, does it not?"

"Indeed, Angus. And the six shareholders shall be we four, The Brothers, and two more, the friends of our youth, Miles and Elam."

"And the purpose of this agent in regard to the new company?"

"He's an Italian, a Signor Baldacchino. I engaged him the day after Astley arrived on my doorstep, five weeks since, with his preposterous offer for Malloray's. He's a registered purchasing agent, known to Malloray's, and is very trustworthy … I see you have questions?"

"A million, Lennard, but please continue."

"Signor Baldacchino, on behalf of Fratelli Imports and Exports, has been buying shares in Killcaire's Irish Trading Company, and his purchases have had the effect of generating some increased interest among those who invest in the stock market. His acquisitions have heightened the surmise that it's Astley's company that might be the successful tenderer for Malloray's wharf space and trading ports in Italy. He does it in such a manner that the price of the shares has risen gently, about two per cent over the past five weeks, enough of an incentive for other stockholders to invest in Astley's company."

"Very well, so far, all I can see is you enriching the purse of the man you hate."

"Did you know that my grandfather owned stock in Astley's company?"

"No, I did not. Shares that presumably are now yours, Lennard?"

"Precisely. It's because of that shareholding that Malloray's has been able to bring in goods from Astley's wharves in La Corunna. I now own twenty per cent of his business. Mr Baldacchino, by using his own hired associates, has managed to buy another nine per cent, gathered here and there in small amounts, in order to avoid any suspicion falling on him directly."

"I sense a scheme here, Lennard."

"Astley's father left Terrence forty per cent. He's the majority shareholder and sits as the chairman of the board and manager. The eleven per cent that gives him complete control of the business is owned by his acquiescent—and very, very nervous—uncle, a man who can't abide him, but who tolerates him for the annual dividends and the rich profits from the Spanish trade."

"You said he was nervous?"

"Nervous for his investment, Angus."

"Ah ... so you intend to—"

"Yes, once Signor Baldacchino has managed to purchase more of Astley's stock, Robert will announce that Malloray's plans have changed, and the company no longer has any interest in selling docking and trading rights in Italy. I shall get Martin Wilson, to whom I have 'sold' my shares in Astley's—it was merely a paper transaction with no money passing hands—to sell them at less than fifty per cent of their current market value. I'll make sure the transaction is mentioned in *The Times* and, if anyone asks, he can say he panicked, and Mr Baldacchino snapped them up for Fratelli's."

"Martin Wilson is in on your plan?"

"Why not, Angus? He's a businessman as much as you and I—his molly house is extremely profitable. We signed an agreement, not two days ago, witnessed by Mr Drudge, and as a result of the sale, and for his trouble, Martin will be richer by five per cent of the value of the transaction, which did not cost him a penny."

"Dear heavens, Lennard. It's you who should be schooling me in duplicity."

"There's nothing illegal being done, Angus. All's fair when it comes to business."

"But Martin selling those shares at half the market value will cause a panic sell-off of the shares held by other investors!"

"Exactly! And again, all snapped up by Mr Baldacchino."

"But you'll lose a fortune when you sell at such a low price. It still won't help you ... oh, wait a moment. Of course! I understand now. As it was a paper transaction with Martin, you won't have lost a penny. What a stroke of genius!"

"As the company is registered in Messina and its regulations follow those of the Bourbon rulers of Sicily, the names of the shareholders are not public. The final nail in Astley's coffin will come when the bottom falls out of the market. Mr Baldacchino, who made an offer to Astley's uncle a month ago—unsuccessfully, I might add—will once more approach him, offering to purchase his eleven per cent at the same price he did previously. If he is successful, Fratelli Imports and Exports will take control of the board."

"A great coup, indeed, should it come to pass," Angus said. "And once Fratelli's is the major shareholder, what are your plans?"

"Signor Baldacchino will be nominated to be the interim chairman of the board. He'll produce a legal document that gives him permission to act according to the instructions of the directors of Fratelli's. Then, a few months later, he'll declare Killcaire's Irish Trading Company is no longer of interest to Fratelli's, who have decided to sell the business to the highest bidder."

"So, what I presume you're saying is that Fratelli's will sell it to Malloray, Beauchamp, and Fahey."

"Of course. It would be foolhardy for any shipping company not to fight to buy Killcaire's Irish Trading Company. Malloray, Beauchamp, and Fahey will gain his fleet of eleven ships, his trading rights with Spain, and those with the West Indies. That's why I asked you about the coffee."

"I'm sorry," Angus said. "I don't follow?"

"I shall explain carefully. As I said, this plan has been some time in the making, and it's only in these past five weeks that I've been able to put it into action. Almost the day after I came into my inheritance, I went about the business of creating the Fratelli 'empire'. To start it off, and to give it some credence, I invested twenty thousand pounds of my own money, which was enough for Baldacchino to start to buy shares in Astley's business and to provide for a few other investments. The first of those, completed not more than two weeks ago, was to buy coffee plantations. Six of them. In total, two thousand acres spread over Jamaica, Puerto Rico, and Haiti."

"Ah, so once you obtain Astley's trading rights with the West Indies, you will save a fortune in double tariffs, plus import a very large amount of coffee without having to go through Spain, and sell it both in this country and also in the colonies. Am I right?"

"You are, indeed, Angus. With our own vessels in the Caribbean, Malloray's could sail directly from Kingston to the Port of London."

"How much do you think you'll lose in the playing out of this scheme, Lennard?"

"Lose? What makes you think I'm going to lose money, Angus? I expect to double my twenty thousand in the space of twelve months. When Malloray's buys Astley's shipping business for a pittance, we won't absorb it into Malloray, Beauchamp, and Fahey, but keep it a separate entity, and eventually rename it. We shall retain fifty-one per cent ownership. As a new public company, majority-owned and run by England's most successful shipping company, we six shall make a fortune!"

"We six? I still don't understand how?"

"Because, before we float the company, Malloray's will offer thirty per cent of the remaining shares to another company, leaving twenty-nine per cent for public investors."

"Ah! So, Fratelli's will be the invited company, I imagine?"

"Just so, Angus. So, between Malloray's and Fratelli's, we shall manage the new company as we wish, and reap whatever profits it makes."

"Is that legal?"

"Of course it is, Angus."

"But what about Astley? Won't he interfere?"

"Once Astley's company is sold to Malloray's, he'll have nothing to do with it. He'll get the value of his forty per cent shareholding at whatever pittance Fratelli's decides to sell it to Malloray's … I shall make sure he loses a vast fortune."

"I just can't see Terrence Astley calmly lying down and taking this without—"

"I've already pointed out to you that Astley will have no say, Angus. His former company will have been sold. End of story. Robert and I have spoken, and we've decided the new name of the company, to retain familiarity to the Spanish and West Indian companies, will be called Killcaire's Irish and Estuary Trading Company."

"He'll have a fit!"

"He can fit all he likes, but everyone else will see the sense in it. Terrence Astley's old company will exist no more, except as a memory and as a name appended to a new, very successful venture that will have him shrieking impotently as he sees its share prices growing day by day."

"I'm rather puzzled about your twenty thousand pound investment, Lennard. It seems you're staking your own money to make a profit for your friends at no cost to them."

"Just trust me, my friend."

"I shall have to employ you as my investment manager, Lennard. I had no idea how clever you have been. Now, tell me why you thought the coffee plantations were such a wise investment. It's something I've never really thought about."

"To me, it was a wise decision made on the behalf of all of us. Coffee is the future. I'd also like to perhaps make investments in the Far East. Perhaps develop coffee plantations in the Dutch East Indies or on the island of New Guinea, anywhere the climate is suitable. However, we can discuss that at a later time. Consider your share in Fratelli's a gift made from friendship, as it has been to the others."

"I think it's a wonderful idea, Lennard, and I feel quite blessed, yet again, to be counted as one of the dearest of your companions. However, I'm very happy to support this new venture, and I intend to make a financial contribution to the business to enable further investments. I shan't take a no for an answer, Lennard. I'll send you a signed cheque for my share in this coffee and shipping extravaganza, made out to Fratelli Imports and Exports, the moment I return home. You can fill in the amount yourself, as you haven't told me how much you paid for your acres of sunshine in the West Indies."

"Take the cheque to Drudge, Angus. He'll tell you the appropriate amount. You'll be able to sign the Fratelli company documents at the same time and he'll issue you a receipt and mark you down as a stakeholder in the coffee venture, and as part-owner of the future shipping company, if our cards all fall as we hope they will."

"You're a genius, Lennard."

"I will be if this scheme works, Angus. Now, what do you think, shall we shake on it? You too, Miles?"

Miles stood and hugged Lennard tight. "If only our parents could see the day when Elam and I might be so well provided for.

Lennard, you know I'd do anything for you and I'll happily shake your hand."

"As will I, Lenn. Now, why are you smiling so bright?"

"Because of the irony, Angus."

"Irony?"

"Astley will still see his name attached to a company he no longer owns but which is making a fortune."

"He still has his North American and Canadian company, Lennard. He won't be totally destitute."

"Until the day I can link his name with The Cargo in an iron-clad manner, Angus. Then it will be either the hangman's rope for treason, or a quick escape into exile for Terrence Maonaigh Astley, the sixth Baronet Killcaire."

"And another new shipping acquisition for Malloray's and Fratelli's combined?"

"Ah! You're starting to think like a businessman, Angus. There's hope for you yet!"

*****

Travis was sitting on his front doorstep, polishing his boots when Lennard, Angus, and Miles arrived. When the front gate protested with a squeak, the doctor glanced up at them with a cheeky smile and with a slight tinge of embarrassment.

"Good morning, Travis," Lennard said. He glanced up into the cloudless sky. "Nice morning for it."

"Judge me not, Lennard. I've always done my own boots, right from a child. Even aboard a ship when there was a boy to do the officers' footwear. It puts my soul right with the world."

"Lennard squeezes his pimples," Angus said cheekily, over Lennard's shoulder.

Travis chuckled at Lennard's eye roll. "How did you sleep, Lennard?"

"Exceedingly well, thank you. I was exhausted when I got home. Gerald sat on the bed and we talked for an hour or two and fell asleep somewhere about three in the morning."

"No pain? Discomfort?"

"None physical, Travis. How fares Elam?"

"He's sleeping now. Would you like to come inside? I have news."

"Not bad news, I hope?"

"No, excellent news in fact. I'll call Mrs Huskerson for tea."

"None for me, thank you, Travis," Angus said. "I'm awash with coffee."

"Where is he?" Lennard asked, after Mark Huskerson had taken their hats and coats.

"In my treatment room. Have a look but go quietly, please don't disturb him. He's recovering."

"Recovering?"

"Yes, Lennard, recovering. He's very drowsy and shall be for about another hour. Just peek around the door, then join me in the sitting room and I'll explain."

Lennard, with Miles looking over his shoulder, gasped softly after opening the door a crack and peering into the room. Elam was dressed in a nightgown, lying on his back, propped up on the chaise longue, his head swathed in bandages. "What on earth …?" he whispered to Miles, while watching the slow rise and fall of Elam's chest as he slept.

"Come away, Lenn. He looks peaceful enough. I'm sure Dr Holland will explain. He said it was good news."

Lennard pulled himself away. Every fibre of his body called for him to move quietly to Elam's side and to take his hand.

"I checked him all over last night and again this morning," Travis explained. "His rib is not broken. He said they kicked him a bit and roughed him around, but as it was so violent, he couldn't read anything they were saying, so I suppose he was spared the ignominy of their coarse words."

"He was lucky in that aspect of the ordeal. I think I was on the receiving end of those he could not hear. However, I'd like to move on from that subject, for the time being, Travis. It's something I will come to terms with it my own time and in my own way."

"Can you not report it, Lennard? Surely—"

"What am I to say, Travis? A violation of this kind would never be accepted in society were it to become public knowledge. I would lay

he'll need to wear earmuffs, because both cold weather and wetness in the ears could cause a recurrence."

"Perhaps we should move to Spain?" Lennard asked with a chuckle.

Travis smiled. "In the meantime, I'd like him to stay here for the next fortnight, where I can keep an eye on his progress. As this is your house, Lennard, you know there are spare bedrooms if you decide you can't be bothered going home. Anytime you wish."

Although Travis's voice was uninflected, Lennard heard the insinuation behind the words and was sorely pleased with Travis's generosity and acceptance of his relationship with Elam. "Thank you, Travis. I'll speak with Elam when he's awake and see what he thinks."

"I must be getting back to the office, Lennard," Angus said. "Would it be an enormous imposition to ask whether Christopher might take me there and return for you afterwards?"

"No, of course not, if you'll do me a favour."

"Of course."

"You still have your lovely filly, Minerva, stabled at your London house?"

"Yes, of course I do."

"Will you rendezvous with me tomorrow morning at Hyde Park?"

"Hyde Park?"

"Yes, I wish to make the morning social ride along Rotten Row up to Kensington Palace and back, and I'd like you to accompany me."

"Good grief, Lennard. You can't be serious, surely? I've seen the wounds on your arse cheeks. You can't ride yet … think of the discomfort, my friend."

"I'll bandage my backside as best I can, and I have a new pair of thick double-woven black serge riding pants, which will conceal any blood should it seep through."

"But the pain—"

"I need to do this, Angus. I rarely ride at the social-gathering hour of the morning and my new outfit and equipage will make heads turn. It will guarantee a mention in the press, especially as Prince Christian Jost will be accompanying us."

"He will?"

"He will, once you ask him."

"But Lennard—"

"He and I are negotiating a trading route between London and Geestemünde, where the prince has warehouses. There is some substance in the reason for our meeting. You can tell him that I would also be grateful for his presence in public, although I'd rather you not share the reason behind it. I can't have Astley thinking that I'm suffering after what he arranged to have done to me. I intend to go on as if it were of no consequence to my person."

"Very well, Lennard. What time shall we meet?"

"I'll get Christopher to drive me in the carriage with Chester tethered behind, and meet you at Stanhope Gate. Shall we say ten?"

"Agreed. I'll look forward to seeing you then and shall send a telegram if His Highness has other, unavoidable duties. Goodbye Miles, Dr Holland."

"Sir Angus," Travis said, shaking Angus's hand. "May I ask you a question before you go? Although I'm not au fait with everything to do with the aristocracy, I believe you're a viscount. Surely your appellation should be either 'my lord' or simply 'viscount'. Why are you called Sir Angus? I don't understand."

"Ah! Mr Holland, it's one of those British institutional anomalies. In society, of course you're right, that's how I'm addressed, either by 'my lord' or simply 'viscount'. My peers call me Fallerton because I am the Viscount Fallerton. However, the person who holds the office of personal private secretary to any of the senior ministers is always called 'Sir' if he's a member of the aristocracy, no matter what his rank. It's a tradition."

"Understood."

"In any case, please call me Angus, like the others do. You've been so kind to me and my dear wife. I should consider it an honour if you did so."

"Very well, Angus. I should do my best not to confuse the situation and address you by the wrong name or title."

"He's very devoted to you, both of you," Travis said after Angus had left them. "You must be very good friends."

"We six were lads together, Travis. In the days before titles and social mores. It's hard leading a double life. Maintaining a masquerade designed to maintain social levels and to hide friendships, and put on quite different faces in public is quite onerous. Especially difficult when it comes to intimate friends from different classes—a thing most ladies and gentlemen would never allow to suffer in their normal life."

"I never thought of it that way, Lennard. Thank you for explaining, and yes, I do see how difficult it must be. But let's see if Elam is awake yet. His eyes will still be swollen, but I applied a poultice overnight, so he'll be able to see a little and read your words."

"Thank you, Travis. I can't express how much I appreciate what you've done."

"It's what friends do, Lennard. Please, after you."

Lennard and Miles hugged Travis in turn, each man slapping his back affectionately, before making their way down the hallway to Travis's treatment room.

*****

"Bertram!"

"On my way up now," Bertram Fetcher called out, fastening his waistcoat as he made his way up the stairs to Astley's day room.

"Have you seen this?" Astley asked, slapping his newspaper angrily.

"Seen what?"

"Yesterday, Lennard Malloray was riding along Rotten Row with Spratt and Prince Christian Jost. I thought you said he wouldn't be able to sit down for a month."

"I saw it with my own eyes, Sir Terrence. Conall stabbed his arse with his dagger. It wasn't a pinprick. The blade went in at least an inch or two."

"He knows, Bertram. It's the only answer. He knows I'm behind what happened. This act of riding in public with the Prince Saxe-Meiningen was done purposely to thumb his nose at me. Was anything said that might have led him to believe I was involved?"

"No. I promise you Conall was very convincing. The story was delivered exactly as you said it should be."

"And you told the prince I was away in Ireland?"

"Of course."

"Are you still to meet him this evening?"

"No, Sir Terrence. Malloray has invited him to dinner, along with the Chancellor of the Exchequer and his wife."

"Who else will be there?"

"I don't know, I'm sorry."

"What blasted use are you to me if you don't know these things, Fetcher!" Astley threw his newspaper across the room. "I need to get you or one of your men into someone's bed in Malloray's circle."

"Isn't that risky?"

"You've no idea what's at stake. Robert Fahey is visiting a seamstress regularly, he's of no use. Langbourne?"

"He doesn't have regulars, from my knowledge. Once and then that's it. He sleeps with them then moves on."

"That leaves Clyford Billings."

"Langbourne's cousin?"

"No, Spratt is Langbourne's cousin. Billings is the impoverished nephew of General Airey. He's one of the Home Office boys. Probably an agent himself and therefore he knows you work for Spratt, as an agent in my house."

"He's comely enough. What do you know about him?"

"Nothing much. Find out what you can. All I know is that he was 'close' to the fourth son of the Earl of Fermanagh—Henry Donaghy. Killed at the battle of Alma last year."

"So, he could be in need of comfort?"

"Where's Conall?"

"In the bath, sir."

"Put him onto finding out some background about Billings. The usual places: taverns, whorehouses, and the like. Find out what type of person Fermanagh's son was, that's the entrée into his society—to become just like his dead lover. Now, if Malloray suspects I'm behind what happened to him and Elam Walters, then I need to go to Ireland as quickly as possible. I'll return next week early on one of my steamers and make a very public arrival at St. Katharine's Dock, to lock in my alibi of being away."

"Very well, Sir Terrence—"

"There's one thing, Bertram, before you go, tell me, when you were spying through the peephole while my men were at their business with Malloray, did you get hard?"

Fetcher took two paces forward and grabbed Astley's hand, placing it against his crotch.

"You mean like now?"

"You're a filthy trollop, Bertram."

"I would be for you."

Astley withdrew his hand. "Get about your business. I'll think about your offer while I'm away."

"I'll think about it too, sir … while I'm in bed with Conall."

Astley laughed and pretend-boxed Fetcher's ears. "Get out. I'll send a telegram when I'm due to return to London."

There was no benefit to himself, Astley thought after Fetcher had left the room. Consorting with him would make things too complicated. If he wanted to empty his bollocks and the urge was upon him, he had both Conall and Colleen.

He'd think about it while he was away, but the idea of carnal relationships with a man who was sleeping with so many others, some of whom might prove dangerous to him, was not high on his list of preferences.

16. CHAFFINCHES, AND UNTIMELY COINCIDENCES

On Monday, two days after the Chancellor of the Exchequer and Prince Christian Jost had come to dinner, Lennard woke feeling wretched.

The wounds on his backside were directly on the points of flesh where his buttocks pressed when sitting. There was only so much he could do while standing; even reclining on his back was uncomfortable. He reached for the bell-pull beside his bed. Then, when Stephen arrived, asked whether Gerald was still in the house.

The daily ritual of cleansing with gin, followed by the application of Travis's lanolin unguent was awkward. There were too many parts of his body he couldn't reach easily by himself without enormous discomfort. Had Elam not been injured, the ordeal, while still painful, would have been met with no embarrassment. Even with Gerald, with whom he'd been intimate ever since they were lads, and who'd touched every part of his body, he still squirmed at the very gentle touch that his friend applied while carefully massaging cream on his buttocks and perineum, for it was there the bruising had been the worst.

"Dear God, Gerald, have a care," he said, face down on the bed, his rear end elevated by two pillows under his hips.

"I'm sorry, Lennard."

"And you can stop laughing."

"I'm happy for you to return the favour, anytime, Lennard."

"Hoping my thumb might slip, I wager?"

Gerald wiped his hands and leaned forward to kiss the back of Lennard's neck. "There's little redness, Lennard, but …"

"But what?"

"Did Travis tell you the section of the cuts is cross-shaped?"

"He didn't need to. The man who did it withdrew the blade and cut me again in each buttock. The second time it felt different. Just as painful, but I imagined he'd turned the blade because he whispered it 'would ward off evil and infection'."

Gerald settled on the edge of the bed, carefully wiping the bruises on Lennard's shoulders with a clean square of linen dipped in a glass of gin that sat on a table beside the bed. "Would you recognise his voice again?"

"He was Irish, for sure. He tried to disguise it, but when he ordered me to stay where I was after he'd finished, I heard some brogue slip into his voice. There's one thing I would recognise though."

"What was that?"

"The thickness of his eyelashes. Black as coal and stark against the ice blue of his eyes. His breath smelled of cinnamon. He was sucking on a cachou. I saw him working it around in his mouth beneath his mask. The smell was over-powerfully strong when he bit the back of my neck at the moment of his climax."

"Lennard—"

"I shall never smell the fragrance of that spice again without thinking of his disgusting use of my body."

"But you said he was not like the others."

"No, Gerald, and that's what made it worse. He made love to me, caressing my body, as if I was an intimate. I wanted to vomit. In the end, he was just like any other man, animal-like, grunting out his orgasm and pushing into me like a demon possessed. Had he been like the others, I could have closed my eyes and tried to ignore it. But his actions were the ultimate defilement."

"Could he have known you?"

"Well, he knew who I was, of course. But known as in society, or at the wharves, or anywhere else? I think not. There's no way I could not have noticed eyes of such distinction. Remarkable, as I told you, for the clarity of their colour and the richness of his black eyelashes."

"Shall I help you roll over?" Gerald asked, kissing Lennard's cheek once his friend was on his back once more.

"You haven't shaven, Gerald? That's unusual?"

"Ah … yes, that."

"Do I sense an assignation, somewhere a close-shaven gentleman of quality might stand out?"

"Perhaps …"

"Feel free to go through my cabinet of disguises, Gerald. We're much of a size, except for our shoes, and there are clothes fit for all occasions."

"Perhaps I may have already taken the liberty, Lenn?"

Lennard laughed. "Tell me what you've chosen then let me guess."

"As you probably already have worked it out, Lennard, it's Arthur Pencott. I've invited him for a meal at the Raven's Beak after he's finished at Malloray's. And you can stop smiling so broadly or I'll slap your arse."

"I was smiling for no other reason than the look on your face, you big puppy dog."

"He's more honest than most I've met, Lenn, and that's no lie. He reminded me where he worked most evenings and what he did, then gave me the opportunity to retract my invitation."

"What was your response?"

"I merely said to him what he did there was no more than I did, except that I did not get paid for my labours."

Lennard laughed so hard he clenched his buttocks. The pain ran through his belly and he had to clutch Gerald's shoulders.

Gerald waited until Lennard had settled then helped him out of bed.

"Call for Stephen, please. It's about time I got dressed."

"I'll help you, Lenn. Don't bother. It wouldn't be the first time I've helped you naked from your bed and into your clothes."

"You are far too saucy for your own good, Gerald. Has any of us ever told you that before?"

"Each and every one of you, and frequently. Honestly though. After what you've been through, I rather hoped some time alone together would give us a chance to talk about things other than the estate, or Malloray's, or The Cargo, or that horrid Russian …"

"Any news on that front?"

"Yes, I did as you instructed, and made a few discreet enquiries. He's well-known at The Queen's Head, but under a pseudonym. They call him 'The Count' to his face and that other similar sounding word behind his back, because he's known not to pay immediately, but to promise payment with interest at the end of the month."

"And does he?"

"Yes, but it does him no favours. The soldiers say it makes them feel like tradespeople, rather than men in Her Majesty's service. He rarely goes into the pub these days, but sits outside in his carriage and sends his man in."

"He has a man? That's news to me."

"And to me. He's not mentioned in any of the documents. Surly looking fellow, late twenties, that sort of age. His name is Bohuslav something. No one seemed to have heard his last name. However—although it cost me two guineas, an hour of vigorous coupling, and a promise of silence to one of the junior officers with whom I may or may not have consorted in the past—I now know that many of the men don't like him. Not because he doesn't pay well, or isn't enthusiastic and will do anything with or for them, but that frequently after the soldier has ejaculated, Bohuslav is oft-times invited to butter the bun after he withdraws."

"Butter the bun?"

"It's a new expression, Lennard. Use your imagination."

"I'm sorry, I—"

"It means to take the place of the man before, immediately after he's done."

"Dear God. That's more or less what I'd heard already as far as his sexual gluttony is concerned."

"Insatiable it seems."

"But with his servant?"

"Doesn't seem to worry you," Gerald said cheekily, helping Lennard into his trousers.

"I shall ignore that jibe, Captain," Lennard replied. "Elam is far more than a mere servant, as well you know. But I suppose that was supposed to make me smile?"

Gerald winked. "It's he who has you wrapped around his little finger, if you ask me, Lenn."

Lennard harumphed softly, reaching for his waistcoat, which Gerald held open for him. "Bohuslav sounds like a Bohemian name to me," he said.

"Either that or …"

"Or what?"

"Or the former Polish controlled territory of the Ukraine."

Lennard stopped; his mind instantly focused on one possibility.

"The Crimean Peninsula is part of that territory," he said.

"Yes. That was my thought too."

"I shall get Angus to assign a shadow."

"I've already taken care of that, Lennard. I spoke with Angus yesterday, after church."

"And when were you going to tell me?"

"I just did, Lenn. You've had enough on your plate. Now, what are your plans for the rest of the week?"

"I shall visit Elam first thing every morning. On Wednesday, after Travis's invitation yesterday to dine with him that evening, I intend to stay over at Birch House. There's plenty of other business during the week, including a few lunch meetings at the Oriental. On Saturday, there's to be the reveal of the success or otherwise of Travis's operation on Elam's ears. In either eventuality, we shall celebrate, whether the outcome be good or bad."

"Saturday is the fifth of May, is it not?"

"Indeed. Why?"

"Ah, that's another thing you haven't heard. The Grand Duke Vassili Vadimovich Kosorukov and his wife, the Lady Frances, will be having tea with Evelyn Simperknell, the Lady Quaisey."

"Finally!"

"Yes, finally. Your good aunt arranged it."

"Will she be there?"

"Most likely. She asked after you at church yesterday."

"I hope you said I was only mildly indisposed."

"I did. We both know she can see through any deception so it was well and good you decided not to attend."

"I could have sat through the service, but she would have been fussing over me. She senses things far beyond my reckoning."

"Well, just as well there are things she doesn't—"

"Ah, but she does, Gerald. She's no person's fool."

"But she's always trying to get us all married."

"To save our reputations, my friend."

"I doubt I have one worth saving."

"You will do when your uncle dies. Once you've become the eighth Viscount Bussell of St. Cleer, she'll find it her duty to discover you someone charming, amenable, and with an enormous dowry."

"Good grief, Lennard. How on earth—"

"The same way Angus does, Gerald. Continue to keep your lover … or lovers. Close your eyes in the bedchamber and cross your fingers that Aunt Caroline finds you a wealthy sapphist, like Adelia, who's also looking for a perfect match with a man who does not wish for romance, and is desperate for a life without bothersome bachelors seeking her hand."

*****

"Ah, Lady Frances, you have such lovely taste in clothes," Evelyn Simperknell, the Lady Quaisey said, her florid features almost lost in the squidge of chubbiness her cheeks made when she smiled. "I'd never have thought to combine fustian and silk in the same garment. Why, it's delicious!"

The Quaiseys had not been part of her family circle, and Frances Kosorukova felt distinctly uncomfortable, especially after her mother had exclaimed "Really?" when she'd revealed over breakfast that she would be accompanying her husband to visit them for tea, only slightly mollified when she had assured her that it was Caroline, Lady Winchester, aunt of the new Lord Betteridge, who'd arranged the meeting.

She would rather have stayed at home; she was out of sorts today. Yesterday, her husband had promised to visit her bedchamber after he'd returned from his gentleman's club, the name of which she still did not know. However, she'd fallen asleep waiting and he hadn't commented when she had come down for breakfast this morning. She'd played with her food, but had felt slightly queasy, unable to eat anything.

Vainly, she'd wished for a puppy to keep her company, or even better, a child. However, her husband visited her bed so infrequently, and made do in such haste, she thought that eventuality unlikely. Still, she was hopeful. A child would give her something to keep her occupied during the day, apart from having to put up with her mother's incessant hypochondria and her husband's almost constant absence during the evenings and business appointments during the day.

She was, what might be described as, "fond" of her husband. After all, what was any woman in society without a spouse? For that, she was protective of their relationship and of his well-being. She couldn't bear the thought of endless years of black should something ever happen to him.

"My dear?" Kosorukov nudged her for a response. She had said nothing after Lady Quaisey's compliment, but had sat staring at something on one of the cornices opposite where they sat.

"I do beg your pardon, madam. I confess that, as far as my garments are concerned, it's Vassili Vadimovich who's responsible. He chooses all of my clothing," she replied, patting her husband's arm.

It was a matter of supreme irritation to the grand duke that his wife, although referring to him in the Russian way with both his Christian name and his patronymic, often baulked at using her higher-ranked married title of grand duchess. She preferred, in these times of unrest, to go by her maiden name and inherited family title—the Countess Frances Everett, one of the lesser titles attached to the estate of her father, the Earl of Twinton. It made his blood boil. Sometimes, if he felt especially annoyed, he'd introduce her as the Grand Duchess Frances Fyodorovna

Kosorukova. It was never done out of meanness; merely to remind her, and those around them, of her proper station in society.

At home, in St. Petersburg, his wife would perhaps have been a lady-in-waiting to the Czarina … that is, if their family name had not descended into such a tattered condition.

"I simply choose the best dressmaker and tailor in the city, Lady Quaisey," he replied. "They are the ones who have the eye for the cut. I may, perhaps, be involved in the choice of fabric and the matching accoutrements, but that's in my blood. Our family was always known for its taste in all things."

He smiled as carefully as he could. It was another thing in his blood—the ability to appear charming and interested in whomever he was conversing with, while bored rigid underneath. Lady Quaisey, although immensely wealthy, suffered from a complete lack of taste and was insensible to the rules of polite conversation among equals. She had an unrefined air about her, although he saw quickly that she was neither coarse nor stupid. He knew she was the daughter of a wealthy tradesman and a housemaid, who'd married well. He realised her constant prattling was due to a nervous disposition—she was harmless enough, but spoke whenever there was the slightest pause, usually of trivial things that had no meaning in refined company. He'd met these types of women before—afraid of their own shadows, yet impossible to stop once they'd launched into some lengthy diatribe.

"The house is charming," he said, craning his neck around the parlour. "Is it a recent acquisition?"

"Lordy, no!" she replied. If she'd had a fan, it wouldn't have surprised him in the least had she slapped it in the palm of her hand and tittered. "We've had it for nearly thirty years. It's just been decorated … I did it myself."

"Charming," he said, smiling again, while groaning inside at the sheer confusion of the appointment of the room. Clashing silks and wallpapers, badly placed furniture—and too much of it—and an unsightly, life-sized Buddha in bright, red-glazed porcelain, which served as an umbrella stand—an umbrella stand, if you please, in a formal reception room of all places!

"Don't you agree, my lady?" he asked of Lady Winchester, who appeared to be trying to converse quietly with his wife, who seemed flustered for some unfathomable reason.

"It has a particular … unique feel about it, duke," she replied. "The taste is unlike any I'm familiar with."

"I've yet to do the rest of the house," Lady Quaisey said, all smiles. "Yet, for some reason, Lord Quaisey seems reluctant to allow me to go ahead unguided."

"Perhaps you might enquire of the grand duke, Lady Quaisey," Lady Winchester said, anxious not to miss the very reason she was there. Although Lennard had never explained why she should have arranged the meeting, she was aware that he did not do such things lightly. She was determined to see his scheme brought to fruition, and the advancement of the Russian into Lady Quaisey's social circle fulfilled.

"The grand duke, madam?"

"I believe the work he's done at Gloucester Lodge, for his in-laws, the Earl and Countess of Twinton, is *sans pareil*."

"Oh, dear, I had no idea. How wonderful." Lady Quaisey smiled greatly. Then, she too, seemed to notice the grand duchess looked flushed. "Are you quite well, my lady?" she asked.

"Yes, quite well, thank you. Perhaps, Vassili, you might offer your advice to Lady Quaisey? I know it's something that interests you greatly. Please, go ahead, I don't mind."

"Of course, my dear," Kosorukov replied.

"He has done a wonderful refurbishment of papa and mama's house. It hadn't been touched for years …" she added, searching her reticule for her vinaigrette, which she fumbled with, then dropped.

"Perhaps you could ring for something cool?" Lady Winchester ventured, as she reached down to pick it up. "It is rather warm, and the grand duchess looks a little—"

"It's nothing," Frances replied quickly, anxious not to make a fuss and spoil her husband's opportunity. "May is such an odd month. I've been feeling warm all morning."

"We have had a shipment of ice delivered this morning, Lady

Winchester, courtesy of your dear nephew, Lord Betteridge. I'll ring for something light and refreshing."

"I can take care of your wife, Grand Duke," Lady Winchester said. "Please, I'm sure Lady Quaisey is anxious to show you around her house and to seek your advice."

"Very well, madam. I'll leave my dear Frances in your capable hands," he said.

Lady Quaisey rang for her footman and asked him to bring a bowl of ice and, with it, the soda gazogene from her husband's smoking room.

Kosorukov waited, chatting softly with Lady Quaisey. Then, when the man had arrived with the ice and soda, stood from his chair, and offered her his arm. "Shall we?" he asked.

"Yes, of course, Your Excellency. Please, follow me," she said, after a quick curtsey.

Lady Quaisey was all for knocking this down, pulling that out, replacing this staircase, putting in another, moving reception rooms around the upper floors away from their designed purpose. However, she'd looked genuinely surprised when he'd remarked, without artifice, that the house was quite beautiful, and its structure and purpose should remain as its architect had originally intended. All it needed was a new refurbishment of draperies, papers, and furnishings. The carpets, having been woven especially for the main rooms, were astounding.

It was by far the most perfectly designed residence he'd been in since arriving in London, some six years ago. Shame that it was owned by people who did not seem to appreciate its grandeur, nor perhaps would do so after he'd wrought his magic and made the house a showpiece of taste and refinement. Still, it would do no harm to become known as a decorator par excellence—under the guise of a dilettante, but with some hidden benefits for him in the form of private acquisitions paid for by his "clients"; that is, if some more people of the Quaisey acquaintance asked for his guidance once they'd seen the miracle that, given a free hand, he'd no doubt perform. He had to admit it, Lennard Malloray had lived up to his promise, and handsomely, so it seemed.

"Perhaps I could prevail on you for your advice on how to proceed, duke?" Lady Quaisey said, trying to distract the Russian from a magnificent pair of Limoges porcelain figures, each about twenty inches high and exquisite in their detail and perfection of manufacture.

"Hmm …" It was an art-form—pretending lack of interest while reeling in the catch.

"Of course, I'd reimburse you for your time."

His smile was barely one. He was no tradesman. There were ways the nobility negotiated these things. "One does not charge friends for favours, Lady Quaisey. However, if there was an agreeable budget, then perhaps I might accommodate one or two purchases for myself. In that way, it will offer you no breach of etiquette to talk of such tawdry matters as money to repay the kindness and generosity of your acquaintance. Did you have a modest sum put aside for the redecoration?" he asked.

"Phht!" she said, with a wave of her hand. "We've buckets and nothing to spend it on. If you were to agree to help me, you could simply have the accounts redirected to my husband's estate manager."

"Then perhaps you should show me around the rest of this magnificence," he said, moving off down the corridor before she'd had time to agree.

They were descending the grand staircase, after having inspected a quite lovely Dutch masterpiece—a sea battle, painted by a man whose name he simply could not pronounce, even after inspecting the signature. Pennons flying, guns firing, smoke, and broken spars, all amid an angry, white-capped green sea. It was a skilful depiction indeed, only in need of a good cleaning and some minor restoration to the frame. As they reached the fourth step above the first landing, Lady Quaisey's lapdog hurtled down from above, having decided to join them. In an effort to avoid stepping on her little "Pumpkin", she caught the hem of her dress and fell heavily against Kosorukov, who lost his footing and tumbled down the stairs, landing on the marble hallway floor and hitting his head with a loud crack.

"Help! Someone come!" Lady Quaisey shouted.

A footman appeared quickly and called out for some of the other servants to attend, before running to see to the grand duke. Kosorukov sat up groggily, holding the back of his head. He inspected his hand, which had come away bloodied, then fainted.

"Fetch a doctor," Lady Quaisey told her footman, only to be interrupted by Lady Winchester who'd appeared to find out what had happened.

"There's a doctor around the corner in Soho Square," Lennard's great-aunt said, kneeling at the grand duke's side. "Mr Travis Holland. He's an acquaintance of some standing and a great friend of my nephew. However, he's injured himself and can't walk any distance."

"What shall we do?" Lady Quaisey asked.

"Have no fear, all is in hand," Lady Winchester said, cool in the head no matter what the circumstance. "Have your man fetch the carriage. Mr Holland is in residence at Birch House, you know it surely, not more than a hundred yards from here across the square. We'll have the grand duke there in a moment."

She stood, allowing the servants to help the grand duke—who'd come round—to his feet, and drew Lady Quaisey to one side.

"What is it, Caroline?" Lady Quaisey asked, manners forgotten.

"I think we should take the grand duchess with us, Evelyn," Lady Winchester replied, desperately trying not to show her annoyance with the sudden descent into the intimacy of Christian names with someone she barely knew. "She appears to be quite unwell herself. It will do no harm for the doctor to see to her after he's attended to her husband."

"Very well, madam. I appreciate your good sense. I'm far too anxious, as you probably know. I try hard, but all I seem to do is to come across as bumptious, and sound vulgar and awkward."

"My dear, not at all. We should spend some time together. I'll help you overcome your nerves. It's simply a matter of having a more experienced woman to guide you, that's all."

To Lady Winchester's amazement, Lady Quaisey burst into tears and embraced her. She found it rather touching, and yet extraordinary that she should have offered what she had done. Still, no harm was done. She considered herself an excellent judge of character. Perhaps she'd relied too much on gossip and not enough on her own observations.

Evelyn Simperknell, the Lady Quaisey, appeared to be simply trying too hard. Underneath, even in the short time they'd had over tea, Lady Winchester had sensed a quiet, gentle creature, trying vainly to be the person her husband thought should be worthy of him, rather than owning her own shy demeanour.

Such was the case with the wrong woman matched to the wrong man. She'd make sure that the wives she found for Lennard, Gerald, and Robert would be strong, independent and have their own lives. No woman should be beholden to a member of the opposite sex, she vowed. She'd been "owned" in all but name by her father, her brother, then her husband, and after him, her nephew, Hugh.

She loved Lennard as dearly as she might a child of her own. To her, he was the son she never had. She owed it to her nephew, Faris, to make sure that his son was matched well. She knew he loved elsewhere and had done for twenty years, but a wife was the biggest insurance against scandal for men who cared deeply for one another.

*****

Meanwhile, at Birch House, Elam sat on the edge of Travis's examination table, his legs swinging in the air, smiling at his brother and Lennard who sat on a chaise, side-by-side, both appearing to be quite nervous, yet returning his smile with broad grins.

He was used to their nonsense and entirely sick of the bandages around his head. There was cotton packed into his ears that felt uncomfortable, and the pain inside his ear had become moderate; annoying, rather than distracting.

"Why are you two smiling like a pair of ninnies?" he asked, puzzled over their good humour, and yet unable to stop grinning back at them.

"We're anxious to see whether Travis has been able to work a miracle on your head and make you less asinine in appearance," Miles said.

Travis sighed but then joined in the good-natured laughter, before moving to stand in front of Elam.

"Now, I want you to close your eyes, Elam, and please don't open them until I say you can. I'll take off your bandages and stand behind you while I remove the packing from your ears—"

"You still haven't told me why there's wadding in each of them. I know they kicked me in the head—"

Travis lifted one finger to Elam's lips to shush him. "Eyes closed, if you please."

Lennard watched, his stomach in a knot, anxious for the result as Travis carefully removed the bandages around his Elam's head. After placing them on the examination table, Travis moved behind it and placed both hands, cupped, over Elam's ears.

"Open the windows, Lennard," he said.

"Why?"

"Please, just do it. Can't you hear the chaffinches outside in the birches?"

"Ah! Yes, of course." Lennard and Miles leaped to their feet to throw open both casement windows of the room.

"Very well. Now for the proof," Travis said after they'd returned to the chaise.

Gingerly, without moving his hands and using his forefinger and thumb, he withdrew the cotton from Elam's left ear. "Here we are. Let's see if I've been as clever as I hoped I've been," he said, slowly removing his hand from Elam's ear.

Outside, the birdsong grew loud in the room. Lennard, on the edge of his seat, worked the thumb of one hand with the fingers of the other, such was his anxiety.

All at once, Elam's eyes blinked open, and a look of wonder flew across his face. Travis gently attended to his other ear, then gestured to Lennard to speak.

"Elam?" Lennard said, his voice breaking.

"Lenn?"

"You heard me?"

Elam threw his hands over his face and began to sob.

"No, no, don't cry," Lennard said, rushing across the room and taking Elam in his arms. "This is wonderful, not sad!"

"I'm crying because I've never heard your man's voice before, Lennard, and I've forgotten what you sounded like when we were lads."

Within minutes all four men in the room were so profoundly moved that not one of them remained dry-eyed.

Of course, Travis had insisted that Elam's ears be protected for another few weeks, and only uncovered for five or ten minutes every few hours until the surfaces inside his ear canals were healed enough to remain exposed for any length of time. He'd also assured Elam that, although the sound was not yet clear and crisp, he'd soon be able to hear as keenly as any of them.

"I still have to watch everyone's mouth, almost constantly while you're speaking," Elam said after several minutes of banter and laughter.

"That's because you must learn to hear again, Elam," Travis replied. "Your brain 'hears' speech through lip movements. You'll find it becomes easier over time. Now, let's just put some light gauze into your ears—"

"May I have a moment alone with Elam before you do, Travis, Miles?" Lennard asked.

"Of course. I think I heard Mrs Huskerson bringing tea up. Miles and I will give you five minutes and no more. Agreed? There'll be more tomorrow and even more time the day after."

"Thank you, Travis. You too, Miles."

Elam stared into Lennard's eyes for what seemed the entirety of their permitted five minutes, but which, in reality, could not have been more than ten or fifteen seconds. "Put your head against my neck, Lenn," he said. "And whisper low like you do in bed at night. Say whatever it is you haven't been able to speak to my face all these years."

"Elam—"

"Please, Lenn. I know you always protest that you're only purring with pleasure, but I know you're saying something."

Lennard rested his head, where it usually lay and said, ever so softly, "You're far too good for the likes of me, Elam Walters."

Elam laughed. "I love the sound of your voice. It's deep, like my father's was. Nothing like I'd imagined. I didn't hear all of what you said clearly, but enough to wonder why on earth you should say such a thing, and to me of all people?"

"Because, Elam, everyone I've ever loved—my parents, my brother and sister, my grandfather and my uncle Arthur—were all taken from me. I didn't want to say it out loud in case the saying of it brought about misfortune. I—"

Elam stopped Lennard's words with a kiss. A soft, gentle touch of the lips.

"And why now do you confess such a thing? I understand you well enough to realise it's not the miracle that Travis Holland has performed. Come now, Lennard. No untruths."

"When I saw you lying on the footpath, all bloodied and broken, it hit me that the loss of you would be the end of me. I couldn't bear to think of—"

A loud banging and the sounds of voices at the front door stopped his words.

"What on earth?" Lennard said.

"Go to see what it's all about, Lenn. Travis has left his gauze squares here. I'll use the mirror to pack my ears."

"For heaven's sake, wait, Elam. You might—"

"Lennard? Elam?"

Lennard reeled at the sight of his aunt Caroline standing in the doorway, a dark stain of blood soaked through the deep lace collar of her dress.

"Dear God—"

"It's not mine. It's the Russian's."

"Which Russian, aunt?"

"Kosorukov. He had a fall at Evelyn Quaisey's house and has smashed the back of his head. Travis has insisted he stay in his carriage until he can see whether he could be moved."

"Quick, Elam. You can't be seen," Lennard said. "Into the drawing room. Better still, get down into the kitchen."

Lady Winchester marvelled at the conversation but said nothing. Taking Elam's arm as he went to leave, she stared wide-eyed at his attempts to secure the two squares of gauze he'd placed over his ears with a long strip on linen, bound under his chin and which he was trying to tie in a knot at the top of his head.

"I can hear your voice, Lady C," he said. "Travis has restored my hearing."

She clapped her hands to her mouth in delight and kissed his cheek, tying the linen strip into place for him.

"I must leave you. But I'll speak with you as soon as the Russian has gone," he said and then fled the room, leaving her dabbing at her eyes with her handkerchief.

Unfortunately, the slight delay in his departure coincided with the arrival down the hallway of Vassili Vadimovich Kosorukov, aided by Lady Quaisey's footman on one side, and Mark Huskerson on the other. The look of astonishment as the Russian caught sight of Lennard then Elam was remarkable, missed by no one, and yet fleeting as he was ushered into Travis's consulting room.

"What was that all about?" Travis whispered as he rolled up his sleeves in the corridor outside the room.

"I'll tell you later. But please—"

"Doctor!" Kosorukov pleaded loudly, his voice echoing into the hallway.

"I'll speak with you shortly, Lennard. Let me see to this man."

"But Travis—"

Too late. The doctor had gone and had closed the door behind him.

*****

"I'll beg you to hold your head still, sir. I'm sorry if it's inconvenient that you lie on your stomach, but it allows me to see the wound more clearly."

"There's blood running into my eye and into the corner of my mouth."

"Here, your excellency," Travis said, handing the grand duke a wad of cotton batting. "I have no idea where Mr Huskerson can be. I asked him to help me. Please, just for a moment, hold the cloth against your face. I promise you the wound is not deep. You've split the scalp and head wounds often bleed profusely."

Kosorukov mumbled something through the wadding.

"What was that, sir?"

"I was commenting how surprised I was to see Lord Betteridge in your hallway, Dr Holland."

"It's not an uncommon occurrence sir. This is his house, and I lease it from him. The caretakers were the same couple who looked after him and his parents when he was a child."

"And the gentleman with him?"

"Please, duke. Be patient," Travis said, ignoring the Kosorukov's direct question in order to continue with his examination. "I shall apply some erythroxyline to the would before I stitch it, to save you any discomfort."

"Erythroxy ... what—?"

"It's a newly derived alkaloid of coca, discovered by a German scientist only this year, a Herr Doktor Friedrich Gaedcke. Now, only a moment, sir. You won't feel anything but the slight pressure of my wooden spatula as I apply the cream. Your scalp should feel numb within less than a minute."

"How many stitches, Mr Holland?" Kosorukov mumbled again, the linen pad still pressed to his face while Travis gently applied the cocoa paste.

"No more than three or four. Now, are you ready, your excellency?"

The Russian mumbled his consent.

"Very well, I'll start now." Travis counted slowly as he tied off each stitch—one, two, three, four. "You may sit up sir, but please, take a seat in my examination chair next to the table. You're not to move for fifteen minutes, do you understand?"

"Thank you, Mr Holland. I must confess I felt nothing. You're a man of novelty and of skill."

Travis helped the grand duke to swivel on his table then assisted him into the chair, about to place a towel behind the back of his head when Mark Huskerson rushed into the room.

"Quick, Mr Holland, if you please. The lady has fainted."

"Which lady, Mark? Lady Winchester?"

"No sir, it's the grand duchess."

"What—?" Kosorukov said, attempting to rise from the chair.

"Please, your excellency, stay seated. I'll attend to your wife. It's not uncommon for ladies to swoon. Blasted tight corsets have much to answer for. Mr Huskerson will make sure you're not left alone while I'm away. I'll return shortly."

"Are you comfortable, Your Grace?" Mark asked.

"Your Grace is a term reserved for English dukes, Mr Huskerson. Either Excellency or grand duke will suffice. However, with my head pounding, I'm not quite sure I really care."

"Is there anything I can do for you, sir?"

"Ah, yes, perhaps you can. The tall gentleman with the bandage around his head walking down the hallway with Lord Betteridge when I arrived is exceedingly familiar, however, I cannot put a name to his face."

"Elam, Excellency? Why, that's the baron's valet."

"Ah, I see," Vassili said, wondering at the coincidence. He recalled the bee-keeper he'd met at the Sultan of Khartoum had a twin sibling who was in the employ of a gentleman. "He has a brother, doesn't he? My memory recalls hearing such a thing."

"Yes, he does, sir."

"Paul? Is that his name? A twin?"

"No, duke. His brother is a few years older than him, and his name is Miles."

"Are you completely sure?"

"I could not be more sure, sir. I've known them these past twenty years, although I haven't seen them for more than ten until recently ..."

Mark Huskerson's voice became dim in his ears as Vassili Vadimovich Kosorukov began to realise that he'd been led astray. The man in the Turkish baths had not been an identical twin, but Malloray's valet. There could only be one explanation. The man had somehow recognised the Russian grand duke and had created a deception, to avoid any scandal to his master. Perhaps, like Bohuslav, this Elam was Lennard Malloray's private bedfellow? He'd not enquired whether the new Lord Betteridge was of the persuasion, but if he was, he wouldn't be the first nobleman to keep his lover close by as a manservant.

He was about to enquire more on the topic, when Travis Holland appeared through the door, wiping his hands, his face wreathed in smiles.

"My wife?" Kosorukov asked.

"Weeping sir. But for the very best of reasons. May I congratulate you, your excellency. Your wife is with child and you may expect to enjoy a happy event in less than five months or thereabouts."

"I must see her," Kosorukov said, dismayed to find his face wet with tears.

"I'll take her to you presently, sir. Please, to staunch the bleeding, just a few more minutes.

"Oh, dear heavens, doctor. Please forgive my show of emotions. I—"

"There is nothing to forgive, sir. The news of the first child is a joy beyond compare to any man. I offer you my sincerest felicitations."

A child? Could it be so? Kosorukov adored children, never having hoped to have one of his own. His infrequent visits to his wife's bed were carried out with haste and he never tarried after. He thought he'd never become a father and the family name and title would pass to his brother's son.

A child? A son of his own? As the strongest emotions coursed through his body, all thought of the coincidence of finding "Paul" or his twin in the presence of Lennard Malloray flew from his thoughts.

However, at the back of his mind was the anticipation of announcing the news to his father and mother-in-law. Thirty thousand, as promised for the first child, plus another ten thousand a year and a house of their own, away from the prying eyes of the Earl and Countess Twinton.

He could not believe his great good fortune.

17. KOSORUKOV BEHAVING BADLY AND NEWS OF THE CARGO

On Friday evening, some six days after Elam's bandages had been removed, Travis held a celebration at Birch House for his friends.

Angus had also been invited. However, due to a prior engagement at the Royal Opera House in the company of his wife and her parents, he'd promised to escape after the last curtain and to join them at around eleven in the evening.

As Lennard raised his glass in a toast, he realised, when Angus eventually arrived, the full complement of the directors and shareholders of Fratelli Imports and Exports would be seated around Travis's table. He'd really taken to the young doctor—young being a comparative term, for Lennard had but three years on him. He wished there was something more tangible he could do to advance his comfort.

The idea of a match with his cousin, Philomena, was one he intended to foster. She was intelligent, enquiring, and delightful company. Travis could do far worse than marry into a wealthy family, especially one that cared so much about his well-being. It wouldn't be hard to throw them into each other's paths, especially now that Travis had not only garnered a reputation among both the well-to-do businessmen in the City, but also the titled patronage sent his way by both Lennard's aunt and the Baron Hochschild, who'd declared Dr Holland the miracle of the age. Very soon, the list of social invitations would steadily increase, making Travis one of the most sought-after guests for any soirée.

The evening had been splendid, served *à la française*, in order to make Miles feel comfortable. Elam had been served at table with Travis by Mark Huskerson since he'd first been carried into Birch House by Lennard, bruised and bloodied, two weeks beforehand, and had managed some inner reconciliation with his conscience about being waited upon by another servant. However, Miles had reluctantly accepted the invitation. Were they supping at the kitchen table, he could have coped with no qualms. But seated at table in an elegant dining room was a different thing altogether. However, after being reassured that all the food would either be laid out or in chaffing dishes over spirit burners on the sideboard so the men could help themselves and talk freely, Miles's anxiety had been assuaged with little protest.

Over the course of the dinner, Elam had insisted that each of his friends and his brother speak his name, daring them to repeat it four times with different inflections, his face ruddy and excited with each utterance. He still found it novel to equate sounds with his ability to read speech.

By nine in the evening, three courses had successively been laid out in the room. Mr Huilot had arrived earlier in the day after serving lunch at Bexford House, to help Mrs Huskerson with the food. Merrill had travelled with Lennard, Gerald, Robert, and Miles, in order to help in the dining room.

"Would you enquire from Mr Huilot if there's anything that could be ruined among the offerings for dessert if we were to wait for half an hour please, Merrill?" Travis asked. "My stomach is groaning, and I need to let the food settle."

"Would you care for a *digestif*, Mr Holland? I've brought a bottle of his lordship's favourite wormwood liqueur."

"A *digestif*? What on earth is that?"

"It's a distilled liqueur, made from herbs and spices. Bitter, but palate cleansing. It does what the name infers."

"Wormwood should be taken in moderation, Lennard. I'm not sure …"

"Ah, Bénédictine has the merest hint of that herb, Travis. I promise you, once tasted, you'll crave for more."

"Very well, on your recommendation, I'll try some. Gentlemen?"

"Try to stop us, Travis," Elam said. "It was the most pilfered from the cellar at Gresting I can assure you. Oops!"

"I swear you've had far too much to drink," Lennard said, affectionately sliding his hand over Elam's thigh under the tablecloth.

Travis held his glass up to the gasolier, turning it in the light. "Why, it has the colour of brandy, although the liquid seems more viscous," he said before sniffing the contents.

Lennard smiled as he watched the look of delight pass over Travis's face after tasting the liqueur.

"Why, this is delicious, Lennard. And you say it aids digestion?"

"Well, let me say, if you drink half a bottle, it would be easy to forget you'd eaten anything at all!"

Their laughter was interrupted by a discreet knocking at the dining room door.

"Yes, what is it?"

Merrill entered the room. "I beg your pardon, sir, but Christopher is at the front door with a lady and a gentleman. He says it's of some urgency."

Travis sighed then downed the remainder of his glass. "If this is another of your friends whose wife is to be unexpectedly diagnosed with child, Lennard—"

"It's not for you, Mr Holland. They've arrived to see his lordship."

"Me?" Lennard asked, surprised at Merrill's announcement. Merrill found himself unceremoniously brushed aside as the three visitors hastily entered the room.

"Martin?" Lennard exclaimed at the sight of Martin Wilson, beautifully dressed in his guise as the proprietress of Mrs Hedger's Molly house.

"Arthur?" Gerald said, rising from his chair, having noticed her companion.

"I'm sorry to intrude, Lennard," Martin said, glancing nervously at Travis. "But there's been a commotion and I need your help."

"How on earth did you know I was here?"

"We caught a hansom to Bexford House and your under-footman … I'm sorry, I can't remember his name …"

"Stephen," Arthur offered, "told us where you were. He arranged for Christopher to bring us here in your phaeton."

"Please, madam, sir," Travis said. "Unless someone is dead or some catastrophe has fallen, allow me to introduce myself."

Lennard immediately remembered his manners and began to make introductions. "Travis, this is a friend of long standing. Mary—"

"Let's not be deceptive, Lennard," Martin said, fishing in his reticule for a card. "My name is Martin Wilson. I'm the proprietor of Hedger's Molly House in Farrington, and before you jump to any mistaken conclusions, Mr Holland, I've known most of these gentlemen since I was a young man."

"I see … madam," Travis said, reddening slightly. He smiled, gathering his composure, appearing not to be startled by the revelation that the very attractive woman who held out her card to him was in fact a gentleman.

Arthur introduced himself, extending his hand to Travis, who shook it then moved around the table to stand next to Gerald.

"Please, Mr Holland. I'm sorry to intrude. But I would not be here were it not of some urgency," Martin said.

"Is it so urgent you cannot take a seat for a moment to catch your breath?"

"If you don't find my presence unwelcome, sir, I'd be delighted to sit for a moment."

Lennard was not in the least surprised to watch Travis, despite the awkwardness created by the pain in his leg, draw a spare dining chair from the wall and place it next to the table, holding the chair for Martin, as he would have done for any lady.

"It's the Russian, Mr Malloray … I mean, my lord," Arthur stated as soon as Martin was seated.

"Which Russian, Arthur?"

"*The* Russian, sir," he said, glancing at Travis.

"Do you mean Kosorukov?"

"Yes, sir. He pulled a pistol on me and shot one of the lads."

Lennard cursed as he and his friends rose to their feet, each one exclaiming in surprise.

"Is he outside in the carriage?" Travis asked. "Is that why you're here?"

"No, sir," Martin said. "I had a client on the premises at the time who is a physician. The doctor assured me it was merely a flesh wound. 'More blood than bite', he said."

For a matter of a few seconds the room was deathly still, each man looking at the others, wondering who should speak.

Travis broke the silence. "Please, madam, would you be so kind to inform me then of the urgency of your visit if the man is not wounded? And what is so important that you should call upon Lord Betteridge at a stranger's house so precipitously?"

"Lennard ...?" Martin said, glancing at Travis, unwilling to speak.

"Travis, I fear the Russian has done or said something inappropriate, and my friends are simply too hesitant to speak because they neither know you, nor do they comprehend the level of our friendship. Very well, I refuse to hold my tongue. Arthur Pencott supplies services to gentlemen of quality at Martin's establishment and he is also Gerald's beau. Am I correct, Gerald?" Lennard explained.

"Well, it's far too soon—"

"You may take that as a yes, Travis. Hear me out. You may ask questions when all has been revealed, and most likely what I'll have to tell you will have me up to my neck in hot water when the Home Secretary finds out what I may have to disclose, but I know both Martin and Arthur to be trustworthy and not to have come on some fool's errand."

Travis merely raised his eyebrows with a slight smile. "Very well, but let's not be uncivil. As it's not a matter of life or death, shall we find a glass for the lady and gentleman?"

*****

"He did what?" Lennard asked, not sure if he'd heard correctly.

"He asked for Arthur but when I told him he'd found a sponsor and would no longer be available, he started to become violent," Martin said. "I adhered to the story you'd asked me to tell him, Lennard."

"Today, I believe, is the eleventh of the month. He's not due for his regular appointment for another four days. Has he ever arrived unexpectedly at any other time?"

"Never. My lads are usually spoken for in advance. Most of my evening clients are regular callers. They have excuses at home for certain days of the week when they're expected to be away, and they always ask for the same companion. It's rare I have gentlemen arrived unexpected, except during the day, because they know arrangements are usually already in place."

"But you said you offered him someone in Arthur's stead?

"Yes, a new recruit, if I may be so bold to use the term. He is, or rather was, a junior officer, discharged from service after being run over by a gun carriage. He walks with a limp, not unlike Mr Holland here. Very comely indeed, fair of countenance and strongly built, possessing the necessary attributes for one of my lads."

"But he rejected him?"

"Yes, Lennard, that's when he became violent. He smashed my china cabinet front with his fist, swearing he'd rather couple with a beggar than a cripple, and asked what I'd taken him for."

"Good grief."

"He was exceedingly drunk. Fortunately, a few of my other lads were either between callers or waiting for one, so they were able to restrain my new man, who, I'm sure would have taken to your Russian and thrown him from the first-floor window, and without opening it first!"

"But?" Lennard asked.

"But we'd barely managed to calm him down when Arthur, who'd been playing cards upstairs with the slops boy, wandered into the room to see what the fuss was all about."

"You should have heard the language, my lord," Arthur said. "He started raving about Karl Paulsson, your valet Mr Walters, some

Turkish fellow, and shouting almost incoherently about being the victim of abuse and deception. He's not a fighter, sir. Not in the sense of using his fists, but he has a violent streak. He was about to take to Mrs Wilson when I grabbed him by the wrists, shouting at him to calm down, but he yelled at me, saying that it had been reported to him that I'd been with Captain Langbourne on Monday last, supping at the Raven's Beak, and asking me whether I was aware that Gerald was one of your ..."

"One of my what, Arthur?"

"Conquests, sir, but he did not use that word."

"And what word did he use, Arthur?" Gerald asked.

"Captain Langbourne, I ..."

"Out with it. If I'm to be insulted, I'd like to know the depth of the injury."

"He called you one of his lordship's mustard-pots. I apologise for the coarse term."

Gerald chortled and placed his hand on Arthur's shoulder. "I've been called far worse and on many more occasions than one. No need to apologise. Now, had he called me a prickless sodomite, then I truly might have taken offence."

One by one, all the gentlemen—bar Travis—began to chuckle. He merely shook his head. It crossed Lennard's mind that no doubt Travis had heard a lot worse aboard ship and thought the epithet mild.

"As I was saying," Arthur continued, "he became very heated and started yelling, squiffied almost legless, thrashing around, knocking over the furniture. That's when he broke free and pulled out his pistol. Fortunately, I was quick enough to deflect his aim by headbutting him. That's when he shot Freddy, the lad who took the flesh wound. It took four of us to subdue the Russian. He wouldn't listen to reason, daring me to deny that Captain Langbourne was my new keeper. He said he'd never have believed it, had not come from Asprey's trollop—"

"Asprey? Are you sure you heard the name correctly?" Lennard asked.

"I thought he said Astley," Martin offered. "But I could be mistaken. Why? Does the name mean anything to you, Lennard?"

All at once, the tone of the room changed as Gerald, Robert, Miles, and Elam turned to stare at Lennard.

"Conall Leddy," a voice announced from the doorway in the sudden silence that ensued. "One of Terrence Astley's twins, Lennard. He's Astley's bum boy."

"Angus?"

"I'm sorry to arrive so early, but I was called away from the opera at the end of the third act."

"How long have you been standing there?"

"Long enough to put two and two together. Good evening, Martin, Arthur, gentlemen? Is there perhaps something left over from dinner? I'm starving and I bear tidings of great importance."

"Your news can wait until after you've eaten, Sir Angus," Travis said, ringing his handbell to summon Mark Huskerson. "Please take a seat, won't you?"

"I do apologise for letting myself in the back door. It's something that I often did as a lad in this very house, but I thought my news could not wait."

"This evening has already been an occasion of unexpected tidings, Sir Angus. I doubt yours will be more surprising than what I've already heard so far."

"I wouldn't place a wager on it, Travis. Now, is that some of the Gresting claret I see on the sideboard? I'd kill for a glass."

*****

Travis inspected Martin's hand carefully, after he'd removed the glove.

"You say you knocked him out, madam?"

"One punch, sir. I've never seen anyone so agitated. He threw off my boys and leaped to his feet, hands outstretched as if he was going to throttle poor Arthur. However, I hoisted up the edge of my skirt with one hand and let fly with the other. The Russian fell flat on his back."

"Martin was a roustabout at the markets," Travis explained.

"I was a porter, Lennard," Martin protested. "Roustabouts are thugs."

"As I remember you, at age seventeen, Martin," Angus said, with a laugh, "thuggery was your middle name, if I dare propose."

"You need to pay attention to your pronunciation, *Sir* Angus, for you have said the word incorrectly."

"Dear God," Travis murmured, with the slightest of eye-rolls.

"Forgive me, Mr Holland. Despite my frills and flounces, I am still very much a man and spend my daylight hours dressed not unlike yourself or the rest of my friends as they go about their daily business. My costume is for convenience and convention. Houses such as mine rarely thrive when managed by a gentleman."

"Madam, you owe me no explanation."

"So, where is the Russian at the moment?" Lennard asked. "Did you put him in a carriage and send him home?"

"No, Lennard, I asked him to sit down to dinner and offered him a glass of my best claret and a free tupping, gratis and pro bono. What do you think I did? We tied him up and locked him in the cellar. I have no idea what he was yelling about, but there's no doubt it was indiscreet. And, knowing you work for Angus, it was most likely very sensitive. It was Arthur who said we should find you as soon as possible."

Angus cast a glance at Lennard then cleared his throat. "I think the time may have come, my dear friend," he said. "We need to speak very plainly to the grand duke and reveal to him the extent of our knowledge, and present him with options in order to avoid the supreme penalty."

"Surely not this evening, Angus," Lennard replied. "Can't it wait until the morning?"

"Yes, it can wait until tomorrow. However, as to the reason that I was fetched from the opera just before the end of act one of Mr Berlioz's *Benvenuto Cellini*, that cannot wait."

Angus reached into his jacket pocket and retrieved an envelope, passing it to Lennard, who read it quickly and asked Travis whether he might borrow a writing implement.

"I have this at hand," Travis said, producing a propelling pencil from his inner breast pocket. "I have one in every jacket. It's a habit I've been unable to break."

"Thank you, Travis," Lennard said, taking the pencil and beginning to decipher the code of telegraphic message which he'd discovered inside the envelope. He glanced up at Angus halfway through, who had started on a plate of food, delivered by Merrill.

"How did this get here so quickly?" Lennard said, his forehead creased with concentration.

"Optical telegraph from Marseilles to Lyon, thence electric telegraph to Paris and on to London. It arrived in the office at half past eight this evening, and one of the night clerks fetched me from my box at the opera. No doubt there's a copy for you at Malloray's or at your home, Lennard."

"Please forgive my lack of manners, Travis, but this is urgent, and I apologise in advance. However, I think it might be ruder to leave the room," Lennard said to his companions before turning to Robert. "The *Malmaison*. Do you know her?"

"I assume you mean the paddle steamer and not the chateau owned by the Empress Joséphine de Beauharnais?"

"Yes, the steamer, I'm sorry, Robert," Lennard replied.

"She's a passenger vessel, side-wheeler, of about fourteen-hundred tons. She sails the route from Marseilles to La Rochelle, thence St. Katharine's Docks. Arthur would be able to tell you more about her, for he worked there before coming back to us. Why do you ask?"

"This telegram was sent by one of our crew aboard the *Cutler's Edge*. It seems the chicks have flown their nest and have boarded the *Malmaison* in Marseilles. One of our men is on board in case The Cargo disembarks in La Rochelle."

Gerald, Elam, Miles, and Christopher—who had stayed in the room and was seated near the fireplace—let out a gasp.

Lennard held up his hands to quieten the barrage of exclamations and questions, apologising to Travis, Martin, and Arthur who seemed astonished at the sudden reaction of the other men.

"I'm desperately sorry, Martin and Arthur, but I simply can't tell you what this is all about."

"Then I shall, Lennard," Angus said. "As I'm the *chef de mission* in this affair, it is for me to decide who hears what. Besides, I have my reasons."

"But, Angus—"

"Why on earth do you think I gave you a copy of *La Vie Secrète de la Marquise Fonteneau*?"

"You mean …"

"Yes, Martin has been one of our agents for over a decade now."

"Really? I'm astounded."

"As you should be. If an agent's identity is to be kept secret, then concealment is of the utmost importance, don't you agree? Besides, you'd be surprised who among the aristocracy and the business brokers in the kingdom frequent Mrs Hedger's. Isn't that so, Arthur?"

Arthur Pencott blushed deeply. "I am never told their names, Sir Angus, only what titles I should use."

"As for you, Mr Holland," Angus said, "it seems only fair that you learn something of the affair we are tiptoeing around. You will be treating several of the people involved in the tale and I would hate to put you in a compromising situation."

"That's very kind of you, Sir Angus … although I hesitate to be included, only because of the nature of the seriousness that my good friend Lennard seems to be radiating across the table."

"I beg your pardon, Travis, for my grave countenance," Lennard explained. "However, I bow to my superior's decision. You too may find some earnestness in your heart after he discloses what I fear he may be about to. But, Angus … why does Arthur need to be involved …?"

"Arthur Pencott is not unknown to me, Lennard. You may draw your own conclusions as to how."

Lennard glanced at Arthur, who seemed to be studiously avoiding Gerald's eyes. That is until Captain Langbourne whispered something in his ear that made him raise his eyebrows and smile. Lennard's conjecture was that Gerald had said something like "me too, and for years."

"We may also be in need of someone else with fighting skills. Gerald may not be enough if and when we come to intercept and deal with the Turkish bodyguard."

*****

Plates and extra spaces made at the table, dessert was served just as Clyford arrived, clutching Lennard's copy of the telegram, with excuses that he'd been out to dinner himself and had returned home not twenty minutes beforehand.

Relieved to discover that Angus had beaten him to it, and that Lennard had seen the telegram, he asked if he should return home, but Lennard asked him to stay, introducing him to Martin, the only person in the room he did not know.

Angus had explained that he'd delay his explanation until after dessert, which Lennard knew would cause some consternation, especially to Travis, who'd lost a brother in the Crimea. However, with no urgency to attend to Kosorukov before the morrow, Lennard soon settled and found himself in excellent conversation with Arthur, from whom he gathered there had been nothing but courting between him and Gerald thus far.

Lennard could not help but see the attraction Gerald felt for the man, for away from the docks and talking of books and nature, Arthur's face became illuminated, such was his joy in reading and discovering the world around him. His enthusiasm was very infectious.

Mr Huilot had prepared more than enough food, and there was plenty for the extra guests. A cheer of delight went up when champagne arrived to celebrate the success of Elam's operation, and to accompany the spread laid over the table and on the sideboard.

Trifle, lemon flan, raspberry fool, and a large jelly set with early strawberries and blackcurrants, all accompanied by pots of cooled custard and whipped cream. Lennard aimed to have a spoonful of each of the desserts but owned he had been beaten by the time he reached for a slice of the *tarte au citron*, declared heavenly by those who'd already partaken.

The table cleared, Travis asked for the door to be closed. Angus began to tell the story of The Cargo, including the latest news received. At the same time as its exposition, Kosorukov's calumny was woven into the tale. Many were the cries of dismay from those who were not already privy to one of Britain's greatest secrets.

At the end of his discourse, Angus looked around the room. Those already aware of The Cargo and Kosorukov sat solemnly, most likely ruminating on the urgency of the situation now that not only had the

Russian overplayed his hand, but also, perhaps, that the pretender and his bodyguard might be heading for Britain.

Travis stood with his back to the room leaning against the mantlepiece, his shoulders heaving with the effort to breathe, and his injured leg trembling almost violently. "No!" he shouted, turning to face the company. "This cannot be! It's beyond heinous. Treachery is not strong enough ... why, if I could—"

Lennard was at his side in a trice, taking his upper arms and holding them firm. "Look at me, Travis," he commanded. "Take several deep breaths. I know this is—"

"It's treason! That's what it is, Lennard. Treason! Why—"

"Stop. Please, just do as I say. We've all been in the very same state in which you now find yourself. Anger is the first of emotions and the foremost in all of our minds, but that convulsion of the spirit does not allow clear thought, and I believe I know why Angus has revealed one of the nation's greatest secrets to those of you who would not ordinarily be party to information of this magnitude."

Travis took several deep breaths, as Lennard had suggested, his jaw tense all the while and stiff in the body.

"Angus?" Lennard asked over his shoulder. "If you would be so kind?"

"It is as Lennard has divined. Of course, something so important would normally be kept among very few. But, as I said earlier, each of you is connected in some way to one or two of the players in this Shakespearean tragedy. I hope I may avail upon you for help. It is merely fortuitous that Martin and Arthur are here, but I've already thought of how they might be used, if they're willing to put their shoulders to the wheel in the name of Queen and country."

"Help?" Martin said, visibly shaken. "Of course, Angus. I can only speak for myself, but I'd be more than willing to help—although I've no idea how I could contribute."

"Thank you, Martin. There is much to be done and all at once. One small group of people will not be able to attend to everything. We will need several, each focused on a different endeavour and at the same time. I don't wish to bring people into the equation with whom I'm not already acquainted. All of you, bar Travis, who is now a new-found friend, have been acquaintances of many years—some of you decades—and it is upon you that I sincerely hope I may depend."

Travis gradually relaxed and drew Lennard into an embrace, an unusual gesture for him as he'd once told Lennard that he hadn't grown up in a household where demonstrations of affection between men was an acceptable thing to do. Even his brother, Percival, had merited no more than a strong handshake and a slap on the back, despite the closeness and affection the brothers had held for each other. "Perhaps brandy or port? Then I shall be at your disposal, Sir Angus," he said. "I need to realign some of my thoughts and take in much of what you've told me."

"Of course, Travis. I'm sure everyone probably needs to draw breath. Perhaps you won't mind if we open a window? I'd rather like a cigar and it's a little stuffy with so many of us in the room."

"I'll do it," Lennard volunteered. Then, stopping briefly at Travis's side, asked whether it might not be time to cover Elam's ears once more. It had been an ongoing process during the course of the evening, allowing Elam ten-minute intervals of hearing speech.

With the window open, Lennard leaned against the windowsill, which rested in the small of his back. Gerald joined him and they spoke softly while Merrill placed the port decanter on the table, distributed glasses, asking each guest whether he'd prefer brandy, after which, he carried Lennard's Thermidor around the room.

"You brought your own cigars, Lennard?"

"I doubted Travis would have any, Gerald. From memory, he smokes cigarillos. Now, tell me about Arthur Pencott. He says you're 'courting'? That's unlike you, Gerald, you're usually a straight into the rowboat sort of fellow."

"Despite his appearances and worldliness, he's actually quite shy, Lenn. Have you seen him dockside? Striding around giving orders, brooking no nonsense, a man in charge who has no qualms about knocking a few heads to get work done. Then, there's his work at Mrs Hedger's. Such a contrast. Yet, when he's talking books and asking questions about history, or words, or nature, he's as soft and gentle as one could ever hope to meet in a man."

Lennard smiled. He'd not seen this side of Gerald before and found his vulnerability charming indeed. Although they'd been friends for nigh on twenty years, the affection between them had been jocular, almost brotherly, despite their bedroom antics. There'd never been any softness; not ever. Lennard loved seeing it new in Gerald's countenance.

*****

Half an hour later, the room cleared. Travis suggested that the party might repair to his sitting room, where more comfortable accommodation would be found, and so that Mr Huskerson might attend to cleaning the dining room after they'd vacated the room.

"I shall send Clyford to France," Lennard said, once his friends had settled comfortably. "You have nothing that may prevent you from leaving, do you, Clyford?"

"Nothing that can't be delayed, my lord. I imagine you'd like me aboard the *Malmaison* when she docks in La Rochelle?"

"Yes. We'll need to formulate a plan before you go. But your visit shall serve two purposes. First of all, you can visit the Gräfin Mecklenburg-Strelitz in Paris to see whether she's received any more missives from her lover. I'd also like you to present her with a jewel, one which I've ordered from Rothschild's. It's a show of gratitude and may appease her sense of discomfort—every woman likes to feel appreciated, and it may be an enticement for future sharing of information."

"Good heavens, Lennard, that's extraordinary thinking," Angus said.

"To be frank, and vulgar with the talk of money at the same time, it cost little. The parure I've ordered for my aunt's birthday set me back close to fifteen-hundred guineas. The addition of a broach, so fashioned that it may be transformed into pair of diamond and emerald earrings, was added at minimal cost by the jewellers, anxious to maintain my custom."

"There was a letter arrived for you advising that Lady Winchester's jewellery is ready. Do you wish me to collect it at the same time, my lord?" Clyford asked.

"Yes, Clyford. I was intending to have you go to Paris in any case, so this new development will serve two purposes. Please ask Mr Drudge to draw a bill of exchange for Rothschild's. You should take two men with you when you travel."

"One should suffice, my lord," Clyford said. "I can take care of myself."

"One will return directly to London with the jewellery, Clyford, the other will accompany you to La Rochelle. I'm sure we have a vessel at our disposal that will wait at Calais for a day after delivering you to France, is that not so, Robert?"

"We now send a company mail packet to the continent every day, Lenn," Robert offered. "There's no need for a vessel to wait."

"I'd prefer to keep this as clandestine as possible. Do we have anything available that could serve this solitary purpose?"

"There's the new steam launch, the *Achilles*. A little smaller than the mail packet, but speedy with it. She's designed for coastal trade, but the Channel, unless there's a gale blowing, should be no problem for her."

"Is there a chance she could sail to La Rochelle before returning to London?"

"That's easily arranged."

"Very well, here's what I have in mind."

"I see you have taken charge, Lennard," Angus observed.

"You may correct me or interrupt me as you wish, Angus. However, I've been working on The Cargo case for many years and have had contingency plans in place for any eventuality. This latest revelation about La Rochelle is merely a matter of reworking another scheme that Elam and I have already formulated."

"Proceed then, my friend."

"Clyford and the two men we send will return to Calais after business is concluded in Paris. All three will proceed aboard the *Achilles* to La Rochelle, where Clyford will wait with one of the men, while the other will return to London with any correspondence from the Gräfin Mecklenburg-Strelitz and the jewellery I've purchased for my aunt. Clyford will book passage to London for two aboard the *Malmaison* before she arrives. They can wait until passengers disembark, in case The Cargo comes ashore, before boarding themselves. If the pretender and his bodyguard do not leave the vessel, Clyford and our other man are to occupy the cabins they've booked aboard her and make themselves known to our man from the *Cutler's Edge*. Clyford will communicate our plans for the apprehension and disposal of The Cargo."

"Surely you don't mean to do away with them on board the *Malmaison*, Lennard?" Angus asked.

"No. My plan has always been to never allow the pretender to step foot on British soil. We shall intercept the *Malmaison* mid-stream in the Thames while she waits for the pilot to board her. The Cargo will be 'escorted' from the vessel and disposed of in the Thames."

There ensued not a small amount of muttering between the men, only interrupted when Arthur spoke. "I should like to be one of the two men to accompany Mr Billings to Paris and return aboard the *Malmaison*, sir. That is if Mr Fahey can spare me from Malloray's for as many days as it may take to proceed with your plan."

"Arthur? Why on earth would you—"

"If there's to be any violence, my lord, you may depend on me to overcome the fiercest of antagonists. At St. Katharine's, I was oft asked to escort valuables, owing to my ability to use my fists and to be a sure shot with a pistol. I'm capable of defending either myself or my charge with knives and cudgels. I hold no fear of any man or in any situation. I'd be grateful to be given the opportunity."

Angus clapped softly. "Bravo, Arthur. Spoken like a true patriot and a man of great courage."

"Thank you, Sir Angus. I've never been abroad, but I imagine those Frenchies can offer nothing more in fighting than anything I've seen before."

"Very good," Lennard said. "I shall work out the details over the next few days, leaving plenty of time to discuss what's to be done before you leave. When will the *Malmaison* arrive at La Rochelle, Robert?"

"From what I remember, she's about the same tonnage as our *Prince William*, Lenn—"

"Slightly less, if I may say," Arthur added. "And her steam engine is newer. I should say she manages about seven or eight knots if the sea is kind."

"You, sir, are wasted on my docks," Robert said, with a broad smile. "If I'd known you had such knowledge of vessels, I'd have had you at my side in the office."

"And I may have had cause to refuse, Mr Fahey, if you'll excuse my apparent lack of gratitude. I love being outdoors more than anything—other than my reading of course, and that's how I know about ships, sir. For a long while, there was little to read other than my cheaply bought novels and shipping news from the newspapers, posted on the notice board outside the main office at St. Katharine's."

"Very well, Arthur, let's call it seven knots. Marseilles to La Rochelle can be what? Two thousand nautical miles? Let me see," Robert said, mumbling to himself, using his fingers to count. "I make that about twelve days. Very slow indeed."

"So, according to your calculations, the *Malmaison* should arrive in La Rochelle around the twenty-third of the month."

"Yes, Lenn, which means we can expect her to be waiting for the pilot, opposite Greenwich, most likely on the twenty-seventh or twenty-eighth of May."

"We have two weeks to get organised," Lennard said. "That brings me to Kosorukov."

"I wish to interrogate him, Lennard," Angus said. "Unlike you, I have no personal connection with the man. I cannot be compromised, and, if I do discover something about Astley while I'm about my questioning of him, I won't be tempted to be swayed by extremes of emotion."

"Very well. However, I'd like to know what your plans are as to his future?"

"I'll need to speak with Sir George before I can give you any answer, Lennard."

"Hanging's too good for him," Travis blurted out. "The man has been passing secrets to our enemies. Who knows how many lives of British fighting men may have been lost because of his treasonous correspondence?"

"We shall use him well, have no doubt about it, Travis. However, we must protect the reputations of his family in London. Gone are the days when entire clans were wiped from the face of the earth because of one person's sins. The Earl of Twinton is a powerful man and we must protect him and his house from any scandal. I promise you there will be punishment in accordance with the level of his calumny, and it will be meted out with due severity. However, as to the way in which it is to be carried out? That must rest in the hands of the Prime Minister and Sir George."

"If you discover anything ..."

"To do with your brother or the circumstances of the loss of the *Prince*, I will pass on whatever I learn. I promise you."

Lennard had never seen Travis so distressed. He took his arm, squeezing it firmly.

"And what of me, Angus?" Martin asked, having listened calmly to the discussion.

"Ah, yes, Martin. I have a special task for you. Do you still have your children?"

"Children?" Travis asked, surprised at such a question.

"It's not what you may think, Mr Holland," Martin said. "Despite my profession and the knowledge of such things, my house is for gentlemen of quality who prefer the company of adults. My children, as Angus calls them, are my crowd of street urchins. Homeless children for whom I provide a hot meal in the evenings, and space in my basement to sleep if any of them feel they are in danger."

"Most generous, madam," Travis said, appearing slightly embarrassed that his question may have been misinterpreted.

"I hope I shan't confuse you during daylight hours, sir, when I appear in your company as a gentleman?"

"Indeed, not. I rather hope I am sensitive to the appearance of gender. Please accept that in the many years I've served in Her Majesty's navy, I travelled to many parts of the globe where many male members of local communities live out their lives as women, and vice versa. Your disguise is not unknown to me and I consider it nothing remarkable."

Martin smiled, thanking Travis. He turned to Angus. "My children?"

"I'm sure that we'd all like to know why Terrence Astley's male lover was following Captain Langbourne. If he reported the fact to

Kosorukov, there can be no other explanation that it was not mere coincidence. Astley is abroad as far as I know?"

"He's been abroad since the fifteenth, Sir Angus," Clyford said. "He left the day after dinner at Bexford House."

"Then why is his companion so interested in Gerald?"

"Perhaps it's not just Gerald," Lennard said. "I know Astley's behind the beating of Elam and the misuse of my person. Perhaps this Conall Leddy has been assigned to follow us all, to see whether retribution is planned?"

"Thus, my reason for asking about Martin's 'children', Lenn."

"What do you wish me to do?" Martin asked.

"No one notices children, the way they would if they were being shadowed by an adult of either sex. Can you arrange for some of your little ones to play outside Astley's house in Bayswater, both at the front and at the rear and observe the comings and goings?"

"Of course, if you'll provide me with an address. I suppose you want this Conall Leddy fellow followed?"

"If that's not too much of an imposition."

"How shall they know him?"

"He's about your height," Angus said. "Black hair, missing the earlobe of his right ear—"

"The right ear, you say? And he's Irish? That's the mark of someone sold into prostitution—like a slave collar, only it can never be taken off, even after emancipation."

"Astley bought him and a girl from a brothel in Tralee when Leddy was seventeen years old."

"Anything else about him?"

"He's very comely. Has a mouth on him—swears a lot. Thirty-two years of age and with the most startling blue eyes one could ever see … Lennard? What's wrong?"

"Please don't tell me he also has the thickest black eyelashes, so dense they appear to be made up with kohl?"

"Well yes, Lenn. But how on earth could you possibly know that?"

Lennard turned his back on the company, his shoulders tight with anger, trying as hard as he could to not shout out his dismay.

"If and when you find him, Martin," he said, turning into the room, red-faced and obviously furious. "I'll give you twenty guineas to have him delivered to my door. I don't care how it's done, but I want the man."

"Lennard, you've no need to offer me money. I'll gladly do anything you want out of our long-standing friendship."

"The money's not for you, Martin, although you could keep it if you wish. It's for the thugs you'll have to pay to beat him senseless and to drop him at my front door tied up in a hessian sack."

Those who did not know the unspoken words behind Lennard's impassioned plea stared in wonder. Those who did, nodded with tacet understanding of his rage.

18. INTERROGATIONS, CONFESSIONS, AND OUTCOMES

Vassili Vadimovich Kosorukov had been drunk. Drunk and angry.

It was an explosive combination. After a terrible family quarrel on his sixteenth birthday, he'd avoided mixing alcohol and ire. On that day, he'd lost control and had stood up to his father. As a result, he'd been horsewhipped and locked in an outside earth cellar for a week in the middle of winter. Since then, he'd tempered his anger through sheer willpower, and controlled his overindulgence in spirits by keeping company that would force him, by virtue of good manners and etiquette, to maintain strict self-control.

It didn't mean that he didn't get angry, or drunk. While he was still in Russia, he'd taken out his rage on maids and stablemen, beating the former with his fists, and forcing the latter to indulge in unwanted acts, humiliating them in the doing of it. It was what his kind did with serfs. They belonged to the landowner, as did the cattle and the crops in the field—they existed to be used by the aristocracy. He felt no remorse or shame. If the maids complained, they were dismissed. If the men proved to be adequate, even though unwilling, they would be rewarded with a coin. Sometimes, the lure of the silver outweighed the humiliation, and they'd seek him out for more. It made him feel powerful, far beyond the reality of his situation as the eldest son of an impoverished former great house.

But it was drink that was the bane of his life. Forced to restrain himself in company, he frequently took to the bottle at times and in places where he could not get into trouble. Last night, angry and in his cups, sitting in his carriage in Cowcross Street, opposite Mrs Hedger's Molly house, had been neither one of those times nor places.

He banged on the door with both fists. He had no idea how long he'd been locked up, but his head pounded with every percussive impact, so soon stopped. Even yelling loudly brought no reply. A jug of water, a tin mug on a small table, a chamber pot, and some rags in an earth closet off the room in which he'd been confined were the only "luxuries" he'd been afforded. He checked his timepiece. It showed half past nine—he'd been here for over twelve hours.

"Stand back!" a voice came from outside the door. "I have a pistol and I'm not alone."

"I don't know who you think you are—" he shouted, his voice cut off as the door was pushed open, knocking him backward. He landed on his backside, legs splayed.

"I know precisely who I am, sir," a strangely familiar man said, behind him two brawny louts. "Now get to your feet and come outside, up the stairs, where there's something to break your fast."

He stood slowly, brushing off the seat of his trousers, then pushed his way past one of the men who'd come into the room. He growled at the sight of the pistol pointed in his direction, but then followed the third man up the stairs into a bright open room, in which was a table set for three.

"Good morning, Vassili," Angus said, already seated at the table, drinking coffee. The smell of it pervaded the room and made his stomach heave. "Would you like something to eat?"

"Sit," the man holding the gun ordered. Then, when Kosorukov did as he'd been told, passed his pistol to one of the bulky men who'd accompanied him up the stairs, taking the third place at the table.

"Where am I?"

"Where you were last evening, duke. One floor below," the man replied.

"And you are?"

"My name is Martin Wilson, and this is my house."

"You're Mrs Hedger's husband? Brother?"

"No sir, I am she."

"You have me at a disadvantage, sir. I don't understand your meaning."

"Have something to line your stomach, Vassili," Angus said. "There's much you don't understand as yet, and I advise a little sustenance before we have a little chat."

"A chat?"

"More of an interrogation, duke. However, it can be as amiable as you wish it to be."

"What about these two?" Kosorukov asked glancing at Martin's two companions.

"They are merely bystanders, agents of Her Majesty's service, deaf and voiceless when it comes to the great secrets of our nation. They'll observe … for as long as you're amiable. I'm sure that's something you do understand, *n'est-ce pas*?"

Vassili Vadimovich Kosorukov wiped his forehead on the linen table napkin next to his breakfast plate, swallowing nervously. He passed a watery smile at Sir Angus Spratt.

*****

"How was his absence explained, Angus?" Lennard asked.

It was three days after the dinner at Travis's and Lennard had finally been invited to meet with Angus and Sir George at the Palace of Westminster to discover the result of Kosorukov's extended interrogation.

"I sent a message to his wife and his father-in-law," Sir George said. "It was one suitable for our future plans for the grand duke."

"Would you care to enlighten me?" Lennard asked.

"All in good time. If I tell you now, you may jump to the wrong conclusions."

"Very well, Sir George."

"The Prime Minister will join us shortly, Lennard," Sir George said, checking his fob watch. "In the meantime, I've ordered tea and coffee. Thank you very much, my lad. My wife is delighted with your new blend of coffee and asked me to enquire of you when she may obtain more?"

"There's half a hundredweight in the warehouse, Sir George, but if my designs go according to plan, Malloray's will import it directly from the Caribbean without a third party being involved."

"Really? Do tell …"

Before Lennard could answer, the gentlemen rose to their feet as the Prime Minister entered the Home Secretary's parliamentary office.

"Gentlemen," Lord Palmerston said, removing his hat and passing it to his manservant. "I beg your pardon for my tardiness, but I've been lobbying votes. That damned Astley has disappeared at the most untimely moment. I wish to God that I didn't have to depend on his clique for every motion in parliament."

"It seems perilous to be quite so dependant on one man, Prime Minister," Lennard said. "What would happen if anything should befall him?"

"I trust nothing shall, Lennard," Palmerston said, his eyes narrowed.

Lennard held up his hands. "Despite my constant dreams of doing so, I swear that these hands will never touch him with violent intent."

"That statement hardly allays my concern. However, I'm here to talk about Kosorukov. What news?"

"Lennard knows nothing yet, Prime Minister," Angus said, "and the Home Secretary little more."

"Then it's best if you start at the beginning, Fallerton."

Lennard sensed the Prime Minister's irritation, which was most likely due to Astley's absence. From memory, he doubted he'd heard Lord Palmerston refer to Angus by his title more than thrice, and one of those times was when he'd been trounced at bezique after drinking too much red wine.

"Once the grand duke realised his situation, he became very stubborn indeed, asking what I could do to him, asserting that he was a relative of the Russian royal family. To which, of course, I stated that it was the royal family of a nation with whom we were not only presently at war, but also, after hostilities ceased, a strong friendship would be bound to ensue, mainly because of the relationship between our Queen and Czar Alexander, for whom she bears great affection—he courted her when she first came to the throne and was most delighted with him."

"And Kosorukov's reaction?"

"Ah, it was as one might have suspected. All excuses, lies—obstinate to the end, until …"

"Until?" Lennard asked.

"Until I asked him whether he understood the rules of slavery under Pedro the Second, Emperor of Brazil."

"You threatened to sell him into slavery?"

"No, not him, Lennard, but his brother, wife, and their child."

"Good heavens, Angus—"

"It was a threat in word only, Lennard. I made it clear to him that there are no rules when it comes to war."

"I beg your pardon. The mere thought of it …"

"Then I assume you will free any slaves on the coffee plantations you have purchased in the Caribbean which continue to practice the heinous affront to mankind?"

"Most assuredly. The directive has already gone out."

"Kosorukov was dumbfounded, calling me every name under the sun and in every language he knew. He only shut up when I reminded him of the numbers of our men who may have lost their lives due to his treachery and treason. He countered that in wartime men die, to which I replied, 'Sir, you are mistaken. In war, it is not only men who suffer, but also women and children too'."

"So, he will cooperate?" the Prime Minister asked.

"Fully, sir. In accordance with what I propose to offer him, with your agreement of course, in lieu of a public execution."

"By Jove, that would draw a crowd," Sir George said.

"But it cannot be allowed to happen," Lord Palmerston replied. "Such a thing would reflect badly on the Earl of Twinton, and most likely upon us too. Tongues would wag, asking what the point was of having a Prime Minister and a Home Secretary who could not keep an eye on subterfuge carried out for years, right under their very noses."

"Indeed, Prime Minister," Angus said. "What I have in mind is to arrange things so that the Russians sense no change of atmosphere. Kosorukov's coded messages will continue as usual in letters sent by the Swedish guard to his sister in Stockholm. The only difference being that we will instruct what is to be written. The third bombardment of Sevastopol is due to commence in June, less than a month from now. I have great hopes the war will be over by the end of this year, or at the latest twelve months from now. From that point on, Kosorukov's intelligence to the Russians will have no currency. Therefore, I ask you, what's to be done with the man?"

"He can't be suffered to remain in this country," Lennard said heatedly.

"No, Lennard, in that you are entirely correct. However, Kosorukov is not only devious but also wedded into one of the leading houses of our country. I propose that after the birth of his child, he is to be offered a position at our embassy in Paris, where he will remain, under threat of 'accidental' death if he ever steps foot again on British soil—"

"No! This cannot be—" Lennard protested.

"From the outside, it may seem like a reward rather than a punishment. However, Vassili Vadimovich Kosorukov will find himself a slave to the Crown, obediently acting as one of our agents for the rest of his life, perpetually followed by our people and allowed no privacy in his personal life."

"But he's a—"

"Slave to his physical needs? Is that what you were going to say?"

"Yes, Angus."

"He can keep his Ukrainian lout and make do with him. I'll make it clear that if he strays from his wife's bed or far from Bohuslav Melnyk's prick, I'll have him castrated with a rusty ploughshare."

Lord Palmerston raised his eyebrows, smothering a smile. Sir George, however, was intemperate in his laughter. Lennard merely frowned.

"As for his meetings with the guard, Paulsson, they must continue unchanged at Mrs Hedger's house on the first and the fifteenth of each month. It's a precaution in case the change in his routine is noted. We must assume that he's being observed not only by us, but also by other interested parties."

"But we can't allow them to spend time together unsupervised. Who knows what they might scheme between them?"

"That's why either you or I will be in attendance during their meetings."

"But what if they …"

"Lennard, if you tell me you've never observed such a thing, I shan't believe you. Take a pistol and a book. Just keep your ears open and hope that all they do is talk, and if they do become intimate, I'm entirely sure you'll find distraction with the words on the page in your novel. We will bring instructions to their meetings for what Paulsson will write."

"But surely this could be done alone with Paulsson at any time, Angus."

"Indeed, it could. But if at some later time Kosorukov is able to deny any knowledge of what was in Paulsson's missives to his sister, then his complicity would be hard to disprove, if you or I could vouch otherwise. Besides, Kosorukov will be able to put into his own words that which we wish to be conveyed. We can't have any discrepancies to be noted."

"And if Paulsson changes the words before the letter is sent?"

"If we discover any such thing, it will be the rope for him, his sister, and his parents."

"Another threat in words only?"

"Karl Paulsson has no noble family's reputation to protect, Lennard."

*****

After the meeting, Lennard and Angus walked down to the portico, waiting together while their carriages were fetched.

"I have something to ask you, Angus," Lennard said.

"Is it about the reason for Kosorukov's absence from his home? I remember I said I'd tell you later."

"No, it isn't that. I suppose you concocted some story about his future plans as attaché in Paris and time spent at Sir George's country house to discuss it. Am I correct?"

"Close enough, Lennard. You want to know why Kosorukov met with one of Astley's men, don't you?"

"I am more than curious, Angus."

"Kosorukov sent a message to Astley, asking for a meeting. However, as he's abroad, Conall Leddy came in his place."

"Is that what he told you?"

"Kosorukov wanted to know whether you were … you know, of the persuasion. It seems he had no idea. He was trying to reconcile the reason that Elam should have given him a wrong name and have appeared at your side at Birch House. He had no idea about yours or Astley's personal preferences when it came to companions and wanted to reassure himself that it was as he'd convinced himself to believe—that Elam had been at the Sultan of Khartoum without your knowledge and had made up a story out of embarrassment and to cover the fact."

"But that still doesn't explain how Kosorukov came to know about Gerald and Arthur."

"Pure circumstance, Lennard. On the same night that Gerald and Arthur had supped together at the Raven's Beak, Leddy and his 'sister', Colleen, in company with the man I keep as an agent in Astley's household had decided to dine at the same establishment. They arrived in time to see the men leave together in a handsome cab."

"No doubt to drop Arthur off at Mrs Hedger's."

"Just so. It seems our enterprising Irish man has compatriots everywhere, including one of the publican's servants, one who waited on table for Gerald and Arthur. After the passing of coin, names and occupations were revealed."

"I still don't understand why Leddy would find it so important to tell Kosorukov."

"Because when our Russian enquired whether Astley knew anything about your bedfellows and preferences, he seemed astounded to learn that Gerald should be one of them. However, when Leddy revealed who Gerald had been consorting with, Kosorukov was not only astounded, but furious. That's why he turned up at Martin's drunk and incoherent. He wanted to know if it was the truth. He might have left, had Martin not told him that Arthur had found a gentleman patron and would no longer be available. Unfortunately, Arthur, innocent of Kosorukov's presence, arrived from upstairs to enquire about the noise. That's what tipped the scales into violence."

"It seems far too coincidental that Astley's Irish lad and the girl, along with your agent in his household, should just happen to be at the same pub out of hundreds in London."

"I'm meeting with him this evening and shall bring up the matter."

"He's to be trusted?"

"He feeds Astley bits and pieces—only those I want him to know—and he reports back to me thoroughly. I've no reason to doubt that he's truthful. Besides, I think he suspects that I know he's one of my prince's dalliances."

"He is?"

"One must prevail with patience for true affection, Lennard. Bonds of steel and reluctant promises only lead to betrayal, deception and ultimately, heartbreak. Some men are not made to be monogamous: they must come to that conclusion by themselves once their appetites have been whetted."

"Does His Highness know?"

"Of course not. Besides, it would do no good to broach the subject. He never asks what I am about when he is busy."

"As you mentioned knowing Arthur for some time, I suppose you mean Mrs Hedger's?"

"No, my dear friend. I haven't been paying for connections with Arthur or his fellows at Cowcross Street if that's what you think."

"I'm sorry, I don't understand," Lennard said.

"At times, you are incredibly naïve for such a man of the world—even though those terms are contradictory."

"Me? In what sense, Angus."

"The reason I gave you the book. Think about it."

"What? No! I can't believe it ... you've been sleeping with Martin?"

"For over fifteen years, Lennard. Who do you think loaned him the money to buy the house in Farrington?"

"Oh ..."

Angus laughed. "It's good to trounce you once in a while. Somehow, I always believed you'd suspected. You never slept with him yourself, did you, years ago, when we first met him as a porter at the markets?"

"No, my dance card was far too full. However, I do remember talk of his prodigious member."

"There's none to match it, my friend. But that's not the reason I like his company."

"I shan't enquire."

"Perhaps at another time. I see our carriages advancing along the line. We'll meet tomorrow perhaps. Where will you be?"

"I'll be at Malloray's in the morning, after which I'm meeting the Earl of Twinton at the Oriental to have yet another discussion about his blasted tea business. Robert insists I should be there. What shall l say if Kosorukov's name comes up?"

"He's back at home now, duly chastised, his tail between his legs. As far as the earl knows, the grand duke was meeting with the Foreign Secretary at his country house to discuss the probability of his offer to work for Her Majesty's government in Paris."

"I see."

"Now, here's Christopher. Before you go, Lennard, if Martin does manage to find Leddy and bring him to you, what will you do with the lad?"

"I did have several ideas, a few of which included punishment such as he afforded me, but there's no guarantee that he would find any displeasure in that."

"If you believe he'd accommodate such abuse because he was once a prostitute, Lennard, you are mistaken. Even prostitutes are human beings, and their trade is conducted by means of commerce, not by coercion and unwanted violence."

"I find myself reprimanded, Angus. You are right. However, during our earlier conversation with Lord Palmerston and Sir George, you have given me much to think about on how I may deal with Conall Leddy, should he be delivered at my door in a hessian sack."

*****

On Friday, four days after Lennard's meeting with the Prime Minister, Sir George, and Angus, he was at home, happier than he'd felt in ages.

Elam had returned that morning, accompanied by Travis, who had given strict instructions about the continuing treatment of Elam's ears: how often they should be covered, how carefully the gauze should be packed in them, and the admonition that when he bathed, he should insert wax plugs to prevent water from entering the ear canal.

Mr Huilot had prepared the most magnificent duck and oyster pie with freshly picked asparagus for lunch, and so Travis had been invited to eat with them. As a special treat, and because Elam was inordinately fond of him, Geoffroy had been granted a day away from his uncle's side at Malloray's.

Elam and the lad had pulled back the Turkish carpet in the day room and had laid on their stomachs playing skittles while Lennard and Travis talked about forthcoming social occasions to which the doctor had been invited. Lennard had been only too happy to offer advice about dress, what was expected, who Travis should talk to, and the most tiresome ritual of all: deference.

"If in doubt, Travis, my advice is to wait for someone else to address the person first, with the following word of caution: if one gentleman addresses another by the name of their title, for example 'Buckingham' instead of 'Your Grace' when referring to the Duke of Buckingham, you should avoid repeating such a familiarity. Only noblemen of equal rank or of close familiarity should speak so to each other. When in doubt, if you know their rank, it's simpler to call them merely, duke, or earl, or viscount, whatever. Sir, otherwise, if you don't know their title."

"They all need insignia, as we do in the navy," Travis said. "How on earth do people negotiate such hazardous waters."

"If I were you, Travis, I should find someone already of your acquaintance, preferably a lady not your own age but your senior, confess your awkwardness and ask her advice. If you can manage a pretty blush at the same time, you'll find the evening passes easily and you'll have gained the reputation for being a charmer, worthy of further advancement within her circle."

"Try not to stare at their bosoms while you're at it," Elam called out over his shoulder.

"His hearing has improved remarkably," Lennard said with a chuckle. "And for that, I am forever in your debt."

*****

At seven that evening, just as the household was about to sit down to dinner, Christopher arrived in the dining room doorway.

"There's something just arrived for you, Lennard," he said.

"Something?"

"Something you've been waiting for," Arthur announced, appearing behind Christopher. "It's in a sack, as you requested."

"Please, Arthur, come into the room," Lennard said. "No one will bite you."

"I'm sorry, my lord, but I'm scarcely dressed appropriately."

"None of us cares, do we? Gerald, perhaps you could fetch a chair?"

Gerald jumped to his feet and took Arthur's arm, leading him into the room.

"What shall I do with Leddy?" Arthur asked.

"Where is he now?"

"Still in the sack, in the back of a dray in your stable yard."

"What condition is he in?"

"Untouched, sir. Mrs Hedger said to bring him to you bound but not beaten. She surmised you'd spoken in anger."

Lennard owned that he had then rung for Merrill, asking him to set two more places for dinner. One for Arthur who, although protesting, sat next to Gerald, the other for Conall Leddy, who was brought into the room by Stephen and James, his under-footmen.

"Sit, if you please, Mr Leddy," Lennard ordered.

When the man did not move, a shove to the middle of the back propelled him toward a chair, which James held ready for him.

"Mr Malloray—"

"Sit, I said. I did not invite you to speak. We will go ahead with our meal, which I invite you to partake with us, but during the course of the evening I shall ask questions of you. If you answer truthfully, I promise you will leave this room unbloodied and uninjured, your fate to be decided by your own choice. Do you understand me?"

Leddy nodded, red-faced and breathing heavily, his head bowed, fidgeting with the cuff of his coat sleeve.

"Do you dine at table with Astley?"

"Yes."

"Then I have no need to instruct you. We dine *à la russe* in this household. I'm not sure how you eat at home, but please ask if you are confused."

"Thank you, my lord, but I have no appetite."

"Then you may sit in silence and watch, responding only when I pose a question to you. Do you understand?"

Conall nodded.

"Speak up, man. I've never known an Irishman to hold his tongue when there's a chance he may not live to see another day."

Conall Leddy's head shot up, staring in amazement at Lennard. "I thought you said—"

"I said *if* you answer truthfully, sir. 'If' is a loaded word, making whatever follows it dependent on another thing. Now, look around the room. Is there anyone here you don't know or recognise?"

"No, my lord."

"Please tell me why you are acquainted with all of us."

"Sir Terrence charged me with gaining recognition of all present sir, and also of your private secretary, Mr Billings."

"Why?"

"He believes you're behind the interception of the *Pendragon* and the seizure of his vessel, his warehouses, and the house at St. Just in Roseland."

"And why does this give him cause to spy upon me and my friends?"

"He is obsessed with you, sir. He wishes to know everything about you."

"So, am I to assume that before your meeting with the Russian grand duke, that you, your colleague Colleen, and another gentleman were not at the Raven's Beak by accident, and you went there to spy upon my friend, Captain Langbourne?"

"No. That's not the case. We sup there frequently, especially when Sir Terrence is abroad or out to dinner himself. It was Mr Fetcher who noticed the captain as we arrived and as they were leaving. I paid the man who attended to their meal to tell me who Mr Pencott was and what his business."

"How does this Mr Fetcher know my friend?"

"You'd best ask your friend, Sir Angus Spratt, my lord, if I may be so bold."

Lennard banged the table with his fist so hard that the crockery and silverware rattled. "You will answer my questions, Leddy. I'll have no insolence."

"May I say something before I answer?"

"You may proceed," Lennard said, ignoring Robert's raised eyebrow.

"He shall kill me. There's no question that when he comes to learn that I may have spoken about him, he'll have me gutted. You think what he ordered to be done to you and your Mr Walters was harsh, my lord? He saw that as a divertissement. You have no understanding of the depths of cruelty of Sir Terrence Astley, my lord. There'll be no refuge for me in this country, or my own. He'll hunt me down and provide sport for his dogs, tear them off me when I'm half-dead, and draw out my guts while I'm still alive and force them down my throat. You think I'm exaggerating, don't you? Well, I've seen it done more than once and most recently to your man who was planted aboard the *Pendragon*."

"Dear God," Gerald said, half-rising in his seat.

"Soup is about to be served," Lennard said, gesturing for Gerald to remain seated. "Let me think on what you've said, for I sense that, no matter how alarming, what you've said is most likely true. I've seen the cruelty in his eyes and I've always supposed it could be manifested physically. What you've told me turns my stomach. However, I freely admit that it does not surprise me. Very well, I shall not be the architect of your torture at Astley's hands. After the soup plates have been removed, I shall put an offer to you that will have you out of his clutches for as long as you live. If you tell me everything, there's no reason you won't die in your bed an old man."

As James approached Leddy, his ladle ready to serve Mr Huilot's excellent *Consommé Henri Quattre*, the Irishman demurred, but Robert spoke quickly and earnestly across the table to him in Gaelic, after which Conall thanked James and accepted a bowlful, which he ate slowly, keeping his eyes down all the while.

"What did you say to him?" Lennard asked Robert, in French.

"I said to him to mind his manners. It is the Irish way to accept hospitality from both friend and foe, and that he should listen to your offer if he didn't want to end his days locked in the bowels of a prison hulk, selling his arse for stale bread."

"Our man aboard the vessel. Could this man have been telling the truth?"

Robert continued to eat his soup and shook his head. "Our fellow hasn't been seen. I'd say it was most likely true and I think you do too—I saw the knowing of it in your eyes while he spoke."

The soup plates cleared. Lennard waited until James and Stephen had left the room. Merrill stood waiting next to the dining room credenza, glancing at Leddy, in case the man should make an attempt to bolt for the door.

"What ships do we have leaving port this week, Robert, and which destinations are they bound for?" Lennard asked.

"Two days hence, on Sunday morning, the *Star of the Orient* sails for Ephesus. On Tuesday, the *Grand Caraque* returns to Batavia, thence Surabaya on the island of Java before proceeding to the port of Canton. A week from today, the *Admiral Hartford* sets off for the port of Melbourne, after which Sydney town with a shipment of portable houses. Why do you ask?"

"These are your choices, Conall," Lennard said. "Depending on how much you wish to share, and how forthcoming you are with information, you may choose to sail on one of those ships."

"You are sending me into exile?"

"I'd be sending you to the bottom of the Thames with an anchor chained around your waist had not my very good friend, Sir Angus Spratt, reminded me of your history, sir. Bought as a chattel to be used as a bed slave by a pig of a man and ordered to do his bidding. No doubt with the threat of violence held over your head. Am I correct?"

"I do not always go unwillingly to his bed, but yes. He punishes me with floggings and rewards me with his body and a purse, or sometimes allows Mr Fetcher into my bed."

"Fetcher, the man you supped with at the Raven's Beak. Can he be the same fellow who works for Sir Angus and also sleeps with a member of the royal household at Kensington Palace?"

Conall Leddy's eyes opened wide.

"I know more than Sir Terrence appreciates, sir. Now, pay heed to me. I will have a direct answer to the question I am now about to put to you—"

"Before I answer, sir. The choice of destinations. None of them seems like a punishment, more like an opportunity for a new life."

"Only one of them is, Conall. Disembarked in Melbourne Town with ten guineas in your pocket and the directions to the goldfields. Who knows what might happen to you? But, as for the other ports of call? A man with your looks is bound to be kidnapped and put up on the stand in the infidel market in Ephesus. Why, you'd have your gonads removed in a trice and if you survived the procedure, you'd spend your days getting fat and unloved as a eunuch harem attendant, occasionally forced to service the soldiers of whichever khedive bought you at auction."

The Irishman opened his mouth, as if to speak, but Lennard held up a hand to stay his words.

"I haven't finished. The other choice is the Dutch East Indies, sir. Ruled by cruel Calvinists who can't bear Irish Catholics. In Batavia, perhaps you may look forward to labouring in the mines near Bogor, or in Surabaya, if you choose to disembark there, a slave porter on the docks. And as for Canton, a life tied to a mattress in an opium den, never rising out of the stupor of the brown sticky sap of the poppy, violated until you either died of malnutrition or the pox. Now, my question: tell me what business Sir Terrence has with the Grand Duke Vassili Vadimovich Kosorukov?"

*****

Clyford arrived back at Bexford House late in the evening, having finally finished preparation for his and Arthur's departure for Paris at noon the following day. Mr Huilot had left a cold collation for him, and warmed bread rolls appeared as if by magic the moment he sat at table and took his first sip of wine, ready to start to eat.

"You say he's in the basement?"

"Where else could we put him, Clyford?" Lennard said. "It's hardly a dark and dank prison cell. The basement is on ground level at the eastern elevation of the house. It's light and airy, has a comfortable bed, and the room is well-appointed."

"He'll leave for Australia on Friday next?"

"That was our agreement."

"And he was forthcoming?"

Arthur answered with a smile. "I think he realised there would be an opportunity for him in another land with a new name, the possibilities of a new life, and to remake himself. I've seen that look before, and not once or twice in my own looking glass while shaving."

"Will you stay here tonight, Arthur?" Clyford asked.

"I must return Mrs Hedger's dray, sir."

"I'll ask Christopher to follow you in the phaeton, Arthur," Lennard said. "He can take you to your lodging house to collect whatever you need for your trip abroad tomorrow then bring you back here. Stephen will make a room ready for you."

"Now, the news from Conall Leddy, Clyford. I'm sure you're anxious to know."

"Indeed, I am. Do you mind if I eat while we talk? It's terribly bad manners but I'm famished. I fear I might faint if I don't eat something."

"Please, I don't mind in the least. Leddy was not evasive when I asked him about Astley's connection with Kosorukov. He said it was the one thing that Astley had never discussed in front of him, and when he asked Fetcher, he swore he knew nothing either."

"He mentioned Fetcher?"

"Yes. How long have you known he's been a double agent, working for both Astley and Angus?"

"Since I returned from the Crimea, sir. However, due to the nature of the sensitivity of his placement, Sir Angus asked me to keep my mouth shut."

"Did you know Fetcher was being smuggled into Kensington Palace on a regular basis to service Prince Christian Jost Saxe-Meiningen?"

"Yes, I did. But that's another thing I've kept quiet about. Please don't tell Sir Angus—"

"He's already worked it out and doesn't seem to mind. At least, that's what he told me."

"Did Leddy disclose the identities of the other men?"

"Which other men are you referring to, Clyford."

"The men who savaged Elam and took liberties with—"

"They are out of the country, as is Astley. Leddy gave us their names, however, it will be difficult to find them in the wilds of Ireland. It seems Astley misled everyone and was in London until two days ago. On Wednesday, he left for Ireland, telling Leddy and Fetcher that he intended to do some business in Cork, then sail to La Corunna to see whether he could salvage his reputation and renegotiate trade deals."

"So, he didn't leave the day after he came here for dinner?"

"No."

"Did he by chance—"

"No, Clyford. Only Leddy and Fetcher were present that evening, and Fetcher did not participate, but watched through a spyhole."

"Dear God ..."

"What shall you do with Bertram Fetcher, Lennard?"

"I shall recruit him, Clyford."

"But he's one of Angus's informants. The connection with Astley's household will be lost."

"Astley will have no household, Clyford. Tomorrow, after I've seen you and Arthur off to Paris and while Astley is abroad, I shall visit Simeon Drudge to give him instructions. It will be him who'll announce that Malloray, Beauchamp, and Fahey have decided to no longer offer our wharf spaces and warehouses in Italy to other shipping companies. He'll start the process of short-selling Martin's shares in Astley's company to Fratelli's. Once word gets to the newspaper, Signor Baldacchino will offer premium prices for any shares that come onto the market, sold by scared investors, anxious when they see the dropping value of their portfolios. Fratelli Importers and Exporters will start on their hostile takeover of Killcaire's Irish Trading Company, and Terrence Astley will finally return from La Corunna to find himself well along the road to ruin."

*****

"I love it now that I can hear you whisper, Lenn," Elam said, stretched naked over Lennard's back, gently biting the nape of his neck.

"Does this mean I'll have to temper what I say to you?"

Elam laughed. "I need to hear the filth you've been no doubt growling away and I've not been able to appreciate."

"Filth? No such thing, Elam. Words of affection and pleasure."

Not long after midnight, the members of the household had made their way to their rooms, Gerald and Arthur lingering at the top of the grand staircase, holding hands, and talking softly for a few minutes, before breaking away and moving off along different corridors of the upper floor to their bedrooms.

"Do you think there will be a crossing between bedrooms during the night?"

"I do believe there's been some promise to wait until Arthur returns for any more intimacy than fond words and the holding of hands."

"Strange though, don't you think, Lenn? Considering Gerald's unquenchable thirst for sexual adventure and the nature of Arthur's evening occupation ..."

"Angus reminded me, when I revealed how I'd initially planned to punish Conall Leddy, that the profession does not define the man who works in it. Perhaps it's the same with Arthur—finding that intangible something that rises above the mere physical could be something new. Perhaps he doesn't want to fall into the same type of relationship he had with Karl Paulsson? No one could blame him for taking his time."

"And Gerald?"

"Have you regarded him while he's talking with Arthur, Elam?"

"Puppy dog?"

"A bushel full."

"Lennard …?"

"What?"

"Are you …?"

"Ready? For you anytime, Elam."

"I thought you might be frightened … after what happened."

Lennard shook his head. "Perhaps not that, Elam. But as they say in down at the dockside, 'there's more than one way to shine a penny …'"

Elam laughed. "Or pluck a chicken."

Lennard rolled onto his back and stretched out, pulling Elam close, their bodies pressed together. "Perhaps my hearing is fading, now that yours is restored."

"Why?"

"I could have sworn you said 'pluck'," Lennard said. He kissed Elam deeply, moaning with the wonder of it.

19. EVIL DEEDS REPAID

Lennard had never experienced a fog at sea—or rather, on a river, where he now lay, on the deck of the pilot's ketch with Elam in his arms, a blanket from the captain's truckle bed wrapped around them.

It was unlike dense city fogs, in that instead of choking sulphurous clouds of gritty mist, the fog that surrounded them had no texture; it swirled over the water and poured around them on the deck of the boat. The movement reminded him of the diaphanous, billowing, cotton under-curtains at Gresting Hall, caught in a late summer's breeze when the windows had been left open.

It had been an evening of near-calamity.

They'd taken a special steam train service from Fenchurch Street station to Tilbury. From the station, a carriage had been arranged to take them to the rarely-used, near-dilapidated docks on the river where the pilot's vessel was waiting for them. The reason for the 'near-calamity' had been that not three miles from Tilbury Town station, the engine had let forth a loud report and a hiss of steam and had come to a halt in the middle of nowhere. The night was thick with sea fog; there would have been no way of even knowing exactly where they were, but for a mileage marker at the side of the railway track.

Eventually, after telling Lennard that the engine would be going no further that evening, the engineer had said he knew of a farmhouse, not two hundred yards away, in the direction of the river, off to the right-hand side of the tracks. He'd often noticed it as he'd passed it during the day, and thinking it charming, had made a note of its whereabouts, right where they were, at the three-mile marker.

Although the farmer had been angry at being roused in the dead of night, he'd softened at the sight of a pair of gold sovereigns and had hitched up his dray and taken their party to the dockside. They'd arrived not thirty minutes ago, with barely enough time before they'd needed to cast off.

Lennard, Elam, Gerald, Travis, and Christopher: such an extravagance to hire a special railway service for a twenty-five-mile journey for five men, but which necessitated a travel time of just over an hour, as opposed to four or five hours over uneven road services by coach. However, the Crown had paid for the hire of the steam engine, as they had done for the special pilot ketch and its crew.

"How long before the *Malmaison* is due to heave to, Lenn?" Elam asked, snuggling back into Lennard's arms. Despite himself, he shivered, not for the cold, but the apprehension of the task ahead.

Lennard reached into his pocket and checked his timepiece. It was very dark still, an hour and a half before sunrise. "According to the telegram from the La Rochelle harbourmaster's office, she's due at three. Only another twenty minutes. The time of the dropping of her anchor mid-stream, to allow the pilot to board, should have been arranged by Clyford. Ten guineas will buy a schedule to any man's choosing."

"Look out there, Lenn. Through the gaps of the mist."

"Where?"

Elam extended his hand pointing out over the river to the south.

There was an opening in the gunwale down to deck level, directly opposite where they sat on the ketch's deck, a gap perhaps two yards wide. Lennard thought it odd at first, until he remembered Angus had told him the ship had been appropriated especially for tonight, with a pilot who was in government employ and who would keep his mouth shut. The captain and first mate were also ex-navy men and loyal to the Crown. The opening, although most likely designed to allow free passage of goods to the wharf without the need of a crane, gave them an unobstructed view over the river, which was either completely veiled in mist or briefly exposed in such a manner that he could see lights of the docks at Gravesend on the southern shore of the Thames, opposite Tilbury.

"What are you two looking at?" Travis asked, sitting down beside them.

"The water, Travis. I'm not used to it—such an expanse anyway. I've never travelled on a ship before," Elam said, throwing a corner of their blanket over Travis's knees.

"And you, chained by virtue of your friendship to this brute, the owner of the largest shipping company in the kingdom?"

"Half-owner, Travis," Lennard said.

"Well, it's hardly an 'expanse' as you put it, but at this hour of the morning, calm, with barely a breeze and such thick fog as this, muffling all sound across the water, it's like living in a dream."

"Tell me, my friend," Lennard said, placing his hand on Travis's shoulder, "any qualms about being present this evening?"

"None, except for my gammy leg. Unless you require me to run around the deck, then I am prepared for any exigency."

"Gammy leg? I don't understand the meaning of the word."

"It's a newish word. I heard it first from the son of the Portuguese family of yours who delivers our vegetables. He's a bit of a lad—asked me if my 'gammy' leg caused me problems, because his aunt was a manipulator of the joints and could give me some relief, should I wish it."

Elam laughed, quickly followed by Lennard. "Manipulation of your joints? I think he was hinting that she'd be happy to manipulate another part of your body altogether."

"Really?" Travis laughed. "I shall keep myself for marriage, if I should ever be so lucky."

"I know you to be very capable with your fists and with a pistol, Travis, should it come to that, but I'd rather you stand back and allow us to take charge if any violence should erupt."

"Yes, I understand completely. Sir Angus was very serious about my role this evening. I'm merely here as a qualified medical man and former naval officer, to ascertain that this pretender fellow is truly dead before you consign him to the depths of the mighty Thames. Had I stayed a rural doctor in some leafy, green hamlet, I may have objected to the taking of any life, but during my service to the Crown I've seen things that make me realise that actions come first and then a man's conscience must weigh up the necessity at a time postponed."

"Thank you for coming. Don't worry, Gerald, Elam, Christopher, and I are well-versed in dealing with all sorts of violence—and, of course, there's also Arthur and Clyford for extra reinforcement. It sounds like many men to apprehend but two, but in our line of work, one must be prepared for any unexpected eventuality. Who knows if The Cargo might not be travelling with other companions, unknown to our intelligence?"

"I've never asked about your … training, is that the word?"

Lennard smiled. "In our occupations as intelligencers, Travis, our skills are many. Fisticuffs, the use of pistols and knives, and the many ways one might incapacitate a foe silently, either temporarily or permanently."

"I thought as much, Lennard. Your extreme composure when I attended to your injuries on the night you came to me with Elam gave me thought as to such training. I've seen it often enough with men who know how to look after themselves. But …"

"But?"

"Ah, it's of no consequence. Something not important."

"In our brief acquaintance, I've never known you to waste words. Please, say what you were about to. There's nothing much can either offend or disarm me."

"Something you said to me on the night I treated you, about offering no resistance, and therefore avoiding greater injury. I puzzled over your acquiescence—"

"That acquiescence was to spare Elam's life, Travis. I took no pleasure in it, and I think you would have done the same to save someone so dear to yourself too."

"Perhaps I should, in that you are right, Lennard."

"My friend, it's taken me a very long time to learn to stay calm in stressful situations and not to act rashly. However, I may assure you that my heart beats as fast as any man's, and the feeling of ice in my guts when danger is nigh is most likely the same as yours when you were about to launch into the thick of battle aboard your ship. I'm just as fallible and vulnerable as any other fellow human being—I've just learned not to fall down in a heap in the midst of a crisis, until after it has been averted."

"You would have made a very fine ship's captain, if I may say so."

"Thank you, Travis. That's a compliment I shall hold dear, coming from a man such as yourself."

*****

He felt it in his bones at first, vibrating through the deck of the ship; the barely perceptible rhythmic thud, thud, thud, which grew in intensity until it was accompanied by the sound of simultaneous chuffs of steam and finally by splashes as the steamer's paddle wheels struck the surface of the water.

Elam, who'd been sound asleep, stirred in his arms. Lennard leaned forward and kissed him gently on the forehead. "Look out over the river. Give it a second or two," he said.

Gradually, through the mist, a behemoth drew into sight. Softly glowing oil lamps illuminated her massive form. It was a monumental vision, looming above them as it passed close by, her engines thudding and hissing and her great paddles slapping the water with loud, violent whacks. Their ketch rocked violently in the steamer's bow wave, and as she passed by them, the mighty ship let forth a loud, deep blast of her foghorn, not twenty feet from their bow before she gradually disappeared into the dense river fog.

The first mate roused them, urging them to get to their feet, saying that within ten or fifteen minutes they'd draw up alongside the

Malmaison and board her, using the passenger gangplank, which would be lowered over the arch of the ship's port paddle-wheel housing in order for the pilot to gain access to the deck.

"How long will we have aboard?"

"Depends on how much you've paid, sir," the sailor said. "Normally, the pilot would have a cup of tea with the captain, go through his log, sign off on it, then guide the vessel into St. Katharine's dock, tying her up at around half past seven when it's light and the ladies' and gentlemen's carriages have arrived from all over."

"How will you find the *Malmaison* in this fog?" Lennard asked.

"There are no more than a few suitable anchorages in this area, and they'll be on the Admiralty chart. Besides, in this mirk, the ship will be sounding its foghorn or ringing a bell. Once at least every two minutes. And there'll be a masthead light amidships—a white one, I hope. If we see red and green lights, she'll be under way still."

"Did you know that?" Lennard asked Travis after the man had left them.

"I didn't spend all those years at sea not knowing the procedure to bring a vessel into port, Lennard."

"I'm sorry. Stupid of me really. I think my anxiety, as well-concealed as I'm trying to keep it, may be stronger than I might admit it to be."

*****

Lennard breathed a sigh of relief to see Gerald embracing a man's form at the top of the lowered gangplank. It could be no one else but Arthur.

"My lord, there's a problem," Arthur said, whispering, his voice slightly muffled through the scarf he wore, which covered the lower half of his face.

"A problem?"

"Yes, Mr Billings said to warn you that Sir Terrence Astley is aboard."

"What? How on earth—?"

"He was in the passenger lounge at La Rochelle waiting to board the ship when we arrived."

"That's a complication I could have done without."

"Your money has been well spent, sir. We've had him under observation, as we have the pretender and his bodyguard."

"My money?"

"Mr Billings has disbursed bribes without revealing the reasons for the vigilance he's required. Neither Astley nor The Cargo, as you call them, seem to have communicated. They've mostly stayed in their rooms during the crossing and have eaten at tables far removed from each other in the dining room. There's no reason for any of the three to know me, so I've been able to observe them and can assure you there's been no contact."

"What about in the dead of night?"

"Apart from meals, Astley stayed in his cabin for the entire journey, and the pretender and his bodyguard came to the dining room at midday only. The rest of the time they took their meals in their room."

"Very good, Arthur. There can be no reason for Astley to be on this ship if it's not to introduce himself to The Cargo at some stage—I've no idea how that might be achieved because I know for certain that he speaks not a word of French. Where's Clyford?"

"Waiting on the rear promenade deck. He said to bring Captain Langbourne and Elam, but you and Mr Holland are to stay here. We'll escort the pretender and his bodyguard to you. Is Christopher not with you?"

"He's standing guard down on the pilot ketch. We're not expecting anyone else to arrive, but Christopher, the captain of the vessel, and his first mate are armed and prepared should anyone else have conceived to 'rescue' The Cargo mid-stream before she docks. I can't have been the only one to have thought that such a feat might be possible, although I rather think a show of the pretender arriving, and with supporters of his cause dockside, might advance their cause and lift their spirits. However, it shall never happen."

Lennard signalled for the pilot to make his way up to the captain's cabin, then turned to Gerald. "You have two pistols?"

"Yes, and a knife. Don't worry about me, Lenn, as much as I appreciate your concern. Both Clyford and I have fought and killed many a Turk and Russian during our time in the Crimea."

"Well, make sure you don't kill any this time unless they're down on the deck of the pilot ketch."

Gerald mock-saluted Lennard. Then, to Arthur's enormous surprise, pulled down his scarf, took his face in two hands and kissed him full on the lips, before he turned and disappeared into the swirling fog, which still covered the deck.

"Shouldn't you follow him?" Lennard asked.

"Once I regain my breath, certainly, my lord," Arthur said, with an enormous grin, replacing the scarf.

"Stay safe, Elam," Lennard said.

"No farewell kisses, Lenn?"

"Get off with you. There'll be plenty when you return."

Lennard and Travis smiled, watching Elam and Arthur shake hands before heading off together after Gerald.

"Dear heavens," Travis said, "Before I came to know you and your friends, I had no idea there would be any affection, such as between you and Elam."

"Are we not men, like any other?"

"Indeed, you are, Lennard, and I am poorer for not realising it years ago."

"None of us asked for this life, Travis. It wasn't one day that we woke up and decided that we'd prefer male companionship. Many men, like Robert and Miles, who may have indulged in early manhood, move away from intimacies with others of the same sex. Elam, Gerald, Angus, and me? Well, we've made peace with our desires, and as arduous as it has been at times, we have managed so far to keep our private lives just that—private."

"Certainly, wealth has paved a smoother route, Lennard."

"I wasn't always wealthy, Travis. In fact, my friendship with Elam was easier when we were penniless, sharing two rooms in Jermyn Street. Our future will be much harder to keep confidential, and less happy in many ways."

"Less happy?"

"As a man of substance, my life can no longer be spent behind a desk as third secretary to Sir George Grey while sharing my public life with my manservant at my side. Like Angus, I fear that both Gerald and I will be obliged to marry, and not to the people we love, but for the sake of propriety and to disguise our true natures. Could you do that, do you think?"

"No. In all sincerity, I own that I could not. Is there any way you could perhaps …?"

"My aunt Caroline is my matchmaker. She will choose wisely, and Elam and I will go on as we always did, but in more private circumstances. It burns in my heart to think that we may only act freely when behind closed doors, not out in the street, jesting and behaving like childhood friends, a situation readily accepted for a penniless member of a well-known family, even though observers might frown and tut-tut. There's a certain charm in close male friendships of long standing, no matter the difference in their classes—depending on the situation, of course."

"Have you ever thought of buying him a title?"

Lennard stared at Travis for a moment or two. "The thought never crossed my mind."

"It doesn't need to be an aristocratic title, Lennard. I can't believe you didn't think of it. There's many a country holding with a 'lord of the manor' attached to it."

"It's an excellent idea, however, it would still cause raised eyebrows. Why would we be living together? No. Unless I relinquish the title, master and valet is the only solution. There's always been a valet's truckle at the end of the master's bed in many households, and Elam's official 'closet' is in a room adjoining mine. We will manage. However, your suggestion has given me an idea—"

Travis interrupted Lennard by turning away from the ship's railing, upon which they'd been leaning while they talked.

The tall, gagged, and bound Turk was unmissable, but it was his companion that made Lennard gasp. As round as he was short, with bulbous bovine eyes and dark greasy hair parted in the middle, the pretender could easily have passed for a cousin of Her Majesty, such were the physical similarities of their facial features and complexions.

"Please, keep your pistol aimed between the pretender's eyes," Lennard said to Travis.

"Consider it done, Lennard," Travis replied, standing with his arm extended and braced, ready to shoot if required.

"*Monsieur*," Lennard said to the pretender. "*Enfin nous sommes ici, tous ensembles.*"

"You are French?" the man replied in the same language, his voice light and slightly broken.

"My mother was French," Lennard replied.

"We may be here altogether, as you so stated, sir. But who are the *we*?" The pretender smiled slightly, then spoke in a quick torrent of Russian to the bodyguard, abruptly halted by Clyford, who spat something back at him in the same language.

"Ah, your friend who spoke to me in French when he invaded my cabin speaks Russian too?" the pretender said. "What about Turkish? Any of your assembled company?"

"I know you speak none," Lennard replied. "Neither that, nor English. Did you ever wonder why you were neither schooled in the language of the country in which you were raised, nor in the language of the country over which you believed you were destined to rule? It was designed on purpose, to make you an impotent pawn, sir. One who may be directed by others in charge with no voice of your own."

The pretender did not answer, but narrowed his eyes, angrily wiping his nose on the sleeve of his nightshirt. It was the gesture of defiance by a powerless man; one who found himself not only captive, but no doubt apprehensive that he would become the victim of some calamity—one he most likely would be unable to avoid.

"The Irishman ..." Clyford said to Lennard in English, slightly raising his eyebrows, his face indicating he was worried. They'd decided not to use names in front of The Cargo.

"You know where he is?"

Clyford shook his head. It disquieted Lennard, who wanted to get his charges off the ship as soon as possible. Looking around, he saw that Elam was missing.

"Have you seen Elam?" Lennard said to Gerald, who stood behind the Turk.

"No, I thought he'd returned to you ..."

"Take these two down to the pilot vessel. I'll find him."

"No, sir, that's unwise. You don't know the vessel," Arthur said. "I'll go."

"Very well, be quick about it though."

"Who are you?" the short, round man asked after Arthur had disappeared into the swirling fog behind them.

"Who I am is of no interest to you. What shall I call you?"

"How about you start with 'Your Majesty'," the pretender said with a sneer.

Lennard took two steps forward and slapped the man hard across the face. "Don't be insolent," he snapped.

"How dare you! I'll have you cut into ribbons and your bones fed to the crows—"

Lennard slapped him again then pointed his pistol at the Turk, who he'd noticed had been rebalancing his stance subtly, ready to jump, making sure the balls of his feet were firm against the boards of the steamer promenade deck.

"Your friend here, Kadir, will be the first to die if he even thinks about moving," Lennard said, glancing at the Turk, who growled at him through his gag.

"What, you think discharging a firearm in the dead of night won't have men swarming out here to see what's going on?" the pretender said, spitting on the deck at Lennard's feet. "You're more of a fool than I thought."

"The use of a firearm would be a last resort, sir. But I promise you, blood will be spilled."

"Godon!" the man said, reeling with the threat. Lennard smiled at the mildness of the French epithet, which showed how much the pretender had been protected from the real world and strong language. "You wouldn't dare ..."

"Make both of these creatures aware of Kadir's situation," Lennard said to Clyford, then watched the Turk's reaction when Clyford jabbed it with the point of the man's long, oriental sword, which he'd obviously confiscated from his cabin when he'd apprehended him. Kadir cursed through his gag.

"Ironic, isn't it, if your Kadir should be impaled by a *kiliç*?" Clyford said, in his impeccable, unaccented French. "Sliced open at the waist to the spine. It would take but two short, quick movements of the blade, cutting right through the kidney. Such a lot of blood and thrashing about," Clyford added, his sword now hovering at the man's waist, just under his ribcage. "Gagged, you might scream when the blade enters your body, Kadir, but my orders were worthy of a Janissary in their violence—your quick incapacitation, followed by immediate decapitation. You shan't go to paradise with your body in one piece."

Clyford murmured something else in Russian; the Turk's and the pretender's eyes widening in horror.

"I just told him that I'm not inexperienced with this form of mutilation. I may have added some colour," Clyford explained, in English. "I've only killed three Russians by slicing off their heads, and that was on horseback at the gallop."

"What's keeping you?" Christopher said from behind them, at the top of the gangplank. "We became worried." The pilot's first mate stood next to him.

"Arthur went looking for Elam," Lennard said. "Help take these two down to the ketch and secure the Turk to the mainmast. You can tie this barrel of a creature to a hatch cover. If I haven't joined you with Elam and Arthur in five minutes come back. Go with Christopher, if you please, Travis."

Lennard watched as Christopher and the seaman jostled the pretender to the top of the gangplank, disappearing from sight then returning a few minutes later. With Gerald and Clyford assisting, the four men manhandled the Turk in a similar manner, only more roughly. The bodyguard's muffled protests cut off when Gerald punched the side of his head.

They could not have been gone for more than a few minutes when Lennard heard scuffling and footsteps. He cursed the thickness of the fog, which had risen from the river and covered the deck, obscuring the dim light of the oil lamps at the bow of the vessel and on the wheelhouses. He could barely see a few paces in front of him. As the footsteps came closer, he drew his pistol and began to slowly move backward.

Elam appeared first. "Ah, there you are. Here's something for you," he said.

Astley was flung at his feet, propelled by Arthur's boot, placed on the man's backside.

"You!" Astley spat, raising his head, his eyes dark with anger. "You fucking pup! Always getting in the way—"

Lennard saw red, and before he could temper his reaction, kicked Astley square in the mouth so hard that he thought he may have broken his jaw. Falling to his knees, he grabbed a handful of the Irishman's hair and pulled his head back, forcing him to look straight into Lennard's face.

"You're done, Astley. Finished!"

"What, are you going to kill me here? An Irish lord, a man and his clique upon whom your Prime Minister is dependant for holding power—"

"You didn't listen to me," Lennard shouted. "I said you're done! Your part in this ridiculous charade is over. Your gun smuggling efforts have been exposed, and your goods and businesses have been stripped from you. Your baronetcy has been nullified, and the moment you step on the dock you'll be taken away and hanged in public within days."

Astley did something Lennard never expected. He laughed then spat a mouthful of blood into Lennard's face.

"You'll have the devil's own task to prove any of this at trial."

"Trial? There will be no trial. You've been found guilty in absentia of treason, which needs no jury or communion of your peers, and the sentence has already been passed. If you only had any idea of the number of your so-called supporters who've disavowed you, who've denounced you, who'd provided evidence of your collusion in this delusional scheme. And then, the proof, you asked? Ah, well, both your Conall and Colleen, and your former man, Bertram Fetcher, were only too happy to provide testimony, share the secret hiding places of your documents, and swear to your misdeeds in front of a judge in exchange for impunity."

Astley sneered. "The words of a catamite, a slut, and a traitor to the Crown. Who'd believe Fetcher?"

"Everyone did, you fool. We knew most of what they had to say anyway. You've been watched and followed for years. If you buy people, Astley, they're always, always, open to a better offer. You above all people should know that."

"I'll kill them, all three of them."

"If you're talking about Conall, Colleen, and Bertram, you won't get a chance before you swing, Terrence. Conall is on his way to a new life in Australia. Colleen is halfway across the Atlantic, bound for her aunt in Louisiana, and Bertram is very happily ensconced in my service, newly employed as a spy for Her Majesty. Clyford tells me he has a very pretty cock—"

"You dirty, fucking—"

"Mind your mouth," Lennard said, pulling Astley's head back so far that it became impossible for the man to speak. "Now get to your feet."

Arthur pulled him upright while Elam secured his hands behind his back with a length of rope he'd unwound from around his waist.

"I should have had my men kill both of you. I should have had my men take turns with your catamite first while you watched, impotent while they strangled him after they'd finished abusing his body. As for you, you miserable—"

Lennard drew back his arm and punched Astley so hard, he heard his knuckles crack. As Elam bent down to pull him to his feet, the Irishman started to scream to call for assistance, but Elam was too quick, pulling off his bandana and thrusting it into Astley's mouth.

"You coward, Astley!" Elam growled under his breath against Astley's ear. "Four men beating me and five holding Lennard down to sodomise him, and yet you call for aid when there's but three of us? What sort of man do you call yourself? You yellow-bellied, snivelling—"

With enormous effort, Astley spat out his gag. "Untie me and fight me, man to man, Elam Walters. Then we'll see who's the coward."

Lennard drew Elam aside by the elbow, then stood so close to Astley that their noses were almost touching. "If I had my way, I'd push you overboard with your hands tied behind your back."

"Then why don't you!"

"Because I promised the Prime Minister I wouldn't lay hands on you, and you'd answer to him and the nation by swinging at the end of a rope in front of a crowd of thousands. Don't worry, I haven't forgotten what you and your men did to me and to Elam. I'd pull your guts out through your throat before I flung you over the ship's rail if I hadn't promised to not kill you."

"You both only got what you deserved," Astley growled, blood running down his chin and onto his bare chest. He turned to Elam, "I'd have sliced you open from your balls to your neck myself, had I been there. As for your slatternly lover, Lennard Malloray, I hear he enjoyed every pox-ridden inch of unwashed pizzle that discharged its foulness into his bowels. I'd have—"

Elam roared in anger and before either Lennard or Gerald could react, pulled a dagger from his boot, leaping onto Astley, knocking both him and Arthur to the ground. He spread his hand over Astley's mouth to stifle his cries and began to plunge his dagger over and over into the man's neck and chest.

"Dear God, Elam, what have you done?" Lennard said, having pulled him from Astley's body. Blood covered Elam's face and hands, Arthur's shirtfronts, and had begun to flow across the deck.

"He couldn't die by the rope, Lennard. He'd have become a martyr. He'd take advantage of his death speech on the gallows to put forward his agenda of sedition and revolution. He had to die, and I was happy to kill him. You promised not to touch him, but I didn't. And I'd do it again, given half the chance, and with my bare hands—"

"What's happened here?" Gerald called out, appearing from behind them, alarmed at the sight of so much blood. "Arthur, are you injured?"

"No, not me, Gerald. It was—"

"It was an accident, Gerald," Lennard interrupted. "That's what happened here. Astley's dead. Now, let's get his body down to the ketch. We can talk about what came to pass later, once we're well away from this vessel. See if you can find something to wash the blood off the deck. Get Christopher or the captain's mate to bring up a few buckets of water from the river."

The ship's foghorn sounded, and its bell rang shortly after.

"I think we must move, and in haste," Arthur said. "The pilot can't delay much longer, and the *Malmaison* must be ready to heave to in the Thames near St. Katharine's dock in less than an hour."

"Elam?" Lennard whispered, his arms tight around him, as if he was afraid his friend might break free and throw himself on Astley's body once more and tear his eyes out.

"If you think I regret what I did, Lenn. You're sadly mistaken."

"We need to get off this ship, my friend. Swallow a few times and take a few breaths. What's done is done. Listen to Arthur, we must make haste."

"The anger, Lenn … I couldn't help it."

"I know, my dearest friend. I understand better than any man. It was, as I told Gerald, an accident, and that's how it will remain. Now, come, let's get away before we are no longer able to."

"What shall we tell the Prime Minister?"

"Trust me. I've had an idea already."

20. THE TERRIER AND THE RAT

Travis was tending to Astley's body by the time Lennard and Elam arrived on the deck of the pilot's ketch. "How did this happen?" he asked, staring up at Lennard.

"It was an accident, Travis."

"Six stab wounds, two in the throat and four in the chest is unlikely the result of an accident. I know you hated the man—"

"I did not kill him, Travis. Please, can we discuss this later? I need to think how we can deal with this unfortunate turn of events."

Travis stood slowly, his gaze flicking between Lennard and Elam. He saw at once the smeared blood on Elam's neck and hands and fell silent. "I am at your service should you need another mind to help. I am not unused to finding solutions."

Lennard glanced at his timepiece. "We have an hour at best."

"Shall we talk away from these two?" Travis asked, glancing at the Turk, who was bound by ropes to the mainmast, and at the pretender, his wrists tied and fastened through the hatch cover of the ketch.

"There's no need, Travis. Neither speaks English."

"However, the expressions on men's faces are a universal language. Let us at least turn our backs."

"I've a better idea. The bow has a lading bench. We can sit there. Both men are facing away from us and we can talk freely."

"Shall I keep an eye on them?" Arthur asked.

"No, come with us, Arthur. I may have to ask you to perform a disagreeable task."

"My lord, I—"

"No, put your mind at rest. If there's blood to be spilled it will not be at your hand if that's what you're thinking. Grab yourself a rag from the captain's mate, dip it in the river, and you and Elam clean yourselves up while we talk."

Once the men had gathered in the prow of the vessel, Lennard exclaimed, "Damned Astley! He was supposed to be in La Corunna."

"There was no time to send a telegram, my lord," Clyford said. "Our vessel developed problems with the engine, and we pulled into the harbour twenty minutes before the *Malmaison* was due to depart. Fortunately, we already had reservations, made in Paris and confirmed by telegraph. I saw him immediately we entered the assembly area, and it was sheer luck he happened to be busy talking with one of the shipping company officials and did not see me. We waited until he embarked then boarded at the last minute. He was almost the last of the passengers to go up the gangplank, and the nearest telegraph station was in the harbourmaster's office, some miles from where we were. There was no way we could have let you know."

"No one is blaming you or suggesting you should have done anything other than what you did, Clyford. I'm eternally grateful … to you both," Lennard added, placing his hand on Arthur's shoulder.

"Well then, Astley is dead," Travis said. "I'm sure this changes everything. What was your original intention?"

"That we sail to Benfleet, where we shall spend the day, returning this evening by train to Fenchurch Street."

"Benfleet, on Hadleigh Ray? Why there?"

"Because our departure from Fenchurch Street station last evening was noted in the logbook as a special service departing at six in the evening. The train on which we travelled was not entered into the journal. As far anyone will discover, we were travelling to spend last evening and today with His Highness Christian Jost Saxe-Meiningen and Sir Angus, whose family has a country house overlooking the river. We supposedly boarded the train at six last evening in precisely the way we actually did hours later in the middle of the night, by using the waiting room on the private platform, so as not to be observed."

"I had no idea Benfleet was connected to the railway."

"It's a very new connection, only opened earlier this year. Angus's father had a lot to do with the extension of the line from Tilbury Town. I believe he put up close to eight thousand."

"I'm sure no one will question our whereabouts, Lennard. However, I understand that precautions, put in place for any eventuality, are part of your trade?"

"Indeed. My plan was to question the pretender and to take care of him and his Turk somewhere before we arrived at Benfleet then spend the day sleeping."

"Our sojourn will be mentioned in the Court Circular, Travis," Gerald explained, "along with our names. Officially, we'll have been at Angus's country house playing cards, having a splendid day walking in the countryside, and far away from anything that might have happened aboard a French paddle steamer."

"What about the crew on this vessel? How do you know they won't gossip?" Travis whispered, checking to see that neither man was close by.

"Canada, my friend. They're being sent to the Port of Quebec as new employees of Astley's former whale oil and fur trading fleet, which, as you may have read in the newspapers, has been the victim of a hostile takeover. Malloray's has acquired it through the association with their new business partners, Fratelli Imports and Exports. They'll be set up with a house and land, and the opportunity for a new life, one far away from the dreariness of hard labour aboard a river vessel on the Thames."

"And you believe there could be no possible connection made between The Cargo, Astley, and the pilot ketch?"

"None whatsoever. Clyford and Arthur took the precautions of going through the Russian's and Turk's belongings—that's why they took so long returning to us while we waited on the promenade deck. They threw everything overboard. As far as the *Malmaison* is concerned, our two friends—the pretender and his bodyguard—and our dead Irishman will have disembarked along with the rest of the passengers at St. Katharine's dock in a few hours from now."

"It seems like you thought of everything then, Lennard ... except for our arrival time in Benfleet. We shan't get there until late this evening, even with a good wind. This ketch is laborious—I know her type and this particular vessel is particularly sluggish in the water, especially with so many of us on board."

"Ah, but Travis, in less than an hour from now, we'll be climbing the ladder onto the most powerful and speediest of Malloray's propellor driven vessels, the *Cutler's Edge*, which is waiting for us a few miles east of Tilbury. It's all been arranged, you see."

"Then, if I comprehend you completely, nothing has changed in your original plans except for Astley's unexpected embarkation on the same vessel as The Cargo."

"The reason for which, until I question the pretender, we still don't understand," Lennard said.

"I think I can provide an explanation," Clyford said, producing a letter from the inner pocket of his jacket. "Astley had this in his portmanteau. I found it when I was going through his belongings."

"And?"

"And it's written in French," Clyford explained to Travis, passing the letter to Lennard. "It's a letter of introduction. Astley spoke not a word of the language, and therefore this missive lays out the details of what the pretender should do. Basically, once the *Malmaison* docked, The Cargo should follow him, board Astley's coastal steamer, then be taken to Cork, where members of the clique were to meet him."

"You know this man?" Lennard called out to the pretender in French, after having read the letter, indicating Astley's body.

"No, who is he?"

"Let me speak with him, my lord," Clyford said to Lennard. "He's afraid of you. I'll speak with him in Russian. Perhaps he'll reveal something to me that he might not be able to finesse away in French—it's not so nuanced a tongue as the language of diplomacy."

"Very well. See what he knows. Use whatever tactics you wish, Clyford."

It was almost immediate that Lennard realised Clyford had adopted one of the intelligencer's stock-in-trade tricks: he smiled and talked softly, almost confidentially, glancing anxiously at Lennard from time to time. It was a ploy oft used, and one of the first to be taught—a strategy to make the person who was being interrogated believe that they might have an ally, and perhaps offer something up as appeasement, to avoid harsher treatment at the hands of a less sympathetic questioner.

"When I showed him the letter, I thought he might faint," Clyford reported no more than three or four minutes later. "He'd only been told that an intermediary would approach him while the passengers were assembling on the promenade deck of the *Malmaison*, ready for disembarkation at St. Katharine's dock, and not before. The pretender said he was devastated to learn just now that the man lying dead at his feet was his promised contact."

"How forthcoming do you think he might be if you were to question him more?"

"Although he's shocked, I think he still believes he holds an upper hand. He's recognised me as doing your bidding, my lord. He knows you're in charge. I think he's unlikely to tell me more."

"If you've already detained the clique who supported him in Britain, Lennard, what information do you hope to gain by questioning him further?" Travis asked.

Lennard sat quietly for a moment before answering, his gaze wandering out over the river, catching wisps of fog as they swirled, not quite touching the surface of the water, trying to find the "Terrier" within him, that Sir George valued so much. "As Gerald, Clyford, and Elam will tell you, Travis, the Home Secretary considers me his best rat catcher. I'm good at burrowing down into the hidden tunnels that men call their secrets, until I catch my prey and drag it to the surface."

"I sense that I am not going to like what may happen," Travis said.

"Thugs and common criminals don't understand that an interrogator's greatest weapon is fear. During the Inquisition in Spain, they used to show men the instruments of torture, to hopefully wring forth a confession without having recourse to bloody their own hands. It's the threat of agony that is normally the most successful. I've seen many a man such as our pretender—effete, yet stubborn; haughty, yet vulnerable. What is his greatest protection, do you think?"

"The clique who've fostered him both here and in his homeland?"

Lennard shook his head. "No, Travis. I've been trained to notice details. He's entirely dependent on the Turk. Kadir is his rock. Without him, he's a feeble, ungainly creature with nothing but conceit and words with which to fight. If what Clyford says is true—that the pretender believes he still holds an upper hand—and I doubt my private secretary not, then this creature thinks he will survive. It's hubris and the belief that he is special among men that gives him such confidence. However, the Turk is the keystone to his resolve. Once Kadir is removed from the equation, or the threat of the keystone's removal is seen as a real possibility, the arch of the pretender's own construction will tumble into ruins."

"So, how will you proceed? I'm sure you have a plan in mind."

"I intend to incapacitate his protector in such a way that the pretender believes his bodyguard is dying from poison, then use the dangled possibility of a last-minute antidote as a way of loosening the pretender's tongue. However, as you know, neither man can leave this ship—alive, at least. So, you must not interfere when I disable the Turk, but you must object and cry out to try to stop me when I show the pretender my instruments of persuasion. That will assist in his belief that I won't shirk from inflicting pain. Don't worry, the others will play their part too, but I shall tell the pretender that you're a physician, at hand to see how much pain the pretender can bear without me disabling him permanently. I shall start with a glowing poker held a few inches away from his eyes."

"Dear God, Lennard."

"Don't worry, my friend. Remember, it's all theatrics."

*****

Lennard sat on the deck next to the pretender, his canvas roll of implements laid out at his side. Pliers, horseshoe pincers, cramping irons, tongs, each one with wooden handles, designed not to transmit the heat into the hands of the person that wielded them.

"The captain's mate is heating up his charcoal stove to red-heat," Lennard said to the pretender.

"You barbarian!"

"It can all be avoided if you tell me what I need to know."

"What have you done to my servant?" the man snapped, wide-eyed, unable to keep glancing at Kadir, whose head slumped on his chest, breaths barely perceptible.

"It's a slow-acting poison. You have about twenty minutes before an antidote needs to be administered and before it will be too late. If you continue to remain silent, and your friend dies because of your intransigence, that's when I'll start to place my 'playthings' among the coals."

Lennard had injected the Turk with a quantity of tincture of poppy, a dose that he knew would eventually kill Kadir. He had no choice; the man had to die. However, he had no stomach for shooting a servant simply for obeying the wishes of his master, no matter what the Turk might do if unrestrained. He looked as strong as an ox. Travis had growled as Lennard had drawn up the dose, whispering urgently that it was too much, to which Lennard had questioned, sotto voce, whether being thrown into the Thames to drown alive, or being despatched by a bullet through the brain at close quarters would be preferable.

"You are a fool!" the pretender shouted. "My friends will tear your flesh from your body. When I'm king, I shall—"

Lennard stopped the man's speech with a hand over his mouth, squeezing his nostrils at the same time, until the pretender started to struggle, vainly trying to breathe.

"Listen to me!" Lennard said. "Friends? Do you mean the people who schooled you in neither the language of the country over which they said you were intended to rule, nor in that of the land in which you were raised? Even a modicum of sense would have made you realise you were being kept in the dark. Why, look at you, sir! Unkempt, poorly clothed, travelling for three years in disguise, fleeing from one town to another, with only a manservant as your companion. Do you really think that if you were intended to be the king of our great land, you'd be treated in such a tawdry fashion?"

"You know nothing!" the man spat.

"In that you are mistaken, sir. Your plot has been uncovered and your 'friends' have been disclosed, disavowing any knowledge of you in their haste to protect their reputations. There are lords and ladies, men and women, high and low, now in disgrace for the rest of their lives. Shall I tell you what I think would have happened to you when you arrived in Ireland? The moment you stepped ashore, your protector would have been shot dead on the spot, you'd have been seized then kept drugged and docile, manipulated by men who cared nothing for you, but who are obsessed with the opportunity to seize power and to rule the kingdom themselves in your name."

"How dare you—"

Lennard slapped his face hard then rose to his feet. It was obvious to him that Kadir was already dead, so he drew out his pistol and said, "How dare I what, sir? This is how much I dare." He shot the Turk through the temple.

The pretender shrieked, loud and long, howling with fear.

"Are you to be next?" Lennard shouted.

"No, no, no ..." the man blubbered.

Lennard crouched down once more and waited. When the sobs had subsided, turning into irregular hiccoughs, Lennard spoke. "Well then, first of all, your name, if you'd be so kind."

"My name?" The pretender stared at Lennard, red-eyed, his lips quivering, then spat directly into Lennard's face.

*****

The jetty into the Thames at the back of Marwick Castle was one of the longest on the estuary, nearly a hundred and fifty yards in length, mainly because the foreshore was shallow in that part of Hadleigh Ray.

Travis and Lennard stood on the afterdeck of the *Cutler's Edge* while they watched the magnificent steamer approach the end of the jetty. Two blasts of her horn reverberated through the decking beneath their feet.

"This is the new future of travel by sea, Lennard," Travis said.

"She's beautiful, isn't she? Neither Robert nor I have had cause to step foot aboard her. This is my first time."

"I know one or two of the crew. Odd isn't it, that retired naval officers should find employment aboard a private vessel."

"Who do you know?"

"The purser and one of the lads who's handling the hawser—the tall one, with the ..."

"Gammy leg?"

Travis chuckled. "That's the one. Odd that I should find anything to smile about after what's happened."

"What was done had to be done."

"I understand that. You must realise I'm no stranger to death, Lennard, but it's always been the result of illness or war—sometimes, both."

"There was no pain, Travis. Other men may have been more violent, but I'm not one of those, unless there should be a threat to those I love, or if it's been unavoidable."

"Tincture of the poppy ... there are other, less costly, and yet more effective concoctions."

"Perhaps I can employ you as a consultant, Travis?"

"No thank you, Lennard. However, I can send you a volume and you can ask me questions."

"Ah, there's a sight you don't see every day," Lennard said, pointing out over the jetty.

"No, it cannot be."

"Yes, Angus told me of the static railway line along the wharf—similar to those laid for pit ponies in the mines. Horse-drawn, as you can see, but what an excellent labour-saving device. The length of that jetty would exhaust men pushing carts back and forth to load and unload vessels."

"What on earth is Angus wearing? Even at this distance, he looks ... sparsely dressed."

"Matelot pants. It's how he spends his life away from work during the warmer months of the year. Bare-footed, stripped to the waist, and with his hair unkempt, flowing out in the breeze like some golden Alexandrine god."

"I do believe the prince is wearing even less," Travis remarked.

"I think you're right! It's a *lungi* ... an Indian loincloth."

"Dear God," Travis said, chuckling.

*****

Lennard stayed on board the *Cutler's Edge*, waiting for Angus to join him. He'd asked Elam to tell him to come up to the deck.

"Is everything all right, Lennard?" Angus asked, turning to wave at the open horse-drawn "carriage" that had just started to roll off along the jetty carrying the rest of their friends. "No problems with The Cargo?"

"They're at the bottom of the Thames, Angus. Arthur bound them together with chains and pushed their bodies overboard."

"You're trembling, Lenn."

"There's something you should see. Come with me."

Angus followed Lennard to the aft deck, upon which was a large metal box, butted up against the outer wall of the vessel's superstructure, the purpose of which was to hold ice and cooled confections for deck lunches or parties. When it was not in use, it was covered with two paillasses and piles of cushions, designed as a resting place out of the sun for guests who wished to doze.

"Steady yourself," Lennard said, flinging open the lid of the container.

"Jesus in heaven!" Angus said, staring in disbelief at the bloodied corpse of Sir Terrence Astley, the sixth Baron Killcaire.

"I swore I would tell no one else how he died. Only Elam, Arthur, and Gerald, who were there at the time and who bore witness, know. However, if anyone ever finds out we were involved, you're to promise me one thing."

"What is it?"

"No, Angus. You must promise first, on the love you hold for we six, The Brothers plus two."

"I see. It's an oath of that magnitude."

"It is. No one must know. And I'm only telling you now because you were there when I swore to the Prime Minister that if the chance ever arose to kill Astley, I'd stay my hand."

"Then it was not you?"

"Promise me first."

"I love you, Lenn, I always have. You and our fellow friends. I know you would never ask me to do something, invoking that love, were it not to protect another person. Very well, I swear."

Lennard opened his arms and Angus moved into them, kissing him on the cheek as he did so. The lid of the box slammed shut, reverberating for an instant.

"It was Elam, wasn't it?"

"Yes, Angus. But, if there's ever any discovery, then you must stay silent when I own for Astley's death."

"Elam is so gentle. He must have been sorely tried, Lenn. Unless it was to stop Astley from harming you? The wounds look savage and placed as if to obliterate him."

"He goaded us something dreadful, Angus. You can't imagine what he said, what filth spewed from his mouth—"

"I'm sure that I can, Lenn. I suppose you're telling me, and swearing me to silence, because I would have eventually divined which of you had killed him."

"Yes, and I don't want Elam to the burden of hiding the fact from you. He cares for you as much as any of us, and I fear he might want to withdraw from you to hide his guilt. He says he'd have done it again with no remorse, but I feel the band of iron around his heart that won't allow him to feel regret."

"That night when you were both ... it must have been terrible."

"Elam is reconciled to the treatment afforded him, as I would be had my abuse been punches and kicks. However, I shall bear the scars of what his men did to me for the rest of my days."

"Then you must allow us to help you heal those scars, Lenn."

"In the few hours since we left the deck of the *Malmaison* carrying Astley's body, I've had time to reflect, to weigh up what is most important in my life. I suppose I always knew it was you, my friends, and the thought of losing any of you ..."

"Surely there'd been no possibility of that?"

"Had Astley not been found in his cabin, had the pretender and the Turk been heavily armed. Had we been intercepted by members of the clique with the same idea as us, to board the paddle steamer as she lay at anchor in the Thames, had—"

"Had the heavens opened and you been struck by a bolt of lightning. Had a cannonball flown through the air all the way from the Crimea ..."

Lennard laughed. Angus was so rarely flippant these days, not like he had been as a youth, and it made Lennard realise he'd been worrying far too much about "what ifs". He also knew that worry was the inevitable result of having performed something grim and dangerous. An after-taste of what might have been. Despite all best-laid plans, at the point of action, there was always the possibility of an element of recklessness brought about by something unexpected and in the moment. At least, that's the way he'd seen it happen more times than he'd care to remember.

"Come, release me from your arms, Lennard, and let's join the others. We can decide what to do with Astley after you get some food in your belly and a few hours of sleep."

"What to do with Astley? You know me, Angus, I've already come up with a plan."

"Oh, my Terrier, what will you do with your mangled rat?"

"Feed him to his dogs, so they may see the possibility of their own fates as they feast upon his corpse."

*****

"Where did you get the dagger, Lennard?" the Prime Minister asked, declining another serving of Mr Huilot's most excellent boned, stuffed chicken.

"From Gerald, sir. Even Clyford had one, brought back as a souvenir from the battlefields of the Crimea."

"I must say, it was a stroke of genius, Lennard, leaving Astley's body on the barge steps of the Palace of Westminster ... not to mention the thirty pieces of silver. That didn't go unnoticed."

Lennard had told the crew to pack Astley's body with ice and keep it in the metal box until he could obtain the dagger. In the early hours of the morning, two days after Lennard and his friends had returned to London, the crew of the *Cutler's Edge* had splayed out Astley's corpse on the river landing of the Houses of Parliament, the letter to the pretender skewered to his chest by the Russian dagger, and with it, a bag tied on a cord around his neck containing thirty Irish shillings.

"I was pleased to hear that the discovery of his body created a suitable commotion."

"When I announced it in the house, the deathly quiet that followed was unlike any other I've heard, Lennard," the Prime Minister said.

Lord Palmerston beamed as he cast his glance around the table at the seven other male guests: Lennard and Elam, Gerald and Arthur, Angus and Travis, and the Home Secretary, Sir George Grey. "The Crown owes you gentlemen a debt, one which may never be fully repaid."

"May I speak for my companions, Prime Minister," Angus said. "In offering that duty to the Crown begs no rewards."

"Still, you have done us a great service, despite the problems I shall have with Astley's party, Lennard."

"It had to be done, Prime Minister—the public display I mean. Had he simply disappeared, and his body never been found, his supporters may have held out hope that he'd merely gone into hiding and would one day return and reignite the agitation of his followers."

"But the letter to the pretender, the dagger, and to top it all, the Irish shillings? Brilliant, my boy. All the clues laid out in such a manner there could be no disavowal of his calumny by those who were part of The Cargo plot. Most probably the general public will believe it has something to do with his arms smuggling and why he was stripped of his title and wealth."

"I do feel for his family," Travis said. "They should not be held responsible for his actions. From what I understand, he had little to do with them."

"I've taken care of that," Lennard said. "Not more than a few weeks ago, when Astley's uncle finally accepted our offer for the shares in the shipping company, we were able to enact our hostile takeover.

I've arranged with Simeon Drudge to provide an annuity for Astley's widow and children, to the value of one per cent of the profits from our new venture, and for them to remain in his house, the deed of which is in trust for his eldest son, still a child, until his twenty-first birthday."

"That's very generous, Lennard."

"Not at all, Travis. She'll receive an income that might be considered a fortune in her part of Ireland, but which will be barely noticeable in our revenues. It's, as you said, not their fault that Astley was a—"

"Cad?"

"Quite, Travis. That's a very polite word for an extremely unpleasant man."

"I've had little time to dwell on the information you learned from your interrogation of the pretender, Lennard," Lord Palmerston said. "However, from what I noted, there was little of value."

"The man may as well have been a mole, Prime Minister. Kept in the dark, seldom allowed free access to anything without Kadir at his side."

"He'd been castrated," Travis said.

"What?" Sir George looked astounded.

"Yes, when we stripped him, before he was dumped in the Thames, I performed a cursory examination. At first, it appeared that his testicles had atrophied, but I saw that he'd been neutered quite roughly. The scars indicated cautery to stop the bleeding."

"Good God," the Home Secretary said, pressing his linen table napkin to his mouth.

"Docile, kept ignorant, dependant on others? Yes, he was groomed and prepared," Lennard said. "Not for the life of a king, but for a life as a malleable pawn."

"It's quite sad, to be honest."

"Perhaps, Sir George," Lennard replied. "But the problem with any cause, such as The Cargo plot, is that if there remains the slightest hope, someone or some group will espouse it at some time in the future. When fires are extinguished, one must not only douse the embers, but spread them far and wide, and bury them thrice deep."

The Prime Minister was about to speak when Merrill and Stephen arrived in the dining room with the roast, Miles following them, ready to carve.

Despite an entreaty to join them, Miles refused, much to Elam's sadness. It had become apparent that the brothers had their own destinies to follow, each of them happy in the situation in which they now found themselves. Elam at Lennard's side, and Miles as butler and master of the house.

"I'd like to propose a toast," Lennard said before his guests began to eat. "To our friends, the Prime Minister, the Home Secretary, and to Her Majesty the Queen. For without her, none of us in our great nation would enjoy the benefit and luxury of our lives and the comfort of our surroundings. Rich and poor, we have all prospered under her reign. The alternative, had it come to pass, would not have been worth considering. To Her Majesty!"

The gentlemen stood at table in Lennard's fine dining room and raised their glasses, echoing his toast to the Prime Minister, the Home Secretary, and to the Queen.

*****

At the conclusion of dinner, Martin Wilson arrived, with him Clyford, Robert, and Geoffroy. They'd been to see *Still Waters Run Deep*, at the Olympic Theatre in Wych Street, in the Strand.

"I don't believe I've seen you dressed like a gentleman, Mr Wilson," Travis said, as they shared a glass of port.

"Neither have I, you, Mr Holland," Martin quipped, admiring Travis's very elegant, new formal evening wear.

"Touché," Travis said.

"While I have you alone, sir. May I put a proposition to you?"

"It depends, Mr Wilson."

Martin chuckled. "Nothing untoward, sir. It's a professional engagement. I wonder if you'd be interested in checking my gentlemen every week for … ailments of the trade?"

"Venereal disease?"

"Yes, indeed. I'd be happy to pay you two guineas each for the six of them."

"Twelve guineas?"

"Yes, a week. Is that not enough?"

"Well, no, sir. It's an extremely generous sum—far more than I may have suggested had you asked me my fee. Perhaps I should call on your house to make arrangements?"

Lennard arrived at their side at that moment. "You're going to visit Mrs Hedger's, Travis?"

"Yes, Lennard," Martin replied. "I've offered Mr Holland all six of my boys and will pay him two guineas each."

"My, my, Travis, that's impressive. You must have hidden talents indeed and stamina far beyond mine if this is true!"

"What's this?" Angus asked, hearing the laughter, and joining them, followed by Gerald, Robert, and Arthur.

"Nothing, Angus," Travis explained. "I'm afraid I am bearing the brunt of not a small amount of teasing."

"If they're teasing you, Travis, then may I welcome you?"

"Welcome me?"

"Yes, sir. Such familiarity can only mean you've passed from our acquaintance to the inner circle of our very close friends."

"He's been one since I first met him, although neither of us knew it at the time," Lennard said, with great affection.

Travis, much moved, embraced each man in turn, slapping their backs as he hugged them.

"And now there are seven," Elam whispered into Lennard's ear.

"Eight, if you include Arthur."

Elam smiled, then unnoticed by the other men, brushed the back of Lennard's hand with his own and entwined their fingers, passing a smile at him as he did so.

21. THE THIRTIETH OF SEPTEMBER, 1860

Lennard slipped out of the noise and the light, closing the balcony door carefully behind him.

The night was glorious. The moon full in the sky, slightly rose-orange due to the smoke from across the river where his neighbour had been burning stubble during the late afternoon. Patches of it still smouldered at ten in the evening. He inhaled, the air was flinty and smelled faintly of burning grass and leaves.

It was the evening of the third autumn ball he'd held at Gresting Hall; a custom that had laid dormant for over fifteen years. It had lapsed because his grandfather Trefford had spent the last five years of his life living in London, and during that time had gradually foregone major social events, retreating to his books and business affairs conducted at the Oriental Club. Lennard, however, with his aunt Caroline's urging, had resurrected the erstwhile harvest festival, inviting many of his friends, old and new, from London to stay the weekend.

With the newly constructed railway from High Wycombe passing by Hazlemere and the Gresting Estate, then through the corridor of land belonging to Lord Quaisey before it rejoined the mainline to Birmingham at Saunderton, travel to and from London had become easy and comfortable. For the first time in two decades, all twelve bedrooms of the great house were occupied, and several of the neighbouring estates had also put up visitors.

He lit a cheroot and moved out of the light spilling from inside, leaned on the stone balustrade of the long promenade gallery outside the ballroom, which ran along the eastern elevation of the house, and looked out over the newly-extended lake. It had been Gerald's idea to enlarge and deepen the former shallow lily pond, and although reticent at first, once he'd seen it filled for the first time, it had appeared to Lennard to have always been there.

Could it have been five years now since Sir Hugh had died? He found it difficult to believe. The early years of awkwardness, of finding himself in a new skin in a world then foreign to him, now a distant memory, like that of the evening on the Thames when the Turkish pretender and Terrence Astley had taken their last breaths.

"Hello there," a voice came from behind him.

"Oh, hello, Travis. I didn't hear you come outside."

"I saw you sneak away."

"Too much of a good thing ..." Lennard started to say, then chuckled as he saw Travis's broad grin and accompanying raised eyebrow of disbelief at his assertion.

"I'm not the only one to have noticed you put on a brave front when there's more than a dozen people at a gathering, Lenn. You'd rather be down at that cottage of yours in Falmouth with Elam, mucking about in that American catboat you and he put together, wouldn't you?"

Lennard smiled and nodded, glancing shyly at his friend.

"How will you manage at my wedding?"

"I'm not unused to crowds and behaving as is expected of me, Travis. It's here, in Gresting, where I grew up, that I most feel the need to get my feet in the dirt. Here, and down there in Roseland St. Just. I can't tell you how wonderful it is to take a few days in Falmouth, just Elam and me, reading, walking by the sea, or out on the estuary fishing. It's a literal breath of fresh air. As for your wedding? I shall be as pleased as Punch to walk my cousin Philomena down the aisle to you."

It was Travis's turn to smile shyly, but during the course of the five years of their acquaintance, he'd become one of the group so felt no hesitation at placing his arm around Lennard's shoulders and squeezing him.

"A little bird told me—"

"Before we talk of your little bird, Travis, I'd like to talk to you about your wedding present from me."

"I've told you, I'll accept nothing."

"But you must, I'm afraid. It will appear very badly if I don't give you something. Just imagine the snide smiles if one of the wealthiest men about town seemed to be miserly when it came to the marriage of his own second cousin to one of his best friends. I am the head of the Malloray family after all."

Travis rolled his eyes. "What did you have in mind?"

"Three things, Travis. The first being a honeymoon aboard the *Cutler's Edge* to Danzig, where you'll be met by the Prince Christian Jost Saxe-Meiningen who'll take you by train to Paris, where you and Philomena will stay as my guest in the hotel we own. He lives in Paris these days, so he'll be at your command. Clyford tells me the *Maison Crillon* is superlative in its accommodation. Surely you'll allow me this small gesture?"

"That's far too generous and you know it."

"The second gift is one which you will be unable to refuse, because it will come as part of Philomena's dowry. I intend to gift her Birch House."

"What?"

"Yes, Travis. I've no need for *two* houses in London. Bexford House is big enough. Anyway, as you're to be her husband it will become yours by law. You need worry no more about rent or returning favours and you can carry on your practice there, unless you wish to rent rooms elsewhere—I hear Harley Street is fast becoming fashionable for society doctors. But, as for Birch House, I know you are very fond of its situation—Soho Square being so close to your wealthy clients. And I'm sure the Huskersons would be delighted to stay on—they've become inordinately attached to you."

"I don't know what to say, Lenn ..."

"Say 'yes'."

"Yes to what?"

"Yes to the third of my gifts."

"Surely you know me well enough to understand that I could never answer yes to a proposal as yet unvoiced?"

Lennard laughed. "It's rather a present that's been a long while in the making, and I've been sorely tempted more than once to reveal its nature to you, only holding back until I was sure it would come to pass. Do you remember when we first met?"

"Lying in a cot in squalor in the hospital, surrounded by the dead and dying while you somehow managed to arrange a tray of tea for you, me, and Christopher? That's a scene a little hard to forget, my friend."

"Do you remember what I promised you at the time?"

"That you wouldn't suffer me remaining in the place for a minute more. That I do remember."

"Not that, Travis. I promised I'd lobby about changes to the hospital."

"Ah, yes."

"Well, it's taken the patience of Job to have it realised, but last week I had a meeting with the Prime Minister and Miss Florence Nightingale. I've donated ten thousand to refurbish the four floors of the east wing of the hospital under Miss Nightingale's supervision."

"Oh, Lennard! That's the best thing I could ever have wished for—"

"Wait, I haven't finished yet. The proviso for my donation is that the new section will be named the Percival Henry Holland wing, in honour of your brother, who gave his life for his country, and as a tribute to the man who presently has his arm around my shoulder, as thanks for his efforts as part of a group aboard a river ketch in the Thames, some five years past."

Travis was still somewhat unsuccessfully trying to control his emotions when Elam joined them. "What ho? Tears at an autumn ball?"

"I imagine much of this is your doing too, Elam?" Travis asked.

"If you're talking about Lennard's wedding gift, I can only hold up my hand for the idea of Birch House, now I'm a landowner myself. I felt it was a fair exchange. Lenn told me the idea of a title of lord of the manor was your suggestion."

Lennard smiled. It had been a difficult task to get Elam to agree to such a thing, and eventually, worn out with the arguments, had just gone ahead without Elam's consent. Fitzhaven Manor was a ruin, fifteen miles from their cottage in Cornwall, but its one hundred acres of fallow land came with an hereditary title. Elam could choose to be called Lord Fitzhaven should he wish. Lennard had bought it, had the title transferred to Elam's name, and had given it to him Christmas last.

"The title means nothing to me, and not many know of it," Elam explained. "However, it will make for easier situations when we go abroad."

"I was about to tell Lennard that a little bird had made mention of your grand tour."

"If the little bird is a sixteen, about to turn seventeen-year-old, tall and handsome young man with the most charming of French accents, then I'll tan his hide," Lennard said. "We've only just confirmed final arrangements."

"So, you're taking Geoffroy with you?"

"And Clyford. We shall be four."

"And how long will you be away?"

"Two years, perhaps three. We intend to do business, Travis. It's not just a voyage around the world. We'll visit all the major ports with which we trade. However, there is a personal element to the first leg of our travels. We were intending to first sail to Italy, now that it's newly unified, but I recently spoke to the others and decided we'd go instead directly to Australia. I'd like to visit the memorial to the *Castle Howard.* Those who were recovered from the sea were unidentifiable by the inhabitants of Melbourne Town, because all aboard were immigrants from Britain. They're buried in a common grave. However, I've always wished someday to pray at the gravesite, and I promised my aunt Caroline to have a stone erected for my parents and my brother and sister."

"Lennard's mother was also Geoffroy's great-aunt, Travis," Elam explained. "So, for him, too, it's a journey of remembrance on behalf of his own grandmother."

"Ah, yes. They were sisters. I remember now. That's how the Beauchamp name appears in the title of your company."

"After Australia, we intend to cross the Pacific to San Francisco, then sail up the coast to Fort Victoria in Canada, cross back over the ocean to Japan—"

"Japan! How extraordinary!"

"Yes, it will be wonderful to see a culture that's been cut off to us Westerners for centuries. After that, we'll return via Canton and India, after which we'll take the overland route through Egypt to Alexandria, board one of our vessels to Italy, returning home by rail and coach through the continent. We, too, shall have our time at the *Maison Crillon*."

"Promise me you'll keep a journal," Travis said, his eyes wide with amazement.

"I'll do better than that. I've sworn to Arthur that I'll write a detailed weekly account of our travels, including any business transactions that might be routed through the docks at Tilbury, and post it from wherever we are. The letters might take ages to arrive, and most probably out of chronological order, but he says he doesn't care."

"He still likes his new position?"

"Likes it?" Elam said. "Gerald has had to concede that Arthur is a better businessman than he. After Lennard and Robert bought up all that land and built new docks and warehouses at Tilbury, Gerald grumbles that he's become nothing but an itinerant, travelling between Lady C's house in Hampshire, Gresting, and Bexford House. He won't stop complaining—but with a twinkle in his eye—that he's living Lennard's life while having to juggle his own schedule to spend evenings at Chadwell St. Mary with Arthur, where he built their house."

"I'm afraid our Gerald is taken to histrionics. Everything is so easily accessible these days by rail. Arthur is but a few hours away by train, no matter which of our properties Gerald is working at," Lennard said. "But, as for Arthur? The man is a marvel. He manages the whole operation at Tilbury, and I'm not backward about telling Gerald how very lucky he is to have found a companion so even-tempered, competent, and devoted."

"And, seeing them together, who'd could guess which of them had spent their lives taking orders and which giving them. Arthur rules the roost at their house," Travis remarked, smiling at his friends. "But who will manage everything you normally take care of while you're abroad on your travels, Lennard?"

"Ah, that," Lennard said. "My aunt, of course. Last year, just after you came to me and sought my permission to ask Philomena for her hand in marriage, she confided in me that she was fearful of becoming restless and bored once my cousin had flown the nest, so I've charged her and Gerald to share the burden of what little I do. Robert will take my place on the board of the Oriental Club while I'm away, and my great-aunt will manage my duties on the committees of the charitable institutions of whose boards I am a member. It will put a few gentlemen's noses out of joint having a lady of her feistiness to contend with, but I think it may do them a bit of good."

"I thought she was heartily sick of business affairs, and it was the reason she signed everything over to you?"

"She says being excessively employed on my behalf will provide an excuse when her gentlemen suitors become too ardent. Once we've gone and she rolls up her proverbial sleeves, she can swear that affairs of business keep her far too busy to become attached to any one man in particular."

"She has so many callers? I'm not doubting the beauty and poise of your great-aunt, Lennard," Travis said. "But—"

"She's a wealthy catch, Travis. Or appears to be. Perhaps the lure of the splendid violet-coloured sapphire and diamond parure I gifted her for her birthday five years ago attracts gentlemen's eyes rather more than her impressive cleavage."

"Talking of your aunt, Lennard. I see her through the windows inside beckoning me. I expect I've spent far too much time with my friends and not enough with my bride-to-be."

"We'll join you shortly, Travis. Please, make some excuse for Elam and me."

"I will do, and thank you again for your very kind wedding gifts, Lenn … Elam."

*****

"Fitzhaven," Lennard whispered after Travis had closed the terrace door behind him.

"Betteridge," Elam replied.

"Come with me."

"Where to?"

"Into the corner where we can't be seen."

"It will be odd, Lenn."

"What will?"

"Returning to England after years abroad, travelling as brothers or cousins then going back to our situation as master and valet."

"I've thought of that myself. However, Geoffroy will be nineteen, perhaps twenty years old when we return. You've seen how keen and capable he is, and with a sense for business and trade second only to Arthur. We'll be in our forties when we return. Perhaps I can hand over the reins of what little I do in the affairs of Malloray's to Robert and Geoffroy, and the running of the estate to Gerald and my aunt between them, should they wish to continue."

"What about the Home Office?"

"As you know, I'm not fond of Sir George Lewis, now that *our* Sir George has moved on to better things. The new Home Secretary is the reason Angus left. I think there'll be a major change and I'm not sure I want to be part of it anymore."

"Angus left because he learned that his father had fallen gravely ill and was given a year to live. As he's to be the next Earl of Marwick, he had to learn—as you did—how to manage a huge estate. There's also the responsibility of making provisions for his mother, and the onerous burden of taking his father's seat in the House of Lords when he passes away. Not only that, but with two children and a third on the way ..."

"Angus, Martin, and Bertram Fetcher, all in the same bed. How he has the energy to father children as well, I've no idea."

"He did tell me once, but it doesn't bear repeating."

"Please, Elam. I'm not sure I want to know."

Elam pulled Lennard into his arms, nestling in the small alcove where the return of the balcony met the outer wall of the ballroom.

"Lenn ..."

"Yes?"

"Did you ever wonder what might happen if we didn't come back?"

"We'll be safe. Ocean travel is—"

"No. I didn't mean that. I meant if we found some part of the world we could live in, without the nonsense of master and servant, like we do in the cottage at St. Just …"

"Does there exist some country like that? Where you and I didn't need to hide who we are?"

"I don't know. But we'll have two or three years to discover if such a place exists."

"You know, Elam. I once had a thought just like that, years ago."

"Tell me."

"It was when we returned to Benfleet aboard the *Cutler's Edge*. Do you remember that day? Angus's wharf, him in his matelot pants, stripped to the waist, his hair hanging loose over his ears and neck, and beside him his prince, dressed only in a breechclout. I thought of you and me, on some foreign shore. White sands, blue seas, living on coconuts and crabs from the sea."

"And an income of forty thousand a year."

"Sent in bottles, washed ashore by the tide—"

"And nowhere to spend it."

"It sounds wonderful," Lennard said, then kissed him.

"Whisper in my ear, Lenn," Elam said. "The way you used to do when I couldn't hear."

"No, Elam. I want far too much to see the light in your eyes when I tell you to your face quite how much I love you."

"Enough, Lennard Malloray, small parcels will suffice. It's a heady drug, your affection, and I'd hate to become addicted to it."

"Why so?"

"Because it's hard enough as it is, maintaining propriety when in company, and I'm not sure I could control myself."

Lennard laughed softly then turned his head to ascertain they were still out of sight and hidden in the shadows. He kissed Elam once more. "That's your ration then, Lord Fitzhaven—for the meantime at least."

"I see your aunt peering through the ballroom window, Lenn," Elam said, peering over his shoulder. "She's looking for us."

"Then I think it's time to make our return to our friends. Are you ready?"

"I shall be in a few minutes. Go on, I'll follow you in a moment."

"Is anything wrong?"

"No, there's nothing wrong," Elam replied. "I just want to sniff the air, feel the evening breeze on my face, and gaze at the reflection of the moon on the lake for a moment or two."

"Very well, I shall see you inside."

Elam watched over his shoulder as Lennard straightened himself at the door leading into the ballroom and took a deep breath before opening the door. A burst of music and laughter filled the air for the short time it remained open, and then Elam returned to lean on the balustrade.

"Thank you, Gresting," he said to himself, casting his eyes out over the lake and the stand of alders behind it. "Had I a glass in my hand, I'd raise a toast to you. Not for the magnificence of your beauty, but for all that you've given me."

The sound of someone tapping on the glass of the windows behind him caused him to look back over his shoulder once more. Arthur, his eyes filled with laughter, beckoned him to join the others. So, quickly wiping the tears in his eyes with his coat sleeve, he straightened himself, like Lennard had done, took a deep breath, then returned to the celebration.

AUTHOR BIO

From the outback to the opera.

After a thirty year career as a professional opera singer, performing as a soloist in opera houses and in concert halls all over the world, I took up a position as lecturer in music in Australia in 1999, at the Central Queensland Conservatorium of Music, which is now part of CQUniversity.

Brought up in Australia, between the bush and the beaches of the Eastern suburbs, I retired in 2015 and now live in the tropics, writing, gardening, and finally finding time to enjoy life and to re-establish a connection with who I am after a very busy career on the stage and as an academic.

I write mostly historical gay fiction. The stories are always about relationships and the inner workings of men; sometimes my fellas get down to the nitty-gritty, sometimes it's up to you, the reader, to fill in the blanks.

Every book is story driven; spies, detectives, murders, epic dramas, there's something for everyone. I also love to write about my country and the things that make us Aussies and our history different from the rest of the world.

I'm research driven. I always try to do my best to give the reader a sense of what life was like for my main characters in the world they live in.

Website – https://garrickjones.com.au
Facebook – https://www.facebook.com/GarrickJonesAuthor

ALSO BY GARRICK JONES

The Boys of Bullaroo: Tales of War, Aussie Mateship and More
(Nov 2018), MoshPit Publishing, Australia

Six tales of men and war, spanning sixty years, and linked by a fictional outback town called Bullaroo. From the deserts of Egypt in 1919 to the American R&R in 1966, the stories follow the loves, losses and sexual awakenings of Australians both on the battlefield and in the bush.

The Cricketer's Arms: A Clyde Smith Mystery
Book 1 of the Clyde Smith Mysteries Series
(July 2019) MoshPit Publishing, Australia

Clyde Smith is brought into the investigation of the ritualised death of pin-up boy cricketer, Daley Morrison, by his former colleague, Sam Telford, after a note is found in the evidence bags with Clyde's initials on it. Someone wants ex-Detective Sergeant Smith to investigate the crime from outside the police force. It can only mean one thing—corruption at the highest levels.

The Cricketer's Arms is an old-fashioned, pulp fiction detective novel, set in beachside Sydney in 1956. It follows the intricacies of a complex murder case, involving a tight-knit group of queer men, sports match-fixing, and a criminal drug cartel.

Was Daley Morrison killed because of his sexual proclivities, or was his death a signal to others to tread carefully? Has Clyde Smith been fingered as the man for the case, or will the case be the end of the road for the war veteran detective?

Australia's Son (Nov 2019) MoshPit Publishing, Australia

A wrongly delivered letter sparks a chain of events that threaten the life of Edward Murray, "Australia's Son", the most renowned operatic baritone of his day.

It is 1902, and Edward has just returned to the Metropole Hotel after a performance of La Bohème at the Theatre Royal in Sydney, when the manager phones his apartment to tell him the police have arrived with bad news.

Edward, and his vaudeville performer brother, Theodore, are shocked to hear that Edward's dresser, the brothers' oldest friend from childhood, has been found dead, stabbed in the back, in Edward's recently vacated dressing room. Following a sequence of gruesome killings, Edward and the detective assigned to protect him, Chief Constable Andrew Bolton, are lured into a trap by a man whose agenda is not only personal, but driven by a deranged mind.

Set around the theatre world of early Edwardian Sydney, the story is steeped in the world of class divides, of music and the theatre. Its themes of murder, treachery and foul play, are ofttimes confronting, but the story is linked throughout by Edward Murray, the man with the golden voice, whose overarching belief is that even in the darkest of times, a sliver of light can mean that hope is at hand.

The House of a Thousand Stairs
(March 2020) MoshPit Publishing, Australia

Warrambool

In Gamilaraay, the language of the Kamilaroi peoples of north-western New South Wales, it's the word for The Milky Way. It's also the name of Peter Dixon's homestead and sheep station, situated in the lee of the Liverpool Ranges.

In 1947, Peter returns from war, his parents and younger brother dead, the property destocked and his older brother, Ron, having emptied out the family bank account and nowhere to be found.

The House With a Thousand Stairs is the story of a young man, scarred both on the inside and the outside, trying to re-establish what once was a prosperous and thriving sheep station with the help of his neighbours and his childhood friend, Frank Hunter, the local Indigenous policeman.

Enveloped by the world of Indigenous spirituality, the Kamilaroi system of animal guides and totems, Peter and Frank discover the true nature of their predestined friendship, one defined by the stars, the ancestral spirits, and Baiame, the Creator God and Sky Father of The Dreaming.

Maliyan bandaarr, maliyan biliirr.

Wheelchair: Antarctica. Snow and Ice
(Sept 2020) MoshPit Publishing, Australia

You can never judge an academic book by its cover. Simon Dyson, a quiet assistant professor, is a man of hidden depths. To the world he presents as a harmless, innocuous, shy and retiring intellectual. However, the man who lurks behind that public persona is far more interesting … and dangerous … and driven.

Wheelchair is a slow-burn contemporary psychological crime thriller about a man who suffers from both OCD and PTSD, a man who is unwittingly caught up in a cross-border war between rival crime gangs—a conflict that almost leads to his death, and more than once.

It's a study of compulsion and of disability, and of the many faces of emotional dependence and sexual compulsion. It’s about how some men cannot just love or make love because their hearts or their bodies lead them to it, but who can only connect emotionally and physically through self-imposed rituals which involve struggle or self-abasement.

The Seventh of December: The Czarina's Necklace
Book 1 of the Seventh of December Series
(Dec 2020) MoshPit Publishing, Australia

As bombs rain down over London during the Blitz, Major Tommy Haupner negotiates the rubble-filled streets of Bloomsbury on his way to perform at a socialite party. The explosive event of the evening is not his virtuosic violin playing, but the 'almost-blond' American who not only insults him, but then steals his heart.

The Seventh of December follows a few months in the lives of two Intelligence agents in the early part of World War Two. Set against the backdrop of war-torn occupied Europe, Tommy and his American lover, Henry Reiter, forge a committed relationship that is intertwined with intrigues that threaten the integrity of the British Royal Family and the stability of a Nation at war.

Neither bombs nor bullets manage to break the bond that these men form in their struggle against Nazism and the powers of evil.

The Gilded Madonna: A Clyde Smith Mystery
Book 2 of the Clyde Smith Mysteries Series
(April 2021) MoshPit Publishing, Australia

Clyde Smith's quiet, happy life, in love for the first time, working as a private detective and journalist, is suddenly thrown into disarray by the appearance, after a three year hiatus, of a body bearing the distinctive hallmarks of a string of murders he hadn't been able to solve when working in homicide.

Forced to cooperate with the new detective sergeant who'd taken his place in the local cop shop, Clyde has to not only deal with the enormous chip on the young man's shoulder, but also with a complex case that involves kidnapping, the re-emergence of the Silent Cop Killer, the historical abuse of young men and boys in orphanages across the State, and a ghost from the past who is out for revenge.

Will Clyde and the new DS be able to find the killer before he finds them? Or will they be his final prize, the last victims in his string of grisly murders? Perhaps only the local psychic, owner of a Romany religious statue, the Gilded Madonna, can provide the clue that might ultimately solve the puzzle, but which will also lead Clyde and DS Dioli into mortal danger.

X for Extortion: 14 Manchester Square
Book 2 of the Seventh of December Series
(Sep 20210) MoshPit Publishing, Australia

After returning from a secret mission in occupied France for His Royal Highness, George, the Duke of Kent, Lieutenant-Colonel Thomas Haupner is looking forward to a cup of tea, a hot bath, and the sleepy head of his American lover, Major Henry Reiter on his shoulder when he wakes up the next morning.

However, along with items Tommy has recovered for the duke, he has also discovered a secret stash of documents, which, when opened, prove to be a poisoned chalice. Tommy and Shorty find themselves caught up in a dangerous web of lies, enemy agents, assassins, and traitors. In an effort to save the reputations of not only their friends, but men and women high in both society and in the government, they themselves become victims of I.K.S., a former World War One international extortion ring, which has risen, phoenix-like, from the ashes of bomb-devastated London.

All available from your favourite on-line retailer

CPSIA information can be obtained
at www.ICGtesting.com
Printed in the USA
LVHW012028280322
714628LV00005B/351